PRAISE FOR MARA WILLIAMS

"Why does childhood sweethearts to estranged friends to lovers have to go *so hard*? I loved all the history between Ophelia and Beau in Mara Williams's *The Truth Is in the Detours*, and I loved watching them fall for each other as adults with all the complications that come with having more life experience. By the time they finally hooked up, I had been dying for it to happen—these two were always meant for each other! Mara Williams is definitely a romance writer to watch."

—Alicia Thompson, *USA Today* bestselling author of *Never Been Shipped*

"Clever, funny, and wonderfully romantic, *The Truth Is in the Detours* tells the story of a woman who finally gets to know herself. It delivers all the best story elements: delicious banter, tension, a road trip, gorgeous California settings, and hot romance. I devoured this sharp story. Mara Williams is a talent."

—Sierra Godfrey, author of *A Very Typical Family*

"A rare gem of a book that captures the beauty and pain of grief, love, and finding yourself, while still feeling like a hug. With sentences that sing and settings that feel like characters, *The Truth Is in the Detours* is the perfect blend of frenemies-to-lovers road-trip romance that will steal your heart and set it racing, and a woman's journey to finding herself as she searches for the truth about her family. An outstanding debut."

—Holly James, author of *The Big Fix*

"Mara Williams's debut is everything I love in a frenemies-to-lovers romance: delicious tension, fleshed-out history, and so much pining! The slow-burn romance between Ophelia and Beau delivers (and then some), and the mystery regarding Ophelia's mom kept me riveted to the pages. Williams levels it up even further with masterful writing and vivid imagery that truly allow the reader to feel like a third passenger on the road trip. I could smell the salt water and feel the sand between my toes like I was right there with them. *The Truth Is in the Detours* is a must-read for this summer!"

—Meredith Schorr, author of *Roommating*

The Truth Is in the Detours

The Truth Is in the Detours

a novel

MARA WILLIAMS

This is a work of fiction. Names, characters, organizations, places, events, and incidents are either products of the author's imagination or are used fictitiously. Otherwise, any resemblance to actual persons, living or dead, is purely coincidental.

Text copyright © 2025 by Mara Williams
All rights reserved.

No part of this book may be reproduced, or stored in a retrieval system, or transmitted in any form or by any means, electronic, mechanical, photocopying, recording, or otherwise, without express written permission of the publisher.

Published by Lake Union Publishing, Seattle

www.apub.com

Amazon, the Amazon logo, and Lake Union Publishing are trademarks of Amazon.com, Inc., or its affiliates.

EU product safety contact:
Amazon Media EU S. à r.l.
38, avenue John F. Kennedy, L-1855 Luxembourg
amazonpublishing-gpsr@amazon.com

ISBN-13: 9781662528927 (paperback)
ISBN-13: 9781662528934 (digital)

Cover design by Sarah Horgan
Cover image: © Rushikanth, © fajarhidayah11, © petovarga / Shutterstock

Printed in the United States of America

For my sisters, who believed it would happen, and for my daughter, who insisted I make it happen.

CHAPTER 1

It's been an hour since the truth fell out of an accordion file.

Well, technically, the document was sandwiched between the pages of *The PennySaver*—filed among my old school projects and Father's Day cards—and flew out when I flung it to the trash. Maybe I should have thought it odd that Dad saved junk mail in a locked cabinet. But yesterday, I found twelve rusted cans of tomato soup in his pantry, so hoarding wasn't exactly off-brand.

It wasn't until I caught my name atop the faded legal document that I paid attention. I skimmed it, but then I had to slow down. I read it word by word, line by line, and reread it a dozen times until I understood the legalese. But it still doesn't make any sense.

Because I can't fathom why my beloved mother—buried thirty years ago—would have lost her parental rights the year *after* the accident that supposedly killed her.

I've scoured the office for more evidence—for any explanation that doesn't indict Dad in deceit. Now, I'm sitting in the middle of the destruction I wrought in my frantic search. The contents of the file cabinet are scattered across the carpet. The desk drawers are open and emptied. The piles I painstakingly sorted into "keep," "donate," and "dump" are now shuffled like decks of mismatched cards.

But the only information I have is this single slip of paper, dated thirty years ago and stashed away like a secret. There's a rip in the corner where a staple must have been, with "page 1 of 10" in fine print at the bottom.

I lift the document to the light, hoping to find a faint watermark that says, "Just kidding! Your life wasn't a lie." But nothing comes into focus but the harsh truth. Mom didn't die when I was a kid. Instead, she lost the right to mother me. And I can't confront Dad about it—because he just took this secret to his grave.

I take a bracing breath, and Dad's scent—a mix of Dove soap, bitter coffee, and tea tree oil—rushes over me like a breaking wave, and I feel like I'm drowning. I don't know when I last had a meal, a shower, or a full night's sleep, so I can't eliminate the possibility I'm hallucinating. I've been barricaded in my childhood home since the funeral two weeks ago, sorting through a lifetime of detritus and keepsakes, and trying to pack away Dad's life and my grief.

And now this—whatever it is. It's all too much to process.

The brassy chime of the doorbell pierces the silence; it's a long-winded melody far too formal for this simple stucco home in the middle of casual San Diego. It's probably a delivery, so I ignore it. I don't want to watch another bouquet wilt in the heat; the scent of decaying flowers is already baked into the drywall.

The doorbell rings again, but my visitor doesn't wait long before going old school. An impatient fist hits the oak in a triplicate pattern. Once, twice, three times, before my name is barked like a summons from the porch.

I scramble to my feet, and the document floats to the floor—weightless despite the crater it's made in my life. I dive for it, sifting through the debris to reclaim it from the wreckage.

But my guest is relentless. "Ophelia!" he yells again, louder this time.

I hop over a stack of files but realize too late that my leg is asleep. My ankle turns, and I wince as I trip over a box, falling to the entryway floor and toppling a lamp in my descent.

The Truth Is in the Detours

The front door swings open, and I register brisk footsteps, but I'm too rattled to look up to check the identity of my intruder or worry whether he's here to make my day worse.

When I feel a hand on my shoulder, my eyes fly open. His face is too close to come into focus, and he's assessing me for injuries—or possibly here to finish the job. In my shock, I take him in through hurried still frames—full pouty mouth, thick black hair, smooth bronze skin, and broad, muscular shoulders.

"Ophelia, are you okay?" The low baritone jolts me back to reality. And shit. I do know that voice—and the familiar furrowed brow and hard scowl. Beauregard Augustin.

I don't know whether he's the exact person or the last person I want to see right now, because he's too many people to process: my childhood friend, my teenage nemesis, and just about the hottest grown man I've seen in real life. And here I am, flat on my face, wearing my grief like rancid perfume and my stained tank top from yesterday.

I tuck my knees under me so I can sit up, wincing from the sting of the fall.

"What happened?" Beau asks, his eyes scanning my face, my body. "What hurts?"

"I'm fine. I just"—I search for an explanation and settle on—"tripped." I'm too embarrassed to check for blood, so I force a laugh. Raw skin skates over my incisor; I think I have a fat lip.

"Are you sure?" The way Beau asks, it sounds like there will be consequences if I'm not. It's how a parent dares a kid to double down when they know they're lying.

I haven't seen Beau this close up in years, other than in photos on his wife's Instagram feed, which are always paired with cheesy captions: "My history professor is hotter than your history professor #hotgeek," or "This man has a doctorate in romance #blessed #PHDofLove." I unfollowed her a while ago; I couldn't stomach it anymore. At this angle, I'm disheartened to learn Beau's glow-up wasn't an Instagram filter. And I'm forced to admit, the years have been kinder to him than me—personally, professionally, and physically.

"What are you doing here?" I ask.

"My mom sent me over for a wellness check. She says you haven't stepped foot outside since the funeral." He takes in the disarray, peering into Dad's office with a sneer, as if he might spot a family of rats frolicking in the filth. "And clearly, it was necessary."

And *clearly*, he hasn't outgrown his tendency to judge me. At least some things haven't changed.

"I'm fine." I scoot back and stand, but stagger forward because the lamp cord is wrapped around my ankle. Beau grabs my waist.

"Whoa, hey." He steadies me and brings his other hand to my shoulder. "Did you hit your head?" His hands are hot on my clammy skin, and for a moment, I want to pretend we're still friends and let him hold me. He used to give great hugs.

But he's here only on his mother's orders; we haven't been friends in a long time.

"No. Really, I'm fine." I stand to my full height to prove my point, but the impact is minimal because I barely come to his shoulders. Man, he's tall. I remember the summer of his first growth spurt when he could no longer sit in his tree house without stooping his shoulders. His joints were so bulbous compared to his skinny limbs that he looked like a stick figure built from Tinkertoys. It was also the summer he broke out with terrible acne. I still see faint scars across his jawline. But that jawline can now cut glass.

I am thrown by all the ways he's both familiar and foreign to me. His glasses are just like the ones he wore as a kid, but his face has filled out, and the style has come back in, so he looks more hipster than nerdy.

"You keep saying you're fine," Beau snaps as his patience frays, and this, too, is familiar. "But this place is a disaster. I think you might have a head injury. And you look like you've seen a ghost."

His words land like a bad punch line. I'm having an out-of-body moment, because I'm listening to myself laughing and can't seem to stop it. What begins as a chuckle becomes a cackle—a roar. I'm hunched over, holding my stomach, and clutching the document like it's a permanent appendage. I can't catch my breath or explain to Beau why I've become the unhinged lunatic he assumes me to be.

You're right, I want to say. *I did see a ghost.* But it wasn't an apparition. It was a court order.

CHAPTER 2

"Phe, what's wrong?" Beau asks as my laughter escalates until tears stream down my cheeks, and I realize I'm not laughing—I'm crying. It's a hysterical mix of shock and humiliation, because Beau—of all people—is here as a witness. I need to pull myself together.

"Nothing," I choke out, gasping to catch my breath. "I'm good." I wave my hands over my face. "I'm great."

Beau glances at me from behind his thick lenses, shrewd eyes trying to crack me like a code. "You're not. But if you don't want to tell me, that's fine. I can call my mom if you'd rather talk to her."

The last thing I need is Leilani Augustin storming in, and Beau knows it. Lani would call me an ambulance, enlist a work party, and force me to talk about my feelings.

I wipe at my eyes as my breathing slows. Beau's staring at me, his focus cutting through my panic with precision. I weigh my options. Perhaps I need help making sense of this, preferably from someone who isn't in my day-to-day life and won't have the opportunity to bring this up again if I pretend this new information doesn't exist.

My family scandal can't lessen Beau's opinion of me—he already thinks I'm tragic. And pompous ass or not, he's the smartest person I know. Perhaps he could help me puzzle this out.

I exhale and hold the document out to him like a smoking gun at a murder trial. *Your Honor, I submit to you proof that my life is a lie.*

"What's this?" he asks.

The Truth Is in the Detours

"My ghost," I say.

Beau takes the paper but quirks his eyebrow at me. He adjusts his glasses and squints while reading. I watch Beau's eyes scan the page, once, twice. Then he reads aloud, as if the words will make more sense if spoken. I track the headlines as he mumbles. "In the Matter of Ophelia Rose Dahl, a minor child . . . Department of Human Services, Petitioner v. Mary Ann Johnson . . . Jackson County, Oregon, Circuit Court . . . Termination of Parental Rights by default judgment . . . failure to appear . . ."

"I don't understand." He offers an apologetic shake of his head. There was a small piece of me that wondered if he knew. If *everyone* knew but me. But I'm surprised I can still read him like he's my native language—he's as shocked as I am.

"This is dated the year after the car accident. My mom isn't dead. She gave me up." Saying it aloud, the information hurts as much on the way out as it did on the way in. Nausea rolls in as the realization lands anew. I press one hand to my belly and clasp the circular pendant at the hollow of my throat. The honed gold is as familiar as the silk of my skin; I've touched it so often that the *M* on its face has faded. I thought it was all I had left of her.

"That can't be true, Phe," Beau says in a shaky voice.

"That's what I thought. But I've had some time to let it settle." I tick off the evidence on my fingers. "Dad never talked about Mom unless I asked. I don't remember a funeral. And we never visited a grave."

Beau twists his face in concentration. "But she was buried in Oregon, right?"

"Yeah. Medford. But it's a short flight from San Diego—it doesn't explain *never* visiting your wife's grave." We'd moved here right after Mom "died." I assumed Dad was running from loss—not from lies.

"Maybe your dad was so traumatized by her death that—"

"She didn't die, Beau." I point to the document. "At least, not in the accident."

"Your scar," he says, his voice dropping to a register that strikes me as kind. His focus drifts to the white gash along my hairline.

I instinctively bring my fingertips to trace the ridge. Beau asked about my scar the day his parents dragged him along to welcome Dad and me to the neighborhood all those years ago. The scar was red and angry then—as fresh as my loss. But it took me months to tell Beau I'd gotten it in the same accident that killed my mom. At least that's the story Dad told me. I was four years old when the EMTs pulled me from the sedan on an icy highway in Oregon. I never saw Mom again, and Dad said she was gone. Why would I doubt him?

"Maybe this document was drafted before the accident. Are you sure you calculated the dates correctly?"

"I know I was never great at math like you were, but I can subtract, Professor."

He growls. "I mean, do you remember the timeline correctly? You were very young."

"I spent Christmas in the hospital after the accident. Dad brought me gifts and a small Christmas tree to cheer me up. I have a picture of it here somewhere." I wave to the calamity I've made of Dad's office. "This document is dated the summer afterward, right before we moved here. I found the deed to the house yesterday, and the dates line up."

Beau is silent for a few minutes, and I can see him processing. I reach for the paper and take it back from him.

"Besides, even if this doesn't mean what I think it means, there are a whole lot of lies packed into this piece of paper. Dad made me believe we were a happy little family when she died. This document uses her maiden name—and her parental rights were *terminated*." My mom's maiden name is in block letters: MARY ANN JOHNSON—clear, legible, unmistakable. "Johnson" is the answer to all my password security questions—email, bank account, the workout app I never use. The name is so common, unlike Dahl, the often-misspelled surname Dad gifted me like an inherited pet peeve.

The Truth Is in the Detours

"Do you want to look for her?" Beau asks. "You could try to track her online."

"Yes." At least, I think so. "But the search hits for Mary Johnson would be infinite. This might take better detective work than Google."

"But you know other things about her, surely?" He shoves his hands deep into the pockets of his joggers. They're the expensive kind—soft, clingy, and revealing all the quad muscles he didn't have when we were young. I drag my eyes away. I'm not attracted to Beau, of course. But this new body of his sure is distracting. I refocus on what he asked.

"Not much. Her birthday was March 8, and she was born somewhere back East—New York, New Jersey, maybe? But I don't know what year she was born, her Social Security number, profession, or . . ." I silently curse myself. It seems so obvious now. Dad didn't like to talk about Mom. And I didn't like to make Dad uncomfortable. So it's laughable how little I know. "I might find more information in there." I point to the office. "But I've gone through most of it already."

Beau scoffs, peering at the garbage heap of paperwork on the floor. "With the grace of a honey badger."

"Yeah, well, next time you find out your life is a joke, let's see if you can search for the truth like a detached detective."

Beau scowls and crosses his arms over his impressive chest. *Wanna bet?* he seems to say. And yeah, if Beau's perfect life ever imploded and he found himself in a similar situation, he'd uncover the truth through a methodical, organized quest using qualitative and quantitative data. He definitely wouldn't tear into the evidence room like a feral animal.

"It will probably help you to get her side of the story."

I wave the paper. "She didn't care enough to fight for me. *'Failure to appear.'* It's here in black and white."

Beau lets the truth sit for a few moments.

"And my dad let me grow up thinking I was motherless." I scrape my mom's pendant across the chain again, and Beau's eyes catch on the movement. He, more than anyone alive, knows how much her absence wrecked me.

Beau speaks his next words while watching my fingers glide over the gold. "Your dad loved you more than anything, Phe. I'm sure he didn't intend to hurt you. If he lied to you, he must have done it to protect you, and to give you a childhood marked with loss but still filled with love."

Grief—heavy, discordant—pushes on my shoulders and yells in my ear. "Maybe, but I can't even ask him why."

Beau moves to me until we're so close it's like we're friends again, when it was normal to reach in for a hug or whisper in each other's ears. "I know, Phe. I can't believe you have to deal with this, too, after everything you've been through." His voice reeks of pity, and my hackles rise. "I can imagine how terrible it must feel to be lied to."

His words are a match to my emotional gas line, which has been leaking for weeks. "How, Beau? How could you possibly imagine how I feel?" He's had nothing but luck and light since we parted ways. I get the reports from his mom. "Do you understand what it feels like to have a dead dad, a not-dead mom, and no fucking answers? Your pity and condescension are bad enough, but don't pretend to understand." My words tumble out of me with the repressed rage of my childhood, the petulance of my adolescence, and the pain I've restrained since my dad took his last breath.

Beau's expression hardens—and we're instantly strangers again. He steps away, and I shiver as the temperature drops. "All right. That's my cue. Let me know when you figure out what you want from me."

His tone feels like a slap, even though I threw the first punch. It occurs to me too late that I may have overreacted. "What's that supposed to mean?"

He steps away, pausing in the open doorway before his dark eyes land on mine. All softness is gone. "I'm trying to give you grace because you're dealing with a lot. But you showed me the paperwork despite my propensity for—what did you call it? Pity and condescension? You dragged me into your crisis like you always have. Not the friends you ditched me for. *Me*. In my experience, it's because you want something."

CHAPTER 3

"Beauregard Makani." I hear Lani's reprimand before she appears in the doorway beside her son. "You were supposed to check on Ophelia, not yell at her."

I drop the document face down on the console table, sending mental telepathy to Beau to keep his mouth shut. I already regret telling him; I don't need to increase the pity tally.

Lani off-loads a stack of Tupperware containers into Beau's arms and leads him back inside with her hand on his elbow. He could easily slip out of her grasp, but Beau is nothing if not an obedient child, even as a grown-ass man in his thirties.

Lani hasn't aged much in the last several years, other than her long hair that's grayed to a vibrant silver and pops against her tan skin. Her face is still soft and round, and her smile lines barely hint at the generosity with which she shares her broad grin.

"I wasn't yelling at her," Beau grumbles.

Now that they're both inside, I see Beau's visit for what it was—a preplanned sneak attack. I'm not proud that I've been dodging their daily wellness checks. I appreciate Lani's care and tenacity, but I haven't been fit for human contact.

She sighs and looks back and forth between us, her kind face pinched in concern. "You two. I don't understand what happened between you, but I should have made you work it out years ago." She grabs my hand, connecting the three of us in an awkward triad angled between moving boxes, bags of recycling, and the evidence of my earlier excavation. I'm worried we're about to have an intervention in my dad's dimly lit entryway. "And you need each other, especially now, with Henry's death and Beau's—"

"We're fine." Beau cuts her off, giving her a murder signal with a tight jaw and narrowed eyes. "Right, Phe?"

"Right." I play along, even though Beau just implied I'm a parasite. I would love to ask him exactly what he meant by that little barb, but I'm even more curious about how Lani was planning to finish her sentence. Why would Beau possibly need me? His life is a fairy tale. And years ago, he made it painfully clear he didn't need me. Didn't want me.

"That's what I like to hear." Lani gestures to the containers stacked high in Beau's broad arms. "Could you please put those in the fridge?"

Beau gives his mother a sidelong glance before heading toward the kitchen.

Lani wraps me in a hug. "Phe, my love." She pulls back and takes my face in her hands to kiss both cheeks. "You know, I like your pink hair. It suits you and is so much better than that Cookie Monster blue you had last Thanksgiving."

Lani shares her opinions as readily as her love, but it's hard to take offense. She studies me. "But you're too thin. You need to eat. I brought Spam musubi, shoyu chicken, and mac salad."

"All my favorites." My stomach growls at the mention of the Hawaiian dishes she raised us on, and my heart warms that she remembered.

But she's not done with me. "And you look tired."

"It's been a long few weeks." I probably look like the undead with undereye bags as blue as my eyes. Concealer is a necessary part of my beauty routine, but it wouldn't help now, even if I cared enough to apply it.

She tsks. "You're working too hard. What's the rush?"

"I have a business to run. And the more time it takes to clear the house, the longer I'll have to float the mortgage." Dad had refinanced

The Truth Is in the Detours

twice, and there's still another decade of payments. He never mentioned money problems, but since his death, I've learned his financial situation was precarious. I need to sell to settle his debts. The house is small, simple, and hasn't been upgraded since it was built in the '70s, but the beach is so close that Beau and I could ride our bikes there as kids. So it'll sell quickly with a few cosmetic touches.

I turn at the sound of footsteps as Beau returns from his assigned task, positioning himself by the front door for a quick exit.

"Well then, it's settled. You need help. Beau will do your heavy lifting."

Beau turns and looks just as surprised by the suggestion as I am—almost horrified. I shake my head and laugh. "I think Beau has more important things to do besides being my personal 1-800 junk hauler."

"He's off for the summer. And he's perfect for manual labor. Look at him." Lani saunters over to her son and grabs his broad shoulders, displaying his brawn as if he's onstage at a bachelor auction.

Beau wriggles free. "I think Ophelia means she'd rather not have *my* help."

He's right about that—his help comes with a side of scorn. Beau and I prove that resentment doesn't fade—it compounds. And we've been generating interest on old offenses for decades.

"Nonsense," Lani says. "You're perfect for this job. You're big, strong, and you could reorganize a landfill." I think she's comparing Dad's house to the county dump, which I can't dispute. When I started cleaning it out, his house was about two degrees shy of a hoarder's compound. I've made a ton of progress on the wreckage in two weeks, but I don't blame them for not recognizing it.

Lani steps to the door, resting her hand on the knob as she casts a warning glance between us. "Beau, you help Phe with whatever she needs. Phe, make sure you eat." She steps onto the porch. "And be kind to each other, my keiki."

The front door clicks in her wake, and Beau and I stare at each other in twin expressions of dismay.

The silence is thicker than the stale air, and the tension hovers alongside the dust motes. "You don't have to stay," I offer, hoping to sound polite rather than petulant.

"And you think my mom won't drag me back over by my ear?" I catch a twitch at the corner of his mouth—almost a flicker of a smile. Miracles do exist.

And it's contagious; I grin at the visual. Lani would need stilts to reach him. She's shorter than I am, which is a feat.

"I'm sorry about—"

But he holds up a hand. "It's fine." It doesn't sound fine, but I'll take him at his word. "Are you feeling better?" He's looking at me clinically, as if he's a medical doctor instead of a PhD. He'd probably check my forehead if we were on touching terms.

I nod. "Can we start over?"

Beau leans against the sidelight, arms crossed. "I think it's a little late for that. A lifetime of baggage is hard to unpack in an afternoon."

I sigh, already regretting my peace offering. "I mean, can we start over from today?" It feels like the longest day of my life, and the sun hasn't had the decency to set yet. The afternoon light is relentless and barrels in through the dusty windows. It's probably hotter in here than outside. June is typically overcast and gloomy in San Diego before it burns off for the summer, but the weather has it in for me, bathing me in sunshine with no regard for my foul mood.

Beau stares at the ground as if considering the merits of my offer, and I get the sense he's contemplating the pros and cons of being stuck here with me versus admitting to Lani he'd abandoned me in my hour of need.

He looks up abruptly and nods. "Of course. Why don't you start with food so you don't faint, trip, or injure yourself again."

I open my mouth to react. Is this his version of playing nice? But he speaks again before I can call off our truce. "I left the Spam musubi on the counter. I know it's your favorite."

The Truth Is in the Detours

He's said the perfect thing to disarm me. My comfort food will forever be a plate lunch with kalua pig, because Lani wanted us to understand and appreciate her Hawaiian heritage.

"Do you want some?" I call as I head to the kitchen.

"No, I'm good."

When we were kids, we'd perch on the stools in Beau's kitchen like we were baby birds at our mama's beak, devouring Lani's snacks before she could finish making them. I thought Beau was the luckiest kid alive—for many reasons. But homemade food was undoubtedly one of them. If Lani wasn't frying up fresh malasadas for breakfast, his dad, Arthur, was making savory crepes or croissants filled with Brie and ham. Beau had the best of both worlds, spoiled by the culinary traditions of his Hawaiian and French heritage. Meanwhile, Dad had two meals he could make that didn't come from a box.

Later, Lani taught me to cook her specialties. To this day, I feel most at ease while experimenting in the kitchen. Lani gave me that gift. And to a lesser extent, my mom. But who knows if my memories of baking with my mother are even real. I don't trust anything about my earliest recollections now.

I shove one of the Spam-and-seaweed rolls in my mouth and load two more on a napkin. I find Beau in the doorway to the office, surveying the damage as I swallow a bite. The salt and fat fortify me. I hate to admit it, but he was right. I needed some food.

"Where do we start?" he asks. "I assume we need to clear out the room and look for additional clues?"

"If there are any." The way Dad kept that document—hidden away in a coupon mailer in an unmarked folder—makes me suspect there's nothing else. Perhaps he kept the court order as an insurance policy in case Mom turned up here and he needed to prove sole custody or something. But I imagine the rest of the document—pages 2 through 10—held information he didn't want to keep. "I don't think I can face the office quite yet. Let's start with an easy win. I've almost finished clearing his bedroom." I went through it yesterday but couldn't bear

15

to go through his clothes. I left that for later, thinking it would be the most emotional job. How naive I was then.

Beau waves me forward in resignation. I sense him calculating how much longer his sentence might be. It makes me want to mess with him.

"Be warned, though," I say. "Henry had some weird kinks."

"Ophelia." His lung capacity must be exceptional, because the exasperated sigh he releases is impressive.

"You think I'm kidding," I say over my shoulder. He's right on my heels as I step down the hallway. "Earlier, I found sci-fi erotica on his nightstand."

Beau groans, and I stifle a giggle. I forgot how much I loved embarrassing him. Maybe I can enjoy myself with Beau, after all.

"There was a stash of weed in his dresser. Vintage *Playboy*s under his bed. My favorite was 'TV Broadcasters Bare All.'" Sifting through Dad's stuff has brought me closer to him in all the wrong ways, and this process might compel me to deep-clean my own apartment to avoid postmortem embarrassment. Not that I have any family left to sort through my junk.

I notice the tips of Beau's ears have turned a satisfying pink. "Just tell me what to do."

"The power." I rub my hands together until he raises his brows. I swing open the door to the bedroom. It's mostly empty, and the brown carpet is a shade darker where the furniture once stood.

I point to the closet. It's the only task left to tackle in here, which I've been putting off. It's the intimacy and finality. Dad will never again wear his favorite Padres jersey or those terrible cargo shorts he insisted were too practical to part with.

Donning my emotional armor, I yank on the brass knobs, fighting with the bifold doors until they collapse and slide wide. Dad's scent is potent, trapped in the fibers of his wardrobe. I want to bottle it in my lungs to savor when his memory fades.

His clothes hang in disordered rows across two short rods— wrinkled oxfords, vintage jerseys, hoodies, and graphic tees silkscreened with puns or names of places we'd visited together. Shorts and pajamas are stacked haphazardly on the top shelf, shoved between baseball bobbleheads, a stash of bite-size Snickers, and Target bags full of receipts and trash. Clearing a lifetime of detritus is equal parts heartbreak and frustration.

Beau assembles a moving box with three efficient flicks of his wrist. I dump the boxers, socks, and threadbare board shorts in one swipe but hesitate as I thumb through the shirts. The mismatched hangers scratch against the rod in a dissonant peal. I stop when I find a hunter-green T-shirt he bought during our trip to Yosemite with a sketch of Bridalveil Fall across the chest. I toss it to the corner to keep.

"You live in LA now?" Beau asks as he picks through a bag of receipts. Small talk. That's something we haven't tried.

"Yep. And you're in Berkeley?" I throw a vintage Chargers hoodie into the keep pile, even though the team betrayed my hometown.

"Oakland, technically."

Of course Beau would correct me. I live in Pasadena, technically, but I didn't insist on precision.

"My mom said you're running your own business?"

I think Beau may be checking off a list of conversation starters he prepared in advance. We used to be able to finish each other's sentences.

"Yeah. I'm a freelance virtual assistant."

"Oh," he says, and it's clipped, dismissive. I'm used to this—people who think "freelance" is code for "unemployed." "But I thought you finally finished your BA?"

I snort. "I did." After so many stops, starts, and transfers that my transcript became a treasure map of mediocre academic institutions. But I run my own business—quite capably, thank you—and there's so much superiority to unpack in Beau's implication that personal assisting is so lowly that it shouldn't require a degree.

"Sorry, I didn't mean to imply . . ." He doesn't finish his sentence. He shoves a handful of candy wrappers into a garbage bag, and I think I see a flash of guilt on his face.

It's not new that Beau is more successful than I am, but he's more successful than 99 percent of the population. He finished his PhD at twenty-seven, is a professor at UC Berkeley, and wrote two books on obscure historical incidents I know nothing about. He was a guest on *The Daily Show* when his second book was published. I watched while eating ice cream from the carton and drinking merlot from a box.

He's also married. And a homeowner. Both of which I am not, unless you count inheriting this hoarder's compound, which I do not.

"How long are you visiting?" I find it strange that he's stayed in town so long after the funeral. His semester is over, but he has a wife at home.

He shrugs. "Another week or so."

"Your wife is okay with you being gone this long?" Inquiring minds want to know: Can she survive much longer without her #hotgeek?

"My parents need help with a few repairs."

It's not an answer, I notice. I'd assume he'd jump at the chance to talk about his photogenic ER-doctor bride, but he doesn't take the bait. Before I can pry, he hoists the box of discarded clothing into his arms. I watch as he carries it into the hallway. He's an impressive physical specimen with a span of back muscles flexed from his shoulders to his ass. I used to be able to pin him while wrestling. My entire body flushes with the thought of trying that now. Not that I would. He's married. And I don't like him. Much.

When he returns, I'm loading another box of worn jeans and khakis. So many boring khakis. "What's it like to have your summers off?" I ask.

"I don't, really. I'm not teaching, but I need to update my dossier for tenure, and I'm taking a research trip for my next book," Beau says, in case I forgot he's a genius academic with an important career. He shoves the last receipts into the trash bag.

I don't know what "dossier" means, but I nod as if I understand what a big deal he is. "I have a busy summer, too. Lots of exciting client projects—travel itineraries to reserve, dog sitters to book, fights to have

The Truth Is in the Detours

with customer service representatives." I can't help but sacrifice myself to the altar of his superiority; it's a self-protection mechanism to poke fun before he does. Beau casts a wary glance my way as he lifts a Crock-Pot from the top shelf. He's either too self-important to understand self-deprecation or wondering why my dad stored a cooking appliance in his bedroom, which is fair.

Beau carries the slow cooker to the hallway and places it beside the other items destined for donation. When he returns, he leans against the doorjamb and clears his throat. "I don't know if I've had a chance to tell you how sorry I am about your dad."

I turn to him, but I don't have anything to offer but the same two words I repeated after each compulsory condolence at the funeral. "Thank you."

I saw Beau only briefly that day when he gave me an awkward hug that neither of us fully committed to. I stumbled into his clavicle before mumbling an excuse and hurrying away.

"I loved Henry, too. And I miss him already." Beau's gaze softens. And there's something familiar in that kind, boyish expression beneath the hardcover textbook of a man. He's paperback Beau: broken binding, creased cover, dog-eared pages, sepia hued.

It was always clear how Beau felt about my dad. They remained close even after Beau and I fell out. I offer a small smile, but it's pained and thin. "He loved you right back."

"Despite this secret, he was a good man, Phe. And he worked so hard to be your everything."

Beau's right. My dad was my person. My home. My emergency contact and first phone call. But I can't give Beau the reaction he's probably expecting. I have too many emotions simmering below the surface to let any of them boil over.

I nod. "He was. Now, if I get kidnapped by a Tinder date who turns out to be a murderous clown with a soundproof basement, no one will know I'm missing." I toss a Stone Brewing Company sweatshirt into the keep pile and turn to find Beau blinking at me as if I've sprouted a tail—with scales.

"Is that an ongoing concern?"

"Well," I say, "Dad was the only person with my location access. We shared an app. The clown was just an example."

"So, like, if you get lost hiking," he tries, editing me in real time.

I snort. "The clown is definitely more likely than the hiking."

We both pause at the sound of the doorbell. I should take the battery out of that thing—the familiar toll is a trip wire on my memories and travels from my ears straight to my subconscious. It's strange how scent and sound can do that in ways the other senses cannot.

"It's probably my mom or dad," Beau says. "Checking to make sure we haven't strangled each other." He heads out to let them in.

The closet is nearly empty. I flick through the remaining jackets before my ears perk up at a familiar pair of voices. I dart out of the room and rush to the entryway as Cherry and Simone slip into the house. They're speaking over each other as Beau stares straight ahead, his entire posture on alert.

"Beauregard Augustin," Cherry hums, reaching in for a hug that Beau somehow evades. She plays it off by leaning against the open door as he escapes to the porch. "I loved your book."

"I'm going to leave you to it, Ophelia. Have a nice night." Beau sounds like an automaton.

"Thanks for your help," I call out. The only sign he's heard me is a stiff nod before he shuts the door.

Beau didn't need that reminder of another thing he hated about me—my friends. I fear whatever fragile truce we just formed is over.

CHAPTER 4

I haven't seen Cherry and Simone since the funeral two weeks ago. When they texted me afterward, I had the impression they had to google "what to say to a grieving friend" before reaching out. I appreciate their new initiative, but this is the worst timing.

Cherry's face is alive with the delight she reserves for the juiciest gossip. "He's hotter in real life than in photos. How did that happen?" She fans her cheeks. "There's no way I would have recognized him if I hadn't seen him on social media—and in *The New York Times*."

It's just like Cherry to appreciate someone once their stock rises. When we were in school, she thought his name was Bartholomew. Cherry moved to San Diego before our freshman year of high school and handpicked me to be her best friend. But I sometimes wonder whether we would have become friends had we met now. Back then, the captain of the football team was pursuing me, and I had all the unearned popularity he attracted. My stock has fallen since—but one of Cherry's best qualities is her loyalty. I may not have my shit together, but her friendship is for life. It's more than I can say for Beau's.

"Phe," she hums, turning her attention to me, "how are you?" She pulls me into a hug and pats my back, swaying until her long chestnut hair sticks to my face in a static dance.

"My turn." Simone steals me from Cherry to wrap me in her long arms.

"We're all yours. The kids are with Austin," Cherry says. "You'd think he'd offered me a full day at the spa by the way he was so proud to watch his own children for a few hours. Meanwhile, I laid out outfits, diapers, and instructions on heating the breast milk. I may as well hire a mannequin to parent while I'm away."

I expected my maternal yearning to kick in when my friends started to breed. But no. The batteries died in my biological clock years ago, and stories like this whack the snooze button.

Simone shrugs and flicks her long blond hair off her shoulder. "I have to say that your sad hetero thing is overrated. Alyanna is taking the kids out all by herself."

"Why aren't you dressed?" Cherry asks me. "We texted you five times."

"Oh." I don't remember the last time I checked my phone. "Sorry, I didn't get them."

Cherry rolls her eyes. "You're a mess, Ophelia Dahl. But we love you anyway."

We head into the kitchen, and I search for something to serve them. The kitchen is spare. But the Spam musubi is still laid out on the counter.

Cherry inspects it. "Is that Spam?" she mumbles before drawing her hand back. "Where's your wine?"

I open the pantry, but I don't hold out much hope. Dad wasn't a fan.

"There's beer." Simone pulls a six-pack from the fridge. She hands one to Cherry and offers another to me, but I decline with a quick shake of my head.

Luckily, there's a beer opener attached to the wall, because I have no idea where the handheld would be.

Cherry sits at the kitchen table before taking a swig of her beer. "Okay, so, spill. What was Beau doing here? And why did he run away like you'd been doing something naughty?" She throws her head back and laughs.

The Truth Is in the Detours

Because he's always hated you, I don't say. It was one of the reasons for our rift. Beau had a list of grievances about Cherry and referred to her as Regina George from *Mean Girls*—never to her face; he wasn't that brave. I thought it was unfair and didn't appreciate what it implied. Which idiotic sidekick did he think I was? "His parents still live next door."

"Hmm . . ." She eyes me skeptically. "Are you fucking him? I'm sure he'd love to comfort you in your time of need."

"Beau, ew, no," I say, too loud. "Married men aren't my type." And even if he weren't married, Beau tolerates me out of familial obligation—and just barely.

Cherry shakes her head. "Beau's not married."

"Yes, he is. His wife is that adorable doctor who looks like she walked off the set of *Grey's Anatomy*," I quip. "And she's an influencer. Dr. Bianca Augustin. I thought you followed her."

They both stare back at me, eyes alight with salacious news. "They divorced. Where have you been?" Cherry asks.

Simone chimes in. "Last year, she posted on her Insta all about fresh starts and new beginnings, broken hearts, yadda yadda, and then Beau was noticeably MIA on her socials when #HotHistorian had been the star attraction. It's so obvious."

"What? Seriously? What happened?" How did I not hear about it? Why didn't Beau tell me when I asked about her?

I lean against the counter, wondering whether Beau's extended stay has more to do with his divorce than whatever excuse he gave me earlier.

Simone shrugs, sitting next to Cherry. "No idea. But 50 percent of straight marriages end in divorce."

"Not true," Cherry snaps, her focus landing on Simone. "Educated professionals who marry in their late twenties have a higher chance of making it, statistically."

I sense they're both projecting.

I stare at Simone as she sips an IPA. The pack has been in the fridge since I arrived. Dad must have been saving it for a special occasion, and I couldn't bear to drink it without him. He rarely splurged on microbrews unless he had people over. But that brand was his favorite.

Cherry waves her arms in front of my fixed stare. "Anyway, why was Beau here?"

"He was helping me pack up the house," I say.

Cherry coos. "How neighborly."

My phone erupts with a telltale ringtone, an instrumental version of Dolly's "9 to 5," and I fish my phone out of my pocket.

"Hello, Juniper. How can I help you?" I coax a professional calm into my voice and pinch my eyes shut as I answer.

"Why haven't you answered my emails?" Her voice is without inflection; the barbed words speak for themselves.

"Sorry, today has been hectic."

"Do you have a pen?"

I reach across the counter to grab a stray purple crayon and press it to the back of a CVS receipt. "Always."

"I need a flight to Singapore on Monday morning. First class. One connection max. Returning in ten days. I will also need transportation and a hotel. The Fullerton will suffice. If not, the Ritz. I've forwarded additional details to your email. Any questions?"

"None. I'm on it."

"Tomorrow, I have commitments until 3:30 and a spa treatment at 4:15. If you have any questions, call me at 3:45." She clicks off, and my headache clicks on.

"Duty calls," I hiss.

Simone jumps up from her chair and approaches me. "Ophelia, it's Friday night."

Is it? I've lost track of the days.

"We came to take you out. You need some cheering up," Cherry says. "We aren't taking no for an answer."

I wince at the thought of going out—in real clothes, makeup, and heels. I'm too feral for any of that, not to mention the hellish task I

The Truth Is in the Detours

must complete for Juniper and the mystery I need to solve about my existence.

"I can't. Not tonight. I have this work thing, and then I need to pack up the house. Dad's hoarding tendencies got a little out of control."

"Pheeeeee," Simone whines. "We never see you."

"It's the first time I've had a babysitter in a month," Cherry says. A babysitter who is her husband. I don't have to say anything, because Simone cuts Cherry a judgmental look that does the heavy lifting for me. "Austin works long hours," Cherry says defensively.

"Thanks for the invite, but I can't tonight."

Cherry offers a little pout but hugs me.

I move them toward the front door, and Simone pauses, surveying the scene. "Do you want us to stay and help?"

I take in her dark-washed jeans, spike heels, silk camisole, and fresh blowout. I shake my head. "No, you go. Have fun. I need to knock this out."

I shuffle them out and close the door before collapsing with my back against the oak. I take in the house, which grows a little emptier every day.

Every dent in the drywall contains a memory—when I played catch with Dad in the family room, when I convinced Beau to set off the toy rocket and it almost set the ceiling on fire, when my half-blind dog, Billy Goat, misjudged the doorway and punched a hole in the wall with his snaggletooth. The ticks on the kitchen doorframe track my height from childhood to adulthood. The walls Dad painted bright yellow when I said the house was dreary remind me he would do anything to make me happy—except tell the truth.

Back in the kitchen, the nearly full bottles of IPA sit on the counter, sweating as the condensation collects on the amber glass.

I load a plate with Lani's feast and sink down at the table to eat alone.

CHAPTER 5

The next morning, I have the window open in the office and the overhead fan circling so fast it's threatening to scatter piles of paperwork everywhere. The room smells like stale paper, worn leather, and the tea-tree-oil lotion Dad used on his eczema—it smells like Dad himself. I gasp for fresh air and swallow a wave of grief that threatens to consume me.

While clearing out the house in a rush to sell, I expected to find surprises—photos, doodles, notes, love letters—tokens to cling to because he left me too soon and too suddenly. But this new truth kills Dad all over again, more permanently than the artery that failed him.

In the last two weeks, I've cleaned out the rest of the house, so the office is my last hope for answers. If I don't find the missing pages of the court order, maybe I can contact the courthouse to track down the entire document—assuming they keep thirty-year-old records.

But before I fall into that bureaucratic quicksand, I decide to search for my mother online, or perhaps I'm procrastinating. I create an empty spot on the floor and open my laptop. My first Google search doesn't produce anything; there are about a million hits for Mary Johnson and Mary Ann Johnson, and very few for Mary Dahl or Mary Ann Dahl. The image search provides a plethora of diverse faces and profiles, but none of them look like the cherished pictures I've clung to.

I catalog the people who might know more. Dad's parents died years ago, and I never knew Mom's side of the family. I asked about grandparents, aunts, and uncles, but Dad's responses were vague. He didn't like to talk about Mom.

I think I'm beginning to understand why.

All our friends, all the people in our lives, knew us after Mom "died," and we left Oregon to settle here in San Diego.

I fall into a rabbit hole of amateur sleuth work. I find websites promising biographical information—addresses, court records, marriage, death certificates, traffic tickets, arrests. But I can't tell which sites are legit and which will implant spyware on my laptop.

I click back to the search window containing all the faces of Mary Johnsons who aren't my mother and slam it shut. There's a knock on the front door before it creaks open. I look up to see Beau poking his head in the doorway of the office. His hair is falling onto his forehead the way it would when we were kids—before he learned how to style it and show off the bone structure that was waiting to be discovered.

"You're back," I say, unable to keep the surprise out of my voice.

"Still need help?" He pauses in the doorway as if waiting for an invite.

I look around. I'm in the eye of the hurricane and not sure how he'll navigate the storm. "I may be beyond help. But if you're offering . . ."

"I am," he says pointedly.

He steps through and hovers beside the seven DVD players stacked in the corner. "Should I ask?"

"Those are relics from Dad's brief stint volunteering to reproduce piano recital videos." He bought seven electronics on the precipice of extinction just to support my short-lived run as a terrible musician. "I'm trapped in the graveyard of Dad's good intentions and short attention span."

Dad was a super volunteer—scorekeeper for my swim meets, assistant coach for my soccer team, and occasional videographer. He was messy in many ways, but I could never accuse him of being unsupportive. Dad fawned over me. But I don't think he had much faith in me. I wanted to try soccer? *Sure, honey.* I wanted to quit after scoring a goal against my own team? *Whatever will make you happy.* He didn't talk to me about failure as an opportunity for resilience. He didn't tell me I'd do better next game. When I brought home straight C's my freshman year? *I'm sure you tried your best.* I was the light of his life, but the shimmer was more disco ball than shooting star. His greatest wish for me was to be fine. Not great. Fine.

"You could sell them on eBay. There must be a market for collectors."

"Huh?" I say, losing the thread of the conversation.

"The DVD players."

I chuckle. "Right."

Beau steps over an open box, sidesteps a stack of self-help books, and crouches a few feet from me, holding a stainless-steel thermos in his hand. "What can I do?"

I flick my chin toward the growing piles I've created to my right. "Storage, donate, dump, recycle."

He scans the room. It's still chaos, but I have made some progress. "How do I know which is which?"

"Social Security cards, keep. *TV Guide*s from 1997, recycle. And if you uncover the truth about my lying parents, let me know."

"Noted," he mutters, and gets to work. "Did you tell your friends about your mom?" He spits out "friends" like most people would say "phlegm."

"No."

"Why not?"

I shrug. In their rush to drag me out, I didn't feel like there was an opening. Besides, Cherry and Simone are friends I escape into, not confide in.

"Is there anyone you can ask for more information? A relative? An old friend from before you moved?"

"Not that I can think of, other than your parents."

"Why them?" An edge of defensiveness crops up, and I remember we're not friends—not anymore.

"Do you think my dad told them something? We moved here soon after the accident. He could have let something slip—or confided in them at some point?"

"My parents wouldn't keep that secret from you." His posture stiffens, and he stares at me from across the piles.

"My dad did," I counter.

"Doesn't mean mine did."

We sound like we're on the playground, arguing about whose parents have more integrity. "Fine. Maybe not. He moved here and started over. Perhaps he lied to everyone, even your parents."

Beau tilts his head to the side, a gesture that is both conciliatory and smug, as if I've conceded the point when, really, I want him to tell me I'm wrong.

"Can you imagine my mom being able to keep that secret?"

As annoying as it is to admit it, he's right. She couldn't.

I notice Beau's bare ring finger as he riffles through the paperwork. He has officially beat me to all milestones—even the unfortunate ones. Dad sent me YouTube videos of every interview Beau ever did. He sent me signed copies of his books, Beau's wedding photos, and a guilt trip for not attending the wedding itself. I wonder why I didn't hear about the divorce. Our parents gossiped and kept us tethered to each other's lives even when we weren't on speaking terms ourselves.

When your contemporaries divorce, it has a definitive middle-age feel to it. It makes me feel older than when my friends were marrying, birthing babies, and buying minivans. And the thought of Beau going through it makes me melancholy for some reason. Perhaps it's lingering fondness for the kid he once was.

"I'm sorry about the divorce," I say, testing the waters. "I didn't know."

He nods but doesn't look at me, focusing on his task.

"You didn't mention it yesterday." I still think it's strange that he'd neglected to tell me when I asked about her directly.

"Surprisingly, my failed marriage is not my favorite fun fact."

"Right. Sorry," I say, deflating at Beau's harsh tone.

"It's fine," he grumbles. I clearly struck a chord, but he's not turning to leave.

It's too quiet, so I cue up music—my favorite eclectic playlist. I quickly cycle through two teeming piles of debris. Turns out, progress isn't twice as fast with two people; it's exponentially faster.

"Ophelia, what the hell?" Beau points to the Bluetooth speaker.

"What?" I halt mid-toss, so the fishing magazine lands in Beau's lap, drawing my attention to thighs that are as thick as my torso. He launches the magazine to its final resting place, and I drag my focus away.

"The music."

"What's wrong with the Fray?"

"Too many things to list. But the DJ is a bigger problem. You can jump genres or decades, but not both."

I scoff. "You live by too many rules." The song transitions.

"No. Just no," Beau moans.

"You cannot have a problem with Aretha Franklin." I hum along, which elicits a deeper frown from my cranky companion.

"I don't. I have a problem with you denigrating legends by shuffling them in with Justin Bieber." He takes a sip from the travel mug he brought along. Black coffee, I presume. I bet Beau is too health conscious for sugar or cream. Or maybe it's tea. Probably green tea—the breakfast drink of the morally superior.

I sip my coffee. It's filled with extra cream and three sugars. Take that, Beau Augustin, with your green tea, antioxidants, and sanctimony. "Don't hate on the Biebs."

"You are a sick woman." He scoops up a neat stack of paperwork to offer to the recycle pile and grumbles again when Aretha finishes her last notes and Taylor Swift throws melodic barbs at her former flames.

"I bet you listen to elevator jazz," I say.

"I have terrific taste in music, thanks."

"Of course you do, Beauregard."

He grunts before mumbling, "You know I hate that name."

The Truth Is in the Detours

"It's your name," I say. "Do you want me to call you Professor?" I wink and drop my voice to a lower register. "Or Dr. Augustin?"

"Just . . . call me Beau," he says, but his cheeks pink.

"As you wish." I set a stack of loan documents aside to review later.

"And watch the snark. I'm helping you." Beau doesn't look up at me while rummaging through what looks like furniture catalogs.

I nudge his foot with mine. "Did your mom send you back?"

"No." He glances out the window and taps his thigh, which is his nervous tic.

I study him. "I just found out my dad lied to me for thirty years. So my bullshit meter is on high. I want the truth, Beau."

He bites his bottom lip. "I came over because . . . I know you don't believe this, but I know a bit about what you're going through."

I tilt my head and watch him, but I still can't get a good read. "How?"

"Well . . ." He pauses for a beat before looking away. "My—" He starts, stops, clears his throat, and then spits out in a rush, "I'm writing a book on deceit."

"Wait," I say, anxiety and anger mixing as I recalibrate why he's here. Not as an old friend, but as a researcher? Not as someone who once held my earliest secrets, but as someone who wants to capitalize on my most recent one? "Are you trying to use me as content for your next bestseller?"

"No," he says. "Of course not. I meant I've heard stories like yours—in my research. And I thought I could help."

"Other people have found out their dead parent is alive right after their lying parent died?" I'm disappointed I misjudged his intentions and feel like I'm under a microscope—a human subject being studied for strange family trauma.

"Well, no . . ." he stammers. "But I have stories of women lying about their children's paternity. Men with multiple families whose adult children collide years later. Parents who kidnapped their kids to protect them from an abusive parent. And all the people caught in their wake struggling to understand."

I stare him down but feel my anger burn out—there isn't enough air between my emotions for any of them to smolder too long. "That doesn't sound like a history book," I say.

"It evolved from a project I chaired last year." He straightens his posture, adjusts his glasses, and settles into professor mode. I envision him behind a podium with elbow patches and an ink stain on his breast pocket. "We captured oral histories from everyday people and noticed a theme—folks using it as a confessional. The book is a detour for me, but not as much as it may seem. Lies can change history—or our perception of it. Imagine if FDR hadn't lied about his disability or if JFK hadn't lied about his health. The entire twentieth century could have unfolded differently. Half of what we *think* we understand is fabricated—which can change the study of history itself."

I look away, absorbing his admission. "You want me to be a research subject—a lab rat?"

"Of course not. You're not . . . I wasn't . . . Forget it. I was just trying to help." He sighs.

"How?" I challenge.

"Well, I can't help until you figure out what you want." Beau folds his arms across his broad chest and bites his bottom lip. His focus is thrown over my shoulder at the bare wall, but then he returns it like a laser beam. "So what do you want, Ophelia?"

Get right to the fucking point, why don't you, Beau. "The truth."

"You sure?"

"Yes." *Not at all.*

"Well, *that* I can help with."

CHAPTER 6

I pluck three glossy photos from the bottom of a drawer. We've been at this for almost a week. I've taken loads of stuff to a consignment store, made three trips to Goodwill, and paid several visits to the dump. Beau has stopped by for a few hours each day, helping me dig through the worst of the detritus to find clues. We've thinned the debris, leaving only a few piles to contend with. And we haven't killed each other.

"Look at these," I say.

Beau accepts the pictures between careful fingertips and squints at the worn photo on top. "You look like a rainbow sherbet ice cream cone."

"Well, I couldn't have you upstage the bride."

The photo captures our backyard civil ceremony, presided over by his older cousin, Shelley, with my incontinent one-eyed mutt, Billy Goat, as our witness. Someone had strung wildflowers on his tree house to create a makeshift altar. Beau was dressed as Spider-Man, complete with the plastic mask, and I donned my favorite dress from that summer—a rainbow-striped tube top connected to a chiffon chartreuse skirt. Beau is shooting fictional webs at the camera with flexed wrists as I hold a bouquet of wilted dandelions. We were five, I think. But the day lived on in infamy. Dad called Beau my "first husband" for the next decade.

"Can I keep this?" Beau asks, looking away.

"Be my guest," I say, although I'm unsure if he's serious.

He sets it on the chair behind him before returning to his earlier task. "I'm leaving tomorrow."

We're almost done, but I glance around the space to hide my disappointment at losing my sparring partner. It's been nice having him here. There's something familiar and comforting in the way we finish each other's sentences, even when we're bickering. We've found a few clues—Mary's place and date of birth, my parents' marriage certificate, and a few photos I hadn't seen before. They will come in handy. But I haven't found pages 2 through 10 of the original legal document. And there is no letter from Dad explaining everything he never told me.

It's like finding blank pages at the end of a book.

"Where are you going? Home?"

"No. I have to do some book research. I have several interviews set up—beginning in SoCal and traveling up the West Coast."

"Oh." I look away, biting my bottom lip. He's stuffy, distant, and sometimes arrogant, but I'm accustomed to his company now. "Thanks for all of this." I brush my hands against my shorts. "For an academic, you are surprisingly good at manual labor."

He shakes his head but otherwise doesn't react. "Are you staying here or heading back to LA?"

I shrug. I don't know what's worse: wallowing in the space that has borne witness to my pain or fleeing to a place with no memory of Dad at all. Beau's trip sounds more interesting than either of my options. He gets to escape.

"Are you meeting with the liars or their victims?" I ask, deflecting.

"Liar—" He clears his throat and closes his eyes. "The people with secrets."

"Sounds like an uplifting vacay."

"It's work." He heaves a box into his arms, and I wander into the kitchen to refill my coffee. When Beau steps through the doorway a moment later, I'm at the window staring out over the brown lawn and the cracked walkway linking the porch to the sidewalk. My Realtor has hired a contractor to do a bit of work—exterior paint, cosmetic touches,

The Truth Is in the Detours

minor repairs—before the house goes on the market. But I suspect the new buyer will scrape and rebuild. And that will be it. My childhood, as misleading as it was, will be wiped off the map.

"Want me to help you do some online research to find your mom before I leave?"

I turn to see him leaning against the doorjamb with his arms crossed. He looks so handsome in the fractured light coming in from the kitchen window—the sunbeam highlights the hard angles of his cheekbones and the soft lines of his mouth. I want to collapse into him, let him wrap those impressive arms around my waist, squeeze away all my pain, and maybe kiss away all my confusion. I look away and shake off the absurd fantasy. I may not recognize him in that body, but I can't forget he's Beauregard Augustin. He's quicksand and would drag me deeper into self-doubt and melancholy—he can't be my escape.

"What's the worst lie you've heard so far?" I ask instead. We haven't talked about his book. I think it's bizarre he wants to speak to liars and paint their deceptions with watercolor words.

"I haven't ranked them. Because I'm trying not to pass judgment."

That's peculiar. The Beau I knew had a metaphorical gavel on hand for every moral infraction. "Then what are you trying to do?"

He hesitates for so long I'm not sure he'll respond. But then he drops his voice to a whisper. "I just want to understand why."

∼

Lani invites me to dinner for Beau's last night in town. I'm too tired to be good company, but she will do most of the talking. She has a feast of sweet and sour chicken, sweet rolls, and corn spread over the counter. The scent of her food, mixed with Lani's perfume and the essential Augustin of it all, is comforting but mournful.

When I peer into the kitchen, Beau's dad, Arthur, is pouring wine. He looked youthful and alive on the podium at Dad's service, delivering a eulogy that feels euphemistic in hindsight. But here, in the overhead lights, I see how much Arthur has aged. Dad had been here, watching a Padres game with Arthur and Beau, when he had his stroke. Arthur and Lani followed him to the hospital, and Beau was the unlucky soul who called to tell me. He tried five times before leaving a voicemail—I didn't have his number programmed in my phone, so I thought it was a telemarketer. But when I raced into the hospital after fighting traffic from LA, I caught a glimpse of Beau and his parents still in the waiting room.

Arthur turns and smiles at me now, lines cutting deep grooves in his cheeks. "Ophelia Rose," he says in his soft French lilt as he reaches for me. I step into him, and he kisses my cheeks before cupping my shoulders in his hands and leaning back to assess me. "You don't look well, ma puce. I thought Beau was helping you."

"He is," I say, defensive for both of us. "I'm just tired." I ran out of moisturizer two days ago and haven't been sleeping well. I know I'm not looking my best. But thanks, Arthur, for noticing.

"You'll eat. It'll do you good." He hands me a stemless wineglass and clinks it with his own. "So nice to have you here. You sure you must sell?"

"My bank account is definitely sure."

"Ahh," he sighs. "But we're too old for new neighbors. What if they're young people who play terrible music and don't tend to their yard?"

"Papa, Ophelia is a young person who plays terrible music and doesn't tend to her yard," Beau says as he walks into the kitchen and digs in the fridge for a beer. But he winks at me, and something about that intimacy makes my stomach flutter.

"Hey," I say as Arthur chuckles.

"We can forgive you everything, ma puce. But I can hold a grudge against squatters who take over your home." Arthur grins.

It's strange to see that Beau has grown up to look so much like Arthur; he favored Lani as a kid. But now, Beau's a mix of both—with

The Truth Is in the Detours

Arthur's height, jawline, and bad vision, and Lani's gorgeous tan and thick hair.

Lani follows Beau into the kitchen and greets me with a fierce hug. She pulls back, and I lean over to pick up the item I brought along. "I finished going through everything." I slide a heavy leather case onto the counter. "And I want you to have these."

"Oh, Ophelia," Lani sighs. "We couldn't."

Arthur leans in, opening the latch and lifting the lid to reveal rainbow rows of ceramic poker chips. "But Henry taught you to play with this set."

"You both taught me to play. Besides, you need the practice more than me now."

Arthur gasps and then chuckles. "Ah, ma puce." His eyes go glassy as he looks at my dad's heirloom set. "If we accept these, you must promise to come home to play with us. Maybe for your birthdays—we can have a tournament like old times." He glances from me to Beau and back.

Beau and I look to each other at the same time—our gazes locked. The thing is, Beau and I share the same birthday. He was born promptly at 8:00 a.m., and I came screaming into the world at 8:00 p.m. Dad used to say that the fact we were born under the same sign proved astrology was bullshit.

We celebrated together throughout our childhood. We visited the San Diego Zoo when we turned five, Disneyland at ten, and SeaWorld at twelve. But we'd always come back here for a poker tournament and cake. Separate cakes because Beau's preferred flavor was the wrong one. Who the hell likes carrot cake? He still hasn't forgiven me for blowing out his candles when we turned nine. But he was lagging, and I was ready to kick ass in Texas Hold'em.

Arthur wraps an arm around my waist and kisses my temple as Lani squeezes my hand. It sounds so tempting—something to look forward to at the end of the summer—but Beau says, "Not possible. The semester starts that Monday, and I'll have to be home by then." Just when I think the ice is thawing between us, he freezes me out.

Lani flashes him a scowl for killing the moment before saying, "Dinner is almost ready. Just waiting on the rice."

"Phe, can I borrow you for a minute?" Beau says from behind me.

I peel away from Lani and Arthur to follow Beau to the backyard. I step onto the covered lanai as he closes the glass sliders behind us. I catch a glimpse of his tree house, although it's shrouded by the overgrown branches of the giant oak tree. The sight of it makes my chest ache with nostalgia. We got up to so much trouble out there.

"Remember when I forced you to kiss me in the tree house that summer before high school?" I release a soft chuckle. We've never talked about it, and I don't know what possessed me to mention it now.

"I didn't think you remembered that." Beau swallows hard and looks toward the structure. "But you didn't force me."

"I totally did. I had to drag you into it, like everything else. Just like when you were too nervous to climb those rocks in Joshua Tree, or too worried about getting caught to sample my dad's scotch at that holiday party, or too anxious about sharks to learn to surf." As a kid, Beau wouldn't try anything unless I dragged him out of his super-size comfort zone.

"Not true." Beau clears his throat, folds his arms over his chest, and leans against the column. "I just didn't want my first kiss to be like that."

My body heats in humiliation. Why did I bring this up? My ego can't afford any more hits. But it was a good kiss. I would bet the last measly dollars in my bank account on it. "You didn't want it to be like what?"

"Like practicing for sport." Beau flips his focus to me, and I see Beau the boy—and all that vulnerability—underneath the confidence his adulthood has borne.

"It wasn't like that," I say, disagreeing with him on instinct.

He scoffs. "Yes. It was. You said you wanted to practice. But you didn't tell me it was because you had a crush on Matty Jones. And a week later, we started high school, and guess who was on the arm of that meathead?"

Okay. Maybe he has a point. Maybe I studied *Cosmo*'s "Complete Kissing Guide" as Beau reread *Great Expectations* three times for his Summer Honor's English assignment. And maybe I was bored as he highlighted passages until his fingertips were stained yellow. Maybe I didn't want to embarrass myself during my first real kiss and thought Beau and I couldn't possibly screw up our friendship. Maybe I was wrong about all of it.

Especially when I assumed kissing Beau would feel like kissing my brother. Because it definitely didn't.

But I wouldn't dare tell him any of this. Or admit that if Lani hadn't called us to dinner, I may have kept kissing him. And if he hadn't acted so weird for weeks afterward, who knows if I would have ever dated Matty at all.

But that's ancient history.

"I was so nervous," Beau confesses. The admission startles me, and I look away. "I thought for sure you were going to tease me or rate my performance."

"You did just fine," I say before I think better of it. Our gazes lock, and I can't discern what he's thinking—but I'm replaying that first, sweet kiss like it happened yesterday. He tasted like strawberry Starbursts, smelled like coconut sunblock, and pulled me close like he'd done it a hundred times before.

Beau swallows once, and I feel my pulse rage through my skin—but he looks away first, and I exhale a shaky breath. It's just nostalgia, I tell myself. Everyone's pulse races when thinking of their first kiss.

"Why'd you bring me out here?" I ask.

Beau studies me for a heartbeat, and I shiver despite the warm night. He clears his throat. "I'm not sure how much you've looked into it, but I did some research." He pauses. "The document you found means child protective services had grounds to terminate your mom's rights. It wasn't a typical custody dispute. A parent can sue for custody in Oregon, but they can't sue to get the other parent's rights terminated. And a parent can't waive their rights voluntarily unless someone else is stepping in to adopt."

"What are you trying to say, Beau?" I don't like where this is going. It sounds ominous.

"I just want to make sure you're ready for what you may find."

"I am," I say, even though I absolutely am not. I swallow, the emotions suddenly too big to keep at bay. I have only a handful of memories of my mother, but they're like specks of spilled glitter clinging to me years later—a day at the beach, a dance party in the kitchen, baking cupcakes, singing at the top of our lungs with the car windows rolled down. I don't understand what happened all those years ago, but I can't imagine it's as bad as Beau is implying. My mom wasn't abusive. I would have remembered. I would sense it. Right?

"Okay." Beau exhales and hands me an envelope.

"What's this?" I glance at him before turning it right side up.

"Some possible leads on your mom. I've narrowed the search hits based on the personal details we found. There are a few addresses for a woman who could be her—a list of places she lived over the last few years and her dates of residency." He drops his volume. "You can search for her when, if, you're ready."

"How'd you find these?"

"One of my former grad students is a whiz at archival research. She owed me a favor."

I peel open the envelope and unfold the paperwork, skimming the words. There are pages of addresses and personal details on several Mary Johnsons, but Beau has highlighted information about one woman in her late fifties whose footprint is on the West Coast. There's an address in Oregon and a few in small Northern California towns—Redding and Fort Bragg. This reality of my mother's existence delivers another truth bomb on parchment. I shove it back in the envelope.

"Sorry if I overstepped." He folds his arms. "But I told you I'd help. And I didn't want to head out without giving you some leads."

The Truth Is in the Detours

"No. Thank you. This is . . . Wow." He called in a favor for me. It's overwhelming—as is the information he found. I fan myself with the envelope, suddenly flushed.

"You don't have to follow up. But if you want to, you'll have a head start."

Beau found her trail. Dad could have found her. My mother could have found me. That grief thing bubbles up again, like a black hole, eating into my soul. It's so damn lonely grieving a beloved parent who betrayed you and realizing you wasted a lifetime of grief on a parent who didn't deserve it. I should have saved it all up for this moment when I would have to mourn them both: the fiction and the reality.

"Are you going to be okay, Phe?" Beau tries to capture my gaze and stoops to meet me at eye level. But I evade him.

"Yeah. Of course." I think of returning to Dad's house tonight, knowing that Beau won't stop by to help or irritate me. Or going back to my apartment and working all day without my nightly call from Dad. It's just so lonely. "Where did you say you're going again?" I ask as an idea develops, filling my empty well with possibility.

"Up the West Coast."

"Up to Northern California?" I prompt.

"Yeah." There's a note of suspicion in his voice.

He should be suspicious. My thoughts are tumbling down this hill like a boulder—untethered and dangerous.

"Take me with you," I blurt out.

His eyes widen, his lips part into a soft O, and he quirks his head to the side. "I'm sorry?"

"I can be your assistant. Take notes, plan your calendar, that sort of thing." My words rush out of me without a tether to rational thought.

"Don't you work?"

"I can work anywhere. I'm a *virtual* assistant. But I could be your physical assistant."

His eyebrows disappear into his hairline, and he pushes his glasses up his nose.

"Get your mind out of the gutter. I mean, your actual assistant. In-person, concierge-level research assistant."

"I haven't sold this book yet. So, no advance. No money for an assistant."

"Your last book sold a gazillion copies and got you onto all the cool talk shows. Aren't readers salivating for another one of your thousand-page tomes?" His books are an essential public service so all the social climbers have something to discuss to make themselves look well read and cultured.

He folds his arms across his chest, his armor locking into place. "It's too dissimilar to what I've published thus far. So I'm looking for a new publisher. My agent is shopping around my proposal." His tone shifts to the lofty register of a lecturer. "But I must prove that I, as a historian, can write a compelling book about human behavior. I thought a deeper dive into first-person accounts would allow me to show that history is no more than a loose collection of stories we were told, informed by the perspective and integrity of the teller—"

"You launch into academic lectures faster than a drunk uncle launches into sexist rants at Thanksgiving dinner."

He sighs, cracking a small smile, and I hold up my hand. "I don't want you to pay me. I think the time away could be good for me. And I can help you." I have more oxygen by imagining time away from my reality. Maybe I'll use it to search for my mom. Maybe I'll use it to clear my head. Either way, it's better than my current option—standing still.

"I work alone," Beau says.

I laugh. "Okay, Batman. Consider me Robin. I'll even wear tights if you ask nicely." I bat my eyelashes and cock a hip. His gaze skitters over me before darting away, replaced by a weary frown. "And . . . maybe we can take a detour to track down my mom." The addresses in my hand are calling me like a siren. It's probably a terrible idea, but terrible ideas have always been the ones I like best.

He opens his mouth, closes it, and opens it again. "You and me. On a road trip? Together?"

"Relax. We're not taking the kids to the Grand Canyon. I won't make you play I Spy or Twenty Questions. It's for research. Your book. My life. Win-win."

"You'd be willing to take instructions from me?" he asks skeptically.

"I did clarify that 'physical' assistant was an unfortunate word choice, right?"

"Ophelia," he grumbles, and there's that adorable blush again.

"I will obey your every command, Professor."

His cheeks go even redder, but he lowers his voice, growing sterner. "And you won't go off script during the interviews?"

"I'll be so on script, I'll be sprawled on top of it."

"Many interview subjects are fragile," he says.

"As am I," I argue.

"You're fragile like a bomb," he mutters. "And are you sure you want to find your mom?"

"No," I admit. I'm sure of almost nothing right now.

"Then why come?"

I shrug. "I'll have the option," I say, and then try some vulnerability. "And I won't be alone if I choose to look."

He paces away, dragging his hands through his hair, knocking his glasses askew. I watch as he carves a path on the patio. "Fine," he finally spits out. "But I control the music. You can't talk the entire time or complain about camping or cheap motels."

"Camping?" I gasp.

He narrows his eyes, and I lift my hands in surrender. "I love camping. Sleeping on dirt is character building."

He releases a long, low breath. "I'm going to regret this, aren't I?" He leans against the post, his head hung in defeat.

I pat his shoulder. "Don't worry, Professor. Regret is also character building."

CHAPTER 7

Late the next morning, we settle into Beau's Subaru hatchback with our bags shoved in the back, my laptop at my feet, and his miserable indie bullshit playing at a monotonous volume. Lani packed three grocery bags full of snacks—li hing mui, teriyaki seaweed, macadamia nut cookies, mango slices, and kettle chips. She hovered and cooed about how adorable it was that we were taking a road trip.

"It's for work, Mom," Beau had grumbled.

But Lani was undeterred and stood in the driveway to send us off with as much vigor as wedding guests waving to the newlyweds.

"So, what're the sleeping arrangements on this trip?" I ask, about a day later than I should have.

Beau casts me a wary glance. "You'll have your own room at each stop."

"Are you worried I'll use a Sharpie on your face while you're asleep again? Because I promise I learned my lesson." I laugh.

"It took me a week to wash that off, you know. It looked like I had a flower tattoo on my cheek."

I swallow another laugh, because it sounds like he's still holding a grudge.

"Yeah, well, you superglued my eye shut while playing doctor," I say. "Which will take a lifetime to forget."

"You know I felt terrible about that. And you were the one who told me it was Visine."

The Truth Is in the Detours

"So you've claimed. But that's not how I remember it."

I dig into the li hing mui as Beau slips into the second lane on the 5. He darts his focus to me and wrinkles his nose. "Remember, those are prunes covered in salt," he offers. "Don't expect me to pull over every ten minutes when you get the runs."

"Don't expect me to hold you when this depressing music makes you cry."

He turns up the volume with an impatient flick of his wrist.

"Much better!" I shout over it. "It will drown out the sound of your tears."

He shakes his head at me. "It's mellow, not depressing."

I pick up his phone, where the song title scrolls across the screen. "This song is literally called 'Sorrow.'"

"I like this band."

"And I like music that doesn't make me question my existence. I don't need a soundtrack to do that."

He fights a smile. "Fine. But I reserve the right to drop you at a bus stop if you play bubblegum pop."

I scroll through his phone and settle on a playlist of acoustic singer-songwriters. Just shy of Top 40, skirting indie. He watches me, and his brows pinch together, the well-worn groove between his eyes becoming more prominent. He waits a beat before settling back into the driver's seat, appeased.

Since we packed up this morning, Beau has been Professor Augustin, determined to establish our new working relationship. As soon as I slid into the car, I entered his office. His anxiety is oozing from him. This is going to be a long trip.

"First crisis averted," I say. "We got this."

"We've been driving for ten minutes, Ophelia. The fact we've had a crisis at all is the noteworthy bit."

José González is strumming the guitar through the speakers while Beau swerves around a gaggle of rubberneckers who've paused to inspect a Prius with a flat tire.

"Who's our first liar?" I ask.

Beau gives me the side-eye.

"Where's our first stop?" I inquire instead.

"Barstow."

"Well, there's your answer. I would be an asshole, too, if I had to live in Barstow."

"You'd *be* an asshole?" he grumbles under his breath.

I ignore him. I am a big person. "You couldn't find a rich fraud in Malibu or somewhere? There must be a bunch of dishonest people with ski lodges, vineyards, beachfront homes . . ."

Beau waves a hand toward the coast as it stretches out beside us. "It's not too late to drop you off. I'll even throw in a sleeping bag so you can sleep beachside."

"Ha!"

"You sure you don't have things to do here?" he asks.

"Nope." I'd finished clearing out the house yesterday afternoon and packed up the things I want to keep, storing them in the attic for now. It's not much to show for sixty years of existence. But a life full of lies has a way of washing the nostalgia from the blood. Clearing out my childhood home after discovering Dad's deception is the opposite of grocery shopping when famished. I may live to regret the indiscriminate purge. But it was therapeutic to toss all the trash he'd hoarded.

I met with the real estate agent, Ronald, at the crack of dawn this morning. He has a contractor who will start renovations immediately. I downgraded his expectations about the improvements I could afford. He downgraded my expectations about my desired sale price.

"You don't have important things to do in LA?" Beau tries.

"I have a plant. But it's probably dead by now."

"That's rather pathetic, Phe." He tries to soften the judgment with the endearment, but it cuts too close to the artery.

"Yeah, well . . . what's waiting for you at home?"

"Not much, actually."

The Truth Is in the Detours

My eyes skitter over his bare ring finger, his tense posture. "Right," I say, and glance out the window. "You looked perfect together on Insta. What happened?"

"I don't want to talk about it." Beau taps his thumbs against the leather-clad steering wheel and squints at the road ahead.

"Well, at least you did the thing. The engagement. The wedding. Met the major heteronormative milestone. My longest relationship was in high school—Matty. And you know how dysfunctional that was."

"You don't still talk to that asshole, do you?" There's a bit of venom in his voice.

"No." But I don't want to admit how long our tumultuous relationship persisted after high school. No doubt Beau would judge me. There was no love lost between them. "As an adult, my longest relationship was only six months—with a mediocre tattoo artist. Three years if you count friends with benefits, but most people don't." I shrug, looking to Beau, who doesn't appear to be listening. "Romantic commitment is a requirement, apparently."

"Ophelia," he growls. "Fifteen minutes and you've broken two of my boundaries. Controlling the radio and talking endlessly."

"Fine. I'll shut up."

He grabs the phone and launches us into Death Cab for Cutie.

~

When Beau mentioned a West Coast road trip, I'd pictured palm trees, redwood trees, grapevines, and sandy beaches. I didn't anticipate we'd head inland to the brutal desert—to sparsely populated towns where hope came to die. When we pull into Barstow, the temperature is over 100 degrees. The panorama is flat and sizzling—sand blankets the shoulder with tufts of cartoonish plants emerging from the plain like a Seussian dystopia. Stucco homes litter the landscape, set behind treeless streets and chain-link fences.

"How fast can you type?" Beau's voice is raspy after hours of silence.

"Like lightning," I say. He casts a skeptical glance my way. "Seriously."

"Some of our interview subjects are reluctant to be recorded. So taking dictation would be helpful."

"See, I can be helpful," I say. "Who's up first?"

"Natalia Bridgewater," Beau says, but offers no details.

"How'd you get people to volunteer?" Lies rely on secrecy. Sharing their truth with a stranger so he can bind it into a bestseller is the antithesis of that.

"I have several hundred nameless confessions from people eager to unburden themselves behind the veil of anonymity. But they were short and created more questions than answers. I put a separate call out to folks for in-depth interviews. I've done dozens over the phone, but some didn't feel comfortable giving me their stories unless they could meet me, shake my hand. I don't understand their motivations, but I guess we'll find out."

Beau turns onto a short road that dead-ends at a dusty lot, with two boxy homes perched along the same side of the street. We stop in front of a beige house that blends into the desert backdrop, the lone pop of color a flamingo-pink patio umbrella. The heat rushes in like a swift tide when I pop out and hoist my backpack to my shoulder.

As I stand, Beau is right there, caging me in behind the open door. "Type quickly. Speak minimally," he says.

"Sit there and look pretty? How very *Mad Men* of you, Beauregard." I brush the wrinkles out of my navy shirtdress. It's paper thin and sleeveless to help me survive the apocalyptic temperature, but the collar and belt add notes of professionalism.

"This has nothing to do with . . . I'm not being . . ."

"Sexist?" I finish for him.

He growls. "You volunteered to be my assistant, not my partner. It has nothing to do with you being a woman. But you haven't done the research or established the relationships with the subjects."

"If you call them 'subjects' to their faces, you might need me to do the talking."

He folds his arms across his wide chest. I imagine this might intimidate some poor research assistant, but I remember when I made him pee his pants by coming out in full costume to lip-sync Britney Spears's ". . . Baby One More Time." He can pretend to love serious music and be a serious professor with professional standards, but I recall watching soap operas with him in identical mud masks and hair curlers.

"Fine," I say. "But if you revert to academic snobbery, I'm intervening for your own good." I reach up to fold the collar of his polo, and he startles at the contact, frowning as he stares at my fingertips.

"What are you—"

"Making you look pretty," I say. "In case we need to switch roles." I pat his shoulder and smile before snaking around him toward the house.

He circles my wrist and beckons me back with a gentle tug. "And no judgment."

I startle at the feel of his warm hand on my wrist but cover it with a chuckle. "I'm not the moral warden in this partnership, Beauregard."

He grinds his molars and narrows his eyes but ultimately releases me, and we walk side by side toward our first interviewee.

Natalia Bridgewater swings the door open before we step onto the porch, with an outraged Yorkshire terrier at her heels. "Shh, Georgina, shh," she scolds.

Natalia is not who I expected had I been given time to form an expectation. She must have been a tall woman in her youth, but she's stooped over a cane, her spine bent like a tree in a storm. Deep grooves stretch across her forehead and make wells down her cheeks.

"Ms. Bridgewater, hello. I'm Beau Augustin." He extends his hand, a warm smile blooming on his lips. "And this is my assistant—"

"You said it would just be you." Natalia scans me from head to toe before darting her cloudy gray eyes back to Beau.

"Ophelia will be taking notes. I understand you had reservations about me recording the conversation. Everything will be anonymous."

Natalia releases a small grunt, and Georgina growls in agreement. "Ophelia? Like that tragic *Hamlet* character? Do your parents hate you?"

"Jury's out, actually," I say, offering a placating smile.

Beau laces his fingers in mine and squeezes. It's so quick, and his hand is gone before I can reciprocate the gesture. Was it to comfort me or warn me to stay quiet? Either way, it startled me enough to accomplish both.

"Ms. Bridgewater, I can assure you—" Beau begins, but Natalia holds up her hand and opens the door wider as Georgina scuttles back into the dark hallway.

"Well, come in. I don't want the neighbors to see you lurking."

I scan the street behind us—it's so empty that an illusory tumbleweed cartwheels by, but I step through the threshold into the dark, spartan space. Natalia guides us into a living room with a beige love seat positioned in front of a square window too small for the wall. She takes a tentative seat in a rocking chair, and Beau and I sit on either side of the love seat. The cushions are old and plush, so we sink into each other, our thighs pressed together until I clamber to hug the armrest with one elbow. I lift my laptop from my bag, flipping it open to the empty Word doc with "Liars" typed at the top of the page. Beau does a double-take, his frown deepening before he reaches across me to hit the backspace with the tenacity of a woodpecker.

All right, no snarky titles. Got it. I retitle the document "Very Important Book." Beau shakes his head, clears his throat, and turns to Natalia. She has the dog on her lap, who lets out an aggrieved, swallowed bark.

"Thank you for speaking with me. As I mentioned when we spoke on the phone, I am interested in the impact of secrets. I'm not writing a salacious book; instead, I want to uncover how history may have gotten it wrong—especially family histories."

Natalia says, "Yeah, well. I read *On Death's Door* and *Homes Withheld*. So I get what you're going for. I like the way you look at things."

"I am grateful for your trust." Beau smiles and tips his glasses up his nose before settling back on the sofa. I fall into his side again. "We're here to listen. So please, begin wherever you feel would be most helpful."

"The beginning is as good a place as any," Natalia sighs. "Fifty years ago, I killed a man."

CHAPTER 8

Natalia runs through her story without interruption as I capture her words on the keyboard. My fingers cramp as she fills in the details. Her story is a series of dead ends and tangents, but I transcribe it all, knowing I'll need to make sense of it later.

"I had a headlight out, so the accident was my fault. I fled. It was instinct, self-preservation. I didn't find out he'd died until days later when I saw it in the paper. That's when I learned about the kid he left behind. I probably should have turned myself in, but my daughter was a baby then, and her dad was a deadbeat. So I didn't want to feed my kid to the foster care system. Instead, I made amends my own way and made sure my daughter was raised to be better than me." Natalia takes a sip of her iced tea, her hand slipping around the condensation, her knuckles pale as she grips the glass. "For decades, I anonymously sent cash to the guy's wife and son. And I raised my girl." Natalia is silent for several minutes, but Beau waits. He's a patient interviewer.

"My daughter, she grew up to be a teacher. You may have heard of her." Natalia grabs a stack of newspaper clippings from the wooden end table and waves them toward Beau. He leans forward and takes them from her shaking hands. He skims the articles and then passes them to me. I scan the headlines as Beau continues with the interview: *"Area teacher saves school from gunman," "Teacher's quick*

The Truth Is in the Detours

thinking averts tragedy," "Children are safe at home tonight thanks to brave schoolteacher."

I remember this incident. The gunman came into the cafeteria during lunch, and a teacher knocked him out from behind with a metal folding chair. He got off one shot. It clipped the principal in the shoulder, but there were no other casualties. It could have been catastrophic. I find the teacher's name in the second paragraph—Mandy Bridgewater.

"My daughter wouldn't have been there that day. You don't grow up to be a hero if your mom is in jail for killing someone," Natalia says. "You wanted to know how choices change history? There's a whole lot of kids who wouldn't be here today." She lifts her chin and knocks her cane against the hardwood.

And wow. Maybe. But that's some mental gymnastics she's doing to justify her own immoral choice.

"My lie almost ate me alive. But as much as I regret my mistake, I don't regret my secret," Natalia says.

"Why share it now?" Beau asks, his voice like a salve.

"I'm not a young woman, Mr. Augustin. And not a healthy one either. I'm sending a letter to the family tomorrow—because my doctor told me the treatment stopped working." She points to a sealed envelope on the coffee table. "They say the truth will set you free. I don't know about all that. Because people don't deal with the truth all that well. We use it for vengeance. An eye for an eye, making the whole world blind. But I'm running out of time to try my luck at making my peace. And I thought maybe you'd do my truth some justice."

~

The sound of Georgina's piercing bark is still ringing in my ears when Beau turns into a gravel lot. The red neon sign of the greasy-spoon diner spells D——ER, the *i* and *n* burned out, forcing us to use our imaginations to fill in the blanks. My imagination is filling in the blanks with E. coli and salmonella. But I'm not about to complain. There aren't any other choices in this wasteland. My stomach is bursting with sour sludge after I ate all those li hing mui on the way here; I need sustenance and nutrients to balance it out.

I pull my backpack out of the car before following Beau inside, sending a prayer to the weather gods that "Der" has AC, but it does not—proving no god anywhere has answered any of my prayers.

Der is a relic of a restaurant with peeling, checkered linoleum and seafoam-green vinyl booths. The grease hovers in the air, coats the surfaces, invades my nostrils as I peer into the kitchen. *Sorry, stomach lining. You're not getting any help here.*

Beau slides into a booth and grabs a menu, his face pinched into an expression more sullen than usual.

I plop down across from him and struggle with the menu, which is the size of poster board. "Do you think we'll get vegetables on this trip at some point?"

"There's a salad on the menu," he says.

"Really?" I fumble with the menu and knock his in the process. He scowls at me. "You should have snacked in the car," I say. "Lani packed snacks because she knows you get hangry."

"I'm not hangry," he snaps.

"How can you be so charming to Natalia, a literal killer, and be so grumpy to me?"

"Natalia is helping me with my book."

"*I'm* helping you with your book."

He shakes his head, but his lips curl into a small smile. "Natalia didn't frame me for using crayons on her bedroom wall."

"I was six," I say, holding back a giggle.

"It may have worked had you not written, 'B-O-W was here.'"

"Your capacity to remember every wrong I've ever done is . . . something."

The Truth Is in the Detours

"I'm sure I don't remember *every* wrong." Beau grins. "I'm a historian, not a savant."

I shake my head, although I'm enjoying his teasing. It's better than monosyllabic. But the interview is still sitting with me. "What do you think about Natalia? About her deciding in hindsight that not confessing meant her daughter became a hero years later."

"You don't think the ends justify the means?" he asks.

I drop my voice and lean forward. "That poor family had no closure. It's not like Natalia's lie was a victimless crime. You disagree?"

"Not necessarily. But I want to approach the book without bias. I'll let the readers decide."

"I think the man's widow and child get to decide. What if the child grew up to be a mass shooter because of his trauma? Does it nullify Mandy's good deed?"

Beau sighs and rubs his temples. "I'm not writing this book to pass judgment." There it is again, and something about that comment strikes me as more personal than professional.

"Why are you writing this book?"

Beau waves the server over and doesn't answer me. A thin guy, with a man bun and an apron, approaches from the counter.

"What can I get ya?"

"The spinach salad," I say.

The server, Dan his name tag says, shakes his head. "You don't want that, trust me."

"O-kay," I laugh. "What do I want?" Nothing like a man to tell a woman what she does and doesn't want. I need vitamins and minerals. But I've been a server, which leads me to trust him. I'd rather lose my suffragette badge than my stomach contents.

Dan bites his lip and tilts his chin. "The burger's all right. Grilled cheese if you don't eat meat. Also, the fries are legit."

"Burger and fries it is." I smile and notice his fantastic blue eyes—a blend of Tiffany boxes and the diamonds they enclose.

"You got it." His focus lingers on me as he takes my menu.

Beau clears his throat. "I'll have a chicken sandwich. And water."

Dan nods, looking Beau up and down before sauntering away. Beau glares after him.

"You have two speeds," Beau grumbles under his breath.

"Dare I ask?"

"Fight or flirt."

"I'm sorry?"

"What *do* I want?" he mimics in a register too high.

"You think I was flirting?" I chuckle. "Oh, Beau, if that's your idea of flirting, your radar is malfunctioning, but I'm happy to give you lessons."

"I don't need lessons." His cheeks pink softly.

"You might. I'm sure someone will flirt with you—someday." I'm sure people flirt with the man all the time. But he probably doesn't notice.

He glares at me with a surly expression, which could also be considered smoldering. Poor Beau. His late-stage hotness must be wasted on a bunch of introverted PhDs too distracted by academia to notice his pouty lips.

But then I gasp. "Oh my God. Your students."

He folds his arms across his chest, making his biceps pop. They're defined, with raised veins working hard to feed all that muscle. "What about my students?"

"I bet they flirt with you all the time. 'When are your office hours, Professor?' 'You're so smart, Dr. Augustin.' 'Is my thesis good for you, Professor?'"

"Gross, Phe." He frowns and fiddles with the napkin dispenser.

"Doesn't mean it's not true. I bet you're dressed in jackets with elbow patches in your students' fantasies."

He groans. "They're barely legal."

"I'm not implying that you encourage it. But c'mon. Of course they objectify you. Teacher fantasies are canon. Hotness isn't even required." The issue with teasing him is that it sears the images into my brain. I've

The Truth Is in the Detours

never had a teacher kink, but Professor Augustin is doing it for me. He's had such a glow-up during our long estrangement that he looks like a hot stranger—and I need to remind myself that the history between us is thicker than his gorgeous head of hair. Unlike some anonymous dude at a bar, I already know all the reasons Beau and I aren't compatible: temperament, intellect, animosity. Now if I can only convince my libido he's not for me.

"Only you could manage to insult me while objectifying me."

"Oh, please. I didn't say *you* weren't hot. You look like a Hollywood heartthrob playing the part of an academic. You're probably the subject of coed fan fiction starring Professor Benedict August."

"Are you always this crass?"

If he thinks this is crass, he really doesn't want to know what I'm thinking. "Are you always this prudish?"

His gaze collides with mine, and something heavy passes between us.

"No," he says in a tone that makes the little hairs on my arms stand up and a warmth brew somewhere it shouldn't. Because I immediately imagine him in a hundred nonprudish scenarios—most of them sans clothes.

Well then.

I look away first and don't say anything until the food comes.

～

I can't tell whether it's the ice maker or the vending machine hissing outside my motel window. Whatever it is, it's in its last days. We're in Lebec for the night, a tiny town at the base of the Grapevine off the 5. Like Barstow, it's desolate. California is spoiled with beauty, but so far, this road trip is doing its best to prove otherwise. Beau took control of the radio on the way out of Barstow and didn't speak much on the two-hour drive. There was nothing to distract me but flat plains interrupted by clusters of gas stations and fast-food chains.

We parted ways in the lobby when he handed me a key. I heard Beau leave his motel room a few moments ago when the door adjacent to mine slammed shut. He must have left to grab dinner. He didn't invite me along, which is probably for the best. Bad things happen when we spend too much time together: bickering, irritation, fantasies. And this has been a ton of togetherness.

I'll catch up on my day job, clean up my notes from this morning, and distract myself with TV while I work. The motel has basic cable. My choices are *CSI*, *Dateline*, and some new medical procedural like *Grey's Anatomy* but isn't *Grey's Anatomy*. I search for a show not fixated on death. I land on HGTV, which tries to convince me I can remodel an entire home for $40,000. Meanwhile, my real estate agent leaves me a voicemail detailing the number of Benjamins I will have to shell out to make modest repairs on Dad's house before selling. I turn off the TV and throw the remote across the bed.

The quiet settles into my bones like fog.

I've lived alone for years. But it didn't ever feel so lonely. I check my phone. I don't have any texts or messages from anyone but clients. I hover over the voicemail button. The devil on my shoulder is enticing me to pour alcohol on my raw wounds. My angel . . . well, I've never had an angel. I press play.

"*Ophelia, love, it's your dear old dad, checking in. How was your date? I hope he wasn't a prick like the last one who showed you a photo of his ex-girlfriend and asked to split the bill on your soda and his three beers. Either way, call me when you get home. I saw a story the other day about catfishing and want to make sure you aren't, you know, caught. Okay . . . well, I love you. Call me. No matter how late.*"

I press play.

"*Ophelia, love, it's your dear old dad—*" but I'm startled by a knock at my door, and I drop the phone.

I freeze. "Who is it?" I yell.

"Creepy dude with bad intentions." Beau's voice seeps through the door in a monotone.

The Truth Is in the Detours

I slide across the bed and open the door. He shoves a brown paper bag into my chest before I get it all the way open.

"Be ready at eight." Beau stalks off to his room.

"Don't let the bedbugs bite," I call after him.

I open the bag to find a large spinach salad and the last of Lani's macadamia nut cookies.

CHAPTER 9

Beau and I have now spent three days interviewing morally bankrupt individuals—at their homes, an Applebee's, a shoe repair shop, and a sad small-town zoo where the animals paced like, well, caged animals. But it isn't until we're waiting in the deserted parking lot of the fairgrounds of a nowhere town that I wonder if this trip was a terrible mistake. We've probably invited a killer, kidnapper, or other variety of psychopath to meet us at a destination of their choosing. And it smells like cow.

We're far from civilization. The fairgrounds is the only attraction for miles—a pavilion, amphitheater, awnings, and collection of picnic tables in the middle of dry, dusty flatland on either side of a two-lane highway.

"Why here?" I ask.

"He works here," Beau says.

"Hmm," I say.

"What?"

I wince. "Just worried we might be meeting a killer carny in a deserted lot."

"He doesn't work for a carnival. He's the manager of the fairgrounds. And isn't that term disparaging?"

"Maybe." I suppose I'll apologize before he slits our throats. "But we are meeting questionable people who could be out to kill us."

"Don't be dramatic."

The Truth Is in the Detours

"Easy for you to say. You're a man, six foot something, and have shoulders the width of a refrigerator. You don't have to carry pepper spray while jogging or hold your keys between your fingers in dark parking lots."

Beau leans against the side of his car and crosses his arms. "Sorry. You're right."

I startle. This is a first.

He continues, "I wouldn't put you in danger. I've had each of the interviewees sign contracts, and I made it clear that my office knows where we're meeting."

"Your office?"

He shrugs. "My agent and my mom have my itinerary."

Lani would send out a search party the instant Beau didn't answer his phone. That's comforting, at least. But I worry we might die of heat stroke before the carny gets the chance to kill us. I'm sweating out of more pores than I knew I had. I'm going to die smelling of body odor and manure. But this is important to Beau, so I ignore the eerie similarity to a common horror trope.

A few minutes later, a hot rod rolls into the gravel drive.

"There he is." Beau slides into our car and nods to me to do the same. We follow the Corvette toward a yellow gate that's been propped open.

"Do you have a weapon? Just in case?"

Beau growls at me—literally growls at me.

"Stay in the car." He parks beside the Corvette under a canopy of solar panels.

"And go crazy with worry? Unh-uh. We live and die together, Beauregard." I step out of the car. "Besides, we face better odds as a team."

"That's debatable," he mutters.

Jeremiah Abernathy, it turns out, is not a murderer.

He is a wisp of a man—my height, thin and wiry, with tarnished shoulder-length gray hair and a handlebar mustache.

We follow him from the staff lot to the covered food court. The place is empty but has footprints of vendor huts that probably peddle deep-fried Oreos during the fair season. We settle across from him on a wooden picnic table. Jeremiah apologizes for the location but chose it because he knew no one would be working today and we wouldn't have an audience.

"It's about my son," he says. "I've lied to him his entire life."

Beau is watching me; I feel his gaze on my profile as I type.

"There was this girl. I loved her as long as I can remember, even though she didn't feel the same. Then she got into trouble in high school."

Beau drags his focus from me when Jeremiah pauses—when it's time to ask the follow-up questions. But Jeremiah offers more without prompting. He was the girl's knight in shining armor when an (actual) carny knocked her up. Jeremiah married her and raised the child as his.

"I was happy for those first few years. I thought we all were. Until she left."

Jeremiah stayed, and never told the boy he wasn't his biological father.

"Sometimes, you do the right thing for the wrong reason—wind up doing some good but hurt everyone anyway."

He shows us a photo of his family. His son towers over him, with one strong arm wrapped around Jeremiah's shoulder and a pretty brunette tucked into his other side. Three boys—all under ten—stand in front. The youngest has his hand in Jeremiah's, looking up at his grandfather with a toothless grin.

"They're my family. I'll never see them any other way. But . . . I'm not sure they'll see it that way if they ever find out the truth."

He exhales a long, shaky breath. I suspect he's a smoker—or was—the rattle in his chest is a telltale sign. "Whew. That's a lot to admit right there. I was married again for twenty years. Never even told my wife. She passed last year."

"I'm sorry, Mr. Abernathy," Beau says.

He nods and wipes a palm down his face.

The Truth Is in the Detours

"How do you think the lie impacted you—or your son—over the years?" Beau asks.

"You lie long enough, you start to believe it yourself." Jeremiah looks from Beau to me. "But now, your generation is obsessed with those genetic testing things. My grandmother had some Native American blood—or so we were told. My oldest grandson is begging us all to be tested. Wants to know how much. What tribe . . . that sort of thing." Jeremiah picks at his cuticles. "I guess lies, no matter how noble, end up coming back to bite you in the ass."

～

Back in the car, Beau lets me be DJ. I choose Taylor Swift, but one of her mellow folk albums, so Beau can't protest. I mean, he can. He is Beau, after all. But he's been quiet, casting surreptitious glances my way for the last hour. Our next interview isn't until tomorrow, and we're finally escaping the inland heat to meet with Anna Thorne, who lives in Santa Barbara in a posh estate along the coast. I expected more of the liars to be wealthy. Law of probability. But our itinerary appears to be a mix of tax brackets.

"You okay?" Beau asks as he merges into the left lane.

"Yeah, why wouldn't I be?"

He speaks as if tiptoeing. "Because that father admitted to lying to his son his entire life."

I should have known this project might cut close to the vein. It seems the longest secrets are family secrets; the people you love always have the most power to hurt you. "Are you going to draw parallels with every person we speak with?"

"Not unless there are parallels." His voice is dry.

"There aren't. I mean, besides the deception." There are, of course. But if I open the emotional floodgates by acknowledging them, I can't sit comfortably in denial. "It's not like Dad can explain his motivations, and it doesn't matter what they were anyway."

"Lying to yourself isn't the solution."

"Are you a historian or a psychologist?" I laugh, but it gets caught in my throat.

"I'm your friend," Beau says, and I snap my head and study his profile. He's focused on the road but casts me a fleeting look. "Or used to be."

There's vulnerability in his words, so I relent. "Lying to myself is all I've got."

"It's going to be a long trip if we aren't honest with each other, at least."

We drive for another few minutes in silence while the monotonous landscape blurs by without interruption.

"It matters," I admit. "But I'm too raw to process it, especially since I can't interview my dad for answers."

"Your dad loved you, Ophelia. You were his world. I don't know what the story is. Or why he lied. Or why she left. But I knew your dad, and he must have had a good reason."

"I don't doubt that he loved me. But he didn't think I was worth the truth or capable of understanding it."

"Phe." Beau's tone is uncharacteristically careful as he sneaks a glance in my direction. "His inability to tell you the truth was about his hang-ups, not about what he felt you were worth."

I shift my focus to the dizzying scene as we race by crop lines on the roadside. It's like an M. C. Escher painting.

"I see what you're saying, but it's hard to believe that when you're the one being lied to."

Beau reaches across the console and finds my hand. I startle, but after a moment, I lace my fingers in his.

"I get that," he says. He gives my hand a tentative squeeze, and the pulse shoots straight to my chest. There's a warmth brewing, something like fondness—or I don't know—maybe nostalgia for a time when it was second nature to hold his hand. When we'd race across the hot

The Truth Is in the Detours

sand to reach the waves and face them together with clasped hands and twin smiles.

Maybe we can be more than our old grievances. Maybe friendship is possible.

But his touch never made my nerve endings dance, and I worry that my emotions are jetting right past friendship to something destined for disaster. Beau is a pumice stone against my shell; he's making it difficult to deflect and protect myself, and he's coaxing me to tip from cautious camaraderie to adoration and delusion.

"We have the stop in Santa Barbara, then Paso Robles, followed by several interviews in the Bay Area," Beau says. But I know the itinerary. I'm not sure why he's recounting it now. "We have a free day after that. Plenty of time to head up north if you want to check out that address in Fort Bragg."

My stomach sinks. "Yeah, maybe, not sure, we'll see." Beau casts a furtive glance my way. Testing, assessing. But he's not going to be able to read me. I haven't made up my mind yet. Do I want to find my mom? Or do I want to skirt past and look longingly out the car window as we pass somewhere she called home after faking her own death and forgetting me?

Beau pulls off the freeway a hundred miles from our next motel and navigates to a rest stop. When he heads to the restrooms, I grab the keys and visit the vending machines. I buy a couple of waters and a bag of pretzels. Sadly, that's the best option. Road-trip snack food has lost its appeal now that it's our steady diet. But I notice Starbursts and buy a packet. They were Beau's favorite as a kid. If we're working our way back to friendship, maybe this can be my olive branch.

While Beau takes a call on the far side of the parking lot, I clear the car of empty coffee cups, take-out containers, and gum wrappers. I dump one bag in the nearest trash can, but it's full, so I take another trip to the women's restroom to discard the second and travel to the dumpster on the far end of the lot to discard the remnants of Lani's expired care package. When I finish, the car is in decent shape.

Beau returns twenty minutes later, and he seems agitated after his conversation. His walk is hurried, and his shoulders are raised.

"I'll drive for a bit," I say, and reach out my hand.

He furrows his brow, and it seems he's been returned to his factory settings—petulant and dismissive.

"What? Do you have to drive because you're the *man*?" I ask.

"That's insulting." He folds his arms across his chest.

"I'm an excellent driver."

"I assume you've gotten better since jumping the median on University Avenue?"

"That happened one time, Beauregard. I saved a cat's life."

"And killed your dad's Civic."

I open my palm. "C'mon. Give me the keys."

"I left the keys in the car with you," he says.

"Oh, right." I flash him a grin and reach for my pockets. I don't have any pockets on this sundress. "I had them with me when I . . ." I trail off as I retrace my steps. I check the console. I must have put them back when I dropped off the water bottles and snacks.

But I didn't.

I didn't drop them on the floor of the passenger seat. Or the driver's seat. Or in the cup holders. Or in that annoying dead space between the seats and the gear shift. I'm on my knees, peering under the seats, when I hear a growl from behind me.

"Ophelia," Beau asks, "where are my keys?"

CHAPTER 10

Beau presses his fingers to his temples. "So, you cleaned out the car and threw stuff in not one, not two, but three separate trash cans—into any of which you may or may not have tossed my car keys. Keys which are now nestled beside three-day-old fast food, dirty diapers, and who knows what else?"

"I didn't drop the keys in the trash. They must be in the car." They must be.

"They are *not* in the car. We've spent ten minutes tearing the car apart." Beau looks like he might erupt any minute—his jaw is tight, his shoulders tense, and his words so clipped that each syllable is a dagger. It doesn't help that it's a solid 90 degrees out here. The pavement makes it feel like 100. We're both sweating and dirty, and Beau hasn't eaten in at least four hours, so he's hangry. I consider giving him the Starbursts I bought him, but I don't think they'll prove to be the token of our rekindled friendship I hoped they might.

"I didn't throw them out," I insist.

"What did I say about us lying to each other?"

"Maybe I dropped them while I was walking *to* the trash cans."

After another fifteen minutes spent scouring every conceivable path I could have traveled, I must admit my new theory is bogus, too.

Beau paces along the sidewalk while tapping his fingers on his thigh. He's so angry with me that it's giving me a stomachache. He's always exasperated with me, but this is on another level.

"I'll look through the trash cans," I say.

He stops. But his face doesn't soften at my sacrificial overture. Instead, he looks disgusted.

"And rummage through rotten, baking trash?"

I almost gag just thinking about it, but if it will even the score between us, I will do it.

I dive into the car and pull out a couple of plastic bags shoved into the glove compartment. I storm by Beau to the trash can, sliding the bags over my hands.

He eyes me for a moment before he sighs and follows me in three quick strides. "Give me one. I'll help you."

"No. I fucked up, and I will fix it." It may as well be my superhero tagline.

The trash can is a four-foot-high stone receptacle firmly planted on the concrete. There is no tipping it over to analyze the contents. Beyond the first layer, I will have to dive in. I move aside a McDonald's bag before finding a dog poop bag partially open. I hold my breath as I turn a tennis shoe over, hoping the keys will drop out, but no such luck. Bags of questionable debris hide soggy paper towels, banana peels, receipts, and half-eaten hamburgers.

"Ophelia, stop. You aren't going to find them."

"That's the spirit." I keep my head down on my task.

"The keys are heavy. The more you move shit aside, the more likely they are to fall to the bottom, and you'll contract hepatitis from someone's used syringe." But the way he's looking at me, I suspect he's considering I might be a justifiable casualty.

"Do you have a spare key?"

"If I had a spare, would I have been on this hellish scavenger hunt for . . ." He looks at his watch. "A half hour?"

The Truth Is in the Detours

I concede I got us into this mess. But he acts as if I threw them into the fires of Mount Doom. I refrain from saying so and asking whether he's impressed I still remember the reference—despite having watched *The Lord of the Rings* only because he forced me. "Know how to hot-wire a car?" I try instead.

He gestures to himself in a wild head-to-toe pattern. "What about *this* gives you the impression I would know how to hot-wire a car?"

I take the opportunity to inspect him. He looks ready to shoot eighteen holes of golf, not steal a car—polo shirt, flat-front shorts, and crisp white Nikes. I suppose he has a point. "Okay, then, what do you propose we do?"

"I'll call a locksmith. See if we can get a key made." He frowns at his phone, holds it up like he's in a Verizon commercial, and stomps away. He calls over his shoulder, "Don't touch anything or go anywhere. And do *not* lock us out."

~

The nearest automotive locksmith is a hundred miles away and can't make it here until tomorrow morning.

Instead of staying at a quaint beachside motel near Santa Barbara, we must crash at the Imperial Motel and Saloon along a dusty patch of land somewhere on Route 166. It's the only motel within a five-mile radius of the rest stop. But the motel won't have our room (singular) ready until after dinner. There's a small music festival nearby, so we were lucky to snag a room at all. They've promised it will have two beds, so there's that. But Beau can't storm off and pout on his own, and I can't wash this day off me. There's no lobby, and unless we want to make another five-mile trek back to the rest stop, we don't even have the car to retreat to for solitude. So, the saloon it is.

My plan is to get drunk enough to forget I ruined our seedling reconciliation. I hadn't realized I wanted his friendship until it became a possibility. But it stings, nonetheless.

The saloon is aptly named—brick walls, exposed wood beams, and a long shellacked bar with leather swivel stools. The space is flanked by a raised stage at one end and a mechanical bull at the other. It's packed with people all dressed for the country music festival. Beau's prep-school golf uniform looks out of place in the herd of cowboy hats and leather boots. But my summer dress is white gingham, so I pass. Take that, Beauregard.

Beau storms directly to the bar and settles on a stool. He's wide and commanding, so everyone moves out of his way. I am neither of those things, so the sea he parted collapses before I trudge through.

After a string of excuse-me's, an accidental hip check, and one elbow to the boob, I stumble onto the stool beside Beau and wave to the bartender.

"You need food," I say.

He glowers at me. "I need my keys."

"I'm sorry, Beau. I really am—"

He holds up one hand to shush me and the other to his temples to indicate I'm the source of his headache.

"I'll buy you food. And unlimited shots. And dessert. And breakfast tomorrow. I'll drive the rest of the way."

He doesn't flinch.

"I'll let you make the music selection even if it's all My Chemical Romance and Dashboard Confessional." I rest my elbows on the bar and crane toward him, but his posture is rigid.

"I don't listen to emo music," he says.

I catch the bartender's eye; she nods and strolls over. "What am I getting you? Beer? Wings? Fries?"

"Three fingers of Maker's Mark. Neat. And a steak." He narrows his eyes—a challenge, it seems—but I grin.

The Truth Is in the Detours

"You got it. Anything for my old friend." I loop my arm around his and squeeze. He freezes but doesn't move away. I consider it a win.

I order and hand over my credit card for our tab as the band warms up. The bartender drops off Beau's bourbon and my IPA. Beau shoots it and gestures for another.

The bartender complies, and Beau takes another three fingers in a long guzzle. I wince. "I'll hold your hair for you, but I'm not sure I can carry you to bed, so you might want to slow down there, Professor."

He ignores me and waves for another.

"Punish me, not your liver," I mumble.

He doesn't respond.

The band starts up, and the crowd becomes a mass of movement and noise that melds with guitar chords and drumbeats. Country music. Beau can't possibly be interested, but he's fixated on the stage—spinning around so his back is to me for the entire set.

I nurse the same beer; I'm prepared to make good on my offer to be his bodyguard tonight. He might need one.

I slip off the stool and weave through the crowd to the restrooms, standing in line for the women's as ten guys cycle through the men's.

When I emerge and fight my way back to the bar, my seat is taken. A petite blonde in a ballerina-pink sundress and cowboy boots has made herself at home, straddled between the edge of my stool and Beau's lap. She has a manicured hand on Beau's bicep, her head thrown back in a fit of giggles. I understand the allure of the bicep—it's been distracting me for days. But Beau doesn't mingle in large crowds or go out of his way to talk to strangers. My bodyguard instincts activate. I don't trust her. I charge over, ready to send the girl away. How dare she take advantage of my drunk friend. But as I approach, they slip off their stools, and Beau pulls her to the dance floor with a hand spread wide on her lower back. I feel the ghost of that touch like a slap.

Beau doesn't dance. Not during family dance parties as a kid. Not at our awkward middle school socials when I begged him to be my partner, and never in high school. He had a girlfriend for a while—a pretty cellist who never spoke. They came to homecoming, but I couldn't figure out why, because they didn't leave their table, talk to anyone, or smile.

But I gawk as Beau begins to line dance. And he's grinning. Not grimacing. *Grinning.* The girl leans close and puts her hands on Beau's hips to guide him. He trips after her for a few moments but picks it up, moving with an ease I wouldn't have predicted. I sink down at the bar as the bartender slides our food in front of me. I pick at my dinner, craning my neck to check on Beau. He's over the lost keys, apparently. Or maybe this is his payback. A passive-aggressive *See, I'm not a grump. I just don't forgive you.*

He has another drink in his hand. Not bourbon. Rum and Coke, perhaps. Whatever it is, he's not doing himself—or his future hangover—any favors. Cowgirl is standing behind him with her palms wrapped around his waist, cheek pressed to his scapula. I don't like it. And I don't know why. I roll my eyes and return to my dinner, fiddling with my phone.

It lights up with a text from Cherry as I scroll through a listicle titled "14 Signs You're Careening Toward Rock Bottom."

Cherry: I have a meeting in LA tomorrow. Take me out and remind me what it feels like to be single and carefree.

I'm not in LA, I reply.

I thought you cleared out of your dad's place last week.

I did. I'm here. I raise my hand above the crowd, capture a panoramic shot of the line dancing, and then take a pouty selfie of me alone at the bar. I send both.

WTH? Where are you? Who are those people? What is happening?

Research. I hit send and put my phone down as I finish the last warm sips of my beer. It dings a few more times in rapid succession, but I ignore it.

I want Beau to come back and spar with me. But I spy him drain his fourth (fifth?) drink, and wish he'd soak up the liquor with the expensive porterhouse I bought on my credit card. We have an interview tomorrow. Dealing with a hangry Beau is challenging enough, but a hungover Beau with a grudge? Brutal.

The front desk texts me that our room is ready, so I have the bartender wrap up Beau's steak. I trudge across the parking lot to the reception desk, retrieve our bags and key, and drop everything, including the prized untouched steak, in our room. I verify there are two beds with a big-enough gap between them that I might avoid the aroma of alcohol seeping from Beau's pores while we sleep.

I want a cool shower and to slide between the sheets and forget this entire day. But Beau isn't answering his texts. If he can't find me—or our room—I may take the blame for that as well.

But when I return to the saloon to search for him, he's not on the dance floor, or at the bar, or in the back hallway. I scan the perimeter and finally spot him in a crowd huddled around a gated area. There are whistles and catcalls and a tremor in the sea of people. I rise onto my tiptoes.

He's standing beside a mechanical bull. Beau's new country girl is astride it, holding on with one hand while she waves to the crowd like a beauty contestant. I've seen merry-go-rounds move faster. She looks great, though—she plays the bull-riding country princess well. When her ride ends, she steps off to raucous applause and beckons Beau over. Shit. I push myself off the wall and fight my way through the crowd.

This will not end well.

Beau tried to learn hula to appease Lani when he was six, skateboarding in fifth grade, roller-blading a few years later, and then mountain biking, hockey, snowboarding. He does not excel in activities requiring balance. He broke a wrist, had two mild concussions, and required a patchwork of stitches. And that was before he was legally allowed to drink his body weight in alcohol on an empty stomach.

"Beau," I call out as he swings one long leg over the saddle. "Beau," I shout with more urgency. He flinches—so I suspect he hears me—but he slides on and motions to the guy in the corner. I push through a wall of denim and cowboy boots and reach the roped-off arena as the bull lurches forward. It starts slow and Beau is in control—one hand wrapped around the strap and the other in the air for counterbalance. His body is loose, face relaxed in an easy grin. He's acquired a cowboy hat from someone, and it's casting a shadow over one eye. But after thirty seconds, the bull jerks to life, spinning, tilting so low that only Beau's grip is saving him from being thrown. His dance partner hollers, and other voices in the crowd cheer him on as I hold my breath. He regains his balance and offers me a smug grin. But then the adventure starts. It was child's play before—the speed ratchets up, the bull bucks, and Beau's bent spine makes him look like a crash-test dummy. He hangs on as his hips lift from the saddle and slam back into place. He survives another two, three, four jerking revolutions before he's thrown over the top of the bull, catches his shoulder on the horn, and lands headfirst on the ground. I gasp, and the crowd roars.

I make it to him in four leaps as he pops up and raises both hands in the air. Another collective roar fills the room as the band starts back up.

"Beau!" I shout over the music. He spins to face me as his new friend collapses into his side, wrapping an arm around his waist. His eyes are glassy, his shirt is torn, and there's a trickle of blood sliding down his chin.

"You're bleeding," I say, moving closer.

She tugs him toward the outer rim of the arena. "I've got him."

"No," I say. "He's bleeding and hurt. Playtime's over."

Beau smiles and looks between us, revealing teeth coated in a film of new blood.

"C'mon, John Wayne. Let's get you to bed." I scoop his arm in mine.

He stumbles after me, offering a small salute to his dance partner before slurring, "I like the sound of that. Take me to bed, Ophelia."

CHAPTER 11

It takes fifteen minutes to corral Beau to our room. As one leg moves in the right direction, his other rebels and almost topples us. I use his elbow and belt loop for leverage. He smells like dirt, bourbon, and his new girlfriend's perfume.

I prop Beau against the wall while I fiddle with the key, and he tumbles through the threshold once I wrangle it open. He sinks against the closet, sliding until he's seated.

"I need to get you to bed," I say.

He gives me a thumbs-up and flashes a lethargic smile but doesn't move. "You know how long I've waited to hear you say that?"

I laugh. "You should save that line for someone you actually want to seduce, Cowboy."

I squat and wrap my hands under his shoulders, heaving him up and coaxing him across the room until he lands on the mattress and curls into a ball.

"No sleeping yet. Concussion protocol. You hit your head when you fell. Come here." I tug on his hip and get him propped on the pillows. I use my cell as a flashlight and look into his eyes.

He bats me away with both hands.

"I need to look at your eyes. I watched Arthur do this after you fell from the tree house."

He circles my wrist in his palm, and I drop my phone. His hand dwarfs mine—and the brush of his fingertips against the pulse point of my wrist makes me shiver. His eyes find mine, and my arousal dissipates when he asks, "Do you even know what you're doing?"

I hesitate but offer a tepid "Your pupils need to contract at the light—or something." He doesn't argue. So, either he doesn't know, or I'm right. His eyes look normal—other than bloodshot.

"Don't fall asleep," I order.

He releases a sound that might be a laugh and closes his eyes.

"Awake, Beauregard," I scold again, and he salutes, widening his eyes like a child trying to stay awake on New Year's Eve.

I run a few washrags under hot water in the bathroom and return to dab at his mouth. I tug gently on his lip to assess the damage. There's an angry wound on the inside of his bottom lip; he must have bitten it on the way off the bull.

"How are your teeth? Any loose?"

Beau pinches each tooth between his thumb and forefinger and tugs, wincing as his finger glides over the cut. "Nope."

"Good. Your parents paid a lot of money for those perfect teeth." I hand him a bottle of water and a cup. "Rinse."

He takes a tentative sip.

"Spit. Don't swallow." I hold the empty cup under his chin.

He chuckles, repeating, "Spit, don't swallow," as the blood-tinged water spurts into the cup.

"Nice juvenile sense of humor. Good to see alcohol makes you less uptight." I wipe his chin. The bleeding has stopped, so I turn my attention to the gash on his shoulder. His shirt is torn, but the scratch is superficial. "Okay. Can you take this off? I need to clean your shoulder."

His smile is a tease as he tugs on the hem—it's surprisingly playful and seductive. He struggles a few times but grabs hold, sliding the shirt up before it gets caught on his head.

"Smooth." I slide onto my knees in front of him to help remove it without aggravating his injuries. Beau falls back onto the pillows, exhausted by the small effort.

I am a lecherous jerk for noticing in his current state, but holy hell, Beau is beautiful. Adulthood has been kind to him—and his abdominals, lats, and shoulders. There's a landscape of smooth, tan skin spread out before me, and I want to explore every inch of his topography.

"Phe," he sing-songs, "you're staring at me."

"Am not," I say as I drag my eyes away from his clavicles, which look like crowbars atop his broad chest. "Just checking you for injuries."

He laughs and lolls his head to the side. "Sure."

"You're cocky when you're drunk," I hiss while I swipe a wet washrag over the long scratch on his shoulder.

"You're attentive when I'm half naked."

I steer my focus away from the even expanse of silken skin and shake my head. "Where'd you get those, anyway?" I ask, gesturing to his six-pack.

Beau grunts, "Where? What?" He looks down abruptly, as if he's never looked in a mirror. It makes the muscles flex.

"You're a brain, Beauregard. You're not supposed to have a body, too."

He makes a sound like "pfft" that I'm not sure how to interpret, until he says, "How evolved of you. I'd never insult your intellect because you have that body."

I scoff. "You insult my intellect all the time."

"Do not."

"Do too." I hold his gaze, and he looks confused before closing his eyes.

"Do you have a first-aid kit?" I ask.

"In the car," he says.

Of course.

I find makeup-removal pads and a hair scarf in my toiletry bag and make a crude bandage that I hope will keep the cut clean for the night. "I'm a regular Flora Nightingale."

The Truth Is in the Detours

"Florence Nightingale."

"Whatever, Professor. All those degrees didn't teach you to avoid a mechanical bull while drunk off your ass."

He sighs and closes his eyes. "I always fall for the wrong women."

I finish wrapping the scarf around his shoulder and tie it off with a makeshift knot, settling beside him on the bed. "Oh, I don't know. The cowgirl was cute."

He opens one eye in a skeptical glance that looks more like sober Beau instead of sloshed Beau.

"This is like our old slumber parties in the tree house," he mumbles.

"Plus alcohol and head injuries." And more nakedness, muscles, and tan skin.

He sighs, throwing his head back on the pillow until his throat is bared to me.

I riffle through my purse on the nightstand and find a bottle of Advil.

"Here." I hold two pills above his palm, but he opens his mouth and sticks out his tongue. So, maybe not sober. "You might be hurting tomorrow."

"I'm fine." He spills the water down his chest as he swallows the pills, and I wipe it up with the washrag. His eyes follow the movement before he lays his hand over mine, trapping it between his chest and palm. His skin is burning through the cotton of the cloth, and I feel the filtered contact everywhere. "Thank you for taking care of me."

"Anytime." I try to pull back, but he resists and pulls me closer until I'm hovering over him, and it's taking every ounce of my restraint—and dignity—not to slither against his naked skin and find a home there.

"I was a dick about the keys. It wasn't your fault."

"It was totally my fault. Maybe you do have a concussion." My words come out breathy as I lean over him, and he reclines like a Calvin Klein model—every hard-bodied inch of him exposed but untouchable.

"You didn't know." He finally releases me, curling into the fetal position until his warm, taut body bends around where I sit on the edge of the bed. I try not to stare at the way his oblique muscles bunch in that position. I want to touch them to see if they are as firm as they look.

"Didn't know what?"

"It's better this way. I should have tossed it myself a long time ago."

"What are you babbling about, Professor?" I try to focus on the conversation, but he's almost naked and so close to me.

"My wedding ring."

"All right, you're delirious. Time for sleep."

Beau yawns and inches closer and drapes a solid, warm arm around my waist, his eyelids heavy. He has a fat lip and a pale bruise blooming on the bridge of his nose under his glasses, and now he's disoriented. I'll need to wake him in a bit to ensure he's responsive. Binge drinking and head injuries cannot be a healthy combination.

But then I stumble back through his last drunken comments, piecing them together. Is he confused, or confessing? "Beau, shit, was your wedding ring on that key chain?"

"Affirmative," he says through a yawn.

I duck and brush his hair away from his eyes. "Oh no. Beau, I'm so sorry. I'll go back tomorrow. I'll find it." Fuck. No wonder he was so upset. But who does that? Who puts their wedding ring on a key chain?

"It's the last sad relic of my marriage—and my therapist says I get too attached to things." Beau tugs at my waist and pulls me until my back is against the headboard. He rests his head in my lap, closes his eyes, and sighs. I hold my breath and remind myself that he wouldn't touch me if he weren't drunk. But it's hard to remember that when he's shirtless and holding on to me like I'm a life preserver.

And yeah, he's really fucking hot.

The Truth Is in the Detours

I cross my arms over my chest, resisting the urge to caress the broad expanse of his back, melt into the affection, and acknowledge how good it feels for him to touch me.

"It's like when my mom cleaned out my room and donated that Matchbox car you gave me. I didn't speak to her for a week, even though I knew I was too old to play with it—just like I'm not going to wear that ring. Better to toss things that remind me about what I can't have."

CHAPTER 12

Beau sleeps the whole way to Santa Barbara, flinching when I hit a pothole or turn a corner. He was monosyllabic and surly when the locksmith called this morning, waking us both from where we slept entangled in each other. I tried to sneak away last night, but his arm was clamped around me like a lap bar on a roller coaster. When the phone sounded the alarm and the morning light streamed through the windows, he scrambled out of bed, creating a cool void where his warm, hard body had been.

I gave him a few painkillers, and he took them like a grown-up. I miss hot-mess Beau. There's evidence of him behind the swollen lip, bruised face, and deep-purple bags under his eyes. But the personality is all angry professor.

We haven't talked about our sleeping arrangements. But I haven't stopped thinking about how he splayed his hand against my stomach and pressed his hips into my backside, or how his breath tickled my nape.

He wakes now as we exit the freeway, straightens in his seat, and cranes his neck to watch as the car hugs the Pacific Ocean, and the white tips of the sapphire waves taunt us as we pass. We have another interview in Paso Robles tomorrow, so we can't even enjoy downtime on the coast. We'll likely get back in the car and head inland without our toes touching sand.

Two identical keys and a temporary cardboard tag dangle from the ignition. Gone is the keepsake metal key chain engraved with the face of Half Dome; missing is Beau's house key, his parents' spare, and his wedding ring. I wonder if he'll ever mention the ring again, or if a night in a saloon is like a weekend in Vegas and I'm supposed to pretend he didn't give me a glimpse of his soft underbelly—still struggling with a broken heart.

"Did you get her number?" I ask.

"What?" Beau croaks out before grabbing his water bottle and draining it in three swallows. He grimaces, slumping back against the window.

"Carrie Underwood."

"Who?"

"You really need to work on your pop culture references."

"You need to work on basic knowledge of historical figures."

"Focus, Beau. The cowgirl. Did you get her digits?"

He doesn't answer as I pull up to a stoplight. I glance at him as we wait, but he keeps me in suspense until the light turns green. "No."

"Why not? I think she liked you."

"Because I don't even know what town we were in last night. I live hundreds of miles from here. What's the point?"

"Are you always so practical?"

He crosses his arms over his chest and groans. "When have you known me not to be practical?"

"Well, last night, you battled a mechanical bull after two dozen shots of whiskey."

He ignores me and flips down the visor to study his face in the mirror. "Do you have anything that could cover this?"

"Sorry, my makeup wouldn't work. You're about three shades tanner than me." He flips the visor up, sinking back in the passenger seat. "Embrace it. You look hard and mysterious. It toughens up the whole uptight academic thing you've got going on."

I turn onto the private drive and punch in the gate code Anna Thorne provided before pulling to a stop in the curved driveway. The sprawling Spanish estate stretches along the cliffside, hogging the view like a spoiled child. We're nestled in a grove of jacaranda trees. The purple blossoms are faded, and the thinning branches provide a window to the curling ocean beyond the bluff. "Do you need extra backup today?"

"I've got it." He runs a hand through his hair, straightens his spine, and adjusts the angle of his glasses. "But thank you." He smiles for the first time today—it's thin and pained but looks genuine.

"Anytime."

Beau twists toward me in his seat, his eyes cast down. "I," he begins, hesitating. "I don't usually lose control like that."

I laugh. "You didn't lose control, Professor. You downed that bourbon like it was on your to-do list." I nudge his arm with the back of my hand. "You're a bit self-destructive but otherwise a likable drunk. I wouldn't mind a second date."

"Don't count on it." His lips are chapped, cracking along the bottom.

"Here." I dig in my purse and hand him a tube of ChapStick and two more Advil.

Beau swallows the medication in a long guzzle and slathers on the balm, studying me. "You're surprisingly maternal, considering."

The words drop like a clang.

Beau slips out of the car, and I follow.

"I'm maternal, considering what? That I'm such a flake?"

He turns to me in the driveway, his expression contrite. "What? No. I meant, you know, you're not known for . . ." He sighs. "You're free-spirited, not the den-mother type."

"Ouch." I shut the door with more force than necessary. "Do you know how many times I've heard that same shit? I'm fun, but not relationship material. I'm good for a night out, but not a dinner with the boss. I'm fine to be introduced to the guys, but not to Mommy."

For some reason, I expected Beau to know me better than that.

"Whoa." He steps closer, his posture softening as he wraps his hand around my upper arm to still me. "I'm sorry. I'm being an ass because I have a raging headache and a fat lip, neither of which is your fault.

The Truth Is in the Detours

What I should have said was thank you for taking care of me. I'm grateful for your maternal side."

"You're welcome," I say. As frustrating as his constant irritation is, his gratitude is even more confounding. His warm eyes are burrowing into me, making me feel . . . things. I look away and step around him toward the front door, stage-whispering over my shoulder. "Now let's pretend to be surprised that our kazillionaire isn't a saint."

∼

"Okay, Anna was the worst so far," I say.

"Worse than the hit-and-run?"

"Yes. Because her mistake was a choice, not an accident. And she abandoned her friend."

Beau grunts, crosses his ankles, and closes his eyes, drinking in the warm afternoon sun. We'd finished our interview and picked up sandwiches. I convinced Beau to grab a spot on the warm sand of Mesa Lane Beach so we could eat lunch before another long drive. But he's terrible company. I console myself with the opportunity to watch the waves and pretend I'm on vacation. I'm jealous he'll grow another shade tanner, while I'll probably burn.

"Explain to me what you think she did," he says.

Anna Thorne and Jocia Antwon were college roommates who dreamed up the perfect clubbing purse—a handheld clutch with a wrist loop, belt clip, and cross-body strap. It had just enough room for a credit card, lipstick, cell phone, and condoms. They'd designed the prototype from their dorm room. Anna was a Hollywood princess who talked her daddy's friend into investing. When Jocia started to have ideas of her own, Anna told her the investor wouldn't take them on as a partnership, even though the investor had made no such stipulation. Anna built a purse empire. Jocia was cut out and left behind.

I swallow a bite of my turkey-and-avocado sandwich and wipe my mouth with a napkin. "You were there. She betrayed her friend."

"Uh-huh." Beau draws his knees up and drapes his arms over his eyes. My phone rings, and Beau winces at the noise.

"Hey, Cherry," I answer, plugging my other ear against the noise from the waves.

"Where are you?"

"Santa Barbara."

"What the hell? I'm in LA for one day and you're not here? Come back," she says. "I have one night to get out and rage. Austin is doing the overnight shift."

"I won't be back for a few weeks." I would have fun with Cherry if I were in town. We always have fun. If she hasn't been my best support for the last several weeks, it's because I haven't given her an opportunity to practice. I've never been the girl who needs a pep talk when a relationship ends, or a girls' night in with ice cream and movies after a career disappointment. I'm the friend who will throw on lipstick and a little black dress and look for a distraction at happy hour. Cherry doesn't know what to do with me right now. But I don't know what to do with me either.

"Who are you with?" she asks.

I hesitate before answering, "No one," and glance at Beau, guilt nudging me in the ribs. But I don't want Cherry's inquisition. I don't want to explain what I'm doing or why I've come. I don't want to listen to her make assumptions about the "hot historian" or make lewd jokes about the sex I'm not having. I don't want her to belittle this trip or Beau's intentions.

"What's going on, Phe?" she exhales in a dramatic sigh. "Last I heard, you were selling the house and going back to LA. And now you're on some road trip? Are you okay?"

Beau peeks up at me through his forearms, squinting into the sun. His brows are knitted together, and his posture is stiff. I press the phone closer to my ear, but who am I kidding? Cherry has no volume control. Beau can probably hear the whole conversation.

"I needed to get away. But, hey, I'll send you some restaurant recommendations. I have a friend who—"

"I don't need your concierge service. I need a night out with my best friend. And you need to have some fun. What good is a single friend if you can't entertain me on my one kid-free night?"

Beau whistles and stands up, brushing the sand off his shins and staring out into the sea.

"I can't, Cher. But I'll make it up to you when I'm back. Promise. I gotta go."

"Ophelia," she whines.

"I'll call you soon," I placate.

I hang up, and Beau shakes his head and strides toward the shoreline.

I stand and follow him. "What?"

"Some things never change." Beau steps into the retreating surf, letting the foam roll over his toes.

"What things?"

"Cherry Stewart is still a terrible person."

"Hey, she's my friend."

"Really? Because it sounds to me like she's only ever wanted you to be her accessory, like a pretty purse on her arm."

"Jesus, Beau." I get it. He doesn't respect me. But he's out for blood today. "Ouch."

"You just lost your dad, and she's more concerned with you serving her selfish needs than being there for you."

"That's not fair," I say, but his words sting. "I usually like distraction when I'm upset—she wants to give me that."

He shakes his head and turns toward the surf as the tide retreats. "Was it worth it?"

"Was what worth it?" I've had a lot of patience for him today, but he's speaking in riddles, and I'm tired, too.

"The social capital you earned by ditching me. Because it looks to me like you're a bit like Anna. You traded me in to get ahead. But where did it get you?"

"What are you talking about?" Hungover Beau is the price to pay for carefree, drunk Beau. I knew he was too good to be true last night.

"You were my best friend, Phe. We had all these plans of what we'd do in high school. And then we stepped onto that campus, and I was the nerdy friend you had to shed to capture the cool kids' attention." He picks up a rock from the beach and skips it across the waves. It jumps once before sinking.

I turn the wheel on my mental camera shutter, searching for evidence, for any recollection I can dredge up to understand his version of events. That's not the way it happened, was it? I thought we grew apart. "Beau, I don't remember it that way at all."

He scoffs. "I was 6'2" and 140 pounds with acne and glasses too big for my head. I was the only mixed kid in our school, and with a stupid name. And you were, well, you." He waves an impatient hand over me as if I'm exhibit A. The wind blows my sundress against my body, and I feel exposed, naked in more ways than I can articulate.

"What does that mean?"

He glances over and looks me up and down, his face pinched into a frown. "You know you're beautiful. This isn't the moment to fish, Phe."

I stammer, struggling for a retort. I've never received a compliment drenched in so much vitriol. "I didn't drop you."

"You kissed me—and the next week, you were drooling over older guys and clinging to the popular crowd. You loved the attention and didn't need me anymore."

I'm not ready to have this conversation—or to excavate those years. They were awkward and exhausting, and I've tried to bury the impact of the choices I made then. "That's not true. I just knew you didn't approve of any of them. And there came a point when I couldn't deal with your judgment. You had your smart clique, and I had my friends."

The Truth Is in the Detours

"It's not judgment when it's based on fact. Cherry and Simone are so shallow they are essentially well-coordinated cardboard cutouts. And Matty was a seventeen-year-old jerk with a five-o'clock shadow who preyed on my fourteen-year-old best friend."

"But you weren't judgmental at all," I snap.

"I didn't judge until I had to pick up your pieces over and over again. Every time they got you drunk and you needed a ride home. When you'd ask me to lie to your dad for you. Every time one of your 'friends' stabbed you in the back. All those times Matty would lose interest, and you needed a pep talk. When he refused to wear a condom and almost got you pregnant. When he cheated with that volleyball player from La Jolla."

"She was a basketball player from Del Mar." Of all the useless retorts, I chose that one. But I'm confused and angry. I don't know how to have this argument when I've repressed the evidence and buried it under twenty years of more recent memories.

He scoffs. "Not the point. But glad you've gotten over it."

"Hey, I'm not the one with the long list of grievances."

"Right. Because *you're* the bigger person here."

It hurts that he sees me this harshly, even in the rearview. He'd cataloged my adolescent insecurities and missteps. He was keeping score. He assessed me and found me lacking.

I may not recall everything the way Beau does, but there are flashbulb memories that haven't faded. And I hate that Beau's not entirely wrong. In all my worst moments, he was the one to glue me back together. It was Beau who drove me to the free clinic—twice. It was Beau who answered my call when I needed to be rescued. But I didn't know he resented those rare moments when I had the courage to reach beyond our distance to find my old friend.

The wind whips fiercely at my face, pulling errant tears from my eyes to my eardrums as I remember when our friendship finally ended for real. The day he left for Harvard, I met him in the driveway and gave him a box of stationery stamped with my address. I hoped it would be a way to start fresh and wipe away the missteps of high school. The thought of him not being next door made my heart hurt. But Beau handed them back to me and said he didn't think it would be a good idea to stay in contact. "Our lives will be too different," he said. "I'll be at Harvard, and you'll be at community college. We need to stop pretending we're still friends. We've both changed." I held back my tears until I got home but then cried for hours, and I've flinched at the mention of his name ever since.

"Beau, I always knew you were the bigger person. And our lives have proven that. Professor. Author. Checkbook-balancing homeowner with organized closets and extra sheets. I *know* you're better than me."

He growls and throws another rock into the surf. "Listening to how Anna discarded her friend, and hearing you refuse to admit to Cherry that you were with me just now, it reminded me how that made me feel back then. You've always thought of me as 'no one.' You owned me, and you knew it. You kept me on a long leash but tugged on it to make sure I was still tethered. And I was pathetic enough to heel."

I can't access the memories as freely as he can. I remember we grew apart and lived in two different worlds—but found each other when we needed the comfort of our friendship. Did I take advantage of him? I hadn't meant to. "It wasn't like that. And if it was, I didn't know I was doing that. I was a stupid kid and obviously made some terrible mistakes."

He turns to me, his face like stone as the waves careen toward shore. "And my mistake was trying to be your hero when I was your doormat. And here I am, doing it again."

CHAPTER 13

I want to put us both out of our misery. Beau doesn't want me here, and I don't know the point of this escapade anymore. I should have listened to him all those years ago, because he was right. We should have stopped pretending to be friends. I have to chalk this up to another bad decision. Perhaps Beau will add it to his running tally.

I'll catch a train tomorrow—it will take eight hours, but it's cheap. I have to survive one more night, and if I'm lucky, we'll check in to our separate rooms as soon as we get to the motel. I can take an Uber to the train station in the morning and never see Beau Augustin again.

Beau plays a podcast during the drive to Paso Robles. Two hours of Malcolm Gladwell is two hours too many for me in my state. He turns on the navigation when we take the exit into town, and I exhale. Our destination is only four minutes away. He pulls onto a long drive bordered by grapevines in front of a ranch-style home, cutting the engine.

"Where are we?" I ask.

"We're staying at my friend's place tonight."

"What?" I straighten in my seat and reach for the mirror, running a hand through my hair to tame the mess. I smell like sunblock and have a light dusting of sand coating my shins. This house is only a few steps down from Anna Thorne's place—and we're staying here?

"Relax. He's happily married. Flirting will get you nowhere."

I turn to glare at him. "I thought we were staying at a motel. And now I have to impress some genius friend of yours for the night."

"He's not a genius—he's just a friend."

"What does he do?"

"It doesn't matter." Beau sighs as if I'm the most tiresome person in the world. "It will be fine. They're good people."

I wish there were a train leaving tonight. "I'll catch an Uber to a motel."

"Don't be ridiculous," he snaps as a bearded man with salt-and-pepper hair steps onto the porch and trots down the stairs. He's average height with a wiry frame, dressed in board shorts, a faded yellow T-shirt, and flip-flops.

Beau steps out of the car and offers a wide, generous smile that looks like sunlight. I wither, aware of how little he's shared it with me. It's a beautiful smile. Bright white teeth, a hint of a dimple under his right eye, a warmth that radiates like static. He hugs his friend in a tight embrace, unmarred by the apologetic bro pat that men often use to neutralize affection.

"It's so good to see you," the friend says. I hover near the car door.

"Thanks for having us," Beau says, without any evidence of his hangover. He's practically giddy, the bastard.

"What the hell happened to you?" the friend asks, taking in Beau's fat lip.

"He thought he was a matador," I say.

"Carlos, this is Ophelia Dahl. Ophelia, this is Carlos Navarro. We went to undergrad together."

"A Harvard grad," I say, and attempt to keep my inferiority complex from shitting on the introduction.

"But don't hold that against me." Carlos shocks me by pulling me into a hug. "The famous Ophelia. We meet at last."

I accept his embrace but am perplexed by the greeting. Beau looks away, moving to the trunk to grab our bags.

"You sure it's okay I crash here?"

Carlos laughs. "Yes. I've been dying to get dirt on Beau for years. Do you like wine? I can ply you with alcohol to get the secrets."

I relax as Carlos links his arm in mine and leads me up the porch steps. I hear Beau trudging behind us. "I do like wine. But I will dish even stone-cold sober."

～

"Beau spent the entire night staked out at the window, with a flashlight and a whistle," I finish. Carlos laughs and pats Beau on the back.

"I was protecting both of us from an alien invasion," Beau says.

"He never could handle scary," I say. "He had nightmares after *Scooby-Doo.*"

Carlos's wife, Serena, comes into the dining room carrying a round of after-dinner drinks and sets one in front of each of us.

"Thanks," I say, taking a sip. I think it's port. It's sweet and decadent.

"Be careful, Ophelia," Beau says, his tone light. "I have way more stories on you than you do about me."

I'm grateful he has managed to hide his disdain for me in front of his friends.

"But they aren't interested in those stories, Professor. Your friends, your embarrassment. I don't make the rules." I shrug.

Carlos tips his glass to me. "She's right. We aren't out to humiliate the newbie."

I scroll through my phone. "Here." I hand it to Carlos, cued up to a collection of photos copied from an album I'd found in Dad's stuff. Beau as Spider-Man, as Cinderella, in a tux for our fifth-grade promotion.

"Ahh, this one is adorable." Carlos turns the screen toward me. We're at the beach, and I have Beau buried up to his neck in the sand as I pose above him in a Wonder Woman bikini. We're about six years old, I think. Carlos keeps scrolling before sharing a picture of Beau in braces and headgear, circa ten. "That's quite a look, Beau. If only I could have flashed this photo in college when all the pretty girls ignored me for you."

"Hey," Serena says.

"Except you." Carlos kisses his wife on the cheek when she settles next to him.

"But to be fair, who knows what would have happened had I met Beau first." Serena winks at Beau, and he gives a slight bow. "We did have that one night. What could have been."

"Ooh," I say, "do tell."

Serena laughs. "I got drunk. Slipped into Beau's bed by accident."

"We were roommates in the dorm," Beau explains. "And nothing happened." He holds up both hands.

"Nothing below the waist anyway," Serena amends, and bursts out laughing while Beau pleads his innocence.

"Was Beau the sensible friend in high school?" Serena asks. "He always tried to reason us out of everything fun in undergrad."

"We didn't hang out in high school," Beau says, his tone clipped. "Ophelia dated the quarterback."

"Beau was valedictorian," I volley back. He holds my stare like a dare.

"Ophelia was homecoming queen." He spits it out as if he's outlining my criminal record.

"Our high school held a pep rally to congratulate Beau on a perfect SAT score." My dad came to support him. It was humiliating.

"Ophelia was so popular she sparked a trend when she shaved half her head and dyed the rest orange. She had all the poor freshmen running around looking like Beaker the Muppet."

"Our principal proclaimed March 30 Beau Augustin Day when he was accepted into every Ivy League school."

"Ophelia forgot I existed because I wasn't cool enough." Beau's voice ascends in the otherwise-silent dining room.

"Beau rejected me because I wasn't smart enough." My voice cracks.

The Truth Is in the Detours

Beau breaks eye contact first, and I follow his gaze toward our shocked and silent hosts.

"I'm so sorry," I mutter. "Excuse me." I push my chair back, and it skitters against the hardwood floor in a discordant clang. Beau reaches toward me, but I walk quickly out of the dining room, through the living room, and out the patio doors. The night is stifling—there's no breeze to push out the triple-digit daytime heat or dilute my anger or regret. Carlos and Serena welcomed me as an old friend, and Beau and I just litigated decades of resentment after they cooked us filet mignon.

I step off the patio and into a grove of trees. There's a porch swing hanging from a towering oak. I sink in, pushing myself back and forth, regretting my juvenile behavior. Why do I let him burrow so far under my skin?

I hear the crunch of feet along the tanbark and turn. I expect Beau, but it's Carlos.

"May I?" he asks.

"Of course." I scoot to one side of the swing, and Carlos sits, falling into sync with my rocking. "I'm so sorry. You and Serena have been lovely hosts. I don't know what came over us."

He laughs. "It's fine. We're married. We're comfortable with bickering."

We sit in silence a few beats before he continues. "I met Beau at freshman orientation. We bonded immediately—two middle-class brown kids among the rich white elite. He talked about you a lot." Carlos throws a testing glance my way and notices my shock. "All his crazy stories starred Ophelia Dahl. He had a photo of the two of you as preteens pinned to his bulletin board."

"Seriously?" I gasp.

"Scout's honor." He holds three fingers in the air. "He told me about that time you got married. And the time you convinced him to jump from your loft onto a bed below, and he broke his arm. He told me about your first kiss." My mind reels back to that memory, and I blink several times. "Don't tell him I told you," he adds. I hold up three fingers, and he chuckles. "He also told me you two fell out. And he missed you."

I try to square this with the version of Beau I know. The one who disapproved of my friends, mocked my lack of knowledge of "important" things, and severed the final ties of our friendship before he left town. But it squares with the hurt he shared earlier. He thinks I ditched him and sacrificed my best friend for popularity. When really, I made no such conscious choice. We grew apart, and I let my teenage years happen to me. I've let life happen to me.

I didn't throw Beau away, but I didn't hold on to him tight enough. And I see now that it's probably the same thing.

"Beau is one of the best and most loyal guys I've ever known. He's guarded. Doesn't always know how to express what he feels. But he shows it. You just have to pay attention," Carlos says.

Carlos pats my leg and stands, walking away before I've had a chance to process what he's said. I watch him slip in through the patio doors as a shadow emerges from inside. But I look away, unable to make eye contact as Beau approaches. I feel the swing rebound when he settles beside me.

"I'm sorry," we say in unison. We both do a double take before Beau gives me a small smile.

"I don't know why I become a five-year-old with you. It's an old habit, I guess," he says.

"Same," I say. "Poor Carlos and Serena."

He shrugs. "They're fine. I once had to mediate an argument when Carlos shaved his head and got a temporary face tattoo before going home to meet her parents. They owe me."

I chuckle and watch as he bounces his knee.

"I'll catch the train home tomorrow and get out of your way." I should get back to my life, or I don't know—make a new one.

"You can't leave." He sits up straight and turns to face me, his expression earnest.

"Beau, this isn't working."

The Truth Is in the Detours

"Sure, it is. I have more notes than I could capture on my own. I have a partner to bounce ideas off of. And . . ."

"And what?" I lean toward him.

"We have one more stop before Fort Bragg."

It's the first chance to track down my mom. The approaching destination looms like a ticking time bomb, and I'll be forced to confront my indecision. "She didn't want me. I'm not convinced I should chase her down to find out why. My ego is fragile enough as it is."

I feel his gaze on my profile before he whispers, "Phe."

I turn and am lost in the glare off his lenses from the patio light. I can't read him with the barrier between us. I want to slide them off and find the truth in his gaze. "I'm sorry," I say. "For high school. For being a selfish teen who didn't know how to be a good friend. For not knowing how all those years impacted you."

"It's okay," Beau says.

"It's not," I say, and his smile in return is faint. "But you were wrong about a few things. I didn't tell Cherry I was with you this afternoon because I didn't want to share you with her. This trip—and you—matter too much, not too little. And all those years ago, you weren't my doormat, Beau. You were my safe place. I may have been the cat on her ninth life playing in the street. But every time I saw a headlight, I ran toward you." I reach for his hand. He flinches, but then turns his palm up, a shy invitation. I thread my fingers in his, and he delivers a warm squeeze. "I was an idiot teenager. Insecure. Self-centered. Myopic. And you were so much smarter than me. And you knew it."

"I never thought I was smarter than you." Beau looks earnest, but I know better.

"I know Lani asked you to tutor me—that semester I almost failed geometry. I overheard you talking in your yard."

He quirks his head.

"You refused and said, 'Mom, it won't make a difference.' That one hurt," I admit.

He squeezes harder and nudges my shoulder with his. "Oh, Phe. If I said that, it wasn't because I thought you were stupid. Because I've *never* thought that. But how would that have gone? Me tutoring you? Would you have let me? Listened to me? Or would you have convinced me to do your homework and ditched me to hang out with your friends?"

I let his version of history penetrate. Is there one truth? Or many? While Beau and I were busy jumping to conclusions, our truths jumped onto different tracks, launching us into alternate realities and resentments. But his opinion mattered so much to me then, even if I pretended it didn't. That one overheard sentence was like a splinter in my self-esteem. "Maybe. I never thought about it like that. School was always so easy for you—and you knew what you wanted and what was important to you. I was lost, Beau . . . When high school started and Cherry and Matty both pursued my attention and affection, I got caught up in it. And I finally felt special when I had always felt less than. It didn't help that I was so jealous of you."

He laughs, and it's loud and throaty. "Of me? We went over this. I was a geek with terrible skin and the silhouette of a praying mantis."

I giggle before slipping into my dad's lower register. "Beau mowed our lawn this morning. Beau got a perfect score on his SATs. Beau helped his dad build a deck. Beau's valedictorian speech was the best I've ever heard. Beau's going to Harvard."

He hangs his head, chuckling softly.

"And it got worse after high school. He sent me your dissertation. Clips of your interviews. Signed copies of your books. Your engagement announcement—" I stop, suck in a breath. Shit. I suck at apologies.

"Well, I failed there, so that should have evened the score a bit." I'm grateful to see a small smile tugging on his lips.

"Hello?" I laugh. "My relationship track record is so dire it's about ten thousand leagues under divorce. Good try."

Beau exhales, parts his lips as if he's going to speak, and then changes his mind.

"What?" I whisper.

The Truth Is in the Detours

"Henry didn't mean to make you feel inadequate."

"He did." I know Dad loved me—but he didn't think I was capable.

"No," Beau says, a bit more forcefully. "He didn't. Your dad thought you walked on water. When you manipulated him to get what you wanted, he marveled at your genius. When you climbed down the tree to sneak out, he was awed by your athletic ability."

I let out an incredulous laugh. "Then why did he always compare me to you?"

"He didn't. He was"—he pauses—"making a suggestion."

"A suggestion?" I shake my head, confused.

He clears his throat. "He was trying to be a matchmaker. Albeit an ineffective one."

I sit up straight, trying to let this version of reality land. Did Dad want me to date Beau?

Beau continues, "I mean, if you were a parent, who would you rather date your daughter, Matty or me?"

I exhale. My dad loved Beau. It makes sense, I suppose. "Fair point. Matty was a prick."

"Colossal prick."

I nudge Beau with my shoulder. "And you were a saint."

"Hardly." Beau swallows and leans into me a fraction of an inch. "Remember when Matty was caught cheating on that final paper?"

"Yeah." How could I forget? Matty turned in a plagiarized paper and couldn't walk at his graduation. He almost lost his football scholarship to San Diego State.

"I sold him that paper, laundered the sale, and anonymously tipped off the administration."

"Beau," I gasp. "You didn't."

He nods, with a guilty little wince. "It was right after you called me for a ride because he'd left you stranded at that college party. When I showed up, the party had ten guys to every girl, and you were wasted. Anything could have happened to you."

I am ashamed to admit that I barely remember that night. It doesn't even rank in the top-ten most despicable things I let Matty get away with.

"Do you remember when he started losing his hair?" Beau asks.

"Before homecoming his senior year." The guy was so vain he wore a baseball cap under his homecoming crown. I narrow my eyes, "What did you do?"

"I mixed Nair into the pomade he kept in his gym bag."

I gasp and cover my mouth as I cackle. "Beauregard Makani Augustin, I didn't know you had it in you."

"You had just gotten back together with him after he—"

I hold up my hands in surrender. "Don't remind me." I was still learning the definition of self-respect. We had a tumultuous love, hate, and repeat relationship for years.

Beau shrugs, a sly smirk on his lips. "I wanted to punch him in the face, but we both know he would have kicked my ass. So clandestine sabotage was my only option."

"You didn't have to fight my battles, Beau."

"I know. But I was an idiot teen," he parrots. "Insecure. Judgmental. Bitter. But I figured out you wanted me to leave you alone after prom."

"What about prom?" I search his face, but he looks away.

"Oh, c'mon, Ophelia. It was a long time ago. I've let go of that grudge. But don't pretend you don't remember."

"Seriously. I don't know what you're talking about." I search my memories of prom. Matty and I danced. He got drunk at Cherry's after-party. I never even saw Beau.

"Phe." Beau finally looks at me, giving me a glimpse of buried pain. Whatever he sees in my face must convince him. "You seriously didn't know about it?"

"Know about what?" My patience frays as worry sets in.

He sucks in a breath and releases it slowly. "Senior year. Cherry called me right before prom and told me Matty bailed on you, and you were devastated."

"What?" I can feel my pulse in my skull. "Why would she—"

He levels me with a stern look. "Because she knew I'd come to your rescue and wanted to make me feel small. She wanted me to know that I may have gotten into a fancy college, but I was still nobody to you guys."

I don't want to believe this—and it's disorienting to learn yet another piece of my history that I was blind to. I may have neglected our friendship, but I never did anything purposely to hurt him. *Never.* I would have killed my friends if they messed with him. "What happened?"

He shrugs and looks away, suddenly shy. "I rented a tux and tried to come to your rescue."

"Beau," I say, unable to find better words.

"And you can guess the rest. You didn't need a rescue. When I got there, you were already dancing with Matty, so I left. But Cherry saw me. Which is what she wanted."

I bring my hand to his cheek, relishing the feel of his stubble against my palm. He sucks in a breath but yields when I draw his focus to mine. "I'm so sorry. I had no idea. I wouldn't do that to you. And I'm pissed that she did."

"Thanks," he says, swallowing hard. We're inches apart, the tension of the confessions arcing between us. But I'm feeling something else. Something dangerous. I drop my hand.

And then it dawns on me. "Is that why you refused to speak to me after high school? Cut me out entirely? You told me our lives were too different, and I assumed you thought you were better than me."

"I thought you'd tried to make a fool out of me. I was . . ." He trails off, and I see his pupils dilate and dance before he says, "Hurt."

"So was I." Tears clog my throat, but I swallow them back. "I missed you so much." All this time, we've shared different histories, different truths. I lean my head on his shoulder, incapable of keeping my distance anymore.

"I missed you, too. But I felt like I lost my best friend much earlier—to a bunch of assholes."

I snort-laugh as he leans his head on mine. I'm nestled in the crook of his neck, and it feels nice and safe. He smells like summer—coconut from his sunblock, with a hint of detergent. It reminds me of swinging in the hammock in his backyard, our heads on either side, our feet tangled together. "You didn't lose me, Beau. I lost myself."

He slides his arm around my waist and cinches me to him, and our breathing falls into sync. "Well, I'm glad you're back."

I'm sure there's no intent in his embrace, but my nerve endings are misreading the platonic signs. He's so warm and solid that I could stay here for hours. I could crawl into his lap, find his pulse point with my lips, and investigate all those muscular ridges I viewed last night. I could let his fingertips wander under the hem of my dress. I startle at the visual, straighten my spine, and withdraw. He drops his hand and clears his throat.

"Me too." I am swimming in the scent of coconut and the heat of his skin.

"Friends again?" he asks.

"Friends again," I say, and gather the courage to turn to him. His lips are soft. His eyes are wide behind his glasses, searching mine. I swallow once, pushing away a strange urge to lean into him and seal the deal with a kiss.

"But I still think you're chaos." He smiles slightly.

This is good. Better. Familiar. "I still think you're uptight."

He clears his throat. "Then all is right in the world."

We're silent for a few moments before Beau says, "Stay in this with me, Phe. Don't go home yet."

But suddenly, I wonder if I should leave for reasons other than our old resentments. Because this new closeness scares me more. Unfortunately, though, it's also too tempting to resist.

CHAPTER 14

Carlos and Serena send us off the following day with warm hugs and two bottles of wine made from grapes grown in their private vineyard. Beau must have told them about my dad, because Serena pulled me aside after breakfast and slipped a book into my purse. "This helped me when I lost my mom last year."

I was touched by her thoughtfulness, but I'm not a self-help-book type of gal. Dad put me into therapy as soon as I got my period—as if puberty might trigger the latent feelings of motherless longing. My therapist recommended a slew of books based on quackery of all stripes. I never finished them.

I pull the book from my purse when we're on the road, curious about Serena's brand of pop psychology, turning it to the front cover and creaking the binding. But it's not an encyclopedia of motivational hogwash.

Beau casts a glance at the white cover. "What's that?"

"Poetry." I flip to the first page.

"Mary Oliver," Beau says. "Wouldn't have guessed you'd be a fan."

Our ceasefires are so brief that the white flag may go on strike. "Contrary to what you assume, I can read."

Beau lowers the music, and his tone grows serious. "Mary Oliver cuts right to the soul, and you have never been comfortable going there."

I shake my head. "Relax. I don't understand poetry anyway."

Beau sighs. "You belittle yourself far more than I ever could."

I fan through some pages and land on a poem—it seems benign enough. It's about moths, of all things. I read through it, surprised at its simplicity, its clarity. But then the message sneaks in, and I suck in a breath. It's about pain. About avoidance.

A ball forms in my throat, dry and burning, and I swallow several times to clear it, looking out the window before closing the book with a thud.

"Not your thing?" Beau asks.

I shake my head but don't look at him. He reaches his hand to my shoulder and squeezes once but lets me be.

~

After our Paso Robles interview, where a middle-aged woman named Shauna confesses to stealing money from her employer, we have another three hours of driving before we're able to settle in for a few days in the Bay Area. Tomorrow, we have an interview in Berkeley, near Beau's house. The plan is to stay there and knock out several interviews before heading up north, with a possible detour to Fort Bragg to chase my mom's shadow. But I kick that decision down the metaphorical road.

I turn on our compromise playlist—acoustic covers. It's random enough to keep me entertained, and mellow enough to match Beau's morose disposition. I work for a few hours as Beau lapses into an introvert coma. It suits us both.

"Are you sure you don't mind me staying at your house?" I ask once we've pulled off the freeway.

"Why would I mind?"

"Aren't you worried I might find your hidden porn? Or see your Netflix queue and learn you're a fan of trashy reality TV? Maybe you still sleep with Snuffy, or don't know how to fold a fitted sheet and the contents of your linen closet will bury me as soon as I open it." I gasp. "I bet you have a Monica closet like in *Friends*."

The Truth Is in the Detours

He doesn't respond. My powers of irritation are waning.

"Your entire place is decked out in mahogany bookcases with leather-bound volumes of Chaucer, Shakespeare, and Dante. You have Tiffany lamps and leather chesterfield sofas. You wear a smoking jacket and sit in the parlor puffing on a pipe in front of a roaring fire. You don't even own a television because it's too plebeian."

He shakes his head. "Plebeian?"

"Did I use that wrong?"

He rolls his eyes.

"I know. It's worse than that. You're worried I'm going to push on the wrong bookcase and find your secret room, filled with your old *Star Wars* figurines. You still play with them and have a fetish for Ewoks."

"Gross," he groans. "There is something wrong with you."

"Probably. But you're officially my friend again, so what does it say about you?" I grin at him with all my teeth.

"That I'm charitable." He offers me the crumbs of a smile.

"You are a closeted bro and have a pool table instead of a dining room table, Budweiser signs, and one of those paintings of dogs playing poker. And pinups of *Sports Illustrated* swimsuit models," I guess. He ignores me. "You're a secret hoarder. Your house is jammed with boxes of 'As Seen on TV' deals. You order them too fast to open the boxes, so you've yet to use your Ove Glove, Snuggie, or ShamWow."

He chuckles at this one. Finally.

"Okay, Professor, which is it?"

"I guess you'll have to wait and see."

Alas, it is none of those. Beau lives in North Oakland near the Berkeley campus in a classic Craftsman with gray shingle siding shrouded by two towering pine trees. It's a grown-up house with a facade that screams history professor and has three wide steps up to a generous covered porch and double-glass French doors. When we pull up outside, I'm irritated at myself for not calling it—Arts and Crafts charmer for the academic.

He trudges up the steps and I follow, watching him fish a spare key from under a planter box beside the front door. "That's the first place a thief would look," I say.

"Well, if robbers did use my keys, they were more considerate than you, since *they* didn't lose them." He flashes me a wry smile.

I'm surprised when he opens the doors to an empty space, save a few boxes stacked along the far wall. There's an entryway with rich oak built-ins and two rooms flanking each side. I think it's supposed to be a living room and dining room—but there's no furniture to confirm. Beau's steps echo as he heads to open the windows. It's cooler here than our recent stops, but the sun streams across the wood floors, creating a greenhouse effect.

"Um, were you actually robbed?" I ask.

"No." Beau pulls my bag from my shoulder.

"I guess I lost the bet on the whole hoarder thing." I walk over to the oversize fireplace, with a solid mantel flanked by empty bookcases in a rich dark stain. "Where's all your furniture? Your pretentious artwork? The textbooks you read for fun?"

"I got the house. She got the stuff."

"Wow." I scan the emptiness and am struck again. This is a house meant to hold a slouchy couch, overstuffed armchairs, wool rugs, and cashmere throw blankets. I imagine a live-edge table in the dining room, oatmeal tufted side chairs, and custom art that Beau found while traveling overseas. He needs side tables to hold warm lamps and reading glasses, a bar cart for his bourbon and lowball glasses.

"She came a few weeks ago, packed up the rest of it."

"Geez. It looks like the Grinch was here. Not even a crumb too small for a mouse."

He walks through a corridor flanked by columns and more empty bookcases.

"She cleaned you out." I find him in the bright white kitchen, digging through the Shaker cabinets, leaving each open to reveal bare shelves. "Jesus. What did you do?"

He freezes and looks at me, incredulous. "What did *I* do?"

I hold up my hands. "She must have hated something in this house: your tacky leather recliner, or a battered desk only you could love. There's no way she wanted every spoon, trinket, or mug, and yet"—I look around—"this is an action of a woman scorned."

He lets the pantry door bang closed and opens another, growling when he pulls out an orange Dutch oven. It's one of those fancy ones my friend Janna has that I covet.

"That's something," I say. "She hates cooking, then?"

He places it on the counter and rubs his temples. "It's a message."

"Let's hope it's not a boiled bunny."

He exhales loudly and leans on the counter, his spine curved, shoulders near his ears. I think of my vulnerable Beau two nights ago, mourning his lost wedding ring. I don't know that he'll ever trust me enough to tell me what destroyed them. But he doesn't need to tell me specifics to communicate he's in pain. I shift around the marble island and place my palm on his back, rubbing between his shoulder blades. He jumps at the contact, but then leans into it.

"I guess the message isn't as sinister as that?"

"It was our first purchase as a couple. We bought it for a cooking class we took together."

"And the message is?" I ask.

"If I had to guess, she thinks if she makes me miserable enough and leaves a trail of breadcrumbs of happy memories, I'll find my way back to her." He exhales the confession.

"She wants you back?" I ask, and draw my hand away.

He shrugs. "That's her story anyway."

I try to picture her—the Instagram doctor on his arm for all those years. I remember she was pretty. But what I recall about those photos was Beau's smile, so genuine that the rare dimple below his eye would appear when he looked at her.

"And you don't?" I try to hide my skepticism.

He doesn't answer but shifts away to finish his scavenger hunt. Other than the cast-iron pot, there's a cheap I HEART NEW YORK mug (souvenir?), a couple of champagne flutes (wedding related?), and a ceramic teapot painted with freesias (daily ritual?).

"How do you feel about these breadcrumbs?" I ask once he's scoured the space and deposited the meager contents on the island.

"Like I want to smash them and mail the pieces back to her in an envelope."

"Whoa." I draw back. "I understand that impulse. I recently tossed thirty years of memories to spite my lying father. But"—I glance over the sorry stash—"this is all you've got in the world. So I have another idea."

∼

"Honey, I'm home." I push through Beau's front door an hour later, but he doesn't respond.

I set up everything in the kitchen and get to work. It's an HGTV dream kitchen: double ovens, a six-burner stove, marble countertops, and undercounter lighting. If there were more than one pot, I might be giddy and cook all night. Wide windows overlook a redwood deck and small lawn, and I flash back to Beau's life in happier times. I bet they hosted dinner parties and served signature cocktails while their genius friends discussed string theory.

I get to work on dinner, using the Dutch oven and camping gear Beau found in his garage. It's not ideal, but it'll do. I have the ingredients almost prepped when Beau finds me. He's freshly showered in worn Levi's, frayed at the hem, and a white Henley. He steps into the kitchen and studies me, puzzled. "What are you doing?"

"Making new memories, Professor. Come on in." He walks over, his bare feet shuffling across the wood floor, and leans his hip against the counter. I pour two glasses of prosecco in the flutes and push one toward him. He pulls back.

"This seems a little sacrilegious." Aha. Definitely wedding flutes.

The Truth Is in the Detours

I shrug. "Objects only have the power you give them. But this is your object. Your memory, your choice."

He takes a deep breath and picks up the flute. "To making new memories with old friends."

I clink my glass to his. "And saying fuck you to manipulative ex-wives."

He laughs and tilts his head to take a sip. "What are you making?"

"A simple version of cassoulet."

He raises his brows. "You cook?"

"I'm thirty-four years old and live alone. Of course I cook."

"Huh." He takes another sip from the flute.

"I cook, I read. Your opinion of me is really growing today, Beauregard." He stares back at me with a bemused expression. "I figured I'd try a fancy dish in a pricey pot in a model kitchen before I go home to my electric range with only two functioning burners." Something about cooking calms me. As a kid, I would shadow Lani in the kitchen, following her liberal instructions—a pinch of this, a dab of that—learning to cook by taste and feel. Some of my earliest memories include sitting on a stool in a tiny yellow kitchen while my mom baked.

"You know," Beau says, "cassoulet began as a peasant dish. They would throw in whatever they had, which is why it has so many meats and flavors."

I pause before adding the bacon and sausage back into the pot and shake my head while I stir. Leave it to Beau to narrate the history of food while I do all the cooking. Useless academic.

"Did you finish your inventory?" I ask.

He nods. "She left the bed, so there's that."

"More happy memories?" I tease.

He doesn't acknowledge me, and my joke backfires, because the idea spurs a canvas of images across my mind—starring Beau's bare chest, biceps, and broad shoulders. With a cameo by the cheek dimple and his pouty mouth.

Two hours later, we spread a quilt out on the dining room floor and have a picnic using Tiffany champagne flutes, aluminum camping bowls, and plastic utensils.

"This is delicious," Beau says after his third helping.

"It's not authentic. The real dish takes three days. But—"

"This is an impressive counterfeit. And it beats fast food and gas station snacks."

"Amen." I hold up my glass for another toast.

"You can take the bed. I have an air mattress I'll use in the guest room," Beau says.

"No way. I'm not sleeping on your bed full of happy memories."

"Ophelia," he growls. He makes that deep, grumbling sound so often it's begun to appear in my dreams. Now, I get goose bumps whenever he does it.

"I'm perfectly capable of sleeping on the floor, thank you. I might have to sleep off my food coma right here." I lay back on the quilt like a starfish. "You can find me here in the morning."

"Thanks for all of this, Phe. I was dreading coming home," Beau says.

"You helped me dig through my debris. I can help you collect your breadcrumbs. We're friends again, remember?"

His lips tilt in a small smile, and he reaches across the blanket to grab my hand. The heat of his focus and the sensation of his palm in mine ignite a simmer low in my gut. I hold his stare but can't read his expression or comprehend the confusing feelings I must be broadcasting—affection, fondness, desire.

Tension resonates between us like a taut thread, until he breaks eye contact and moves so quickly, I don't have time to react. He hoists me up in one clean move as if I weigh nothing, throwing me over his shoulder as he stands.

"Beau, what the hell?" I scream, trying to keep the thrill out of my voice as he walks to the back of the house. My heart is racing, and I'm

The Truth Is in the Detours

holding my breath and praying he hasn't had too much prosecco to carry me competently.

"You're not sleeping on the floor," he says. "And I'm too tired to argue with you."

Unfortunately, he keeps his hands off all incriminating body parts, but I feel his forearm banded around the back of my thighs like a tease, and I have a clear shot of his tight ass as I hang over his shoulder.

"Put me down," I cry, but he's already swinging the door open to his bedroom.

He tosses me on the bed like a sack of potatoes, and I swallow a scream. I'm panting as he hovers at the foot of the bed, and for a fleeting moment, I imagine him kneeling on the mattress, nudging my legs apart, and climbing on top of me.

But he backs away, watching me, his expression inscrutable. "Good night, Phe," he says softly. "Thanks for dinner."

He closes the door with a gentle click, and I collapse against his two-million-thread-count duvet. That was the hottest moment of my life, even though Beau didn't even intend it to be.

It's official—I have a problem. And it's tall, dark, and grumpy.

CHAPTER 15

Beau is gone when I wake in his bed of happier memories. But there's coffee and fresh pastries on the kitchen counter with a note telling me he went to campus for a few hours to get some work done. Apparently, today's interviewee canceled because his confession had something to do with his ex-husband, and they'd decided to reconcile.

While I wait for Beau to return, I knock out six billable hours and send invoices for last month's work. I dig through the Oregon court records online to try to find the complete file regarding my mom's parental rights. My search finds 212 case records for Mary Johnsons, 32 for Mary Ann Johnsons, but no cases earlier than 2012. I call the Jackson County courthouse in Oregon, where I learn I can request archived case files, but only in person. I still need to decide how much effort to expend in searching for someone who abandoned me.

But I do not think about Beau throwing me over his shoulder and carrying me to bed.

By late afternoon, Beau still isn't home. Even without furnishings, this house is one of the nicest places I've ever stayed. His bathroom is bigger than my bedroom. Double vanities, a shower large enough to pirouette in, and a deep clawfoot tub with polished chrome feet. I blast an eclectic playlist, soak in the tub, and pretend that this luxury is not a once-in-a-lifetime opportunity. Bianca spared the beach towels—souvenirs from Maui—so I wrap myself in a bright-pink towel covered

The Truth Is in the Detours

in palm fronds, step out into the bedroom, and smack directly into someone's chest.

I hear a scream but don't realize it's mine until an unfamiliar voice breaks through my terror. The person facing me is a woman about my size who yells, "Who are you?"

"Who are you?" I bite back, gripping my towel closed.

"You're in my house. I get to ask the questions."

"Bianca," I say as I catch my breath. She is as pretty as her photos—with a dark pixie cut highlighting perfect cheekbones and charcoal eyelashes that must be enhanced. Round hazel eyes blink at me in incomprehension.

"Again, who are you?"

"Ophelia." I hold on to the towel with one hand and reach out my other to shake hers. She glances at it in confusion, and then back to my face.

"What are you doing here?"

"I'm staying with Beau for a couple days. We're old friends," I add.

"Oh," she says, clipped, and it sounds like recognition as her gaze does a quick assessment of me. "Where's Beau?"

I've never been married or divorced. So I'm not the authority on this type of thing, but I don't think this dynamic is normal. She takes all his stuff and then shows up asking questions? I haven't pressed Beau about Bianca—his marriage is a giant bruise. But maybe I should have asked if she was the dangerous, jealous type. She's a taut bow, and I'm a naked, vulnerable target.

"He's not here, and I'm not sure when he'll be home. But I'll tell him you stopped by."

"I'll wait," she says. Thankfully she leaves the bedroom with a backward glance.

I close and lock the door behind her and fire off a text to Beau. SOS. Ex-wife is making a surprise appearance. I was kidding about the boiled bunny. But I'm not in danger, am I?

A few dots pop up, indicating he's typing a reply, but they disappear. I wait, but it's in vain. Nothing. No reply. He's leaving me to fend for myself with the jealous doctor. She probably has scalpels in the car. She could clean the crime scene using latex gloves and disinfectant and frame poor Beau for the crime. She'd probably inherit the house and refill it with all its rightful contents.

I get dressed in a hurry, throwing on a pair of jean shorts, a tank top, and my flip-flops, and pace before talking myself down. She took the Hippocratic oath. And she was married to Beau. She's probably harmless.

I find her in the living room, waiting in one of the camping chairs Beau set up last night. She stands and twists toward me when I approach from the kitchen.

"Would you like some coffee? Water?" I ask.

She smiles, but her cheek quivers a bit. "I know where everything is."

I'm sure she *did*—before she took everything. But I understand the territorial point she's making.

"Of course," I say. We hover in the barren room—not sure what to make of each other. Would Beau want me to be polite and welcoming? Would he want me to assure her that I'm not a threat to their relationship—whatever the status is? Or would he prefer I ask her to leave? Because he's been silent on the subject of his marriage, I have no idea how to play this. I want to ace this fragile friendship we've reignited, but I don't know how.

"So, what was Beau like as a kid?" Bianca asks, and I hesitate, confused by the question, and she clarifies. "You grew up together, right? Beau can't possibly know more than one Ophelia."

"Right," I say. "Probably not." I know who *she* is because I stalked her on social media when she appeared in Beau's posts. But if she knows who I am, Beau must have mentioned me. I was a part of his pillow-talk canon. Carlos knew who I was as well. I don't know how to process any of this. *Should* I process any of this? Even if Beau did have a well-hidden crush way back when, it doesn't mean he feels anything for me now

The Truth Is in the Detours

other than nostalgia, frustration, and a rekindled friendship. "Oh," I say, remembering the original question. "Exactly like Beau the adult. Smart. Sullen. Impatient. Kind. But he was scrawny then."

She smiles, but it's thin, wistful. It's a strange question to ask. It's something you ask your new boyfriend's family—not the woman you catch naked in your ex-husband's house. Bianca must still be in love with him to seek new information like it's a treasure. And, for some reason, this knowledge makes me uncomfortable.

"You met Beau in school?"

She nods. "At Stanford. I was in medical school. He was getting his PhD. We frequented the same coffee shop near campus and both ordered the same variety of jasmine green tea."

I knew that—the first part, at least. But hearing confirmation of their intellectually superior meet-cute presses on my worst insecurities.

"We met when I moved in next door. His parents dragged him over to play with me, but instead, he organized my toys by alphabetical order."

"Wow. He hasn't changed, has he." She laughs.

The door swings open, and Beau steps into the entryway and scans the space. His eyes land on me and widen before he sees Bianca. I'd told him she was here—I don't know what the shock is all about. He offers a strange blank smile to both of us before moving to me. "Hi," he says, as if his ex-wife isn't loitering in the house she just raided.

"Hi," I say.

And then I stiffen as his hand slides to my lower back, spreads wide across my spine, his pinkie brushing the bare skin above my shorts. What is he doing? He stiffens too, as if he can hear me, and answers in body language, *I have no fucking clue.* He leans down as I turn to figure out what the hell is going on, and his mouth collides with the corner of mine. It's less a kiss than a graze, but he tastes like spun sugar and homesickness and feels like the heat of the San Diego sun. I take a sharp intake of breath, and he hesitates before pulling back, his face awash with horror.

Now I really hope Bianca isn't the murderous, jealous type. Perhaps this is Beau's long con. Perhaps he's finally getting even with me for spraying Sun In on his hair and turning it bright orange before middle school graduation. He wants to kill me but keep his hands clean, so he's using Bianca to pull the trigger.

Bianca clears her throat. "Ophelia and I just met. She was in a towel coming out of our bathtub." Bianca says this with a strangled laugh in her throat, as if we're all in on the joke. But I'm not. I'm not in on any of this.

Beau's hand tightens on my hip, but neither of us speak.

"Beau, I have a few hours before my shift. I'd like us to get dinner and talk. Perhaps Zelda's?"

"Ophelia and I have plans."

Bianca steps closer. "You can make time for your wife. You've been gone over a month—and we need to talk."

"Ex-wife," Beau says.

Bianca crosses her arms over her chest. "Beau," she says softly.

"You know what," I say, still unsure what the hell is going on but determined to remove myself from the discomfort, "I have to finish getting ready. Why don't I give you two a chance to talk." I try to step away, but Beau's hand anchors me to his side.

"You look beautiful. No need to change for our date."

I laugh and turn into him. He pulls me closer so our waists cinch. He wants to play this game? Oh, I will play this game.

"Baby, I can't wear cutoffs to Chez Panisse." I bring my palm to his chest, making gentle circles over his left pectoral. I've been wanting to touch him since I'd caught a glimpse after his rodeo routine. It does not disappoint. I'm not sure I've ever felt muscles this defined before. His breath stutters, and I fear he may punish me later. But I'm not scared enough to stop. I grab his neck and plant a kiss on his pouty mouth. He narrows his eyes but kisses me back, his lips soft and surprisingly compliant. I intend to make it a quick peck, but I stop breathing when he catches my bottom lip between his—and the moment slows to a

The Truth Is in the Detours

crawl. His body is warm, and his lips send a pulse of liquid heat to places unmentionable. Especially with his ex-wife in the room.

I free myself from his grasp and escape to the bedroom, the heat of his body trailing me until I close the door and collapse on the bed.

Bianca's voice drifts through the door. "Really, Beau? Her? If you wanted to punish me, you should have been subtler."

Well, ouch.

I slip into the bathroom, turn on the blow-dryer, and decide to get dolled up for a night on the town. Beau may have been bluffing, but I'm going to force him to make good on his promise.

CHAPTER 16

About thirty minutes later, there's a decisive knock on the bedroom door. But I wait for verbal confirmation it's Beau. I'm not interested in another run-in with Bianca.

"Phe, you decent?" Beau asks.

"I'm better than decent, baby."

He steps through the door as I spin in my little black dress—the only nice thing I packed.

"Holy shit, Ophelia." Beau seems panic stricken. Maybe I should have listened to the conversation and intervened if he grew distressed. What does friendship protocol dictate?

"What happened?" I step toward him, but he shuffles back.

"Nothing. You're . . ." He trails off, and my self-consciousness creeps in.

"I'm what? Is this too short for Chez Panisse? I could change."

"No. No." He exhales, runs his hand through his hair. "You look stunning."

My stomach warms, and I smooth the front of my dress. "Thanks, Professor." I think I may be blushing.

"But *why*?"

"Ummm. You don't have to be so shocked." I should never succumb to flattery with Beau—there's always a catch. "Not everyone can be naturally beautiful like you. I spent more time on my appearance than usual. I put on a nice dress. Brushed my hair. Applied makeup."

The Truth Is in the Detours

"Why. Are. You. Dressed. Up?" He enunciates each word like we're speaking over a bad cell connection.

"Did you forget? You are taking me out tonight."

"I was trying to get rid of her," he sighs. "And you can't just pop into Chez Panisse. Reservations book out months in advance."

"So take me somewhere else. I'm not picky." I sweep my hair to the side and turn. "Zip me?"

He's deathly silent behind me, and I look over my shoulder to make sure he's still there. "Beau?" I prompt.

He clears his throat and tugs on the zipper. His fingers trail up my spine, and the gentle touch is a pebble dropped in a river—I feel him everywhere. I fight a shiver and hold my breath as he fastens the hook-and-eye closure.

I turn to him. His face is set in a frown, the groove between his brows more pronounced. Our gazes collide, and I worry I might do something stupid like beg him to touch me again to see if I'd survive it.

But he looks away—which is for the best.

∼

An hour later, we're waiting at the hostess stand at a tapas joint in Beau's upscale Oakland neighborhood. Exposed brick walls, concrete tables, oversize bronze pendant lights. The facade is all glass, framed by black-mullion windows that tilt open to let in the balmy air. We were able to walk here, which suits me fine, even in my strappy heels better suited for sitting. The night is perfect—and the weather is a delightful 70 degrees—almost chilly in comparison to the sweltering regions we've escaped.

"So," I say as we wait for our table, "why'd you kiss me?"

He chokes out a cough. "I meant to kiss your cheek. And you turned. But then you kissed me. On purpose."

"You kissed me first," I say.

"Did not."

"Did too."

A woman glances over from her small table along the window, prompting her date's attention, who spins in his seat and frowns as if we've just yelled in a theater.

"Right this way," the host says before gesturing to the table adjacent to the disapproving couple. The woman glances up and scoots her chair forward so I can squeeze in.

"I'm sorry," Beau says once we have our menus in hand. "I panicked. I shouldn't have invaded your personal space. And I didn't mean to kiss you."

"You didn't mean to kiss me on the lips. But you meant to kiss me," I challenge. He's mortified, and I can't resist messing with him. It's better than replaying it in my mind.

"Right," he says. "Look, thank you for playing along. She's been persistent lately. I thought if she saw I'd moved on, she might, too. But it was stupid and impulsive."

Stupid seems a stretch too far. It wasn't that bad of a kiss—maybe a bit brief. But I could do better if he gave me another chance. "All's fair in love and lies, I suppose. And I'm not an expert on the whole marriage thing, but I think divorce means she legally must move on."

"We've agreed to all the terms, but she won't sign."

"Oh." Something about this information lands like a brick. He said they were divorced, didn't he? Wait, that was Cherry. *He* never said anything. He was still holding on to his wedding ring like he was Gollum. I should have asked more questions.

"But I don't want to talk about it." He drops his focus to his menu.

I put my elbows on the table and lean forward. "Can we talk about the terms of *our* arrangement? Are we rekindling a childhood love affair? Are we friends with benefits? Did we have a one-night stand? In case Bianca swings by again, I should know my role. Who is Ophelia in the Beauregard folklore?"

Beau glances up from his menu. "Who is Ophelia in the what now?"

"Can I keep calling you 'baby'?"

The Truth Is in the Detours

"No." He pinches his eyes closed. I'm waiting for him to cover his ears. He's too pure for this world. And if I joke about how ludicrous we'd be together, maybe it will remind my libido of the truth of that.

"Professor, then. I can get behind that kink." It would not be a stretch for me at this point. #HotForTeacher.

"Ophelia," he warns as his cheeks turn ruddy, which makes me grin.

"What do I do for a living?" I ask.

He feels my forehead with the back of his palm. "You are a virtual assistant. Do you feel okay? Did you fall and hit your head again?"

"You don't want me to be an underwear model or astronaut? Perhaps something altruistic like a social worker or foreign-aid worker. I could be some hotshot tech executive. Ooh. A venture capitalist. I'll even google it and figure out what it is."

He frowns at me. "You're ridiculous. I want you to be you."

"Oh, c'mon, don't you want to impress her? She's a doctor. I can't be *me* and make *her* jealous."

"Welcome." Our server startles me and pulls my focus from Beau's stern expression. I smile at the tall, well-groomed man standing beside our table. "What can I get you to drink?"

"I'll start with a French 75."

"Four Roses old-fashioned," Beau says. The server nods and slips away to another table, and Beau turns back to me. "You really think I'm a snob, don't you."

"I'm not one to judge your drink choice. An old-fashioned is in vogue right now, but you're an octogenarian at heart."

He growls. "Not because of my drink. Because you assume I'd need you to be someone else, something else, for me to . . . For you to be credible in front of my ex."

I don't want to explore that line of questioning. Of course I'd need to be smarter or more successful to be suitable for Beau, but why have that conversation when it would never happen? Instead, I deflect, hoping for levity. "I thought we clarified she's not your ex yet."

He drops his menu on the table and brings a hand to each temple. "What am I going to do with you?"

Oh, he's too easy. "That's what I'm trying to figure out. Kissing is now precedent. What about cuddling? Foreplay?" I drop my voice to a whisper. "Sexual intercourse?"

"Jesus, Ophelia." He looks around and offers a placating smile to our neighbor over my shoulder, but this finally earns me a real laugh. He hangs his head, and his shoulders shake in a silent chuckle. He's a tough crowd. I had to work for that one. His cheek dimple winks at me, even as he tries to bite back his smile, and the tips of his ears turn red. I try not to think about how funny he thinks it would be for us to be together that way.

"There he is." I tug on his hand. "Being friends again means you have to be amused rather than irritated by me."

"As my friend, you shouldn't ask the impossible," he grumbles, but there's no heat in it.

"We'll work up to it, then."

He shakes his head, and I thread my fingers in his. It's an innocent-enough gesture, but each touch ignites impure thoughts. I remind myself I'm lucky we're even friends. "Seriously, though, are you okay?"

"I'm fine." But his voice is flat and humorless.

"You lie. Remember our deal?"

"I *will* be fine."

"Why'd she come over?" I press.

He shrugs. "I haven't been answering her calls. She doesn't like not having access to me. But I took her key. So she won't be surprising you in the bath again."

That's a relief. I really like that bathtub. And that was expert-level awkward.

"Besides, we leave tomorrow and won't run into her again. It'll be fine."

The server comes back and delivers our drinks. He and Beau chat about the specials as I scan the menu. The options blur in front of

The Truth Is in the Detours

me—I'm bad at all decisions, even mundane ones. "Surprise me," I say to Beau, who proceeds to order a long list of tapas as if he were waiting for me to defer to him all along.

We're leaving tomorrow—and where we go is up to me. We could take a detour and try to find my mom. Or bypass Fort Bragg and drive straight to our next destination. What if I'm left with even more questions? What if I do find her and she's not interested in talking to me? To add the sting of new rejection to the mystery, I don't know if I can handle that. There are so many ways to lose a parent—death, betrayal, disappearance, abandonment—and I'm confronting all of them at once, by both parents.

"What did you tell her?" I ask, to disrupt my internal spiral.

"Huh?"

"What did you tell Bianca? About us? What's the story? Are we in love? Or are we just fucking?"

Beau's cheeks bloom along his sharp cheekbones, and my stomach bottoms out. He's adorable when he's embarrassed, and it makes me curious about what else would make him blush. "She assumes we're casual."

"Oh." I take a sip of my drink and choke as the bubbles catch me off guard. I don't know why that answer bothers me. "And you didn't correct her?"

"Considering we're neither serious nor casual but barely north of wringing each other's necks, I thought it'd be fine to leave her assumption intact."

Ouch. "How did she feel about that?"

He wraps his thumb and forefinger around his glass, letting the ice clink against the edges. "She thinks I'm working something out of my system."

Ouch. Ouch. "What she doesn't know is I'm burrowing deep into your system."

"Like a parasite," he chuckles.

"I'm rocking your world." I narrow my eyes and do my best impression of sultry.

"Like a fault line."

"I'm entertaining all your fantasies she was too tame to try."

His eyes widen behind his glasses. He takes a long swallow of his drink before choking out, "Too far, Phe."

He's probably right. I'm skating on the borderline between teasing and flirting. He's embarrassed, and I'm aroused. I am my own worst enemy. But that flush is so cute, and bantering with Beau is more palatable than thinking about what happens next.

The server slides several small plates on the table—mussels, saffron rice, sweet-potato fries, seared scallops, and crusty bread. "Enjoy," he says.

"Oh, we will," I smile as he returns to the kitchen. "But I might need to know more about those fetishes—paint a picture for me about what I've committed to." I lean forward and place my chin on my hands like I'm waiting for story time.

Beau reaches over and covers my mouth with his broad palm, surprising me enough that I gasp. "Shh," he says. "I beg you." His face is bright red now, but his cheek dimple says hello. An embarrassed and amused Beau is my favorite type of Beau.

But I'm playing with fire, because the more I work him up, the more worked up I get. I've always loved to get a reaction out of him—any reaction. But I'm beginning to wonder whether I misunderstood my own motivations. He releases his hand, and I still feel its imprint across my mouth. His skin smells like citrus and eucalyptus, with a hint of pine and lavender. It's a mix of his hand soap and detergent, the same kind Lani used during our childhood. Tomorrow morning, I'm going to wash all my clothes in it so I can take his scent with me. I've worn everything in my bag twice. It's about time I do laundry—and it'll give me plausible deniability about my other intentions.

"I'll be good. I promise."

The Truth Is in the Detours

He flashes a skeptical look but scoops a few mussels onto his plate, and I do the same, groaning when I try one. "This is so good."

"Mm," he says, scooping up another.

I try the saffron rice and soak up some of the mussel sauce with the crusty bread.

"What's your deal with dating anyway?" Beau says before shoving three fries in his mouth and chewing, his mandible flexing like a bodybuilder. "Are you a commitment-phobe? Cynical? Unlucky in love? You said you haven't had a relationship since Matty."

"I'm touched that you were listening."

He takes a sip of his water, but I catch a mumbled "I'm always listening," as if he doesn't want me to hear.

I swallow and look away. "Oh, I don't know. All of the above, I guess?"

"How'd you finally get away from Matty?"

Beau is hinting at my biggest regret—that I stayed with Matty way too long. After eight years together, our lives were enmeshed. From the outside, we looked like the perfect couple, and there were hundreds of photos as evidence. Photos I burned or deleted eventually. Beau was the only person who knew the truth.

Cherry and Simone thought I was crazy to leave Matty. He was hot, charming, and had parlayed a successful college football run and law degree into a career as a sports agent. He had the promise of money and access to fame. Cherry's now-husband is one of Matty's best friends, and she daydreamed of Matty and me marrying, and all of us raising our families together. But when Matty cheated—again—and gaslit me into believing it was my fault, I was finally done. This time it was with a woman he worked with—smart, beautiful, and educated. Someone he could "relate to" because they had "similar ambitions."

"Persistence." I laugh. "It just took a few tries for the breakup to stick."

Matty was a master of the grand gesture, and each time he told me he loved me over the microphone at a big game, or stood outside my window playing our favorite song, or whisked me away to Palm

Springs in an apology tour, my naive little heart would fall for it. When I resisted reconciliation, he'd say *Phe, please*, with a tone that implied I was making too much of whatever small or large betrayal he'd committed. When I finally got away for good, Matty convinced me I couldn't do any better. And maybe he was right. A decade later, I haven't found Prince Charming—not that I've been looking.

Beau pushes his food around his plate. "Have you ever talked to someone? About Matty, I mean." He clears his throat and refocuses on the tapas, as if he hasn't just offered up psychoanalysis as an appetizer.

"You think I'm not over that guy?" I laugh, but Beau's not smiling. "*That guy?*"

"Some of his behavior was abusive, and you said you haven't had a relationship since."

I want to be flippant and ignore the question. But Beau is leaning forward, elbows on the table, his face awash with interest and concern. Perhaps it's time to be honest about what that relationship did to me. "I think the hard part with Matty was that I cared. Now I don't get attached."

Beau winces. "That's sad, Phe."

Maybe he's right. It's not like I planned on being alone in my mid-thirties, but with Matty, I mistook drama for romance, passion for love, and my perception and reality became distorted. I'm not sure I trust myself to distinguish between healthy and toxic relationships, so it's easier—safer—to opt out.

"It is a little sad," I admit. "But I haven't found anyone worth it anyway."

Beau's look of concern is tipping toward pity, and my vulnerability limit has been reached. "What you need to understand is that the dating market is ugly. You have to be vicious or dead inside. You got out at the right time—like those dystopian movies where the elite make it into the bunkers before the apocalypse. I tried online dating. One guy brought a banker's box to a date because he'd been fired that day. It was filled with stuff from his office—Post-its, paper clips, a stapler, and picture frames. In one of the frames was a photo from his wedding."

"Classy."

"When I stormed out to my car, he asked if we could still 'make out.'"

Beau pinches his eyes closed and shakes his head. "This is what I have to look forward to? You realize I'm single now."

I don't like the idea of him on the dating market—bantering, kissing, flirting with other women—but I don't want to interrogate that feeling too deeply. "Yeah, but you'll do fine. You're like fresh meat for the starving masses."

CHAPTER 17

"What the hell is a Chihuly?" Lowell, a contractor I hire for client jobs, shouts in my ear. There's a power tool humming in the background on his end of the line—jackhammer, chain saw? It's hard to tell. I plug my other ear to drown out the wind. The seal on Beau's windows is busted, and there's a constant hum. Virtual assisting from the car takes creativity.

"Chihuly is a famous glass sculptor. The piece we need moved is 567 pounds of blown glass. I've sent you some photos of the sculpture and the installation apparatus."

Lowell sighs and moves me to the speakerphone. The roar of the power tool grows louder, and I pull the phone away from my ear. There's a pause on his end. I assume he's scrolling through the diagrams and photos I'd texted him a moment ago. "How much did your boss pay for this thing?"

"One million dollars." Juniper was sure to tell me how much it was worth when she'd called this morning with the latest impossible task. Meanwhile, she's paying me less to transport the precious artwork than Beau paid for our fancy meal last night.

"Rich people are stark raving mad," Lowell gripes. I've never sent a job his way without listening to him bitch about it for an hour or so. But he does good work.

"But they write our paychecks," I remind him.

The Truth Is in the Detours

Beau and I approach a toll booth. We're heading north out of the East Bay on one of the not-famous bridges of the region. Beau slows through the booth and then accelerates.

"Ms. Dahl, I don't know how I let you talk me into these crazy jobs," Lowell says.

And I've got him. "Because I keep your life interesting."

"'Interesting' isn't the word I'd use. But I'm not one to swear in front of a lady."

I give Lowell the rest of the details before hanging up and checking the item off my list.

"You found someone to do it?" Beau gawks at me from the driver's side as he turns on a podcast. He'd laughed when I read Juniper's email aloud an hour ago. To think he doubted me.

"Lowell. He will do anything—for the right price."

"You're good at what you do, Phe."

I snort. "Anyone could do my job."

"Not true," he says. "You convinced someone to move a million-dollar glass sculpture on a twenty-four-hour deadline while working from your car. I wouldn't know where to begin with that."

"That's because you are a genius, and geniuses are supposed to leave the peasant work to people like me."

He turns to look at me, but I can't read his expression behind his sunglasses. "Why do you do that?"

"Do what?"

"Undervalue yourself."

It seems obvious, but I don't want to have that conversation with him. I *am* good at my job—but most people don't respect what I do. And if I poke fun at myself, others won't feel the need to knock me down. I shift to look out the window as we pass over San Francisco Bay and don't respond.

"How'd you get into that work?" he asks, and I eye him cautiously, waiting for the derision, but his face is guileless.

"I worked as an executive assistant at a commercial real estate company in LA after college. And I didn't mind the work but felt like a caged animal working in a cube all day."

Beau laughs. "Dramatic, but okay."

I fiddle with my seat belt, running my hand over the satiny shoulder harness. "I was pretty efficient, so I sat in the cube for eight hours a day but had finished my work in five."

"I believe it."

I study him again, searching for sarcasm, but don't see any. "I started collecting virtual-assisting clients and worked in the evenings. Once I had five clients, I quit the corporate gig and have been working in my sweatpants ever since."

"Do you like it?" he asks. "You work for yourself. It's flexible. You're good at it."

"I've had some fun projects. I once furnished a client's vacation home with every fancy kitchen apparatus on the market. I have a regular client who has me meal plan, shop for groceries, and create recipes for her family of six."

"So you like food-related jobs." He chuckles.

"Yes, actually. And I like complex projects. I like solving problems, I suppose. And I like the clients who aren't assholes."

He laughs. "Fair."

After a few moments, I turn my attention to my laptop, where my notes are scattered across the page. We were able to do one interview before heading out of town this morning. "Was it me, or was Chester's story even creepier than normal?"

Beau taps on the steering wheel with his index fingers. "I'm trying not to—"

"Judge, I know. But seriously, Beau." I twist in my seat. "The dude and his twin swapped identities. They traded wives without telling them." I do a full-body shudder. Chester's twin, Charles, died two years ago. Both of their spouses are gone as well. There are five children between the two couples, and their paternity is a confusing mess.

The Truth Is in the Detours

According to Chester, they never worried about it since the DNA was the same. I can't wrap my mind around it. "It's so *Days of Our Lives*."

"But in *Days*, one of the twins would be locked in the basement while the other stole his life," Beau says, deadpan.

"See, this is why I missed you," I say. Beau feigned irritation when I'd watch the soap after school, but I'd catch him engrossed instead of doing his math homework.

"Have you?" There it is again, a sliver of vulnerability.

"I have." And I understand how true it is the moment the confession leaves my lips. "But you don't even need to tell me you missed me. I know you did."

"Oh, really?"

"I'm the only person who doesn't let you take yourself too seriously."

"Hmm," he says, and his lips quirk in a smile before he sobers. "And as the friend who forces you to take yourself more seriously, I'm going to need a decision soon. You have thirty miles before I turn one way or the other."

We either head straight to the next interview or take a detour to Fort Bragg to search for my mom.

Another city blurs by the car window. Our tires eat up a new freeway. I know what I'm running from. Now it's clear that Beau is escaping as well. At some point, I need to figure out if I'm ready to run toward some answers.

"Rarely are forks in the road actual forks in the road, huh?"

Beau has been so patient, but I'm no closer to a decision. He relinquishes the reins on the radio—a treat he offers only when I'm at my lowest. I put on Noah Kahan to keep Beau on my good side. Melancholy makes him happy.

"Five minutes," he says a bit later.

"Let's do it," I say on an exhale. "If nothing else, we can visit Glass Beach and get fish tacos in Fort Bragg."

"You sure?"

"No. But *not* being sure is my natural state."

Beau taps in a new address and takes the exit to a winding two-lane highway through the dense coastal redwoods—trees towering above all others, proud, unapologetic in their beauty.

We roll down the windows and let the fog-drenched air crawl in. Light streams in through the trees at odd intervals, ephemeral spotlights that cut through the canopy to blind me. I close my eyes, tilt the seat back, and pretend I'm not barreling toward a truth that might unravel the thread holding my tenuous memories together.

I startle awake when Beau pulls to a stop.

"Where are we?" I sit up and stretch the kink in my neck. We're parked along a small-town Main Street, sprinkled with restaurants and boutiques—most closed for the day.

He gestures to a side street up ahead to our right. "Your mom's last known address is on that street."

I lean forward as if I might spot her if I squint, and then peer away as my heart takes off on a gallop. "You know, this was a bad idea. Ghosts are better left alone. Right? And one parent breaking my heart is enough for one lifetime. Maybe I was wrong. Maybe we should leave—head straight to Chico."

Beau interrupts my ramble with a hand on my forearm, which stills me immediately. "Phe." His voice comes out soft, as if soothing a toddler in a tantrum.

"What?" I hear the mania in my voice, but I can't stop it.

"I'll do whatever you need here." He nods to our right. "But I got us reservations at a beachfront motel. It has firepits and access to a trail along the ocean." He points to a storefront a few yards away. "And there's a dive bar where you can drink too much, and I'll nurse your wounds until you have enough liquid courage to do what we came here for. Or until you're sure you want to leave."

I slump against the seat and throw my arms across my eyes. "If she wanted me, she would have found me. How desperate am I to chase her across the state and show up on her doorstep?"

The Truth Is in the Detours

He's quiet for a moment before he says, "There's nothing desperate about wanting answers from someone who hurt you."

I peek out from behind my forearms to see Beau twisted in his seat, inspecting me with a deep frown. "You're very wise, Professor."

My phone cuts through the silence, the ringer peeling out an old-school analog ringtone at high volume. Beau fishes it from the console and hands it over.

"It's my real estate agent." I slip out of the car to take the call while pacing on the sidewalk. They probably found a roof leak, or asbestos. Ronald has called almost daily with more requests to mine my bank account.

"Hi, Ronald."

"Ms. Dahl, good news. We have a buyer."

My stomach does a little flip as he fills in the details. The offer is a bit south of the list price, but there's no guarantee there'll be another. Ronald tells me about the conditions, escrow timeline, and that he'll forward the offer as soon as he hangs up.

Beau climbs out of the car as I shove my phone in my pocket.

"Someone's made an offer on the house." I pace beside a closed gift shop.

"That's good, right?"

"Yeah. Totally. It's fast. Which is good. It's just, fast, you know?"

Beau steps onto the sidewalk in two strides, his hands deep in his pockets. "I think so?"

"I have to respond by tomorrow. And then, I don't know. The house isn't mine anymore?"

"That's usually how it works."

I glance toward the street in the distance—toward the address we came to visit. And I'm suddenly aware that I'm following the tracks of one parent while erasing those of the other.

"I thought you wanted to sell?"

"I have to." I won't be able to float the mortgage payments much longer, and I have no business being a landlord. Living in my childhood home is not an option—not with all the ambivalent emotions it conjures; I'd risk suffocating in the memories. The happy ones snuck up on me while I was confined there: Dad's booming laugh, the way his signature knock would resonate against the hollow door of my bedroom—always in a pattern of five, followed by *Permission to enter, Princess?*

I pace two more lengths of the storefront before stopping abruptly. "But what if I accept a lowball offer? What if I sell the house to a psychopath who moves in next door to your parents? They could be one of those weird exotic animal collectors who keep tigers or ferrets in the yard. Can I do a background check?"

Beau stands still on the sidewalk while I pace. His focus follows me with every quick lap, and I don't miss the twitch of a smile that flicks across his mouth. "I presume that might cross some legal boundaries. Privacy, discrimination, and whatnot."

"This feels like a decision an adult should make."

He chuckles. "I hate to break it to you, but you are an adult by any legal standard. You'll be thirty-five in two months."

I collapse with my hands on my knees. "That's officially old. Late thirties." A birthday is coming, without my dad to help me celebrate.

Beau clears his throat. "*Mid*-thirties."

With the same birthday, Beau and I share the same timeline for aging. But who knew he would be sensitive about it? He's successful and gets hotter the older he gets.

"Everyone knows you round up at five," I say.

"But why would you round up when your age is already a round number? With that logic, a five-year-old is ten. A fifteen-year-old is twenty." His voice escalates.

"Please, Beauregard, lecture me on the illogical fear of aging." I'm grateful to be able to bicker with him to distract myself from all the scary choices ahead.

But he sighs. "I don't know how you drag me into such absurd arguments. Look, you need to review the paperwork and make some

The Truth Is in the Detours

decisions. I'm going to drive us to the motel." He stops short as I take two slow inhales. "And find you a paper bag to breathe into."

~

An hour later, we've checked in, grabbed tacos and beer, and are huddled around a firepit at the motel. We have a postcard view of the ocean—a rugged lava-rock shoreline of shallow bluffs, with cypress trees and lavender ice plants clinging to the cliffs. This is a millionaire location on a poor man's budget.

"I'm going to accept the offer," I say.

"You're sure?" Beau's skepticism is ripe.

I eye him over my glass. "We've been over this. I'm never sure." When faced with multiple choices, I eenie-meenie-miney-mo my way through it. Selling my childhood home isn't what I want. But I also don't want to keep it. And I don't really have a choice.

"How do you ever feel good about your decisions?"

I shrug. "I don't." Only people with the privilege of multiple good options can feel confident in their decisions.

Beau shakes his head and leans back in the love seat. His legs are up on the stone surround of the firepit, and the red flames reflect off his lenses and highlight the angles of his face. He's thrown on a pair of gray sweats and a soft black T-shirt. I like casual Beau. It reminds me of *my* Beau—who was always wound too tight but had a silly streak a mile long to tangle with mine.

The sun is low on the horizon, and the sunset flirts with us with cotton candy clouds and ribbons of sherbet. "You scored on the cheap motel with killer views," I say.

"I do my best." He raises his bottle, and we toast.

"Why are you slumming it in all these motels anyway? You have that posh house, two bestsellers, and a cushy professor gig. You could stay at the Ritz."

Beau barks out a laugh and throws back the rest of his beer. "You're funny."

"C'mon, Beau. I saw you on *The Today Show*. You're a big deal."

He continues to chuckle. "A big deal. That's rich."

"You don't need to be self-deprecating with me."

He turns to face me, his expression sober. "My first advance and meager royalties helped pay for the down payment on the house. The second advance barely paid for my divorce lawyer. Book two hasn't earned out. And now I can't even sell the third. My job pays okay. But I live in the Bay Area, so I'm house-poor now that the mortgage is my sole responsibility. And I'm still drowning in student debt. I'm a bit of a pariah as a historian since I didn't go the academic publishing route but went commercial. Oh, and I haven't published enough peer-reviewed articles, so I'm not likely to make tenure anytime soon."

I take it all in—even Beau feels inadequate sometimes. It's a strange sense of solidarity after feeling like such a failure in comparison. "Who knew it could be so hard at the top?" Even behind his lenses, I know he's rolling his eyes at me. "It makes me feel more at peace for being such an underachiever."

The sun sinks, and it looks enormous as it dips into the horizon, blurred by hazy rays that shoot out into the tie-dye sky. We sit in silence as the chatter of groups on neighboring patios escalates. A crescendo of laughter dissolves in the twilight when the sky bursts into a kaleidoscope of pastels, and the surf crashes against the untamed rocks.

"So, you're selling the house. How do you feel about that?"

"Happy I'll be able to pay off my student loans, buy a new car, and ditch my asshole mechanic."

"Emotionally," he prompts.

"Ugh. Emotions." I grab another beer and hold it out to Beau. He shakes his head. No buzzed Beau tonight. How sad.

"You can't avoid them forever. Are you going to look for your mom?" he presses.

The Truth Is in the Detours

I shake an imaginary eight ball and stop to look. "The outlook is hazy. Try again later." I take a long sip. Tomorrow. I'll think about that decision tomorrow.

"How have you survived adulthood thus far by avoiding difficult decisions?"

"How have you survived adulthood by being so certain?"

"Touché." Beau sighs and grabs another beer.

Tonight's outlook is looking up.

Two hours later, the moon is high, and the fire is glowing against the black night. The only clue that we're oceanfront is the roar of the waves rising from the bottomless foreground. A group of guests gave us leftover s'mores ingredients, and I've had two—my hands are now sticky and covered in ash after I rescued my last marshmallow from the flames. Beau refrained, allowing himself only a sliver of dark chocolate. He didn't get those abs by accident, I guess.

Beau grabbed a cotton blanket off his bed and draped it over us. At some point—perhaps after the second beer and before the third—I snuggled up against his side, trying to borrow his natural heat. Friends do this, right? They cuddle under a blanket around a firepit while listening to the waves lap against the rocks . . . right?

His arm is draped over the back of the rattan love seat, and my head is on his shoulder. It's a nice shoulder. I suspected as much from my sneak peek earlier this week. But the snuggle test confirms it. I'm sober enough to realize I wouldn't be suctioned to his side like a barnacle if I hadn't had three drinks, but not sober enough to peel myself away.

The wind picks up, and I burrow closer as he grabs the edge of the blanket and pulls it higher on my shoulder, leaving his hand draped there to keep it from falling again. Cue full-body shiver.

For the last hour, we've been updating each other on the lowlights of the last decade. I know his highlights—his achievements and accolades. So I demanded the embarrassing moments that didn't make it into the bio on the back flap of his books. So far, I learned Beau once tripped down a set of stone steps in front of his freshman seminar students. He broke his tailbone but laughed it off and hobbled back to his office in agony. I admitted that I went on a date and forgot to finish my makeup. I'd done an elaborate smoky eye—"*eye*" being the operative word. It was the first and only date, understandably.

"Worst client you've ever had?" Beau asks. He takes a sip of his beer, and my hair snags on his scruffy chin. He smooths it back, his fingertips brushing against my cheek. I feel the touch long after it's gone.

"Peter Winthrop. He was this controlling, sleazy tech CEO who hired me to track expenses for a renovation of his gaudy house. He sent me a billion nitpicky changes to a spreadsheet via nineteen voicemails."

Beau laughs, and his voice vibrates against my ear.

"And each one began, 'Apologies, I was cut off.' So I had to rewind each time to figure out where the instructions began."

Beau's eyes are glassy, and his grin is wide—and that damn cheek dimple. "What did you do?" He's running his palm up and down my arm, a warm pulse along my cool skin. I try to focus on the conversation, but my brain cells have evacuated to join the party my nerves are throwing at the site of his touch. I don't think he's touched me this way before. But I've complained about being cold, and he's chivalrous. And he does get a little friendly after a couple of drinks.

I clear my throat, remembering the question. "I made the changes and sent him nineteen new versions via separate, detailed emails. And didn't renew the contract."

Beau chuckles, and his breath tickles the stray hairs against my face. I'm overwhelmed when I make him laugh, even when it requires a little help from my friend Stella Artois. Beau's face straightens as I watch him. I'm acutely aware of how close we are, how his thigh feels pressed against mine, and how solid he is beside me. The drag of his hand along my skin feels like an invitation, and my body is begging me to accept. Now.

But this is Beau. My old, new, grumpy friend who is irritated at me more often than not. And I've forced him to cuddle me and tell me bedtime stories against his will. He'd never be this affectionate without alcohol in his system. I pull away and clear my throat. I'm immediately shivering.

"I better get to bed."

He removes his arm from over my shoulder. "Yeah," he says. "It's late."

I rise from the love seat to clear our mess, while he turns off the gas to the firepit. When I open the sliding glass door to my motel room, he steps over the short brick divide between our patios.

"Drink a big glass of water," he commands. "And take some ibuprofen."

"Yes, sir," I say, and toss him the blanket. "Thanks for the distraction. You know, from the emotions I don't want to have about . . . all the things."

He chuckles softly and nods. "Anytime, Phe."

CHAPTER 18

My tongue is the size of a tennis ball when I wake. Drumsticks practice on my temples with the incessant bass of Rage Against the Machine. The sun is high and bright, and a warm beam slants across my face.

I roll over and peel one eye open as the drumsticks grow more insistent.

"Oh-feel-eeee-yahh."

It's not a rock band. It's Beau. I stumble from bed and swing open the door.

"Whoa." Beau says as I collapse back on the bed. "What are you wearing?"

"Pajamas."

"You managed to put those on last night? Even with all those straps?" He flicks his fingers in the air in some crisscross pattern with an expression of pure confusion.

I look at my matching tank and sleep shorts—it's a cheap satin set with thin black lace around the edges. I think I got it at Target. The top has spaghetti straps that cross low on the back. Not exactly rocket science. "I wasn't that drunk."

"Drunk enough."

"You had as many drinks as I did. Why are you upright and so awake?"

The Truth Is in the Detours

"It's the alcohol-to-weight ratio." Beau walks to the coffee maker to start a pot before stealing another glance. "You wear those even without anyone to see them?"

"It's a pair of shorts, Beau." I pull the sheets over my legs. "If a guy isn't around to gawk at her, does a woman even exist?"

He snorts and fiddles with the coffee maker.

"I should ask you the opposite question. Why do you hide all that muscle and skin under so many clothes? Leaving girls to wonder isn't nearly as seductive as you'd think."

He looks at his jeans, boots, and flannel as if he's unaware of what he's wearing. I roll over to the side of the bed, propping myself up on an elbow. He looks away, his cheeks pink.

"You don't have any tattoos," he says, his eyes still cast away from me. "I figured with the ever-changing hair, you'd . . ." He trails off.

"How do you know I don't have any?" I tease. I'm hiding enough skin that he shouldn't assume. I don't, though. Tattoos are permanent, and I don't make permanent decisions.

"We have to get moving. Check out. Make decisions. Drive to another interview. Up." Beau shoves a watery mug of coffee in my face, and I take it. I don't fix my strap when it falls over my shoulder, and he darts his focus away as if I've flashed him full frontal. His cheeks turn ruddy. Maybe he'll get so uncomfortable he'll escape, and I can go back to sleep.

I grab my phone and flip through my messages and emails: photos from Lowell of the Chihuly in its new home, paperwork from Ronald to finalize the sale, new absurd tasks from Juniper, an overdue notice from my utility company. Shoot. I drop my phone on the nightstand and take a sip of weak coffee. "This is terrible," I say.

"You'll have to get out of bed if you want to go to a café for that saccharine nonsense you call coffee."

"Black-coffee-drinking sanctimony," I grumble.

A gray maxi dress lands in my lap before a jean jacket hits me in the head. "Get dressed," he says. I inspect the choices. Not bad.

"You're so bossy." But I stomp over to my bag, fish out underwear, a bra, and my toiletries, and head into the bathroom.

Beau has cleaned up the room and stuffed all my clothes in my bag when I step out a few moments later. He winds my phone charger around his palm and tucks the stray end in before starting on my laptop cord, placing them neatly in the small compartment of my backpack. Next up, my headphones. His packing habits are as tightly wound as he is.

"You don't need to clean up after me."

"I'm sick of listening to you swear like a sailor while you fight with your tangled cords."

I load the car while he checks us out, and he meets me at the curb moments later. He raises his brows in question.

"Let's check out the house. Maybe we can just stroll by?" My curiosity is overpowering my fear. As scared as I am about finding—or not finding—the truth, I can't leave without at least taking this next step.

It's a short drive back to the downtown. When we park and get out, Beau falls into step with me. I've memorized Mary's last known address, so it doesn't take us long to find the boxy cottage with peeling peach paint. There's a white picket fence bordering a dying lawn, and a brick walkway leading to a narrow wooden porch. I freeze outside the gate and Beau verifies the address on his phone.

The thing about decisions—and being bad at them—is that you have to keep making them. Each decision leads to another, and at each juncture, they demand answers.

Beau lifts the latch and wraps his hand around mine, compelling me to follow. He knocks on the door once, then again, before we hear shuffling inside. The door swings open to reveal a wiry, shirtless tween with a shock of white-blond hair falling in his eyes.

In television, during a moment like this, there's suspenseful music, a close-up of the kid's face to suggest he might be the main character's long-lost sibling, before a cut to commercial. But I feel nothing. I don't

The Truth Is in the Detours

know who this kid is, and my curiosity is overpowered by my doubt that I made the right decision to follow this lead at all.

He looks from Beau to me and back. I feel Beau's focus on my face before he snaps into action. "Good morning. I'm Beau Augustin and this is Ophelia Dahl. We're looking for someone, and this was listed as her last address."

"Are you the cops or something?"

"No." Beau clears his throat. "Family, actually."

"Does someone named Mary live here?" I try.

He shakes his head. "It's just me and my mom."

"Steven, who's at the door?" A tall woman—maybe late thirties—peers around the corner. She's dressed in blue scrubs, her hair up in a slick ponytail. She sees us and puts on a polite smile as she slings a purse over her shoulder. "Sorry, we aren't interested."

"Sorry, ma'am," Beau says. "We are looking for a family member—this was listed as her last known address. Her name is Mary Dahl."

The woman shakes her head. "It's just us here. And we've lived here since he was a baby."

Beau looks at the address on his phone and back to the numbers hanging beside the door.

"She was probably going by Mary Johnson," I say. "I have photos."

"I'm sorry, who did you say you were?" She shifts forward as Steven steps back. Her forehead has deep worry lines, and her mouth is curved into a subtle frown.

"Sorry," I reach out my hand, and she takes it, but her eyes don't stray from my face. "I'm Ophelia Dahl. Mary Johnson Dahl was—is—my mother." My throat goes dry, and I swallow twice as I dig through my purse to pull out a few old snapshots. In one, Mary's holding me in her lap. I'm about a year old. In another, she and Dad are at a restaurant, posing with candlelight between them. They aren't the best images—faded from time and shot in terrible lighting. The woman in the photos is in her early twenties—much younger than the middle-aged version who would have lived here.

The woman takes them, studies them. "Well, I can't be sure it's the same person, but I did rent out the cottage in the back to a Mary once. Haven't thought about her in years. Her last name could have been Johnson. Maybe." She shakes her head and looks back at me. "But my son was young, I was in nursing school. I think it was about nine years ago or so. I was sleep-deprived and don't remember much."

"Do you remember where she moved? Whether she might still be in town?"

She hands back the photos. "Sorry. But I don't think she's still around. She worked at a coffee shop on Main Street." She looks up and purses her lips. "I think it was Mug and Muffin. But it could have been the Grind, which closed a few years back."

"Thanks," I say, accepting that this might be a dead end.

Beau slips her a business card. "If you remember anything else, we'd really appreciate a call." Good move, Beau. His card is professional and credible—no one is threatened by a history professor with a kind smile.

"I hope you find her—and that she's safe."

"Thanks for your time," I say.

She worked at a coffee shop. Not exactly a hot lead—but nice of this woman to talk to us.

We walk back to the car in silence, but Beau bypasses the car when I stroll up to the passenger door. "You still want coffee?" he asks.

"Always."

He points toward a storefront with a sign in ornate script. Mug and Muffin. "Two birds?"

"Umm," I say.

"Jesus, Phe. You're a dog with a bone about almost everything, but with this, you—"

"Fine. I need coffee anyway. And a pastry." I want answers, of course. But that doesn't mean I don't fear them as well.

We stride up to the counter at Mug and Muffin a few moments later. It's a tiny café with only a few tables. The glass case showcases

The Truth Is in the Detours

an impressive collection of pastries: eclairs, croissants, ten varieties of muffins, cinnamon rolls, and doughnuts.

I order a vanilla latte and a cinnamon scone, and Beau, predictably, orders black coffee and a protein bar that looks about as appetizing as cardboard.

"We're looking for someone who may have worked here nine years ago. A missing family member," Beau says to the teenage cashier while he presents his credit card.

"I wasn't working here then."

She would have been in grade school, I imagine. "But do you know of anyone who still works here who might remember?" I ask.

"Well, Pamela, the owner, might. She stepped out for a minute but should be back soon."

I collect my scone before sliding into a ladder-back chair around a glass table, and Beau sits across from me. I've downed my latte when a woman in her sixties approaches our table a few minutes later.

"I heard you're looking for a former employee?" Pamela, I presume. "Is someone in trouble?"

"I hope not," I say, hedging, while I pull out the photos again. "I'm looking for my mom, Mary. Her maiden name was Johnson, married name, Dahl. We heard she may have worked here about nine years ago."

Pamela takes the photos. "I did have a Mary Johnson for a time. She was a damn good pastry chef." Beau picks his head up, his eyes wide behind his glasses. "Can't say for sure whether this was her. My Mary was older, but blond too. Hard to recognize her as the gal in these photos. Besides, my memory isn't as good as it once was."

"These were taken over thirty years ago," I chime in.

She tilts her head. "It sure could be her."

"Do you happen to know where she is now?" Beau asks.

She sets the photos on the table. "She was getting married and moving away—somewhere south of here, I think."

"Do you remember his name?" Beau asks, which is brilliant. We could be looking for someone who doesn't go by Johnson or Dahl anymore.

Pamela hums. "No—but I remember his last name was some cartoon character. I teased Mary about it because she was planning on taking it. Bullwinkle, I think it was. Wait. No, maybe it was Garfield . . . or Flintstone?" She laughs and shakes her head, realizing how ridiculous it sounds.

"Do you know if she had any friends in town who would know where she is now?" I ask.

"I'm sorry, I'm afraid I've told you everything I remember."

"If you think of anything else that might be helpful, we'd really appreciate it if you could get in touch." Beau fishes out another business card and hands it over.

Pamela shoves it in her pocket. "Sure. Good luck."

But with clues like this, what we need is a miracle.

CHAPTER 19

Mary Flintstone delivers no search results, which is shocking honestly. Same for Mary Bullwinkle. Mary Garfield is at least plausible but still a dead end. I've scoured social media profiles and online birth and death records. Nothing. The cryptic clue is even more frustrating than knowing nothing at all. The confirmation that she went on living like I didn't exist . . . Well, it's more painful than I can allow myself to think about.

"I can help you look when we get to Chico," Beau says. "And we have more addresses to check in Redding and La Pine."

"Yeah, but she lived in those places before Fort Bragg."

"Someone there may know her, may still be in contact with her."

I throw my head back on the headrest. "I've checked all the names Pamela mentioned. Nothing. Are we going to create an algorithm for cartoon characters? Mary Pooh? Mary McDuck? Mary Jetson?"

Beau ignores me. "We know she's a pastry chef. And got married and left Fort Bragg around nine years ago. We can search county records. Perhaps they got their marriage license there." He taps his index finger on the top of the steering wheel, throwing a quick glance my way.

"Maybe." After all the anticipation, indecision, and reticence, I feel . . . I don't know. Deflated, I guess. I touch my mom's pendant, dragging it across the chain, back and forth.

My mother went on living. Baked croissants. Married a guy. Lived on the coast and took in sunsets. While I grew up without her—missing her, mourning her, honoring a version of her that doesn't exist.

She's never felt as dead to me as she has since I learned she's alive.

When we reach Clear Lake, I notice a cover of smoke marring the bright summer day. An orange, hazy horizon bleeds into an apocalyptic dome hovering above the landscape. Traffic has been slow on the two-lane highway bordering the lake—it's taken us double the time to make it this far. We're Californians. We know what this smoke means, and it always sparks anxiety. In the distance, I note patches of charred earth where an earlier fire left its fingerprint.

It's early July, the beginning of fire season in the drought-prone West.

"Shit." Beau turns on the radio. Static comes over the airwaves before we find reception and a local news station. We wait through traffic updates and a feel-good story about a dog saving her owner before the inevitable news of the fire takes over the broadcast. Beau listens while I scroll through my phone. But my maps won't load.

According to the radio, we're not in danger here, but the smoke is blowing out west. The fire is over a hundred miles away, closer to where we're headed, so the route is closed ahead. "We're not going to make our interview," Beau sighs.

"I'll call as soon as we regain service," I say.

"I hate flaking on commitments."

"It's a natural disaster. I'm sure he won't hold it against you."

"Nevertheless." He cranes his neck to the right and places his palm on the back of my seat to peer into our blind spot, brushing my bare shoulder. He swerves onto the shoulder and accelerates to pull off at the next exit. The momentum throws me back into the seat.

"You can't say 'nevertheless' like an old English gentleman while driving like a maniac. Cognitive dissonance."

The Truth Is in the Detours

He grumbles something under his breath that I can't hear. "We'll be stuck on the freeway for hours. We need to find a place to stay while we still can."

Beau drives toward the town, parking in front of a strip of businesses. Ash has fallen on parked cars, a downy white powder coating the scene like mist. I cover my mouth with my jean jacket to avoid inhaling. Beau leads us toward a coffee shop, and the bell rings above the door as we walk in. I order us lunch while Beau hops on the free Wi-Fi.

When I return to the table, he's hunched over his laptop. "All right," he says. "I found a cabin about ten miles from here. We can take back roads. We'll be housebound, but safe."

～

"The air quality is terrible," Beau says. The ashy sky has a hint of saffron on the horizon; it's an ominous tableau. I miss our postcard sunset from last night. We snake through a short one-lane road, down an unpaved driveway, and pull in front of an A-frame cabin burrowed among the towering pines.

"This is adorable." I glance around the dense forest as we exit the car, my shoes crunching on pine needles and brush.

The ash layer adds ten degrees to the already-roasting heat. Our reprieve from the inland hellscape was brief. Beau strides onto the low-slung porch and punches in a code before the door creaks open. I gather my bags and a few of the groceries we just picked up and follow him in.

"Ahh, look at this place!" I squeal. "It's like that log cabin our parents rented when we went skiing in Big Bear. How old were we?"

"Ten, maybe eleven?" We learned to ski that week—sort of. Our parents dropped us off at ski school while they enjoyed the slopes. Beau never learned to make a pizza without getting the tips of his skis caught on each other. His limbs were growing out of control by that point—they were a lot to manage. I preferred to drink cocoa in the lodge to freezing my ass off on the chairlifts. We both loved the cabin, though. While Beau and I built a snowman, our parents played cards and drank hot toddies.

This matchbox cabin is so similar, and it's drenched in pine details: wide-plank floors, wood siding climbing to the steep peak, and a log banister that leads to a loft. It's a monochrome display of rustic charm with knotty lumber—there's an antler chandelier hanging over a live-edge dining table and floor-to-ceiling windows that bring the forest inside. Dust swirls in the air, suspended in an auburn sunbeam as the crimson sun barrels through the glass.

I dump the groceries on the counter and duck into the back. There's one bedroom with a full bed draped in a vintage blue-and-white quilt, and a single bathroom with a stand-up shower.

Upstairs, there's an open loft with a floral futon. I drop my bags. Beau gave me his bedroom at home—I'm not going to make him sleep on a miniature futon. It's so hot up here. It's too much to hope for air-conditioning, and to keep the smoky air out, we'll be sealed in here like roasting chickens.

I hear Beau stomping around below. "Dibbs on the loft," I say as I hang over the railing. "You'd bang your head on the ceiling up here."

He doesn't respond, so I bound back downstairs and unload the rest of the car before stacking the supplies on the dining table. Beau went all survivalist at the store and filled his basket with bottled water, batteries, flashlights, paper maps, granola bars, canned foods, instant coffee, and beef jerky. I was a bit more optimistic and bought real groceries: a nice cut of meat for dinner, fresh greens, an assortment of veggies, and freshly ground coffee, like a civilized human.

"I thought you weren't worried," I say as I inspect a device he pulled from his emergency kit in his trunk. I've seen one just like it used as a prop in apocalyptic movies.

"I'm not. Because I'm prepared." He's been sullen and pouty since our plans derailed. His ability to cope with detours and surprises is an emerging skill. His tantrums as a kid when plans would change were epic. I note now that they haven't disappeared—they've evolved.

The Truth Is in the Detours

"What is this?" I hold up the device while he stacks canned goods in an empty cabinet.

"A weather radio. It'll alert us if the fires get close or the air quality becomes too unhealthy."

"That's not worrisome at all. Hey, do you know what the Wi-Fi password is? I have some work I should probably do."

"Umm . . ." He grabs the welcome binder and flips through it before starting again from the beginning. "Well . . . shit."

"What?" I open the fridge door and slide in the eggs.

"There's no Wi-Fi."

I turn to gape at him. "No Wi-Fi? What about running water? Electricity? Indoor plumbing?"

He rolls his eyes.

I track back to the long list that Juniper sent this morning. I don't know how much of it I can do on my phone using cell service. I check my cell. "Shit. Give me your phone."

Beau does as he's told, but the lock screen is on, so I wave it over his angry mug to trigger the face ID to bust it open.

"Beau," I say. "There are zero bars. On either phone."

He sighs. "Relax. We'll be here for twelve hours."

But can Juniper's to-do list last that long? I guess it will have to. I pick up the stack of paper bags and look for the recycling, heading to the backyard to check if there's an outdoor container. I throw open the back door, which leads to a small patio, and gasp. "Beau!" I call. "Beauregard!"

"So impatient," he grumbles as he walks over.

"There's a hot tub." I step aside and show him my find.

"So?"

"I love hot tubs." I tug on his arm. "A ten-foot well of steaming water. We can pretend we're on vacation, not hunkered down here avoiding the depressing reality of climate change."

"It's 90 degrees and smoky outside. I'm not getting in a hot tub."

"Please?"

"The air quality is in the unhealthy range," he says.

I sigh but trudge upstairs to the loft to change. "I'll take my chances," I say.

I change into a white bikini and jog downstairs to look for a towel, opening the doors to a linen closet in the cramped hallway when Beau steps out of his bedroom and straight into me.

"Shit, sorry," he mumbles, stepping to the right as I shimmy to my left and collide with him again. I'm almost naked, and he's changed into a thin cotton shirt and running shorts. His chest is a solid wall of heat against my skin. When he sighs, his breath is a warm gust across my forehead.

I release an uncomfortable laugh as he grumbles and steps to the right. I shift, and our chests bump. We're wedged beside the open cabinet and his bedroom door, locked in tight quarters in the sweltering space. I look up to see sweat beading on his temple and the veins in his neck straining. But his eyes rest firmly on the swell of my breasts.

And, *oh*. So this inconvenient attraction isn't one-sided after all. The awareness sends a thrill through my veins—but not dissimilar to the feeling I get during thrasher movies when the girl decides to check out the noise in the basement. It's terrifying. Because while my attraction to Beau is troublesome, reciprocity could be disastrous. And it looks like Beau agrees. His brows are threaded so tight that he looks pained; whatever appreciation he has for my cleavage is against his will.

It's safe to ogle Beau when he's looking in the other direction. But hot-professor Beau isn't a novelty anymore; he's my last tether to home, my oldest friend, and the one bit of stability in my mess of a life. I'm just learning how to be his friend again, and I don't want to screw it up with lust and lose him a second time.

I place my hand on his hip to move him. He freezes, his body taut as a bow, but there's a moment when we sway toward each other. I'm disoriented for one, two. But then I remember the conflict on his face.

The Truth Is in the Detours

I need to do what I couldn't before—put our friendship first. I catch his gaze and wince. He opens his mouth to say something but snaps it shut. "Hold still. And I'll go this way." I steady him as I slip from our corner and toward the back door. I turn with my hand on the knob, spotting him resting against the wall, his focus trailing me before I retreat to safety on the patio.

CHAPTER 20

Beau is a man of his word, leaving me alone to luxuriate in the Jacuzzi. His loss. Or maybe mine. But I'm proud of myself for noticing the needed boundary before breaching it.

When I wander up to the loft an hour later, he's still holed up in his bedroom. After a quick shower, I head into the kitchen to make dinner. Beau wanders out as I put the steak into the oven and pivot to slice the peaches for the salad. He's just showered, and I get a whiff of his soap—it's citrusy and distinctly masculine. His hair is wet and brushed back, and his glasses are fogged. He pulls them off and wipes the lenses with the hem of his shirt as he approaches the counter, revealing a strip of tanned, flat stomach. I dart my focus to his face—but his glasses are off—which is mesmerizing, too. I so rarely get to see his eyes from behind his glasses that I've forgotten what a deep brown they are—how his eyelashes are so thick and straight that it looks like he's wearing eyeliner. It's a shame they're always veiled.

"What can I do?" Beau slips his glasses back on. I try to clear my expression.

"Sit there and look pretty. I got it."

He grabs the sparkling water out of the fridge as I top the arugula with the peaches. "As soon as we get back to civilization, I'll help you search for your mom."

"It's like she really is a ghost."

The Truth Is in the Detours

"We'll check the older addresses when we head north. Someone may remember her." He pours me a glass of water. "We can check the courthouse in Jackson County—try to find the rest of that paperwork."

"Maybe." The ordeal unsettles me—it's a pit in my stomach, a subtle form of nausea that hits me in waves, a throb behind my temples. Do I keep searching? The irony is that I wish I could ask Dad what I should do. He was my moral compass. Realizing that his sense of ethics was shaky makes me question every decision I've made—every time he told me, *You did the right thing, Princess,* maybe it was the wrong thing all along.

"Hey," Beau says, his voice gentle, "what are you thinking?"

I contemplate deflecting, but it's getting harder to stop my runaway thoughts, especially in the face of Beau's gentle nudge.

I sigh. "I'm not sure what I expect to gain even if I do find her."

"Answers?" Beau leans a hip against the counter and crosses his arms over his chest.

"If she'll give them." If she *can* give them. I don't know how much of my own sanity or happiness I can pin on a resolution I may never get.

"An apology?"

"I'm not even sure I could accept it."

Beau watches me, and the heat of his gaze might be the one weapon that can pierce my emotional armor, because I feel defenseless.

"Do you know what you'd say to her?"

I give his question a moment to marinate. It's not like I haven't thought about it, but I've tried to push it from my mind. I don't want to get ahead of myself and feel even more unsettled and confused if I never find her. "Not yet. But I feel like I'll know in the moment, right? Assuming we find her, the state of her life will answer a lot, I think."

Beau sounds like he's making me an interview subject when he asks, "In what way?"

I resist the urge to change the subject or tease him about jumping into researcher mode. It's a fair question, even though I'm not sure I have a coherent answer.

"If she looks like she's lived a rough life, maybe that offers some clues. If she moved on like nothing happened and has another family, kids . . ." I swallow as my throat thickens. I'm not ready to go through the scenarios, because none of them—other than a soap-opera-esque three-decades-long coma or bout of amnesia—can absolve her. I'm consumed by feelings without descriptors, questions without answers, and instincts without reason. Beau's undivided attention is dangerous—he shines a flashlight on my emotional cracks and spotty logic.

I turn on a bright smile, stir the pan sauce with a wooden spoon, and hold it aloft. "Taste this."

Beau startles and laces his palm around my wrist. He opens his mouth and closes his eyes as he tastes, moaning slightly. "Holy hell, Phe."

"Good?" I'm pleased with his praise and so grateful that he's letting me move on. He must sense I've reached my limit.

He hums, his eyes closed and expression vulnerable. This is what he'd look like if he were lost in pleasure. The vision of him seeps into my senses, wraps around my chest, ensnares my belly, and spreads heat down my thighs. How would it feel to affect this man and make him experience something other than irritation? To break down his guard until he forgets himself and his hang-ups? To make him hum like that for other reasons? He opens his eyes, and I'm still watching him. Our gazes lock, and the muscle in his jaw jumps. I dart my focus away and shake off the fantasy.

His attentiveness—and my knowledge of the abs under that thin shirt—is making me forget my commitment to keep my hands to myself.

I clear my throat. "We'll be ready in five minutes. You want to set the table?"

"Excuse me," he says as he reaches into the upper cabinet. His arm passes over my head, his body eclipsing the light from the window. He braces himself with a palm on my back, holding me steady as he grasps two plates and closes the door. Every nerve collects under his palm. I step aside as he opens a few drawers, and then we shimmy by each other again. I feel his heat, still humid from his shower, and a drop of water from the tip of his hair lands on my collarbone. "Sorry," he says, flicking his hair back and moving away, as I let out a slow exhale.

I plate the steak, pour a spoonful of sauce over each, and bring them to the table while Beau follows me with the salad and sliced baguette. We settle at the pine dining table, maneuvering our plates and glasses to make room.

"Hair of the dog?" Beau asks, holding up a bottle of cabernet. He doesn't wait for my answer before pouring me a glass.

"Cheers," I say.

"To detours." Beau holds his glass aloft for a toast, and I clink mine to his as he eyes me with an expression that's wistful, searching, and heavy. I don't know how to read it.

He digs into his steak while I take a steadying sip of the wine.

"Phe," he moans, "why did you hide this talent from me for so long? We've been eating like college students."

"Keep renting me cute little cabins and I will cook for you forever." I clear my throat—and coax the flirt out.

"You really paid attention to my mom, didn't you."

"Well, yeah, your mom taught me a lot." But my mom was my first teacher. She'd set me on a stool with a bowl and wooden spoon, allowing me to mix while she measured ingredients. But I'm not sure I can trust those memories or their significance. "While you were busy reading books, I was in the kitchen with her. And then I watched a lot of Cooking Channel."

Beau laughs—but it's true. You live alone, TV keeps you company. He sighs into a bite, and my pride swells. I love to cook, but it's so much more fun to do it for someone who appreciates it. I would cook when I visited Dad, but he had a simple palate. I knew when he didn't like it because he'd say, *Wow, Princess. This is fancy.* His gray eyes would twinkle as he said it—proud I knew how to cook something he didn't know how to pronounce, but still not eager to eat it.

I think of my small apartment back home with no one to cook for. The loneliness creeps in again. I have loads of acquaintances—people I called friends until I lost the person who had been my world. The calls dried up after the funeral, which was a floodlight on the truth of each relationship like the lights coming on at closing time.

Beau takes another bite, making a sound I will never unhear. It's low and satisfied, appreciative—and it makes me flush with pride and something else I shouldn't name. Because I can't afford to let that noise infiltrate my long-term memory. It's bad enough to know how he looks half naked, but I need to keep my fantasies single-sensory. Otherwise, I might do something stupid and pounce on him and threaten our newly rekindled friendship. He's the person in my life who has known me the longest now that Dad has died. Our reconciliation is tenuous, and I need to protect it from my disastrous instincts. Right now, my reflex is to bake him a flourless chocolate cake to see how much more pleasure I could beckon—and then taste it off his lips. And that would put an expiration date on our friendship.

The last time I lost him, it was because I made the mistake of taking everything he would give me—even if it wasn't good for him. I can't do that again.

Perhaps I could hold his attention while we're sequestered together on our strange crusade for truth. We could slip into bed and let our attraction burn to dust. But if I want to hang on to him after this trip is over—and I do—I need to exercise self-control. I need to build on our nostalgia with these new, potent moments of connection to safeguard our friendship from another estrangement. A platonic relationship will be enough, I think. It has to be—because Beau is bred for monogamy with someone serious, and I am not that person.

"What happened with you and Bianca?" The question is born whole, tripping off my tongue and stumbling onto the table.

The Truth Is in the Detours

Beau freezes but softens when he sees my face. I think I'm more surprised than he is. "Phe," he sighs.

"She's obviously still in love with you."

"She's not," he says.

"She couldn't have been more territorial if she had peed on you."

"Possessiveness isn't love." Beau looks at his plate as he polishes off the peach and goat cheese salad. He's about to finish my painstakingly prepared dinner in under five minutes.

"She is refusing to sign divorce papers," I argue.

"Because she wants control."

I'm surprised that he's answered so many questions, even though his responses are evasive. "You kept your wedding ring."

He chews and considers me. I sense he's contemplating how much he's willing to share.

"When I got married, I expected it to be forever. The ring was a symbol of that hope."

I should drop it, but there's something in his expression that begs me to ask more. There's the barest hint of an invitation. "What changed your mind?"

He sets his fork on his clean plate and takes a long sip of wine. When he answers, he looks over my shoulder. "I found out I didn't know her all that well."

That sounds familiar. I thought I knew everything about my dad, but it turns out I didn't know him all that well either. "Did she lie to you?"

"Something like that." He finishes his glass and pours another. For all his sanctimony about the height of my emotional walls, he's not exactly laying out the welcome mat.

I think of how desperate Beau was to show Bianca he'd moved on by pretending we were together. I didn't know what his goal was then, but now I understand. I had to see Matty and his new girlfriend at Cherry's wedding. I brought along a hot guy from work and had him pretend he was obsessed with me—and I was so grateful for that kindness. It numbed the pain a bit. I wonder if Beau's desperation was the same as mine. Did Bianca cheat on him? Was she as careless with his heart as Matty was with mine? It's unfathomable that someone would be self-destructive enough to cheat on this gorgeous, thoughtful man. Bianca is a doctor—could she really be stupid enough to betray him, hurt him, and risk losing him forever? If she did, I hope she's feeling that loss now.

"So I did the right thing, then?" I ask.

"Interrogating me is never the right thing, Ophelia." But he smiles and flashes me a hint of dimple.

"I did the right thing when I was your emotional-support fake girlfriend. I'd feel like an asshole pretending to be your hot side piece if you were the jerk in the breakup."

"Again, Bianca and I are over, so you're not the side piece."

"But you're admitting I'm hot?" I tap his foot under the table.

I'm teasing, but his eyes dart to my lips, to my neck, before he looks away and blinks to erase the image like an Etch A Sketch. It's as much of a yes as he'll confess. I'm going to need to rewire my flirt instinct to keep us on solid ground. I remember Beau's censure: *You have two speeds: fight or flirt.* I need to find a new default for him if I want to protect this relationship.

"Why didn't I hear through the grapevine that you broke up?" I pull us back on topic. His face is impassive as he stares at me, swirling his wine in his glass. "I mean, Dad told me about every milestone as if I were the future author of your biography. The chain of communication was from you to Lani to Dad to me. In addition to all your laudable accomplishments, I heard about your appendicitis while traveling in Europe and that you sprained your ankle hiking Machu Picchu."

"I feel violated," he says, swallowing another sip of wine.

"As did I. I assure you it was unsolicited. But why didn't I hear about you and Bianca?"

He shrugs, looking over my shoulder again.

"Beauregard," I coax.

The Truth Is in the Detours

"I didn't tell my parents until a few weeks ago. When I was there . . ." He trails off. It's why he was in San Diego when Dad died, I presume. "I wanted to tell them in person. And I didn't want to be home when Bianca came to clean me out. She'd been stopping by randomly for months, picking up a lamp at a time."

I let out a long hiss. "But how long ago did you split up?"

"Over a year ago."

I choke on a bite. "How did you keep it from Lani? Even Cherry knew."

"How the hell did Cherry know?" he snaps.

"I think she picked up on the hints on Instagram. She noticed you were absent in Bianca's recent posts. We all followed her—she's almost Insta-famous, you know."

He sighs. "Well, my parents aren't on social media. And they weren't close with Bianca. She couldn't get away much. I went to San Diego for the holidays this year and explained she was on call. It wasn't a lie. Just not the full truth."

For a year, he managed to withhold it from Lani Augustin, who knows everything about everyone, especially her only son. Lani knew the trouble we'd cause before we could dream it up. *I see you spying that cookie dough. I'll know if either of you steals a bite.* Or later, *I know about the plans for Colton's party. Don't you two do anything you're not ready for.* Two days after Beau told me he'd had his first wet dream, she left a book on human development on his nightstand.

Beau wasn't open with his parents the way I was with Dad. The more Lani pushed, the less he shared. But hiding a separation? How? Why? Was he in denial? Did he want Bianca back? Was he hoping they'd work it out? I can't imagine Beau forgiving a betrayal like that. But I don't know for certain that she cheated. Perhaps I'm filling in the blanks based on my own wounds.

Beau sighs and stands, clearing our plates and striding into the kitchen.

"Why'd you hide it?"

"I didn't want to hear about Mom's hairdresser's son's marriage that was saved through counseling, or worse, I didn't want Mom trying to fix me up with someone new. I didn't want her to become invested in us staying together or—"

"In breaking up for good," I guess.

I follow Beau into the kitchen with the salad bowl and the wine, and he stands over the trash bin and scrapes the plates clean. He sets them on the counter and leans against the lip of the sink.

"I needed some time to process everything before sharing it."

That's fair. If Beau hadn't walked in during the moment of impact, I might have hidden my truth bomb, too. "This is why your mom said we needed each other? We were both going through it."

He nods. "Yeah."

"I wish you would have shared more. Our friendship doesn't have to be so one-sided."

Beau looks out the window above the sink as the smoke-soaked sun descends through the bloodied sky. "It doesn't feel one-sided anymore."

I swallow a swell of emotion—gratitude that he sees the effort I'm making, sadness that it took loss to finally bring us together again, and fear that I may not know how to walk the tightrope of this new dynamic.

"Go relax," Beau says. "You cooked. I'll clean. Go find a trashy paperback. Or play solitaire. Or start a puzzle."

"And stop asking personal questions?" I guess.

"Precisely." His smile disarms me.

I relent and abandon the line of questioning. He's working through it, obviously. But I'm not done with him entirely. I love this cabin in the woods and Beau's cautious friendship. The night seems loaded with possibilities if I can stop noticing how hot he looks fresh from the shower.

"You wash, I'll dry," I say as I find a towel in a drawer by the sink.

I watch the way his arms move and flex as he scrubs the plates under the running water: forearm, shoulder, bicep, back. Who knew washing dishes was a full-body workout?

The Truth Is in the Detours

Beau hands me the dishes and pots one at a time, barely glancing in my direction. He's head down, lost to his thoughts—likely dissecting the private details he didn't want to share with me—and I try not to feel left out. I know what it's like to avoid emotional analysis, but for me, it's too much to even ask myself the tough questions. Beau is so introspective, he probably analyzes his pain from every angle, scrutinizing what went wrong until he's written a virtual dissertation.

Or until he's written a book.

I place the salad bowl on the counter with a clang. "Beau, this project is about your divorce, isn't it?"

Beau flicks the water off and wipes his hands on a towel. "Phe," he says, his voice soft and pleading, and it may as well be a yes.

So Bianca betrayed him, and he wants to uncover how and why people keep secrets. It makes sense, I suppose. A professor would want to understand. Beau would *need* to understand, because there's little about the world he doesn't. Meanwhile, I find life so confounding that only my mother returning from the dead has shocked me.

We finish the rest of the cleanup in silence. Beau systematically puts everything away and stacks and aligns the dishes like he once did with his building blocks. He scrubs the counters and straightens the toaster, the coffee maker, and the spice racks in his wake. I watch—quietly—as he sterilizes the kitchen as if we might perform emergency surgery on the countertops later.

"Do you want to play cards or a board game?" I ask, ready to move us toward safer territory. I hope he'll talk to me about it eventually, but I've pushed him enough tonight.

Beau scans the kitchen, and he must be satisfied with his handiwork because he strides over to where I'm standing and cocks a hip against the counter. He's so close that I can smell the familiar scent of home clinging to his clothes.

"The only game I'm interested in is the quiet game," he says.

There's no reason to interpret his words as suggestive, but I can't help but think of all the ways he could make me speechless—with his mouth, his hands, his skin. And by the look on his face, the blaze behind his dark eyes, and the slight uptick in the pace of his breathing, he may be imagining the same thing.

I should have mercy on us, because we've each veered too close to emotional arteries, and I'm at risk of blurring want with reality. We promised not to lie to each other, but that's not the same as baring our souls and unloading our secrets. So I should retreat to the loft and let Beau decompress in the bedroom, where I can't beg for his touch or his truths.

But I don't want to be alone with my thoughts—not when they've been uncorked by his questions and confessions.

"I don't know how to play that game." I lift my chin to capture his gaze.

Beau's jaw is tight, and his eyes skitter over me, dipping to my lips for a fraction of a second. I imagine him pressing his mouth to mine to teach me, swallowing my words with his tongue—but that's not a fantasy I should follow.

Beau seems to sway toward me, and I grip the counter to hold myself in place, my knuckles white with restraint. But when I think he might lean in and test my resolve, he turns abruptly, stepping out of the kitchen and down the hall. Relief—or maybe disappointment—washes over me as he walks away. I poke my head around the corner, expecting to see him disappear into his bedroom. Instead, he hunts through the bookcase in the living room.

"Here," he says, extending a paperback out to me.

It's not a surprise that his discipline is more developed than mine, but I suspect his desire is not as potent. Either way, I should be grateful that I have a partner in Operation Abstinence.

Beau grabs his own hardcover from the coffee table and sinks onto the love seat. I slide onto the other side, take the paperback, and adjust the throw pillows until I'm comfortable. I open the book. The cover is frayed, with dog-eared corners and yellowed pages. But I let myself go where it leads, enjoying Beau's company even as we sit in silence, in solitude together.

He doesn't even protest when I stretch out and drape my feet across his lap. Instead, he brings one hand to my instep and squeezes.

The quiet game isn't so bad.

CHAPTER 21

"I'm going to head into town to get an update on the highways," Beau says as I hover over my coffee. I didn't sleep last night. The loft was a billion degrees, so I gave up and crashed on the love seat, which was an inch too short, forcing me to curl into an unnatural position that gave me a hip cramp. It was still too hot. I was desperate to open the windows, but the ash on the deck glowed in the moonlight, reminding me of our climate predicament. California is a fickle lover—gorgeous, tempestuous, alluring, unforgiving.

When I finally fell asleep, I had a dream about Beau that I couldn't shake. I blame his absent-minded foot massage—and the book, which got right into the M-rated action on page 11 and kept me there for another thirty pages. I haven't been able to make eye contact with Beau after the imaginary things he did to me on that love seat.

Beau woke me for real at six, banging around in his room like he was managing a construction project. I covered my head with the pillow, but it didn't matter. I was up.

He emerged an hour later, showered and ready to start the day. I am neither of those.

"I'll finish packing," I say as he steps outside with his duffel on his shoulder.

"Ophelia," he calls from outside a moment later.

I tumble off the stool and outside to find him in the driver's seat, with the door wide open, one leg still planted on pine needles.

The Truth Is in the Detours

"Did you leave the passenger door open yesterday?"

"No?"

Beau shakes his head. "I can prepare for fires, floods, tsunamis, earthquakes, and tornados. But Hurricane Ophelia is always my demise." He passes me, his cell phone in hand.

"Ouch," I say. "What happened?" I call as the wind from his tantrum blows by me.

"You left the door open, and the battery is dead. We're stranded."

"If you knew I left the door open, why did you ask me if I left the door open?"

He stares at his phone, pacing near the dining table.

"We don't have cell service," I remind him.

Beau lifts his head and glares at me for a beat before he storms back outside. I follow him, but his legs are too long, and I can't keep up. He rushes by the car and up the long, unpaved driveway.

"Where are you going?"

"To find cell service," he shouts over his shoulder.

I'm still perched on the edge of the porch, jiggling my knee when he appears around the corner an hour later. I release a breath when I spot his familiar gait and trot up the drive to meet him. "You were gone forever. I was worried you were lost."

Beau stops in his tracks, folding his arms across his chest. "I called the tow company, but they don't know when they'll make it out. I knocked on a few doors to see if anyone could give us a jump, but no one answered."

"They may have been scared of the big angry man knocking on their door at eight a.m."

He ignores me and trudges up the porch. "The roads are open—for now. But who knows if the winds will shift. But we have no choice but to wait." Beau heads into the cabin, waving me inside. I follow him in and seal out the smoky air.

"At least it's not a cowboy bar this time?"

"Too soon, Phe," Beau says.

"Beau," I say. He stills, turning to me in the entryway. "I'm really sorry."

He shrugs. "It could have been me."

I laugh. "We both know it wasn't you. What did we say about lying to each other?"

His smile is faint. "I'm working on being more patient and forgiving. Someone told me I might be a little uptight."

I nod. "That someone is very wise."

He chuckles as he passes me and walks toward his bedroom. "But I will feel more patient after a nap. That smoke gave me a headache."

My heart sinks a little as he closes the door behind him.

Hours later, I'm on the floor, leaning against the love seat at the coffee table working on a puzzle of the cliffside of Positano. I've managed to connect all the edge pieces, and it helps to distract me from our quandary, the dead end I've hit in searching for my mom, and the dream I had about Beau. I can't stop thinking about whether he's as focused a lover as he is an academic.

Beau emerges from his room. "Hey," he says, his voice scratchy. The sun is already high overhead; it must be early afternoon. We missed another interview this morning. Our momentum has taken a nosedive, and I'm sure Beau is frustrated.

"Want to help?"

"Probably shouldn't. My head is still killing me."

"I have painkillers," I offer.

"Took some, and the nap helped a bit."

He peers at the puzzle, at the lid, and back. "You should organize the pieces by color."

"'How to Mansplain a Puzzle' by Professor Beauregard Augustin."

He collapses in the love seat behind me, his long legs hanging over the armrest before he drapes his forearms over his eyes. I place my hand on his arm, and he flinches slightly before settling.

"What can I do? Do you need water?"

He lolls his head from side to side. "I'm fine."

The Truth Is in the Detours

He really doesn't look fine.

"Scoot down," I whisper. Beau opens one eye as I crawl onto the love seat and toss a cushion to the floor for more room. He complies, making enough space for me to slip in beside him. When I remove his glasses, he furrows his brows but doesn't stop me as I set them on the end table and bring my hands to his head. "Let me know if it hurts."

He closes his eyes, sighing as I massage his head. "It's good," he chokes out.

I find the pressure points at the base of his scalp, cradling his head with my palms and using my fingertips to release the tension there. His head grows heavier, and I slide toward him to lift it onto my thigh. He stiffens, but I keep going, and he exhales, giving in when I sink my thumbs into the wrinkle between his eyes.

There's something powerful about making this man melt—and I enjoy taking him apart inch by uptight inch. His face grows placid, his lips in their signature downturned arc, but parted and soft. His shoulders drop away from his ears, his eyelids flutter when I hit a spot he likes, right at the top of his head. I trail my thumbs along his scalp until I find the tight band of muscle at his nape. He groans—it's low and gravelly—and the sound does something to me. There's a warmth brewing in my belly, and I hold my breath as I work my hands along his neck to his shoulders. His skin is hot to the touch, silk over taut muscle. I press into the soft tissue above his collarbone and make compressions with my fingertips across the top of his chest, teasing the stretched collar of his shirt before dragging my hands out, where I cup the round arc of his deltoids. I slip to his biceps, sliding under his sleeves to find his shoulders again, but I'm frustrated by the fabric. I don't pause to think before I whisper, "Take this off."

I hold my breath as he reaches for the hem of his shirt, crossing his arms over his stomach. He lifts slightly, revealing a small trail of dark hair, his navel, the ridges of abdominal muscles, before his canvas of silken skin is on full display. I might be salivating. Beau tosses his shirt on the floor and settles with the top of his shoulders pressed against my bare thighs. His muscles tense as he bends his knee and plants a foot on the love seat, his other braced on the floor.

His body is draped before me, from calves to thigh, stomach to chest. I find his shoulders, sliding lower, over his pecs, trying to find a rhythm that feels innocuous—that suggests I am a professional tending to his headache. But he's molten against my skin, and it's making me ache in places that have been hibernating for too long. I notice goose bumps pop up on his skin in the wake of my touch.

I wander lower before he startles me, placing a rough hand over both of mine, stilling me, and pressing my palms flat against his chest. My throat goes dry as his eyes find mine. I swallow, and he watches the movement with parted lips. He reaches his other hand to my nape, threading his fingers in my hair and pulling me toward him. At least I think he's pulling me, because I'm falling over him like water over a ledge until our mouths are an inch apart. And we hover there—in the last measure of reasonable doubt. Beau's hand tightens against my neck, and he arcs up until his breath skates across my mouth and his soft lips meet mine. I have enough time to think, *What the fuck*, and *Yes*, and *Please*, before I jolt at the sound of a loud knock at the door.

"Hello? Did someone need a jump?"

CHAPTER 22

Neither of us says a word as we abandon our hideout like escaping fugitives. Beau deals with the tow truck driver while I throw the food in a cooler and drag our bags to the porch. I offer to drive—reminding us both of his headache and the reason I demanded his nudity—but he shrugs me off. We drive in silence for fifteen miles, too uncomfortable to even look at each other.

Beau drops the radio volume abruptly and mumbles, "I'm sorry about before."

"No, I'm sorry. You know, about getting you half naked."

He winces, flashing that same tortured look from yesterday.

And that's the end of it—the discussion, not the awkwardness. The awkwardness has staying power.

We have a long couple of days ahead of us. We're heading north to Oregon for tonight's interview in Klamath Falls before tomorrow's in Bend.

Our phones startle alive at mile sixteen, dinging relentlessly with alerts, reminding us that we've been off the grid. My heart rate spikes as I pick up my phone, noticing a string of texts. I bypass messages from Cherry and Simone—a group thread that could include anything from memes to requests for fashion advice to information about sleep training and nursing that I have no use for. I haven't confronted Cherry about the little trick she pulled on Beau all those years ago. I'm not looking forward to her making light of something that irrevocably tore Beau and me apart.

I also see messages from Ronald, my real estate agent, and Lowell, with an all-caps update: JUNIPER IS A NUT JOB.

"Shit," I say.

"What?" Beau finally looks at me, and I forget to feel self-conscious that I'd asked him to perform a striptease for me an hour ago.

"The Chihuly transport."

I call Lowell, and he starts ranting before saying hello. "I don't know how you put up with that woman. We got the thing installed to her exact specs—all six hundred pounds of it. It isn't going anywhere—even if the next big one is epicentered below her McMansion. And the crackpot showed up hours late and demanded we move it. Three feet! I centered the fucking thing, excuse my French, but she wanted it off-center because the center was too 'expected.' What the actual fuck? I refused. My guys had already worked a ten-hour day."

Shit. Shit. Shit.

"Oh, Lowell. I'm so sorry."

He grumbles something, says it's not my fault—but it's the last time he'll do a job for her.

I try Juniper, but she doesn't answer. I check my email and find twenty messages from her, demanding updates on the list she'd sent me last night, adding another slew of assignments, complaining about Lowell, asking me to find another contractor to move the Chihuly—again. In the last one—four hours ago—she demanded a response if I wanted to continue to work with her. She fires me, over email, in the final message.

I hang my head.

"What is it?"

"I lost Juniper as a client."

"Oh, Phe."

I straighten my shoulders. "It's fine. It'll be fine. I'll be fine." Maybe it's for the best. Juniper is inflexible and incapable of pleasing. But she's my largest client. I'll have to do some hustling as soon as I get home. At least I'll have the money from the sale of the house to tide me over for a while.

Beau reaches over. I think he's going to grab my hand, but he pats my thigh like a grandparent might console a frustrated child. It makes me feel worse.

I suck in a lungful of air and call Ronald next. I had filled out all the paperwork and sent it back before we left Fort Bragg. I'm not sure what he could need.

"Ms. Dahl, bad news."

"Okay . . . what's wrong, and how much will it cost?"

"Well, the inspection revealed faulty wiring in the kitchen and mold in the garage. There's some . . ." I tune him out, my focus blurring as the yellow lane lines stretch ahead to a vanishing point. Ronald finishes with an explanation of possible asbestos and a crack in the foundation that could be structural.

"What now?" I mutter.

"The buyer could pull out. It's enough to scare anyone off. But I'll keep you posted."

When I hang up, Beau doesn't even ask me what's wrong—Ronald was so loud I had to pull the phone away from my ear—so he must know the score. Beau does the hang-in-there-chap knee pat again, and I want to cry. At least my pathetic financial state is a douse of cold water on our ill-advised sexual flame.

Beau pulls off at the next exit, turning into a gas station and jumping out. He scrolls through his phone as he waits for the gas tank to fill, his expression pained when he brings his phone to his ear. I can't help but overhear. The windows are cracked, and his voice is a deep octave that carries even when he whispers.

"What do you mean you want to renegotiate the terms? What was the purpose of mediation if you were going to change your mind again?" There's a pause. "You and I both know you don't want the house—you work in San Francisco and hate the commute. Stop playing games."

He paces back and forth along the driver's side. "Tell me what it is you want, Bianca."

Beau catches my gaze through the dash, and I freeze as he hangs up and slides his phone into his pocket.

The world we kept at bay is cresting, about to crash over us. Suddenly our almost-kiss seems like a quaint little distraction.

"Hungry?" he asks when he pulls out of the station, as if we didn't just overhear our separate lives imploding.

I'm not. But I nod anyway because it's been hours since I cooked us breakfast, and I know what happens when he skips meals.

Beau pulls into a Wendy's drive-through. I haven't eaten at Wendy's since Dad would take me for a frosty and fries as a kid. But the alternative is enduring Beau's empty stomach.

"I got this one," I say, and reach across Beau to slip the cashier my debit card after we order. He pulls back in his seat as if I have cooties.

"Thanks," Beau says, even though springing for drive-through burgers is the least I can do. He's been footing too many bills.

But his appreciation is premature, because the guy at the microphone says, "I'm sorry, ma'am. Do you have another card? This one was declined." Double whammy: "ma'am" and financial shame. I hand over a wad of cash, but not before Beau gives him his card.

"I'm sorry. That makes no sense," I say as Beau gathers our food.

"Don't worry about it."

But I am worried about it. The only people not worried about money are the people who have money not to worry about. I should have at least $2,000 in the account. I log in to my online banking and wait as the spinning wheel of Wi-Fi inadequacy increases my suspense. I gasp when it loads to show I have a negative balance. I knew this month would be tight, but not this tight—I had to pay my rent, Dad's mortgage, and cover the renovations on the house. I scroll through the transactions before I see the culprit.

Shit buckets.

The Truth Is in the Detours

A $1,500 check was withdrawn. I click on the image and whimper. It's a check to my mechanic I wrote ages ago. In all the chaos and trauma over the last month, I forgot about it.

I note a series of overdraft charges. One after another after another—*twenty* charges. "What the fuck?" I mutter. Even with the zombie check to the mechanic, I should only have one charge, not twenty. But the bank cleared the check before processing my monthly bill pay transactions, which were scheduled to go out days ago. *The bastards.*

Beau looks alarmed as he pulls out of the drive-through and into the intersection, but he's wise and doesn't ask.

I click "Contact Us" and hit the phone number for customer service. Beau merges onto the freeway as I listen to the automated message telling me the wait time is over two hours.

Three hours later, I've advanced from the fifty-third caller to the second when Opus No. 1 cuts off mid-melody. I pull the phone away from my ear to see the call has dropped. "Shit, shit, shit."

"What's going on?" Beau pauses his tedious history podcast, which is the only positive to emerge from my turmoil. So far, I've learned about the history of the American bison, the creation of superstitions, and the biography of Walt Whitman. There is no end to Beau's appetite for useless information.

"I forgot about a check I wrote months ago, and it just cleared." I could lie, but what's the point? If I don't get this issue resolved, I'm not going to be able to hide that I'm broke.

"You don't balance your checkbook?"

I laugh. "Only people who lived through the Great Depression balance their checkbook. That's what online banking is for."

"Online banking can't tell you someone is holding on to a check for months."

I ignore this. "But my bank reordered my transactions to take advantage of the situation and charged me six hundred dollars."

Beau sucks in a breath. "Six hundred dollars?"

"It is expensive to be poor, Professor. I don't recommend it. Why can't we report banks for stealing?" I mentally calculate how much money I have in my savings account and the payments I'm expecting from clients. I can limp along—barely.

"What, like call the police?" Beau scoffs. "You cannot be that person."

"I'm not suggesting we call in the SWAT team. But why do we pardon white-collar criminals and condemn the petty thief? I mean, if you got mugged, you could report it. Just because the perpetrators are bank bureaucrats," I say, and Beau chuckles, "doesn't mean they aren't criminals."

He casts a skeptical glance my way, his mouth pursed in that irritating mask of superiority. "Do you think you can keep your corporate vigilantism under control for this next interview? What if she's a bank bureaucrat who swindled people through excessive fees? Or a teller who pocketed a penny from each customer and amassed a fortune?"

I swallow my panic as he pulls into the parking lot of a dilapidated, windowless building. We've had no luck finding my mom. My career is in jeopardy. The house sale may fall through. My bank account is empty. And calling the authorities, apparently, is out of the question. But I don't have the luxury of giving in to my simmering meltdown, because our next interviewee awaits.

"Don't worry about me, Beauregard. I am always objective and professional."

CHAPTER 23

As we approach the building, I notice a neon sign in the shape of a busty woman in a fringe skirt with eyelashes as long as paintbrushes. "Pandora's Box," I laugh. "I wonder what kind of establishment this is."

"I thought you said you'd be objective and professional," Beau chides.

"Don't worry about me, Professor. Just keep your hands off the professionals."

Beau scowls as I tug on the heavy wooden door, but when we step inside, he places his broad, warm palm on the small of my back, a subtle claim that makes heated fantasies erupt on my skin. We're stepping into a seedy strip club, so I know it's a protective gesture. But my body is reading too much into it. My skin begs him to slip that hand lower and claim me in all the best ways.

The lobby is dim, lit only by a ribbon of pink neon lights. A bald man in the corner doesn't stop us as we slip through the corridor and into the lounge, where guests are clustered at scattered tables and in high-walled booths.

Beau keeps his eyes peeled on the crowd, carefully avoiding the sight of the topless woman onstage while I stare. She pivots around a chrome pole, diving into an inverted split, her black sequin thong staying in place by sorcery. I don't know if I'm more impressed with her confidence, upper-body strength, or whatever witchcraft she's conjured to avoid a wedgie.

"There." Beau points to a petite woman tucked into a pleather booth in the far corner. He wraps his hand around my waist, curling me into his side as we pass a crowd of men near the stage. It is way too soon to be this close to him, because my body reignites like a pilot light, turning every nerve into a flame. He releases me when we reach the booth, where the woman looks up with an unreadable expression. She has a drawn face with puckered wrinkles around her lips, arched eyebrows lined with pencil, and an elongated birthmark on her neck.

"Abilene?" Beau asks, and she nods, gesturing for us to have a seat. A heavy bass line explodes, and catcalls erupt when a second woman takes the stage. She has a tall, athletic build and a silky mane of black hair that looks stark against her pale skin.

Beau gestures to me to slide in first, and I drag my attention away from the spectacle, while he makes a point of looking anywhere but at the performers. "I won't judge you for peeking," I whisper into his ear as he scoots in beside me.

Beau clears his throat, ignoring me, and turns to Abilene. "Thanks for meeting with us." His professorial tone is even mightier in his quest to pretend we're not surrounded by naked women.

Beau nudges me with his elbow as I stare openly at the lady straddling a stool onstage. She's wearing nothing but a bowler hat and tassels, which are swinging in tandem. For Cherry's bachelorette party, we went to an overly produced Magic Mike–type show in Vegas, but I've never been to a club like this—a small town's dirty secret where regular women perform superhero feats, and sad men gape without shame.

"Sorry, I know this meeting place is unusual." Abilene's voice strains against the music and the smoker rattle in her throat. "I work here—cleaning, sewing, fixing costumes, and helping the girls with whatever they need." She shrugs. "We're a little family here, and these girls are like my kids."

"No need to apologize," I say. "They're talented." Beau clears his throat. But I mean it. I'm impressed.

The Truth Is in the Detours

"I figured this would be a good place to meet since no one will listen in. They're too distracted," she says.

"Fair point," I say.

Beau gives the speech I know by heart as I pull a notepad and pen from my backpack. Writing by hand adds a step, but my laptop might draw the attention of the scary buff men positioned at each exit. I don't want to get dragged out of here if they assume I'm breaking the "no video or photography" rule that's plastered on every wall.

"Well," Abilene sighs when Beau completes his intro, "I guess there's no use for small talk."

"We can talk or answer any questions you have. Whatever makes you more comfortable," he says. "Do you want a drink?"

But Abilene shakes her head. "It's all right. No need to stall—my secret is old enough. In fact, she must be about thirty now, a woman herself." Abilene wrings her hands before making fists and shoving them under the table. "I had a baby when I was fifteen. Didn't tell no one I was pregnant. I thought if I pretended it wasn't happening, it wouldn't." Her voice raises at the end of each sentence, as if she's asking us. "I gave birth to her in the middle of the night, and my mom found out the moment the baby cried. All hell broke loose. Mom was pretty religious, you know? All fire and brimstone. And she took over. Told everyone she'd had a baby, that the baby was my sister."

"How did that feel?" Beau asks. "Your mom making that decision for you?"

"Confusing, I guess. My tits were leaking, and I was bleeding out my hoo-ha, and my mom was parading my daughter around like her middle-aged miracle—without any husband or boyfriend to show for it. I'm sure most people in the town knew. But no one would dare call my mom a liar."

"And your daughter doesn't know the truth?" Beau guesses.

Abilene drops her focus to the black lacquered table. "Things got pretty rough, you know? I was rebellious and angry, and a few months later, I came home, and my room was empty. Mom packed my things into two suitcases and told me to leave. Told me I was dead to her. That's when I moved out West. I hopped on a bus and haven't been back home since." Abilene bites her lip and tucks her hands under her thighs. "When I called that summer, she said she'd told everyone I was dead anyway." She swallows a humorless laugh.

Beau grabs my hand under the table, and I feel this protective gesture as a shot straight to my feeble heart. Someone else was fooled by the same lie; another family toyed with their child's heart as if they weren't worth the truth.

I realize I've stopped taking notes when Abilene glances at my hand, which is frozen over the paper. I scribble something—I'm not sure it's English.

Beau clears his throat but sends another pulse to my hand and leans his shoulder against mine as a brace. *I've got you,* he seems to say with his body.

"And you haven't seen her—your daughter—since?" Beau asks.

"Karma, I guess, is a real bitch, because sometime later, I heard my mom died—a heart attack in her sleep. And I thought about coming home, claiming my daughter. Saving her from wherever they'd sent her? But I was like seventeen—and supposedly dead. And yeah, not making a lot of good decisions. So I don't know where she is, or who raised her. And I know she ain't out there looking for me, because she doesn't know I'm her mama—or even alive."

CHAPTER 24

"We have to stop," Beau says, waking me from a restless sleep. "I can't keep my eyes open."

I squint at the clock. It's after eleven.

After our interview, I tucked a sweatshirt against the passenger window and pretended to sleep before Beau could interrogate my feelings. It took me an hour to succumb, but when I did, I dreamed of chasing my mother through a fun house; she'd disappear around corners and reappear as countless clones in the mirrors. "Where are we?"

"Middle of nowhere."

"I can drive," I say, but my yawn calls me a liar.

"Let's get some rest. Tomorrow, we'll wake early to get to the interview in Bend." Beau's voice is raspy, as if he hasn't used it in days. I imagine it's what he sounds like first thing in the morning, wrapped in sheets, showered with dawn sunlight, when he's too sleepy and sated for impatience.

We pull up to a motel with peeling turquoise paint, vibrant coral doors, and a flashing crimson vacancy sign. Plastic flamingos stand guard within a patch of bird-of-paradise beside the front office. "Wait here," he says. "We don't want you calling the FBI if they don't have a room with a view."

I turn to protest but catch a hint of teasing in the set of his mouth, the mirth in his eyes. I'm grateful he's bantering with me—it's more comfortable than an emotional inquisition. I'm too busy asking myself the questions he'd likely ask—and failing to answer them. I don't know how I feel after hearing a story so like my own. My mom wasn't a teenager like Abilene. She was an adult and responsible for her own actions. But Abilene's story does open the possibility that the reason she left is even more complicated than I have imagined. Listening to all these confessions creates more confusion than clarity.

I let Beau set off alone and wait a minute, then five, then ten, before I wander in to find him. I run into the brick wall of his chest when I open the door to the lobby. He emits a gruff sound, and I apologize, but not before getting a good feel of muscle under my palms—tense ridges and hard angles. I rebound off as he steps around me and to the car.

"There's only one room," Beau sighs as he collects our bags. I reach for mine and manage to secure it over my shoulder after a slight tug-of-war before I follow him down the corridor.

He holds up his sleeping bag. "But I'll take the floor," he says. It's a reminder that whatever almost happened between us at the cabin was a moment of weakness and not likely to happen again. I'm hit with a rush of relief—and frustration.

"You'd rather risk motel carpet microbes than share a bed with me? Haven't you seen those *Dateline* episodes where they take a black light to the drapes at places like this that rent by the hour?"

Beau doesn't respond, and I hazard a glance, but he's struggling to open the door. The strike plate blinks red and beeps four times before it flashes green. He swings the door open, but it grinds to a halt as he steps through, and he bumps his head with a crack.

"Damn," Beau hisses.

"Watch out for the door."

Beau glowers at me as I reach blindly for the switch. The hiss of the fluorescent fixture activates before the room is illuminated to show the door blocked by the bed—a full, a single, or maybe a toddler bed—which eats up the entire ten square feet of the room.

"What the actual fuck?" Beau moans.

I swallow my panic and go for easy. "It'll be like old times when we slept in that fort in my closet."

"Jesus, Ophelia, we can't . . . it's not . . ." he stammers.

With all my confusing emotions and stressors warring for control, I don't think I'd survive a close call with Beau tonight, so I'm glad he's decided to be the sex police. Sort of. But I wish he didn't sound so horrified to sleep beside me. I slip inside, crawl across the bed, and reach the sliver of carpet at the base of the bathroom door. When I turn, he's still standing rigid at the threshold.

He blinks over at me, and I take in his expression—dread, distrust, and something else I can't quite name.

I sigh and open the bathroom door. "We're adults. We're exhausted. It'll be fine." I'm not sure even *I* believe me, but what choice do we have?

When I exit the bathroom—showered and ready for bed—Beau is on the edge of the bed. "Bathroom's all yours," I say.

I shimmy by him to drop my bag in the closet. When I do, he sighs out a shaky breath and slumps forward with his head in his hands. "Fuck, Ophelia. What are you wearing?"

I glance at my polka-dot sleep shorts and tank top. "My pajamas. I wasn't aware there was a dress code." He didn't like the other ones either, and I only brought two sets. He's stuck with them.

"And what is that scent?" He exhales an exasperated breath.

I cross my arms over my chest. "Lotion. My skin is dry."

"It smells like cupcakes," he grumbles.

"It smells better than the mildew in here." I bend over my bag to find my sleep mask.

He sighs again.

"What?" I snap. But when I turn to unload on him, he's staring at me with an expression too pitiful to abuse. It's the same way he looked at me when I was in the bikini.

He shakes his head, stands, and disappears into the bathroom.

When he emerges ten minutes later, he's showered—his hair damp and mussed, and his glasses fogged. He's dressed in baggy sweatpants and a long-sleeve T-shirt.

"Umm, it's about 80 degrees in here," I say. The wall-mounted air conditioner is gasping and gurgling as if it has a terminal lung condition.

He ignores me and walks to the opposite side of the bed. I attempt to scoot to the far edge, but there's nowhere to go. This will be intimate. He tosses the covers aside and snarls, "I don't think I'd fit on this bed even by myself."

I flip over, curling into a long C. "Sure you can. We'll just have to be creative. I'll keep my hands to myself this time, I promise."

"Goddamn it, Ophelia, I'm not spooning you. Especially with you in that outfit."

I sit up in a lurch. "There is nothing wrong with my outfit."

"If you were performing tonight, it'd be just the right amount of fabric," he snaps.

Beau's irritation with me is the best reminder to avoid touching. We may be drawn to each other, but Beau is attracted to me against his will—and we're made of combustible material. I mumble about slut shaming and tug on his hand until he drops beside me on the bed with an "Oomph."

I hit the light switch and pull my sleep mask over my face. "It's okay, Beauregard, you have enough fabric for the both of us. It's like you're wearing a full-body condom."

He exhales a shaky breath. "Please. Stop. Talking."

Beau shifts. I turn. I get an elbow to my lower back, a knee in my calf. He mumbles an apology before settling behind me so that we're back-to-back. There might be an inch or two between us, but the void is a chanting, wailing siren.

He lets out a breath. "You smell like vanilla cupcakes."

"What's wrong with cupcakes?" I snap.

"Nothing, Ophelia. That's the point."

The Truth Is in the Detours

I sigh and murmur, "Go to sleep, Beauregard. It's been a day." Between almost kissing him and losing Juniper, the house buyer, and all my money, I'm spent. I don't even know how to process that I sat in a dingy strip club to hear about a family secret reminiscent of my own.

I feel like an open wound and can't deal with Beau's internal conflict. I know his self-control is saving us from disaster, but I wish it didn't make me feel so unwanted. Discarded. As if that wasn't already my prevailing emotion these days.

My exhaustion is deep in my bones, but my restlessness is in charge. My foot falls asleep, so I shake it alive before my hip begins to tingle. When I shift to my back, I knock Beau's shoulder before rolling away and tucking my legs into my chest.

"Ophelia," Beau groans. He probably wants to forcibly still me, but then he'd need to touch me. Finally, he whispers, "Do you want to talk about it?"

"Talk about what?" I sigh.

He doesn't answer at first, and I think he might back off, but finally he says, "How you're feeling after that interview with Abilene." His voice is sandpaper against my raw heart.

"I'm fine," I say.

He turns toward me and props himself on his elbow. "Really, Ophelia? Fine?" His tone is calling me a liar.

I lift my eye mask but can only see his outline as my eyes adjust. I squint until he comes into focus. "I don't know what to say. It hit close to home and made me feel shitty. Is that what you want to hear?" My tone is calling him an asshole.

"I don't want anything, Phe, except for you to know you can talk to me." His words are cajoling and kind, and it's clear I'm the asshole.

I sink into the pillow, pinching my eyes closed and letting my caged fears free. "I feel confused, I suppose. Who was the villain? Dad for lying to me? Mom for failing to fight for me? Me for being a fool?"

"You're not a fool. And maybe there is no villain."

When I open my eyes, he feels closer, a wall of heat and heart enticing me to forget he's not a wall I should scale.

"And what if I never find her and don't know what really happened? How can I reconcile my love for Dad without the truth? How do I start or finish grieving?"

He's so close that I feel the brush of his breath against my temple.

"What if something had happened to Dad when I was still a kid—like with that poor baby? Would my mom have abandoned me to the system?" I steady my breathing. "I was so vulnerable and didn't know it. And now I really am an orphan, and it makes me feel"—I brace myself for this hardest truth—"really alone."

I pinch my eyes closed again, scared of the admission. Deflection is the shield over my emotional soft spots. But I've dropped my armor, which is terrifying and freeing.

When Beau pulls me into him, wrapping his strong arms around my spine and enveloping me against the solidity of his chest, I have no defenses left. When he kisses my forehead and whispers, "You aren't alone, Phe," I'm lost. I'm done. I can no longer resist my need to be near him.

I snake one hand around his neck and tuck my face in his collarbone. He pulls in a breath but clutches me tighter, his exhalations accelerating, and his heartbeat hammering against mine. We hold there, time suspended as my focus shifts from emotional confusion to physical longing. I'm no longer thinking about anything but the nerves he's set on fire—all of them. It almost hurts—this feeling—to be close but not close enough. To have him wrapped around me but not inside me.

We're teetering on the edge of a very bad decision. But oh, he's warm. Warm as sunlight or a crackling fire, hot sand, or a bubble bath. More comforting than all the defenses I've built to keep vulnerability at bay. More tempting than I may be able to withstand.

I shift to my back, and he clears his throat and releases my waist. But before he can retreat, I thread my hand in his hair and pull him onto me.

CHAPTER 25

Beau releases a soft curse but otherwise comes to me with an obedience that shocks me even more than my impulse to demand it. He drops to his elbows, caging me in, and I pull at his waist until his body is pressed along mine. He's already hard, and the feel of him sends a pulse of want deep into my bones. I hitch my leg around his hip, driving him closer. His eyes track mine for an answer to this riddle: *What the hell are we doing?* But when I tilt my chin, brush my nose along his, he groans, and it seeps straight into some primal place that takes charge. And the only answer I can give is: *I have no idea, but let's keep doing it.*

I find his bottom lip and tease it with my teeth, and he sinks his mouth into mine. Small, testing kisses, bites, brushes of lips until we lose ourselves and kiss like we've found a well in the desert. This is the best kiss of my life. This is the stupidest thing I've ever done.

Beau's mouth is overwhelming, stealing my air like it belongs to him. But that's fine. I don't need to breathe. I just need to keep kissing him. I need his tongue and his lips and his entire body sealed to mine. I need to skip the foreplay and second-guessing.

His hands slide to my waist, my hips, under my lower back to lift me closer. I dig into his hair and hold him close as he drags his mouth to my jaw, my neck, and along my collarbone. His breath teases me, and I arch into him, aching to get closer as he toys with the hem of my tank with a soft swipe of his fingertip. He's whispering something about my scrap of a shirt. How I'm killing him. I shimmy out of it, and the light from the streetlamps outside casts a stripe across my bare skin.

He pulls back to take me in and makes a guttural sound from deep in his throat—and then he's everywhere. Rough hands on my ribs, gentle teeth on my nipple, his hips moving with mine in a building rhythm. I tug at his clothes, but he's traveling out of reach, down my body, two fingers hitched into the waistband of my shorts before he drags them down with my underwear and tosses them aside. He crouches forward, trailing kisses up my bare torso, circling my nipple with his tongue, closing his mouth over me until I gasp. When he slips a hand between my thighs, where I'm wet and ready for him, we both whimper at the contact. He watches as I lose control at the feel of him stroking me, strumming me as if he knows me too well. I try to kiss him, but he stays out of range, his face awash in wonder at my pleasure.

Somewhere in the recesses of my mind, I know this is a horrible idea, but my body is in control, and it disagrees. And that tortured look on Beau's face is gone, replaced by resolve—and something that might be relief.

It feels like my skin has thinned and I'm only nerves, keyed up by every touch. The cotton of his clothes scratches me. I'm naked and he's still fully clothed, and I'm impatient to have all of him.

I drag the hem of his shirt along his sides and pull it over his head before he stands and sheds his pants in one motion. He's backlit as he slides onto the bed, so I study him through touch, taste, scent, letting my hands trail across his shoulders, his chest, down his abs. But Beau grabs my wrists, regaining control and coaxing me to lay back on the bed.

He drops a kiss to my navel before lifting his head, his chin grazing my skin, and mutters a soft, "This okay?"

I know I should think about all the reasons it isn't. I should save us from this fever dream. But this is the first thing in forever that feels better than okay. It feels *Yes*, and *More*, and *Please*. So instead, I say, "It

The Truth Is in the Detours

beats talking about feelings," attempting—and failing—to lighten the mood because my voice comes out strangled.

Beau chuckles as he trails his mouth from my navel to my pubic bone, before pressing it between my legs. I gasp at the warmth and contact, sucking in a breath as he spreads one hand over my stomach and hooks the other around my hip. He's still watching me as he pulls me into him and teases me with soft kisses and swipes of his tongue. My mind flashes to a memory of him as a kid hovering over a broken radio, focused, intent, puzzling out how to fix it with patience and dexterity. But then he slides a finger, then two, into me and moans into my skin, and all thought is gone. There's no version of him but this one, the one who has wound me tight enough to explode and is unraveling me with every perfect press of his mouth. I grip the headboard and cry out as he finds the fuse that powers every cell in my body. Beau whispers something I can't hear as my body blurs into static energy and sparks, then explodes.

Beau slows, gentles, but doesn't stop as I shiver and collapse into a puddle. I'm already impatient to feel him on top of me again, so I tug on his elbow to pull him up. When I find him with testing strokes of my palm, he drops his head into the crook of my neck, his breathing labored and heavy. "You smell so good."

"Like cupcakes?" I ask, my hand finding a rhythm as I learn what he likes. And this is safer. Teasing. Banter. Being in control.

"And vanilla and strawberries, and fuck," he mumbles, finding my mouth to swallow the words perched on my tongue. "You're going to be the death of me," he says. And something about that makes me hesitate. I don't want to be his guilty pleasure, the temptation he succumbs to against his better judgment. But as soon as the thought flairs, it's gone, replaced by the sensation of his calloused hands, warm mouth, and delicious weight, by the feel of him in my hand growing impatient and needy.

"Wait." He releases a pained breath and crawls off the bed.

But before I can fear—or hope—that he's come to his senses, he exhales a relieved sigh, emerging from his duffel bag with a strip of foil squares.

And thank God he has them. But, "Why'd you bring those?"

"Same reason I brought snow chains on a summer road trip." He lays beside me, spreading his palm on my stomach, along my rib cage, over my sternum. "I like to be prepared."

But that's not an answer. "Did you think we'd sleep together?"

He laughs, loud, throaty, and then grows serious. "No."

"So who were you planning to hook up with?"

He shakes his head and growls. "We can spar in the morning, Phe. But right now, can I be with you, finally?"

An ache gathers low in my belly as he traces lazy fingertips over my thighs.

"Finally?" I ask.

He hums, dragging his mouth along the column of my throat and inhaling. He didn't shave earlier, and I'm grateful to feel every texture—scruff, callus, satin. "Finally."

He tears the packet open and rolls on the condom as I watch. I've never seen Beau this way—undone, unguarded, uncoiled—and it makes me want to keep him just like this, to protect this sliver of honesty. I think about our first kiss. Days later, we started high school and immediately spun out into different orbits. Will this be another collision that sends us hurtling apart?

But I don't want to think about that right now. I capture his mouth in mine, and he lifts me until I'm settled over his lap, my hands exploring the hard planes of his chest—collarbones, sternum, pecs. He clasps my hips in his grip, and I lower myself over him, holding my breath and pinching my eyes closed as he fills me. Beau releases a string of expletives, and I swim in them—until I begin to drown in *him*, in our movement, a perfect rhythm that sends me climbing again too soon. He tilts my face to his with hands on either side of my face, fingers threaded in my hair. When I open my eyes, he's watching me, and his expression

The Truth Is in the Detours

resembles awe; it's so tender that I can't handle it. I find his mouth open for me and give myself over to sensation—the air on my skin, his coarse palms on my skin, all of him inside and under me.

"You're perfect," he says through kisses. "How can I make you feel good?"

But I can't answer because I already feel more than I can process—hunger and satiety, ecstasy and ache. *Finally,* he had said. *Finally.*

He flips us with an arm around my waist—hovering over me, blocking out light and distraction, and thrusting back into me so deliberately and deep that my breath hitches, and my body pulls taut enough to shatter. "Hey," he whispers in my ear, "talk to me."

"I'm good," I say, but it's inadequate. Language and thoughts are second to the reality of Beau—who has known me longest, been cut by my raw edges, grasped at my undone threads, and held on anyway.

"I wish I'd known." Beau bites my bottom lip and soothes it with his tongue as he hooks my knee in his elbow and opens me wider for him. "That this is what it would take to shut you up."

I laugh, but it comes out ragged, and I think he senses that I'm losing it because he brushes my hair away from my face and tries to catch my gaze. I'm powerless and give in, letting him care for me and take me apart with each glance, movement, and word whispered in my ear.

"Beau," I gasp. "Please—" I don't know what I'm asking for, but he answers anyway, finding me, circling me with the pad of his thumb as he drives deep until I go off, arching under him, legs shaking, clawing at his shoulders, and dissolving. His mouth is open on mine, inhaling my gasps, giving me air, pulling every ounce of pleasure from my body until he gives in and unravels after me.

And as I fall apart, I wonder how I'll ever put myself back together.

CHAPTER 26

Beau falls to my side, one heavy leg draped between mine, his palm on my breast, head burrowed in my neck. His breathing is labored, and I watch the rise and fall of his chest. I curl into his touch, hoping to avoid the embarrassment and vulnerability of the aftermath by staying tethered to the moment. I kiss his scratchy cheek, and he turns and steals a deeper one—it's lazy, contented, familiar, like we do this all the time.

"Hi." He smiles into another kiss, and his grin is everything. "I guess it's about time we consummated that backyard marriage." He drags a fingertip down my torso, and I liquefy underneath the touch.

"How'd you get so good at that?" I mumble, still feeling the aftershocks of him. He played my body like he owns the instruction manual. I didn't even know how to ask for what he knew to give me.

His laugh is a soft burst of air against my throat. "You really want to go there right now?"

But my curiosity is a beast, and my response is an unconvincing, "Umm, no?" I imagine Beau learned his talents with the woman he meant to spend his life with—while I had unsatisfying sex with selfish partners who left me feeling deserving of nothing more. Being with Beau felt . . . *special*, as uncomfortable as it is to admit it. Did it for him? Do I want us to be on the same page? Two weeks ago, I was more likely to muzzle him than nuzzle his neck.

He laughs again and kisses me with his palm on my jaw. "I'll answer whatever questions you have. And then you have to answer mine," he

The Truth Is in the Detours

says. "And if you say you're 'fine,' I'm going to make you stay up all night talking about your feelings."

It's a joke. Sort of. But it feels like a threat.

I laugh uncomfortably.

"I can't believe we just had sex," he says, chuckling. "It's like all my teenage dreams come true." He rolls away, steps into the bathroom, and closes the door behind him.

And that vulnerability I feared? Well, it washes over me like a tidal wave. A stew of unfamiliar emotions brings my body to a boil. I don't know how to behave now that we've slept together while I was still figuring out how to be his friend. I wish I could escape to avoid the dissection of what we just did, the awkwardness of postcoital confrontation, and the threat of spilling even scarier emotions all over this tiny motel room. *Finally,* Beau had said. What did he mean? And, more important, what do I want it to mean?

Did he have sex with *me,* thirty-four-year-old Ophelia, who's lost and alone and never measured up to her potential? Or did he have sex with his teenage fantasy—the popular, too-cool girl who no longer exists? Did he cave to his basest desires? Was he revisiting ancient infatuation while I opened myself up and showed him my heart? Will he regret this if I can't keep my cool?

I'm afraid that what I feel for Beau is beyond attraction. And it occurs to me, too late, that perhaps I have always liked Beau more than I could handle. Maybe it's why he's always gotten to me, why his opinions and disapproval injured me, why I've loved to get a reaction out of him—searching for a scowl or a laugh. Maybe I've always been chasing that feeling of our first kiss—the surprise of it, the comfort of it, the fullness of it.

Kissing Beau feels like coming home.

And he's the last bit of home I have left.

But I don't know how to confess that I have never felt anything like this. I worry that I've been doing sex wrong this whole time. I've been doing everything wrong. I want to touch Beau every day for the rest of my life, and I wish I never knew what his touch would do to me.

This bed may be a cramped tomb for our budding friendship.

And I feel very, very naked suddenly. I inhale, but my chest constricts; I can't get a lungful. Then I start to shiver uncontrollably.

I flip on the light and cover my eyes with one hand, my head throbbing from the glow of the flickering fluorescent fixture. My focus adjusts to the glare as I try and fail to find my PJs. I scamper to the closet to throw on a pair of shorts and a torn Beyoncé concert T-shirt that drapes like a hospital gown. It hides the red marks on my hips from his fingers, the rash on my thighs from his stubble, the skin still fevered from his touch. I throw my hair in a messy bun and slide a hoodie over the shirt. When the faucet stops, I freeze, waiting for him to emerge. I pace along the narrow strip of carpet, bang my shin on the foot of the bed, and swallow a scream.

Beau steps out of the bathroom and halts when he sees me hunched over and spiraling—eyeing me with unguarded wariness. "Hey."

"Hey," I say before dropping to the side of the bed, my leg bouncing so visibly that Beau looks at it with furrowed brows.

"Are you okay?"

"Yeah. Good." I release an unhinged laugh. "Which side of the bed do you want?"

He stares at me, hangs his head, and then grabs his boxers. He slides his legs through quickly, as if my self-consciousness is contagious, and sinks onto the mattress without touching me, which is a feat in this doll bed.

"You gonna join me?" he asks. And there's that irritation I know so well.

I lay back along the far edge with my back facing him, and Beau exhales an exasperated breath.

"Ophelia," he says, "what's wrong?"

And then I'm saved by the fire alarm.

The Truth Is in the Detours

∼

I'm outside on the cracked parking lot with a dozen exhausted travelers displaced from this shitty motel as Beau tries to figure out what the hell is happening. I eat up the pavement with anxious steps. The fire trucks have come and gone. Meanwhile, the alarm shrieks into the void, crying wolf despite the absence of flames.

In my corner of the lot, a weary woman bounces a crying baby while a scantily clad couple argues in hushed tones. Most guests have retreated to their cars, but I have too much static energy to sit. Beau stalks out of the shade of the overhang and into the harsh streetlamps. He's all shadow and sharp lines—brooding and disheveled and so fucking hot. Once he filled out after high school, I could acknowledge that he was handsome in a classic, predictable way—symmetry, bone structure, lean body, chiseled chin. I've never been into predictable.

But I'm afraid he's not as predictable as I thought.

Before I can brace myself, he's beside me, and the reality of what we just did is blaring between us like porn on a colleague's computer in the adjacent cubicle. The punctuation mark on that reminder is his shirt, inside out and backward, the tag marking an embarrassing postsex blunder under his chin.

"It's an electrical issue. An electrician is on the way, but . . ." Beau shrugs.

He slides into the car and flips the lock on the passenger side, pushing the door open toward me. I hang there, my hand braced on the door, and peer in. "So, we just wait?"

"Well, you could call the police, but I'm pretty sure they won't have an electrician available."

I fall into the seat and crank it back until I'm fully reclined, my legs stretched along the dash. The alarm is shrill, even dulled by the sealed car doors. "They won't allow us back inside even though it's a false alarm?"

"It's too loud. I prefer my eardrums intact." Beau drapes his forearms over his face after dropping into a matching incline. His knees are bent at a harsh angle and bump against the steering wheel. His muscles are rigid, his posture tightly wound. There's nothing left of the contented, liquid ease of an hour ago.

"What's up with you?" I ask, turning my head toward him. We're inches apart, but he feels worlds away.

He drops his arms and cracks his eyes open. He chuckles, but it's bitter. "What's up with me?"

"Yeah," I mumble, but lose confidence by the end of the syllable.

"There's nothing up with me, Ophelia." And he closes his eyes again, rolling his head until his chin is tipped toward the sunroof. He's silent, his eyes are closed, but he's too rigid for sleep. I finally give up and stare into the distance. The night sky breaks out into a splintered canvas of scattered stars I once wished upon—when I had the audacity to wish.

The panicky siren mimics the trip wire of my nerves, and my brain distorts the repetitive rhythm into an accusatory chant: *Ophelia, you fucked up.*

CHAPTER 27

"We have to leave in ten minutes." Beau's voice pulls me out of my sleep—and the dream he was starring in. But he's not beside me, whispering into my hair. I squint into the sun, where his silhouette cuts his shape against the car window.

"What?" I mumble, and scoot away from the gear shift wedged in my hip. I wince and sit up, which sends a jolt of pain through my stiff spine. He passes me the motel key through the open window. "You have ten minutes to get ready."

I stumble into the now-quiet room, rinse off, and dress before returning to the car, where Beau idles at the curb.

Once I climb in, he doesn't look at me before accelerating out of the lot and onto the highway. There's a deep, pained wrinkle on his forehead. He tilts his head to the side and winces before pushing on his shoulder with the heel of his hand. A kinked neck. I shift onto my knees and fight the seat belt before drawing my hands over his shoulder. He pulls away, freezing at my touch. The porcupine has his quills out again.

"Relax. I know trigger points, remember?"

He casts me a wary glance but settles, dropping his right hand from the steering wheel and returning his focus to the road. I take it as permission and sink my thumbs into the relentless stretch of muscle across his scapula. I find a stubborn knot, and he rewards me with a sound that reminds me of last night. Pleasure mixed with pain—primal.

I curl my palm around his wrist and draw his arm out into a stretch. His forearm brushes my breast, and he tenses again before yanking free.

"Don't play games with me." His words land like a slap, but I suppose I can understand how he'd read my gesture as a mixed message and not the peace offering it was intended to be.

"I'm not."

His shoulders are up to his ears, his jaw tense. "I don't appreciate being treated like an expired Tinder date one minute and then groped the next."

"Groped?" I stammer. "Expired what now?"

He rubs his forehead. "Maybe you expect me to be cavalier about sex, but . . ." He stops short, tapping his finger on the steering wheel impatiently.

"I don't expect you to be . . ." But I don't know how to complete the sentence because I think he's jumping to the wrong conclusions, and I don't have the courage to correct him. I'm feeling so many emotions about last night—but none of them come close to cavalier.

And he's the one who made me feel like I was his belated teenage conquest.

He laughs, a wry, dismissive sound that signals the end of the conversation. Does he regret last night? Did he feel anything but nostalgia?

Beau is impossible to read—scolding me one moment and smoldering at me the next. Perhaps he wants me, but really doesn't *want* to want me. And why would he? I'm a hot mess, and he's a hot success.

I should ask him how he's feeling—what he wants—but then I'll have to face his answers when I am not ready for my own. My raw heart can't handle it if he admits he regrets me. But I'm not sure my insecurities will allow me to believe him if he says he doesn't. And what if "finally" means what I hope it means? Am I capable of living up to his long-held hopes?

When Beau approaches a Starbucks drive-through for my coffee and carb fix, I try to pay, but he bats my hand away. It's a reminder

The Truth Is in the Detours

that I have an empty bank account, a credit card perilously close to its limit, a money pit to off-load, and an income that was just cut in half.
And I just had sex with Beau and ruined our friendship.
And the escape hatch is closed because I can't afford to fly home.
And I can't find Mom.
And Dad is dead.
I pick up my phone, scroll to my messages, and hit play.
"Ophelia, love, it's your dear old dad, checking in . . ."
And again, *"Ophelia, love, it's your dear old dad, checking in . . ."*
And again, *"Ophelia, love, it's your dear old dad, checking in . . ."*
The pressure is building in my head, and tears seem to be the only release valve for the brewing panic. I slip on my sunglasses and turn toward the window, resting my forehead against the glass, then hit play and give in to silent tears.

~

I excuse myself to the restroom when we arrive for our next interview at an upscale brewery in the heart of Bend, Oregon. I splash water on my face and press a damp, cool paper towel to my eyes. I hate crying. I'm angry at myself for giving in. I kept my eyes closed in the car and pretended to sleep, so now my eyes are inflamed, and my skin is covered in blotches. I'm a mess. I take ten deep breaths and pat the towel on my cheeks before smoothing my hair into a ponytail. The pink is growing out—and I have dark-blond roots that bleed into bubblegum.

I find Beau on the redwood deck of the brewery, which overlooks the Deschutes River. The water bends beneath us, bordered by ponderosa pines, aspen trees, and willow bushes. Paved trails line the river, and joggers and bikers swerve along the path. Oregon's high desert is sunny but temperate, and the escape from the summer heat feels like freedom.

It's not even noon, but the brewery is filling up fast on this Fourth of July. I'd forgotten about the holiday until we were caught behind a parade of bicyclists in stars and stripes while crawling down the street.

American flags hang from lampposts, and the sidewalks are bustling with families flashing patriotic garb. But I'm dressed in black—not feeling the hot dog spirit today.

Beau is at a square table tucked into a private corner. He's drenched in sunlight, staring over the river, one forearm resting on the railing. I stop ten feet away and sneak a photo. He is so handsome it makes my heart hurt. He tilts his chin as I take the photo and scowls at me.

"What are you doing?"

I shrug, swallowing back my whole heart. *I need something to remember you by.* "I haven't caught any photos of our trip. And it's beautiful here."

He drops his focus to his pad to scribble notes—or avoid me. It's hard to tell. I slide in beside him but maintain a sliver of distance, so I don't trigger him again. He thinks I'm being cavalier, but I'm just trying to feel some semblance of control over how I feel for him. I want his hands on me again, and his hands off my heart.

I want to let him have me again, but not let him own me.

But I breathe in his shampoo and the gentle scent of his detergent. As he taps the table with his fingers, I remember what it felt like when he dragged a fingertip up my spine, when he made me go off with a simple circle of his thumb. I shiver and pull my focus over the deck, but he turns, and we're face-to-face. He looks so conflicted; I've seen that look before, but I didn't understand what it meant.

Maybe it's not just irritation. Maybe he feels as out of control as I do.

"Hi," I whisper.

"Hi." He bites his bottom lip as he scans my face before his eyes land over my shoulder. He stands abruptly, and the bench scoots backward by a few inches.

I turn to see a middle-aged man approaching our table. He has salt-and-pepper hair, a close-cropped beard, and a thin build with slightly hunched shoulders, as if standing upright requires too much effort.

"Beau Augustin?" he asks, his voice low and unsure.

Beau reaches out his hand, pivoting to professor mode. "Alexander?"

The Truth Is in the Detours

Alexander shakes his hand. "Yes. Hi." He looks at me as I stand.

"Hi, Alexander. I'm Ophelia. What an amazing location. Thanks for suggesting it."

"It's new, but I've heard good things," he says, already standing a bit taller. "They specialize in Belgian-style ales. Maybe it's early for beer, but I'm going to need one for this." He waves down a server with a nod of his head. He's handsome under that beard, with downturned hazel eyes, a strong chin, and a paternal, outdoorsy look, as if he might leave here to go kayaking with his grown kids.

"It's a holiday. It's never too early," I say.

As we sink onto the benches, a server approaches in a tight-fitting black baby tee with the brewery logo emblazoned on her chest. "What can I get ya?"

Alexander rattles off a specialty ale and a basket of fries as I peruse the beer list and order an ale called the Trinity and some wings. I don't want beer, but Alexander looks like he might bolt, and I want to put him at ease. Beau asks for Perrier and a hummus plate.

"This is a beautiful town," I begin once our server departs.

"You're both from California, right? Have you ever been here?" Alexander asks.

"I was born in Medford, actually. But raised in San Diego. This is my first time back in Oregon."

"Welcome home." Alexander grins, revealing a playful smile with bright white teeth.

Beau clears his throat. "Thank you for meeting us, Alexander. As we discussed over the phone, we are looking to understand how individuals get trapped in untruths—how those untruths affect their families and communities in unexpected ways." Beau is so stiff, and I note Alexander sobering immediately—trading charm for anxiousness.

"Everyone has a story," I say. "And we want to tell those stories without bias. After all, if everyone told their truths, there would be far less shame for all of us."

The server returns, tossing cardboard coasters with images of the Deschutes River before setting two ales and a Perrier on top. "Your food is coming up soon."

"Thank you," I say, offering what I hope is a warm smile. Beau's look is intense. Alexander has grown stiff, and our server scurries away.

Alexander inhales a lungful of air. "My story . . ." He lets it out in a gust. "I'm a widower. Lost my wife to cancer two years ago."

"I'm so sorry," I say, lifting my focus from my notes.

He looks away before taking a long swig of his beer. "Thanks, but I don't deserve it. It's my fault."

"How so?" Beau asks, and Alexander stiffens again.

"Some folks feel more comfortable by starting at the beginning," I say.

"Okay, yeah," he says. "So I met my wife in college. I wasn't really looking for a relationship, but I didn't want to *not* be with her. She was pretty and fun and thoughtful; she'd make me cookies for long study sessions. She'd clean my apartment, do my laundry, that sort of thing. I know that makes me sound like a chauvinist ass. But this is about honesty, yeah?" Alexander spins his beer on the coaster.

"No judgment," I say as Beau offers a slow "Right."

"The relationship moved along. Our friends paired off and got married one by one. And eventually, we got married. Bought a little house. Had two kids. And I did love her, I really did. But I'd never gotten out of the habit of sleeping with other women."

I school my expression, an expertise developed in this process. We've heard so many despicable things from people hoping that the antiseptic of truth will cleanse their shame.

"So you were unfaithful," Beau says.

Alexander nods. "When we started dating, it started out as one-night stands with girls at parties or old girlfriends or casual flings with friends. After we got married, I kept it impersonal."

I hear Beau mutter something under his breath. I think he says, "Thoughtful of you." I step on his foot, and he swallows a growl.

Alexander looks from Beau to me and back, his lips pursed.

The Truth Is in the Detours

"What happened then?" I ask, because Beau has forgotten his commitment to neutrality.

"I didn't want to embarrass her. So I'd"—he sighs—"sleep with women I met while traveling for work until I finally started using apps, but that got complicated, too. I matched with a single mom at my son's school, so I deleted those accounts and decided I needed more anonymity. From there it escalated."

This is when Beau usually jumps in with follow-up questions, seeking to understand the impact. But his gaze is focused over Alexander's head, his body rigid like a hunting dog pointing toward its prey. I understand that Beau is angry with me, but it's clear his reaction to this interview is about more than me. I can't get distracted by wondering about the wounds of Beau's marriage right now, though, because he's checked out, leaving me to pick up the slack of this interview.

"What do you mean 'escalated'?" I ask, nodding at him to continue.

He drops his voice. "I hired sex workers."

I look to Beau, but he won't engage. I nudge him under the table, but he's catatonic. I proceed cautiously. "And your wife? Did she find out?"

He shakes his head. "My wife died of cervical cancer—caused by an STD." Alexander drops his voice so low I crane to hear him over the conversations at nearby tables. "Her doctor said it could have been dormant for years. But she'd only been with one guy before me. And that was thirty years before she got cancer."

"I can't imagine how painful that must have been for your family," I say, choking out an understatement because I don't know what else to say.

"The worst part was, she never doubted me—didn't even ask me. And until she got sick, I hadn't felt guilty. She made me happy, and I think I made her happy. I just had this secret—this habit I couldn't break. But from the day she got sick to the day she died, and for two years since, I've been suffocating on the guilt. Knowing I killed her."

He drops his head into his palms. Beau is motionless, isn't looking directly at him. And I let my empathy wash away my disgust like a tidal wave. Our volunteers are looking for something they think we can give them. If not absolution, then unburdening.

I whisper these words into the wind: "Even with our biggest mistakes, sometimes the consequences are far crueler than anyone deserves."

"But I deserved it. She didn't."

"You're right," Beau says, his eyes trained on the river beyond. "Your punishment is living with it."

~

Beau doesn't speak when Alexander makes his way out of the brewery, and I don't know what to say to him. He's angry at me, perhaps hurt, too, but he lost all impartiality once Alexander admitted to infidelity. Beau's good at compartmentalizing for work—he's a productivity robot. But he refused to engage with Alexander; I asked all the follow-up questions while trying to capture notes before Beau blew it up. I think I salvaged the meeting with my good-cop routine. But Alexander may call and revoke his consent after Beau took a scouring pad to his open wound.

I think we need to renegotiate our agreement. Beau's getting a lot of value from my free labor.

"I have a call," Beau says. "Can you hang out in town until I'm done?"

The pressure is building behind my eyes again, but I blink it away. I want to sleep. Maybe I can handle all these inconvenient emotions after a nap. Perhaps if I get some rest or a moment to breathe, I can process my feelings and be prepared to discuss *us*—whatever *us* is. "Could you drop me at the motel?"

"We're camping tonight." Beau slides his laptop into his messenger bag. "There are shops across the way—a bookstore, a library, a café. I won't be long."

"We're camping?" I need a quiet motel room where I can escape from him for a while, where I can rest and hope it will realign my world.

"I told you we'd be camping," he snaps.

"I thought you were kidding. Or trying to scare me away."

"I wish I were. I booked the site before I knew I'd have an interloper."

"Hey," I say, fed up with his attitude, "this interloper just saved your ass in that interview. You were unprofessional and unkind."

"That guy didn't deserve my kindness," he says, still concentrating on sorting the contents of his bag.

I know Beau's pissed at me, but his animosity toward Alexander is pointed. While I've wondered before whether Bianca was unfaithful, now I'm certain. It's hard not to notice the difference between Beau's normal interview demeanor and whatever that was. He's listened to shocking stories of deception for weeks without batting an eyelash. "Beau, do you want to talk about why that interview . . ." I don't even know how to ask him, especially now that he's so angry with me. ". . . was so personal to you?"

He lets out an incredulous laugh as he drops several twenties on the table, slinging the messenger bag over his shoulder and adjusting the strap across his chest. I look away. I don't need a reminder of what his pecs look like. "I'm not having this discussion with you."

His phone rings, and I glance at the screen on instinct. *Bianca.*

"I'll meet you there in an hour." He motions across the street to an outdoor courtyard. "Hi," he says into the phone. "Let me find somewhere I can talk."

As I watch him stride away, my tears threaten to break free, damming behind my eyes like white rapids tipping over a fall, but I refuse to give in.

CHAPTER 28

We set up camp as two colleagues who can—surprisingly—work together when our passions have erupted and cooled to ash. I know how to erect a tent, sleep on the forest floor, and eat over a campfire. I just haven't liked it all that much since I was a kid. I appreciate the outdoors more when I can retreat to a real bed with a feather pillow.

But I don't complain now. It's a sign I've surrendered.

The hour spent waiting for Beau was a blur, but I vaguely recall children strolling by with American flags painted on their cheeks and the distant sound of a cover band playing classic rock. I don't remember how we got from downtown Bend to this quiet campsite along the river. But I'm pretty sure we drove in silence. Because I didn't say a thing.

It is beautiful here. The wide river cuts a patient path through the landscape, with trees framing the shore like lashes. Mountains rise in the distance, with the last stubborn snowflakes clinging to their peaks. This unspoiled air is salvation after weeks of wading through humidity, heat, and smoke. But I can't appreciate it. My panic has collapsed into exhaustion.

Beau unpacks the cooler—freshly filled with hot dogs and potato salad he picked up at the local grocery. I think he intended to be festive, but instead, it reminds me of dead family rituals.

We heat up the food over the fire. He passes me a bottle of water. I set out the paper plates. We trade the ketchup back and forth. We eat

The Truth Is in the Detours

our dinner with the backdrop of the crackling campfire and churning river. We're polite.

And our indifference breaks my heart.

When we finish, Beau drops another log in the fire and pokes it until the new fuel catches and the embers spark. I lean against a fallen trunk splayed along the campsite, adjusting to find a flat surface to rest against, and drag circles in the packed dirt with a stick. I swat a mosquito when it lands on my shoulder and bat another away near my ear. My fatigue is bone deep, as if the hours of lost sleep are a weight pushing on my shoulders, begging me to give up.

The night has cooled, and my jean jacket is too thin, and I want to climb into a warm bed and sleep for a month. Meanwhile, the two-person tent awaits, taunting us with five square feet of shared body heat and forced proximity.

Beau stands and brushes off his jeans before crossing into the tent—the sputter of the zipper puncturing the silence. Maybe I can wait until he falls asleep and slink in without waking him. Maybe we can pretend we didn't fail our last slumber party by getting naked and having sex so good that I still feel his ghost on my skin.

But he crawls out a minute later, coming into my periphery and dropping something into my lap. It's his Harvard sweatshirt—with frayed sleeves, a stretched collar, and patches of missing silkscreened letters. He settles against the trunk, a foot away, and unfurls a navy-and-yellow afghan, stretching it between our laps as I throw the sweatshirt over my head. The scent of his laundry detergent greets me. I leave my hands in the shirtsleeves and wrap my arms around my chest.

He nods toward a peak in the distance. "The fireworks will start soon. We should be able to see them."

"I used to love fireworks," I say, the nostalgia clogging my throat.

"I remember." His voice comes out soft.

When we were kids, our parents would take us to the Del Mar Fairgrounds to watch the annual show. We'd sit atop our dads' shoulders, holding hands for the length of the spectacle—our stomachs filled with deep-fried wonders and saccharine confections, our hearts filled with the simple joys of childhood. But I can't recall the last time I saw fireworks. Lately, the Fourth of July has meant barbecues or bars—and certainly not camping along a river watching fireworks with my forever friend I just fucked and who just got off the phone with his not-quite-ex-wife.

It hadn't occurred to me until I cracked my chest wide open that this grumpy historian might go back to her. What was it he said when he was drunk and vulnerable? *My therapist says I get too attached.* He's the type of guy who mates for life, celebrates anniversaries with thoughtful trinkets according to Hallmark's traditional gift schedule: gold, diamonds, paper, rock, scissors, or something.

"You talked to Bianca today," I say.

The first cerulean flares stream over the mountain, accelerating with so much anticipation it's like it's holding its breath before dispersing into stardust.

"I wasn't hiding it."

"Right. You made sure I knew."

Above, cornflower blooms unfurl into sparklers before the sound follows like a bomb. I imagine there's music playing near the fireworks—"Born in the U.S.A." and "Yankee Doodle Dandy"—but here, across town and in the remote clearing, it's eerily silent.

"Was I supposed to lie to you?"

"No," I say. But that doesn't feel like the point. He wasn't supposed to schedule a call with his ex the day after sleeping with me. This is why I avoid vulnerability and why I don't feel things for people.

"It's been a shitty day," he sighs. "I don't want to fight with you." He deflates as the sparklers dissolve into mist.

"I don't either."

A bouquet of fireworks erupts overhead—ruby, sapphire, emerald, and topaz—painting Beau's glasses in glitter as he studies me. The bursts accelerate as the show floods the sky with color. But we watch each other. His shoulders are bunched, his jaw pinched tight, his expression

The Truth Is in the Detours

pained. I don't have to wonder what he's seeing on my face: fragility, fear, and some feelings I can't name.

"We need some truths," he says.

And then we both speak at once.

"What happened at today's interview?"

"Why'd you panic last night?"

"I asked you first," I say.

"Technically, I asked you last night when you looked like you might bolt."

"Beau?"

He shakes his head and looks over the fire and toward the river, to the plume of smoke hanging in the sky like a bruise before another burst fills the void with jewels. His face is all hard angles out here in the uneven light. "What?"

"What did Bianca do to you that drove you to write this book?" I need him to confirm it. I handed him proof of my heartbreak on a notarized document when we hadn't even spoken in years. He's still holding back the details of his after sharing my bed. His trauma is what initiated this trip; I'm just tagging along, and I think it's pretty hypocritical—and a little selfish—that he's asked me to dig into my emotional wounds while shielding his.

Beau sighs, pinching his eyes closed before wiping a palm over his mouth. I pivot until I can see him properly. He opens his mouth, but the words are dry and empty, like a rusty motor making several failed attempts to rumble to life.

"A little over a year ago, I spotted a positive pregnancy test in the trash."

I freeze—this was not what I was expecting.

"We weren't planning on kids, at least not then, but when I realized we were about to start a family, I was happy. Ecstatic, actually." He picks up a rock and skirts it across the campsite like a skipping stone. "When she didn't tell me right away, I thought she was waiting to surprise me with an ultrasound photo or engraved rattle or something. And I didn't want to ruin it. But a week went by, then two, and she said nothing. I assumed she was nervous because it wasn't in our plan, or, I don't know, worried I'd panic. So I took her away to our favorite bed-and-breakfast in Half Moon Bay, had a romantic meal, and told her I knew—that I was thrilled. But her reaction was so strange." He clears his throat. "And I should have known then."

I don't ask him follow-up questions even though I have a million.

"But I didn't. We went to her first appointment. I cried when I heard the heartbeat and kissed her when the little bean appeared on the screen. When she'd head off for a shift, I packed her lunch, researched home remedies for morning sickness." He casts a glance my way, and he looks unsure, almost self-conscious. I recognize the rare glimmer of vulnerability.

"She didn't want to tell anyone, which I understood at first. But when she reached her second trimester, I wanted to tell my parents. I wanted her to tell hers. But still, she insisted we wait. I didn't figure it out until I'd already fallen in love with the idea of being a dad, until I'd leaned close each night and whispered secrets into the baby's budding ears. I didn't figure it out until Bianca left her phone in my car one morning. I fished it out from the console because it was rattling against the gear shift, and the preview screen was lit up with texts—graphic messages from this guy she worked with."

My stomach turns over as I take in Beau's raw expression. I don't school my reaction, so I'm sure he sees my brewing anger for the sweet-faced doctor who hurt him.

"It was a Tuesday morning. Not sure why I remember that detail. I had to sleepwalk through a lecture to a group of freshmen while I envisioned my wife fucking another man. But I still hoped it was a mistake, that the texts weren't meant for her." He releases an exhausted breath. "But it was all true. She had no idea which one of us was the father."

Holy shit. My shock gives way to outrage. How does Bianca have the nerve to drag out the divorce after putting Beau through that—to take his things, storm into his house, and demand him back? I slip my hand in Beau's and squeeze, but his is lifeless in return. "Beau, I'm so sorry—"

"She'd been sleeping with this guy for over a year and lying to me about shifts, overtime, and working over the holidays. I don't know if she was ever faithful, honestly. She never did answer that question." He throws another rock toward the river, and this one sinks in the center. "She said she was sorry, that she still loved me. But I refused to discuss it or even look at her, and she left to go stay at her parents' house—or maybe her boyfriend's, I don't know."

"Wait, Beau, Bianca has a baby—with someone else?" I ask.

He shakes his head—a brief, barely perceptible quiver. "She lost the baby. A few days later. And I didn't accept her call, so she went through it alone."

My heartbeat hammers in my skull. Beau lost his family, too. He had said he understood what I was going through, and I dismissed him.

"I know I wasn't a perfect husband. I was often distracted and grumpy, so I was partially to blame. And I wondered, if I had been more understanding, if I had heard her out, or hadn't jumped to judgment, she could have had a healthier pregnancy or at least not gone through the loss alone . . ." He trails off.

"Beau." I gather the courage to inch closer and slide my palms to his jaw, bringing his pained focus to me. "Anyone would have been hurt and angry. It wasn't your fault. That's not how miscarriage works."

"I know." His eyes search mine. I'm not accustomed to the intensity of his unguarded gaze. His deep-brown eyes are so crystalline they appear to have their own light source. "I mean, intellectually, I know that. But my guilt, my heart?" He shakes his head.

"It wasn't your fault," I repeat, but I don't think he hears me because he keeps going.

"When I married Bianca, I meant every word of my vows. And I was so angry at her for destroying that. But the truth was, she wasn't the only one who didn't love enough. She didn't love me enough to be faithful. And I didn't love her enough to forgive her."

Only Beau would feel as if he broke his vows after his wife disregarded the most sacred one. For all of Beau's faults, lack of loyalty is not one of them. I think of all the times he's come to my rescue, even after I hurt him. He's been so loyal to me—and our vows were exchanged in Halloween costumes with wilted dandelions. "That's a lot to forgive, Beau."

"For better or worse."

"Forsaking all others," I retort.

Another firework lights up the sky, and we sit in silence as it fades.

"I know the baby may not have even been mine, but it still felt like mine, you know? The miscarriage still felt like a loss."

"Of course it did," I whisper, and he drops his head until our foreheads are kissing. My guarded Beau is deceivingly soft at his center—so sweet and fragile under all that stoicism and reserve. I want to avenge him. I want to cry for him. I want to kiss him until he forgets the woman who broke his heart.

"And my marriage, as dishonest as it was, felt like a loss, too." His words are barely a hush against the wind, the fireworks, and the rush of the river.

"It was Bianca's loss. She lost *you*. She lost everything. Your wit and attentiveness, your willingness to do anything for the people you care about—even when they don't know how to accept it. Your planning and preparation for every disaster. Your ESP for the perfect budget motel with a view, or campsite with front-row seats to fireworks. You only lost the fabricated version of her."

One side of his mouth lifts into a tired smile. "You've spent the last several weeks telling me I'm a grumpy, pompous know-it-all."

"You contain multitudes, Beauregard."

He barks out a laugh, and it breaks the tension. I'm so grateful for it. I don't know how to make him feel better about all he lost, but at least I can make him laugh. Without thinking, I swipe my thumb across his cheekbone. His expression straightens, his tongue peeking out to wet his lips.

"The truth," he says.

I open my mouth to ask what he means, but he presses a finger to my lips.

"Why did you get so weird last night?"

"Oh." This truth thing is looking like a stupid promise in hindsight. I don't know how to explain. "I guess I got overwhelmed and a little scared."

"About what?"

"About losing you as my friend, and"—I pinch my eyes closed, unable to look at his face, which drills past every barricade to see my soul, and say this next thing—"about everything it made me feel."

"Ophelia," he says, his voice low and teasing, "that is the point. When a man and a woman—"

I attempt to shift away, but he grasps my hand. "I expected to feel pleasure, Beau. But I felt so many"—I gulp in a breath and spit out the last word like a gnat in my drink—"emotions."

I sneak a glance to find him staring at me. I imagine it's the face he wears while struggling with a dataset containing unexplained outliers, or discovering an artifact that changes his understanding of history. *Perplexed.*

"Do you not usually feel any emotions during sex?"

"I mean . . . no?"

"Wow, Phe. That's . . ." His mouth forms a few stalled words before settling on "sad."

And if I didn't feel small before, now I feel minuscule, because it's as I feared. There was nothing special about our night together—for him, anyway. "You always feel something?"

He studies me—I'm an amoeba under a microscope. He speaks cautiously. "I don't sleep with anyone I don't already care about."

"So I must be the exception."

He chuckles and brushes a stray hair away from my face, tucking it behind my ear. "Phe, you were my first friend, first wife, first kiss. My feelings for you are much more complicated than just caring about you."

"'Complicated.' Be still my heart." I pull back, but he tugs me close, wrapping one arm around my shoulders.

"C'mon, Phe. Don't make me say it," he whispers.

"Say what?"

He sighs. "You have to know I had a painful crush on you for years."

"You aren't always so easy to read, Professor." I lean back so I can look into his eyes, trying to decipher his inscrutable expression.

"Well, everyone else knew."

I gather the courage to share my fears, revealing my wants. "But what you said last night, about fulfilling some teenage fantasy. It sounded like you thought being with me was an unsettled score. A check mark completed or something."

"Phe, no." Beau slips his hand onto my cheek and ducks to look directly into my eyes. "I'm so sorry I made you feel that way. I was trying to keep it light because I was overwhelmed and worried you might freak out if you knew . . ."

"Knew what?"

He shakes his head, one side of his lip curling in a reluctant smile. I'm fishing. I know it. He knows it. But I'm new at this, and I need reassurance before I let this man shock my atrophied heart back to life. "That I'm out of my mind for you. And last night was a lot."

"Well, I might lose my mind if I slept with my teenage crush. Nostalgia is powerful. And Zac Efron was a hottie."

"Ophelia," he sighs, refusing to take the bait, "my adolescent crush has nothing on the way I feel about you now. I think you're incredible. No one challenges me the way you do. You're funny, sexy, capable, kind, and loving."

"You tell me daily that I'm ridiculous. That I'm a pain in the ass. Chaotic, irritating, and immature."

The Truth Is in the Detours

He offers me a half smile that I catch in the moonlight. "You contain multitudes, Ophelia."

I giggle and push him away with one hand on his stomach. He rests his palm over mine, and the mood shifts. The fireworks finale lights up the sky like an exclamation point, leaving smoke and silence in its wake. Now it's just us, the wind through the trees, and the river crawling over tumbled stone.

When he speaks again, his mouth is against the shell of my ear. "It was scary for me, too."

My heart trumpets in my chest, and his breath hitches. "Why?"

"Because you've always had the power to break me. And I'm already shattered."

I slide my fingertips over his jaw, and my nails scratch against his stubble. "I don't want to break you. And I don't want to be broken." I hesitate. "But I don't know how to prevent either."

He drops his forehead to mine. "Just keep telling me your truths, and I'll keep telling you mine."

I find his mouth, which is soft and cautious, but I take his bottom lip between mine, and he whimpers before chasing the kiss. It's a give-and-take that was absent last night, a conversation of gentle brushes and desperate gasps as my heart bursts into a fireworks show of its own. I crawl into his lap, my knees pressed into the hard earth, my chest sealed to his. He wraps the blanket over my shoulders, cocooning us as the campfire licks the crisp air behind us. My body is a riot—all senses ablaze and rattling with the *thud, thud, thud* of my heart.

He takes my face in his hands and pulls back. "You're not going to panic on me again?"

I shake my head, but he waits as if he needs to hear it out loud. "No," I say against his mouth. He steals another kiss. "But I don't know what I'm doing."

"You seemed to do just fine last night." His tone triggers a deep ache that wraps around my thighs like ivy.

"Afterward," I whine. "When you want to cuddle and do the whole pillow-talk thing. When we need to pretend to be soft and caring and not tease each other."

He wraps his long arms around my waist and tucks my head onto his shoulder, making small circles on my spine. "You do nothing but talk. For pillow talk, do what you normally do, but after orgasms."

I bite back a smile.

"And you *are* soft and caring—you've taken care of me this entire trip. And I don't know where you got the idea that there would be no teasing. I still intend to tease the shit out of you."

"Really? I can call you 'Professor' when you're a pompous ass and embarrass you with off-color remarks in public?" It's a sonnet to my soul. "I might lose things and forget about checks I've written and leave car doors open."

"All part of your charm."

"Okay." I grin. I gather a lungful of air and exhale as he curls his fingers under the sweatshirt to find the bare skin at my waist. I want to let him strip me in the cold bite of the evening air.

"How many layers do you have on?"

"Too many," I say.

"It's a metaphor for your emotional armor."

I tilt my head back and laugh, but he grabs me by the waist and lifts me off his lap. I grow cold instantly.

"Come on," he says. "Let me get you properly naked so we can practice all that intimacy you're afraid of."

He stands, threads his fingers in mine, and leads me into the tent.

CHAPTER 29

Beau kneels on a sleeping bag and pulls me inside the tent before closing out the world, and I reach for him as my eyes adjust to the light filtered through the nylon. I slide his glasses off, folding them carefully and placing them on top of his duffel bag before tracing the lines of his cheekbones with my fingertips and his lips with my thumbs. He closes his eyes and hums before settling his gaze on my face.

"Can you still see me?" I ask.

"If you stay close."

And it's like that, inches apart, that we undress. His shirt first, and I abandon my restraint and drink him in as I've been desperate to. I touch the raised crescent scar on his rib cage—the gash he earned when following me over a chain-link fence—a remnant of me he's been hiding under his clothes for twenty years. I duck to kiss it, whispering "I'm sorry" into his skin—for all the marks I left behind, scars and hurts both physical and emotional. He tangles his fist in my hair, holding me against him with a trembling palm. I drag my lips over his chest, his clavicle, his neck. His skin is hot, but goose bumps rise to greet every grazing kiss, and he releases small puffs of breath as if holding himself back. When I find his mouth again, he deepens the kiss, pulling me closer, making my body warm with anticipation and need, all my nerve endings crackling to life under his touch. He works to free me from my clothes, and we laugh as the garments catch on my head, my elbow, my belt loop. But with each layer of clothing peeled away, he discards another veil; with every touch, he unleashes another truth, until I'm nothing but a raw heart, beating unprotected as I kneel in front of him, finally bare.

If last night was like jumping headfirst into dark water, tonight is like slipping into a warm bath—impulsivity giving way to intention. He drags rough palms from my thighs to my waist, thumbs pressing into the dip between navel and hip bone, his focus traveling over me like a promise, before he pulls me against him. My body aches with the memory of him—battling between wanting to pull him onto me, into me, and craving to savor this newfound patience. He's still in his jeans, and I scramble to undo his belt, release the button fly, and push them down his thighs with his boxers. I shiver when he pulls back to shove off his boots and kick his pants into the corner before returning to me with a slow-growing grin.

"Come here." He wraps a hand around my lower back and lowers me to the sleeping bags, hovering over me so that there's a hint of contact—a brush of skin on skin that makes me arch to get closer. "I don't know whether I want to look or touch." He drags his gaze down my chest, his hands following, ghosting fingerprints over my sternum, my breasts, my navel.

"Well, I'm freezing. So I vote touch."

He laughs and nips at my mouth, pressing warm lips to mine, tasting me until I dissolve under his kiss and the weight of his body. I forget about the cold and my fears and my insecurities and wonder if Beau has been the right answer to every decision I've ever been afraid to make.

Beau covers us in blankets, and we create a nest under the canopy and take our time. I pay attention to his gasps, to the way his fingertips tighten on my skin, to how his mouth goes slack when he slides inside me. I notice how he shivers when I press my mouth to his neck, I listen to the sound of his groan as I drag my teeth over his collarbone, and I feel the desperate grip of his hands when I say his name over and over and over as I come apart.

The Truth Is in the Detours

"Still okay?" he asks when we're spent and sated. I curl against him, my head on his shoulder and our limbs intertwined.

"I'm perfect and ready for all the intimacy," I whisper.

He laughs and kisses my forehead, dragging fingertips along my spine in a soothing rhythm. But it turns out we're too tired for any of that, and I fall asleep cradled in his arms.

~

It's a slate-gray monochromatic morning, and the scattered cloud cover provides a gentle wake-up call. Beau is still sleeping when I stir, my limbs draped over him like I'm clinging to a life raft. His face is placid— all the worry lines ironed out like crisp cotton. His mouth is soft, and I marvel at the slope of his brow and the curl of his lashes—all the vivid parts of him usually hidden behind his lenses and permanent scowl. I'm getting a peek behind his mask. And I love the view. I check in with myself for panic but find none. We cuddled. We talked. We survived the night—and I wouldn't mind an encore. Or a hundred.

"Hey." A low rumble slips from Beau's mouth before his eyes open. I stay close so he can see me. "Where are we on the freak-out meter?" he asks.

"Zero. But it might escalate if I have to face the morning without coffee."

He chuckles, and that sound—along with his scratchy cheek tickling my neck—tempts me to straddle him. But frankly, I'm sore, hungry, and interested in whether we can manage the morning after without disaster this time.

"Can't have that. Give me a minute."

I nuzzle closer and drag my hand down his chest. He laughs again and halts my progress with a firm grip around my wrist. "But you can't do that if you expect me to get out of bed anytime soon."

I get up first, aware of his eyes on me as I prepare for the brisk morning by layering his sweatshirt over my clothes. He follows me out to start the fire and sets the kettle over the grill grate, because he is a saint who thought to bring coffee. Within a few minutes, I'm caffeinated and ready to start the morning.

The clouds part to reveal a horizon painted with a pastel palette—carnations, violets, and daffodils bloom across the sky while the river wriggles under the sun's touch. The landscape looks alive, gentle, kissed by the same optimism that pulses through me. I hear Beau's shuffle step behind me before his arms are around my waist, his chin perched on my head.

"I'm going to try Mary's address in La Pine after our interview today." I'm ready to face more demons. Admittedly it's easier to look for a demon where you're unlikely to find it. My mother won't be there—according to the records, she lived nearby over fifteen years ago, even before Fort Bragg. But the small town of La Pine borders Bend; her old home is only twenty minutes from here. I may as well check to see if someone knew her. There might be a clue. "I really want to keep going—even if I can't find her. I need to see this through." Perhaps Beau is helping me be brave.

"Good," he says.

I turn in his arms. The sun lights him up, the morning playing on his face like hope. It's still novel to touch him like this, as if we're sneaking out to his tree house for our first kiss. It's somehow forbidden and a given.

We pack up the campsite with an efficiency we've developed over the last few weeks, moving in and out like a traveling circus. Melancholy washes over me as we drive away from the river and the honesty it brought us. But Beau reaches over and squeezes my thigh, a small tether, a reminder that we don't have to lose whatever we found here.

Our interview takes us to Sunriver, a resort town close to the campsite, where Jefferson Riley awaits us in his mountain home. We're in and out in less than an hour. Jefferson is a man of few words, so once he confesses that he faked a law degree and was a partner at a prominent firm for four decades, he had little else to say. My notes on

The Truth Is in the Detours

the conversation are spare, but I capture a detailed description of the gourmet kitchen and fourteen-foot ceilings his deception bought him, as Beau tries to gather information corroborating his claim. Jefferson's lack of affect makes me skeptical. It sounds very *Catch Me If You Can*.

"At least he didn't pretend to be a surgeon," Beau says under his breath as we slip back into the car.

I climb in after him and nod. "I concur."

Beau chuckles and leans in for a kiss. I cup his cheek with my palm and pull back, grinning.

"You find me funnier now that I've let you into my pants," I say.

We grab sandwiches to eat at a park and watch a young family fly a rainbow kite while dragonflies dance over the river. Afterward, we stretch out on a picnic blanket and bask in the golden rays of the warm afternoon. Beau trails a palm along my hip, an instinctive gesture that winds me up while soothing me. He falls asleep, his long body curved toward me with his arm tucked under his head. I lay awake, cocooned under him while I consider my next steps—and the potential consequences. I imagine scenarios. The things that could have led to my mother's abandonment. What must have happened? I would have remembered abuse . . . right?

What do I make of my splintered memories that stick to me like glitter—unseen until they glimmer in the light and steal my breath? The time she picked me up from preschool early to catch sand crabs on the beach. Our kitchen dance parties to the *Footloose* soundtrack. Teaching me to make chocolate chip cookies. The time she turned our living room into an underwater seascape to watch *The Little Mermaid*. The morning she woke me before sunrise to grab doughnuts as the shop opened. I still hear her full, throaty laugh on the first bite of a glazed doughnut.

I slip my pendant back and forth over the gold chain. I'm prepared for this to end badly. To never find her. To find a woman so dissimilar from my memory that she blows away the glitter with a careless exhale. Or worse, to find a woman who erases my dad with her version of events.

I can't lose him twice.

The shock of Dad's death is wearing off. And reality is flooding in.

I let Beau in and opened the dam on all my emotions.

Beau shifts and reaches for me—like a reflex. I cuddle closer and allow the rhythm of his breathing to settle my heart rate. Because as scared as I am, I now have someone to hold my hand as I step into the unknown.

CHAPTER 30

The red cabin is at the end of a long gravel road, burrowed in a small aspen grove a few yards from a narrow artery of the river. After several attempts at the doorbell, I almost give up before the door swings open, revealing a guy about our age, with dark hair that rests on his shoulders and an untrimmed beard. He doesn't say anything and looks from me to Beau and back, waiting for us to get to the point.

"Hi." I coax a smile into my voice. "I'm sorry to bother you. I'm looking for my mother. She disappeared decades ago, but we have reason to believe she may have lived at this house about fifteen years ago. I know this is a long shot, but—"

"What's her name?" he cuts in, his dark eyes narrowing.

"Mary Ann Johnson Dahl." I hand him the photos, and he studies them, flipping through a few before handing them back to me.

"I don't know where she is."

He steps back, begins to close the door before I stammer out, "But you know her?" The blood is rushing in my ears, and my throat is tight. His reaction feels personal, and all the hairs on my arms stand up. Beau must sense something, too, because he places his palm on the small of my back, an *I'm here* gesture that anchors me.

The guy sighs. "I don't know who you are or what you want. But I'm not in the habit of talking to strangers about ancient history."

I shove the photo toward him. "Mary is my mother, and it sounds like you know her."

"Look, I don't remember much. She lived here for a while when I was in high school—she was dating my dad. It got ugly. She left."

"Your dad," I say, hoping he's willing to provide more information. I feel closer to the truth than I ever have—and I can't lose this clue.

"What about him?" It feels threatening when he steps through the threshold, but I don't recoil. I sense Beau coming closer, leaning forward in a subtle warning. He has several inches on this guy, who has quite a few on me.

"Would he know more?" I ask.

The guy grunts. "I doubt it. It's not like they send each other Christmas cards."

"Would he be willing to speak to me?" I ask, doing my best to stay calm despite the information I'm absorbing, despite this guy's hostility.

He crosses his arms over his chest and studies me before looking to Beau and back. "He's not here."

"Could I contact him?"

A gust of wind blows through, rustling the aspens that cloak the small cabin. A set of wind chimes sing in the corner, and it's a dissonant harmony against the backdrop of the moment. The guy continues to stare at us, and I wait him out.

"He moved out of state."

"Would you mind sharing his number?" I ask, undeterred.

He laughs again, but there's less bite in it. "You're relentless."

"Have you ever been lied to?" I ask the guy. His expression clears, and I sense he's listening now. "When I was a kid, my dad told me my mother was dead. I learned she was alive only a few weeks ago—right after my dad's funeral. I'm following breadcrumbs across state lines, searching for clues or answers or closure or . . . something. But I've only hit dead ends. Anything your dad could tell me would be helpful."

He levels me with a hard stare. "I feel bad for you—assuming you're telling the truth—but I have no reason to trust you."

The Truth Is in the Detours

Beau reaches across me to give the guy his card. I notice that my name and number are scribbled on the back. Beau must have prepared for this possibility, keeping his fingertip on the white flag all this time.

"If you could pass this along. It contains our contact information. It would mean a lot."

The guy eyes it like potential poison, but finally grabs it. "Can't promise he'll call."

"I understand," I say. "Whatever you can do."

Beau slips his hand around my waist and turns us. "Thanks for your time," he says as we walk to the car.

"Hey," the guy calls out when I open the passenger door, "all those dead ends you mentioned? They may not be clues, but they could be a sign that you're better off not finding her."

"Ophelia," Beau beckons. I climb in the car, my focus on the rearview mirror as we drive away.

∼

We check in to an inn in Medford that night. It's a short drive to the Jackson County Courthouse where the court order was filed, and I'll have enough time to swing by tomorrow to see if I can access the missing pages—or any other court document that might give me answers.

When the receptionist at the inn asks us how many rooms we need, Beau and I don't hesitate before saying "one" in unison. This thing with us is still new, but when Beau curls his fingers in mine, it feels right.

Beau asked me if I was okay in about a hundred different ways during the drive. The answer is more complicated than yes or no. I was swimming in all varieties of frightening emotions—reeling from the feel of his palm on my thigh as we drove, struck by the stolen kisses at stoplights, and sinking with the realization that we might be chasing a dead woman, after all. My mother's trace ran cold almost a decade ago. She could have died before I realized she was alive. I can't tell if that guy at the red cabin knew more than he let on. I don't know if his last words were intended to be a cryptic clue or a warning.

But other emotions simmer under the surface as well. Jealousy, I think. And anger. While I was growing up and trying to figure myself out—making mistakes, adrift without a mother to model self-respect—she was raising someone else's teenager.

Our room is plain and sterile but has a king bed centered across the wall with a half dozen pillows. I want to fall on top of it. Right now. But I have two days of filth—and Beau—on me.

"Go ahead, take the first shower," Beau says. He must read the longing on my face as I look toward the bathroom. I almost ask if he wants to join me, but I'll feel sexier once clean.

I luxuriate. I use every bath product I brought, which is admittedly minimal. I exfoliate, shave my legs, let the conditioner do its best to repair my dry hair, and moisturize with the cupcake-batter lotion Beau seemed to appreciate the other night. The steam is curling over my shoulders as I leave the bathroom in a scrap of a towel, hoping to grab Beau's attention—hoping he'll help me shut out the confusion for a night.

But he's on the phone near the window, pacing and rubbing his hand through his hair. He startles and swivels toward me. An expression crosses his face too quickly to read.

"I have to go." He turns away. "I know. I hear you. But I can't talk about this now."

I step back into the bathroom to give him privacy. He knocks on the door a few moments later, looking sheepish.

"Sorry," he mumbles.

But I wave my arms in a gesture that appears more erratic than unconcerned, so I pull them back to fiddle with the towel in a useless attempt at tucking in the end. "It's fine." I sneak by him as he hovers at the threshold. I sense his eyes on me, but I shuffle through my bag, busying myself. After a few moments, the bathroom door closes and the water turns on.

The Truth Is in the Detours

When Beau emerges, I'm on the bed with my laptop, catching up on work—a distraction quite different from the one I planned.

Beau settles beside me and plants a kiss on my shoulder before resting his forehead there. "So that was Bianca," he exhales into my skin.

"I assumed." I attempt to keep my voice neutral. I'm not jealous—just confused.

"I'm worried if I avoid her too often, she'll make this more difficult. And I still feel guilty ignoring her calls—like something bad may have happened."

"Beau," I sigh, feeling the weight of his responsibility and my sorrow, "I was joking about being the other woman. But it's not something I'd ever be okay with. Am I getting in the way of you reconciling—"

"No," he says flatly, straightening his spine and putting a sliver of distance between us.

I don't know if I have a right to ask for more. It comes perilously close to asking about our future. Which . . . well, I can't go there. We live on separate ends of the state and lead very different lives—and we're both a bit broken. For now, this trip is enough, I think. We can figure out the rest later.

"If I wanted to reconcile with Bianca—if I thought that was even a possibility—nothing would have happened between us. I'm not that guy."

"Okay." I don't know what else to say. This conversation is too murky to wade into. I don't know how it starts. I don't know where I want it to go. He lost so much so quickly—and if anyone can understand that, it's me. I don't want to hurry him through the grief of losing his marriage and hopes for their family.

"Hey." He tips my chin to him. "I don't like talking about Bianca, but if you need to—"

"I don't," I say quickly.

He draws his brows together, skeptical. But I want to assure him; I know what it cost him to confide in me last night because I know what it costs me every time I let him witness my darkest hurts.

"Okay." He searches my face for evidence of the truth.

But the reality is, I want to feel better about it without talking about it. I want to understand why my nagging insecurity is nudging me in the ribs. I don't know whether my lingering unease stems from concern about what Beau feels for Bianca or what he feels for me. This trip has forced me to recalibrate everything I understood about Beau—how he interpreted our friendship breakup, how he really felt about me during all those tense years, how I misread him. It's easy to believe his version of our history when his mouth is on mine, when he's inside me, and losing himself over me.

But then doubt creeps in.

Because I've always known men could want me—and still not want to stay.

"What is it, Phe?"

"Do you remember your going-away party? Before you left for Harvard?" I close my laptop before hugging it to my chest.

"I remember Henry had to drag you there."

I flash Beau a heavy side-eye. "Not true. I wanted to see you off. But it was hard for me, and"—I hesitate—"I think that's when it dawned on me that you were moving across the country with all this fanfare, and I hadn't even signed up for community college classes. And I realized how much I was going to miss you."

I feel his breath on my temple, a small press of his lips. "I didn't know."

It's silly how much this memory still hurts. "And I asked you to write to me."

"We talked about this. I was hurt about that stunt Cherry pulled." He reaches for my laptop and puts it on the nightstand, as if disarming me, before wrapping an arm around my shoulders.

"I know, but you said our lives would be too different. You said it wasn't worth pretending we'd be friends from across the country when we couldn't be friends while living next door." I don't know what I'm

The Truth Is in the Detours

getting at, but I wonder if he thinks it will be worth staying in each other's lives from across the state.

He squeezes my shoulders. "Well, I did write you. Every week."

"What?" I turn my head, and his nose is an inch away from mine. He kisses it.

"That first semester." He pulls back enough that his face comes into focus. "I missed home so much, and there were all these elitist traditions that I knew you'd find as absurd as I did. I told you all about them and imagined you laughing or sharing some witty barb back. But I never sent them."

"Why not?" I whisper.

"I couldn't let myself hold out hope that you'd write me back. I needed to get over you."

I swallow, mesmerized by his perfect face—which is so familiar and yet all new. I remember being this close to him in the tree house before our first kiss—when we somehow got it all right before everything went wrong.

"Did it work?" I ask.

He hums, and the vibration sinks into my skin. "Not even a little bit."

Maybe that's all the reassurance I need for now. I slide into his lap, and he settles his hands at my hips. We hover, our faces mere inches apart as I slide his glasses off and place them on the nightstand. And then his mouth is a promise on mine—warm, reverent, and patient. We come together and apart, finding new ways to connect, my eyes flicking to his with each retreat, trying to understand what I see in his gaze. It's searching and a little desperate. His eyes are so dark that the iris bleeds into the pupil, a bottomless oil well. It absorbs everything but reveals nothing. But soon, there's nothing to see or second-guess. Our clothes fall away, and his mouth finds every sensitive spot on my skin, his hands untangle my patchwork of nerves until I'm one live wire arcing toward him.

Later, when we drift to sleep to the rhythm of each other's breathing, all my worries fall to the back of my mind like sediment, and something close to happiness bubbles up.

It feels like my head has just hit the pillow when a shrill ringer pierces the silence.

"Hello?" I rasp into the phone after scrambling for it. The blinds of our hotel room are drawn, and I squint at the red analog clock on the nightstand. Five in the morning.

"Ophelia Day-hill?" The voice on the other end of the line is gravel crunching under tires. Beau tightens his grip around my waist, burying his face into my neck. He mumbles something into my hair, but I don't make it out.

"Yes?" I sit up and swing my legs over the side of the bed, preparing for . . . I don't know. An emergency? A quick exit?

"This is Saul Perry. You left your number with my son."

"Hi . . . yes . . . hi," I say again, as my eyes adjust to the dark.

Beau shifts beside me, sitting up against the headboard.

"Oh, shoot," Saul sighs. "I forgot about the time difference again. I'm in Florida."

"It's okay." I clear the sleep out of my voice. "Thank you for calling."

"My son left me a strange message last night with your number. And he wouldn't pick up this morning." He coughs a few times before recovering. "Is this some kind of paternity suit? Because I got snipped decades ago."

I laugh. "No, Mr. Perry. I know who my father is, and I believe my mother met you long after I was born."

He exhales as I give him the highlights, summarizing what I found, the minimal online footprint, my suspicion his ex-girlfriend was my mother. Beau slides out of bed, turns on a desk lamp, and slips into the bathroom. I'm grateful for the gesture of privacy.

"Well, sorry. I didn't think my Mary had kids—a blessing, really."

His words land like a dagger—there's nothing like someone saying it's a blessing you were abandoned, or that it would have been better

The Truth Is in the Detours

if you hadn't existed at all. But I'm not going to get anywhere if I react emotionally. I channel Beau during an interview. "Why do you say that?"

"Well, she . . . I don't like to speak ill of people, especially if she *was* your mom. But she had some issues. It caused a lot of conflict with my boys."

"What kind of issues?" Anger issues, drugs, drinking, what?

He sighs. "I don't know, really. But she was hard to live with. And we'd fight. I don't blame her. She was who she was, and I, well, I wasn't the right match. My boys suffered with all the drama. So I had to choose them, you know?"

A memory flashes in my vision. My mom sprawled on the green bathroom tile, my dad sitting beside her, coaxing her up, brushing her hair away from her face as she stared, unblinking, into the distance. I try to erase the image, but it slithers into my gut, some hybrid of memory and conjuring.

"Any idea where she might be?"

There's static on his end of the line—the hollow whip of wind through a tunnel. "We didn't part on good terms. She left town like she came into it a few years earlier, on fire and burning every bridge she passed."

With that image, I envision my mom barely glancing in her rearview as she abandons her four-year-old daughter to spend Christmas in a hospital—burning her bridge to me forever.

Saul says he'll call if he remembers anything else, but I don't know whether more vague horror stories will be helpful. A few minutes after he excuses himself and hangs up, Beau emerges from the bathroom.

"Who was that?"

"That guy's dad. The one who dated my mom. He has no idea where she is."

The bed sinks under Beau's weight as he climbs in, shifts toward me, and tugs on my hip until I collapse beside him. "Why did he call so early?"

231

"He hasn't mastered time-zone math."

This earns me a soft chuckle. I hear the fatigue in Beau's voice. "Did he say anything helpful?" Beau nestles his mouth against my neck, the question coming through a soft burst of air that makes my skin prickle with goose bumps.

"Nothing that will help me find her. Another dead end." And as dread seeps in, I wonder if perhaps it's a sign that I should stop trying.

CHAPTER 31

I learn two things when the sun joins me in the morning: what that ruckus was the other morning in Beau's bedroom at our cabin, and how Beau earned those abs. It's bad news for me and other lazy fools hoping for shortcuts to the bodies we've always wanted. He disappears for an hour in running shoes and dry-fit garb, coming back sweaty and panting, to begin a half-hour regimen of push-ups, planks, crunches, and other exercises I can't name or do. I watch like a lecher until he's sprawled across the floor like a starfish, eyes closed, chest rising and falling as his heart rate descends.

"Have you been working out every morning on this trip?"

"Most. Yeah."

"So you get up at dawn, exercise like you're in boot camp, and then wake me and feed me pastries?"

"Basically."

"Sabotaging my chance for abs of my own," I sigh.

He chuckles and scans my bare legs. "You're perfect. And buying you pastries is self-preservation. I'm the bastard who wakes the kraken every morning."

I throw a pillow at his head, and he catches it before tossing it back with the force all those push-ups made possible. I should exercise. But I don't have the discipline to punish myself with burpees on motel carpet.

We have two interviews this afternoon, and the courthouse opens in a half hour, so we pack up and settle in the car by midmorning. I send Beau in search of coffee as I venture into the courthouse, waiting twenty minutes until a stooped man with buzzed gray hair and horn-rimmed glasses opens a window and waves me over. "I'm looking for a copy of a court order."

The man squints at me over his glasses. "Most of our records are online these days. Have you tried there?"

"I did, but the case is thirty years old. Nothing came up online." I slide him the cover page of the parental termination, with the Jackson County seal at the top.

His entire face knots up in concentration as he skims. He harrumphs. "This might be in the archives. But I don't know. We don't usually get requests for things this old." He mumbles to himself and riffles through stacks of paperwork behind the counter before producing a multiple-page form with tight lines and small print. "Fill this out. You should get a response either way in six to eight weeks." He gestures to a stack of clipboards resting on the counter.

I thank him and settle into a plastic folding chair in the far corner. Beau finds me when I've completed three of four pages. He sinks into a chair beside me and kisses my cheek.

"What's the verdict?" he asks.

"I fill out this paperwork. And then hope someone follows up . . . someday."

"Who knew private investigative work was so much admin?"

"Sherlock Holmes made it look so glamourous."

After I turn in the form, Beau consoles me with a cinnamon roll and vanilla latte from a nearby café, and we head to our next round of interviews.

We meet our youngest confessor outside Ashland. Xochitl is in her early twenties, with wispy black hair, a round face, and a thin scar across her chin. She asks us to meet her at Wild Horse Ranch, where she lives and works as an agritourism guide for families looking to stay off the grid. She's shy and nervous and doesn't speak until we're settled on a picnic table along a hiking trail.

The Truth Is in the Detours

"I lied to my family—told them I couldn't be a kidney donor for my sister. I told them I got my blood type checked as a first step and that I was type B. I lied. I'm O, the universal donor." She lets out a wry laugh. "Which is so fitting. I've always been the one to give, give, give—while they take. And it was one thing I wasn't willing to give them."

Later that afternoon, we meet Floyd in a small town called Weed, California, which relishes its name with souvenir shops featuring silk-screened hemp and kitschy I LOVE WEED T-shirts. Over a beer, Floyd tells us he's dying from lung cancer. He's hiding it from his family, hoping he can live out his last months without the burden of their pre-grief, while still enjoying his cigarettes without their guilt.

"Are you getting what you need from these interviews?" I ask Beau when I start the car and pull away from Weed. I'm growing skeptical—or perhaps, more accurately, remain skeptical. "What are we learning but that people are inherently selfish?"

What are we doing to ourselves besides triggering our own traumas and learning that liars don't often consider the feelings of those they're hurting?

Beau stares out the passenger window, his arms folded and his shoulders tense.

"I think it's more complex than that. Sure, there are those who are purely selfish—driven by money or power. And then you have self-preservation as a motivation, those who know they'll lose something if they confess. And there are those who may want to keep a bit of themselves separate from their loved ones or are lying to protect someone else."

"I suppose," I say.

"Our truths are pieces of ourselves. No one shares all of them with everyone because of embarrassment or fear or selfishness or shame."

We drive in silence. I wonder whether this project will give Beau closure—and me answers.

I reprogram the GPS, a quick detour that will hopefully bring me a step closer.

"Where are we?" Beau asks as I slow to a crawl in a suburban neighborhood in Redding. He's been head down, typing furiously for the last hour. When he's in a zone, he's so out of tune with what is going on. I could have driven us to Canada and he wouldn't have noticed.

I hand him the list of addresses he'd printed for me weeks ago. Mary would have lived here after La Pine and before Fort Bragg.

"Oh," he says, a note of surprise and admiration in his tone. He almost had to drag me into this mission, and now I'm running headfirst.

Saul and his son's words are haunting me. Who was my mother? A woman not cut out for parenting? Was it that simple? She left, and my dad made the story more palatable?

What was their motivation? Selfishness? Or was it more complex?

I pull up outside a large home in a nondescript neighborhood of mixed-style housing. I'd checked the address on Google Maps this morning, so I know it by sight. Beau follows me up to the door, and I'm drawn to a sign on the facade—REDDING HEALTH COLLECTIVE. I scan the smattering of instructional signs before ringing the bell. A woman's voice comes over the intercom.

"May I help you?"

"Hi," I say. "We're looking for a missing person."

Beau raises his eyebrows, but I smile triumphantly as the door buzzes unlocked.

We step into a small lobby, with two wooden armchairs in the corner and a front desk to the left. Informational brochures are stacked along the ledge. I scan a few titles: "Understanding your Diagnosis," "Seeking Help for Addiction," and "The Benefits of Residential Care."

A woman with a jet-black bob and clear lip gloss beckons us to the desk by clearing her throat.

"Hello," I begin. She nods and purses her lips. "I'm looking for a missing woman, Mary Ann Johnson Dahl, who listed this as a former address."

The clerk's face is impassive when she says, "I cannot disclose the identity of any of our patients. Are you law enforcement?"

"No, but—"

"I'm sorry." She doesn't sound sorry. "Patient confidentiality is nonnegotiable."

"She lived here a little over twelve years ago. Could you confirm whether your organization owned this facility at the time?" What does it mean if my mom lived here?

She eyes me—expressionless—before admitting, "This facility has been operating at this location at least twenty years."

"Hypothetically, if someone listed this address as their home, would they be staff or a patient?"

She stares back, silent for a few beats before saying, "We do not have staff who live here full-time."

Beau wanders to the far wall, looking over a bulletin board.

"Are you sure there's nothing you can tell me? Her family is desperate to—"

"If you don't leave, I'm afraid I will have to call the police." The woman grabs the phone receiver, eyeing me as if she has her hand on a gun.

"We're going," Beau says.

I slip a brochure out of the trifold stand before he hurries me out.

"Read anything interesting?" I wait for a woman pushing a double stroller to pass before striding to the car.

"Not much. But it's obviously a mental-health facility. Long-term care. The posters on the bulletin board were flyers for family support groups."

I hand him the brochure before pulling away from the curb. I turn on music—'90s hip-hop—while Beau reads through the pamphlet.

"It's a general flyer on the organization's services—they do everything from grief counseling to intensive mental-health and addiction treatment. Acute, long-term. I don't know what it tells us." Beau squeezes my thigh, resting it there as the tires thump over notches in the pavement. "We might be able to find more on their website."

I'm piecing it together with Saul's words, creating a new picture of the woman who carried me, birthed me, then left me. She was always a tragic figure in my history, but the tragedy is changing shape into something more complex than life or death, good or bad.

There are too many gaps in this mosaic. Saul painted the picture of an erratic woman. A stint at a mental-health facility seems to support that picture. But Mary's more recent history in Fort Bragg tells a different story. She was a talented pastry chef about to be married to someone with the name of a famous cartoon character—if I'm to believe Pamela back at the Mug and Muffin. Could we be chasing the shadow of two different Mary Johnsons? Or did this one woman have multiple stories to tell?

I don't know if my mother is still alive, or where *her* story led.

But I'm going to find out.

Because whether or not she's worth finding, without answers I'm afraid I'll lose my dad for good.

CHAPTER 32

A rare summer storm comes through and douses the final embers of forest fire that had burned across California for the last week. It allows us to wrap up our rescheduled interviews in Chico and Oroville over the next two days.

On an unusually cool July day, almost three weeks after we began, we finish Beau's project—sitting across from a quiet middle-aged woman, Erin Miller, overlooking vineyards before her shift at a small tasting room. She hid her sexuality from her disapproving family and ruined every romantic relationship along the way. Her body uncoils as she recounts each lie, every excuse about why she didn't marry, every time she told a partner she couldn't bring her home.

"Thank you," she says as we finish. "I needed to tell a stranger first to get the courage to tell my family. I lost the woman I wanted to marry. And I need to win her back."

After Beau and I slide into the car outside the winery, he doesn't turn on the ignition. He's quiet for a bit, staring over the dash and into the vineyard beyond.

"We're done with the interviews," he says, and I may be projecting, but I sense disappointment in his tenor. It feels like we're ending on a whimper—after a stay at a nondescript motel and before another monotonous drive.

I've spent every free moment during the last two days trying to find new leads on my mom. But without her Social Security number or her new name, I'm chasing a phantom. We've run out of addresses to visit. I've scoured obscure social media channels. Beau spent last night sifting through online newspaper archives, and the night before we checked online death and marriage records for every county in California and Oregon.

As ambivalent as I was at the start of this journey, now it feels necessary—a loop I need to close, if not to find my mom, then at least to understand my dad's decisions.

But her trail runs cold, and I may have to accept that I'll never find her.

I fell asleep with my laptop open last night and woke in the morning with Beau curled against my spine—and our time together expiring. We haven't talked. Not about what comes next or what we want. We've existed in a time capsule. I imagine I'll look back on our trip with a strange mix of fondness and pain. I spent the first half of the trip trying to dam all my emotions behind sarcasm and evasion, and now they're coursing through me like a wild river.

"Are you excited about going home?" he asks.

I'm not even sure where home is. The small apartment I haven't missed once, even when sleeping in Beau's car or stuck on the side of the road. Or the childhood home that will likely be sold in a week—for less money than I need to make it worth the loss. The buyers have another twenty-four hours to pull out, demand repairs, or ask for a credit for their trouble. Ronald walked through the potential numbers two nights ago as Beau and I pulled out of Redding and away from my last maternal clue. My focus was a bit spotty. From what I understand, the sale price—with all those California real estate zeros—is an order of magnitude smaller after the credits, commissions, and loan payoff. But I don't have many choices.

I settle for honesty. "No."

"Same." His expression is so earnest it makes my heart swell.

I lace my fingers in his, squeezing tight before kissing the back of his hand.

The Truth Is in the Detours

"We've gotta face it eventually."

He nods. "But you'll stay at my place for a bit?"

The idea is tempting. I wish I could hide out with him. But then what? I checked my bank account this morning—and it's dire. I need to focus on work and land new clients. Without Juniper, my invoices will barely cover my basic expenses. Beau has insisted on paying for most of our travel expenses since I'm helping with his book, but the incidental costs are adding up—meals, extra charges for my mobile hot spot, and lost income.

Beau leans forward, a reluctant smile playing at his lips. He cups my face in his palms and kisses me until I forget our trip is almost over, we haven't found my mom, and my dad lied to me and I may never find out why. Until the only thought swimming through my head is that I think I love this man. I should be terrified, but it feels too natural—too obvious—to trigger my self-destructive tendencies. I don't even have the impulse. Of course I love him. Maybe I always have, but now it's taken on a new shape.

"Okay," I say into the kiss before he pulls back, looking for confirmation in my face. I bite my lip, worried he might find proof of something bigger. "For a couple days."

His phone buzzes on the console, and I startle. Bianca hasn't called him in days, but that doesn't lessen my reaction to the possibility.

Beau grabs it and grins, pushing his glasses back up his nose. He holds the phone out to me. I read Carlos's name at the top of the screen—a short text from his friend.

"Come here." He drapes his arm over my shoulders and holds his phone aloft.

"Wait," I say. "Are you attempting a selfie?"

"Whatever the equivalent is for two people, yes."

"What kind of angle is that? Are you trying to document the texture of my nostrils?"

He snorts. "Oh my Lord, Ophelia."

"And you're leaning forward, so it looks like your head is three times the size of mine."

"It's fine," he grumbles. "Carlos wants to know we kissed and made up."

"In that case..." I tousle his hair and unbutton the top two buttons on his shirt while he groans and huffs. I lean in to plant a kiss on his cheek and snap a photo. The picture is dimly lit, off-center, and blurry. He's scowling at me out of the side of his eyes—embarrassed, I think. But it's sweet, possessive, adorable.

"That'll do," I say. "You may share it." He rattles off a message, and I add, "Send it to me, too."

And just like that, he adds me to their group thread. Serena responds first—a series of heart-eye emojis and an invitation to visit soon.

Carlos offers a subtle note. It's nice to see you're no longer choosing violence.

"Let me feed you and get you home," Beau says as he backs out of the winery.

We find a diner perched along a dusty patch of highway. I groan as Beau turns off the engine. "Really? Another diner?"

"Every experience needs closure, Phe. There's nothing more quintessential road trip than a roadside diner. Last one, I promise."

Closure. I was hoping it would be delivered through means other than greasy grub and pleather booths. This diner is surprising, though. It's been refurbished recently, and the staff are all dressed in a retro rocker vibe, which gives the place an ironic charm.

Our server has a black beehive and two full sleeves of vibrant ink, her eyeliner drawn into a precise cat-eye. Her name tag reads Dorothy, but I'm skeptical. It's probably Madison or Ashley or some other millennial moniker.

We stay on brand—hamburgers and fries for each of us. When we're done, Beau polishes off my fries and insists on a slice of huckleberry pie to share.

The Truth Is in the Detours

"Dorothy" drops it off with a smile and saunters away before Beau pushes the plate in my direction.

"I'm stuffed." But I take a bite anyway. "What even is a huckleberry?" I say through a mouthful.

"It's like a blueberry, but smaller, darker, and not grown commercially."

"That was a rhetorical question, Professor."

"Do you want the genus and species name?" he asks, deadpan, shoving a quarter of the pie into his mouth in one bite.

"Huckleberry," I say, and my mind catches on the word.

"No. That's the common name. You're not very good at this game," he teases.

"No. Huckleberry. As in Huckleberry Hound. Remember that old cartoon blue dog?" My dad loved classic cartoons and would have me watch them with him when I was small. I don't know why I didn't think of it sooner.

Beau shakes his head, but I pull up an image on my phone, and he squints. "I guess. It looks kinda familiar."

"Huckleberry is also a last name. Like Mary's boss mentioned in Fort Bragg." I drop my fork. I could be wrong. I've been nothing but wrong. But I type in "Mary Huckleberry" and click on the image search.

And there, on page 2, I find her. I'd know the line of her profile anywhere—because it's exactly like mine.

CHAPTER 33

I follow the link to a website for Café Huckleberry, a beachfront bakery and café in Elk, only twenty miles south of where we'd first looked for Mary in Fort Bragg. The website is fresh and spare—a white background featuring full-color images of eclairs, croissants, and their specialty, huckleberry scones. The "About Us" section highlights the owners—Mary and Jack Huckleberry—who opened the award-winning coastal attraction six years ago. Their picture features my mother in profile gazing up at a man with silver hair and warm brown eyes. The energy is similar to that of the photo Beau and I just snapped in the car.

Beau pays the bill and ushers us out before I emerge from my haze. We drive for a bit with him clutching my hand, my knuckles white in his grip.

"Talk to me, Phe. What do you want to do?"

"I want to go see her."

"Okay," he says. "Of course."

"But I can go alone. We're done with your project, and I don't want to prolong this wild-goose chase for you."

"Hey." Beau shakes his head. "I'm not leaving you. Let's see this through."

And when we stop for gas, Beau makes it happen, finding a place to stay while I stare out the window. We won't arrive until late tonight, but I can look for her in the morning.

The Truth Is in the Detours

The drive to Elk is the longest stretch of our trip as we cut westward along two-way country roads. The landscape blurs outside the window—meadows, farmland, hay-colored brush. I steer my focus straight ahead. I don't usually get carsick, but my stomach is gurgling—some combination of shock and huckleberry pie.

My mother is really alive—baking confections along the ocean beside her new husband. She's smiling and fulfilled, after ditching me and Dad three decades ago. My feelings cycle through hope, resentment, rage, excitement, and disbelief in a game of emotional roulette.

We arrive at a cliffside cottage in Elk as the sun slips into the ocean. Clad in white clapboard siding and moss-green trim, it's perched on the bluff like a lonely spectator over the churning Pacific, a man-made spec in the wild landscape.

"How'd you . . ." I don't know what I'm asking. How did Beau book an oceanfront cottage on a few hours' notice? How did he know that a secluded bungalow fit my tempestuous mood? How did he read me when I am stream of consciousness written in invisible ink?

Beau kisses me on the temple, lingering for a moment before stepping out of the car. I follow him to the door and wait as he searches on his phone for the key code. He waves me into the cottage—it's an angular bungalow with wide-plank pine floors and a linen sectional positioned in front of a floor-to-ceiling brick hearth. Tucked into one corner is a white-tiled kitchen. A small bedroom on the opposite side has a wrought iron bed, layered with textures of cream, white, and gray. But the highlight is the wall of windows in the living room. They could tempt someone to walk right off the bluff and into the ocean. It's cozy and menacing, soothing and foreboding.

I lean my forehead against the glass, watching as the surf pummels the rocks, as the whitecaps froth and churn before drifting onto the beach pacified. I don't know how long I've been standing here, but the sun has set, and the moon has taken over. I startle when Beau wraps his arms around my waist, pulling my back to his front. He's turned on a light in the corner and brought our bags in from the car.

"What do you need? Food, wine, sleep, distraction, or do you want to talk it out?"

I pivot in his arms until my nose is pressed to his hard chest, and I breathe him in like a palate cleanser. I tuck my arms against my ribs and let him hold me. We sway slightly, his palms making comforting circles on my spine. Perhaps I should work through what I'm feeling and what I might say to my mother. I could write a script and have Beau playact several permutations of how my mother might react. But there are no answers to be gleaned through make-believe, and I need to save my emotional stamina for the real event. Besides, I want to stay in this moment—not because I'm too afraid to face tomorrow, but because tonight is too beautiful to miss.

So I hum, "You."

"I like the sound of that. Do you want to soak in the hot tub? I know you love them."

I pull back, delighted. "You remembered?"

"Hard to forget the image of you in that white bikini." He trails featherlight fingers over my clavicle to push my spaghetti strap off one shoulder as his other hand teases my waist, lifting the hem of my tank top. He pulls my hips to his and drops his mouth to my neck.

I slide Beau's shirt up, and he yanks it off, dropping it to the floor. We strip in fits and starts as he pulls me toward the back deck, fumbling for the porch light. I open the patio door, and the sound of the waves roars to greet us as I step out of my shorts and underwear in one move, letting them fall to the redwood deck.

Beau whistles once—a low release of air—before he says, "I thought nothing would top that bikini."

I'm laid bare in the moonlight, resisting the urge to cover myself because I'm feeling naked in more ways than one. The wind dances across my skin as his eyes heat. "Come here," he growls. I watch as he drops his pants, stepping into the hot tub with an arm outstretched to me. The water is a tonic, so hot it shocks me; the contrast is stark against the brisk night. And Beau is there, wrapping me in his arms

The Truth Is in the Detours

and pulling my thighs around his hips as the water bubbles and churns. Beau's breath is warm on my lips, his body solid, smooth, and slippery. I clasp my hands around his neck and fall into a kiss I hope gives me the strength to deal with what comes tomorrow.

And the thought creeps in again. I love this man. I love him with a certainty that astounds me. I've been sure of nothing in my life, and my lack of conviction has enabled me to float above want, to be satisfied when disappointment could have owned me.

There's an expiration date looming—to this trip, to this version of us—but I'm starting to daydream about making us work. About laying my heart out for him—more naked than I've ever allowed myself.

I love him.

And I'm crying. The tears trail down my cheeks, and tightness constricts my throat as if the love itself has a fist around it. I bury my face into his neck and inhale as his hands thread into my hair and he pulls back to look at me.

"What's wrong?" He kisses my cheek, my eyes, my nose.

"Nothing's wrong," I whisper.

"Why are you crying?"

"I'm happy," I admit. "This moment, right here. And maybe I won't be happy tomorrow. And I certainly wasn't three weeks ago. But here. With you and the moon and sea and the goddamn sky full of stars, I'm so happy that it's overflowing."

He laughs—this rich, delighted sound—and pulls me back into him, brushing lips over mine until our kiss mixes with my tears, and the stars rain over us, and the ocean plays the only song we agree on.

CHAPTER 34

I sneak out of the cottage when Beau is still tangled in sheets, his bare chest exposed to the cool air, limbs splayed across the mattress.

We made love twice last night. Once hurried and desperate, falling onto the sheets when we were still damp from the hot tub. And again, after finishing our road-trip snacks and a bottle of wine. He let me stay in the moment, but I noticed him watching me with that furrowed brow. He was playing carefree to appease me. Something is weighing on him, and I can't discern whether he's worried about me or what he'll face when he returns home.

Café Huckleberry opens in twenty minutes. I could wait until a reasonable hour, when I'm not queasy from lack of sleep as well as nerves and terror. But if Mary's the pastry chef, she's more likely to work the early shift, and I don't want to risk missing her—after traveling across a constellation of points to end up where we started.

I go alone because I don't want a witness in case she confirms that she never wanted me anyway. So I leave before Beau wakes.

It's a sunless morning of taupe clouds too bland to be cheery or ominous. The coastline, which gleamed like a jeweled tiara in the sunset, is indiscernible in the fog.

I head out on foot—walking along the shoulder of the highway until an unpaved trail opens to the beach and dumps me onto packed sand at low tide. I bury my nose in Beau's Harvard sweatshirt, ball my fists in the pockets, and brace against the too-cold July air. And then I see an old red barn with CAFÉ HUCKLEBERRY written in white script on a wooden placard. The building is perched along the highway, right across from the beach. It sits on its haunches, shoulders pressed against other historic buildings that have been transformed into trendy shops and restaurants. The short strip of shops is more tourist stopover than true attraction, a blip in an article on the West's hidden gems. They would all fit neatly into one postcard, and the red barn would be the highlight of the shot. It's bright, vibrant, and memorable—and not just because it's where my "dead" mother bakes the best scones found on the California coast.

I kick the sand off my shoes as I walk up the wooden beach-access steps and onto the road. There are several cars parked in the diagonal spaces in front of Café Huckleberry, and another handful at the store next door.

I wait for a vintage green truck to pass before making my way across the road and straight through the open doors of the café.

And then I freeze.

She's behind the counter, her smile wide as she chats with a customer. Her laugh echoes in the converted barn and reaches me at some primitive level. I remember it—the sound, the feel, the vibration of it. And then I can't hear anything because the volume of my heartbeat dials up to blaring. My face is on fire, my hands numb.

I have to look away from her to steady my breathing. The café is white and airy, with a window to the orderly pastry kitchen in the back. It smells like salt air, sugar, and every memory I wish we'd made.

A man, her husband with the cartoon name, calls to me. He's unloading merchandise onto shelves near the front. I hadn't noticed him when I stepped through, but now he's a few feet away, smiling, welcoming me to Café Huckleberry. And I have a ridiculous thought that he reminds me of Dad. He doesn't look like Henry Dahl. He has dark eyes to Dad's gray, white hair to Dad's salt-and-pepper. Lanky where Dad was wide and imposing. But his smile—it's disarming like Dad's, and the way he offered welcome was so genuine. They both have a knack for making a turn of phrase sound meaningful. When Dad told me that he loved me, I believed him.

Or maybe I'm projecting. Misremembering. Misinterpreting. Because my dormant emotions have roared to life and gone haywire. Sifting between present and past and contaminated by pain and shock and disbelief.

"Thank you," I think I say, but I can't be sure.

I walk to the counter, waiting behind three other customers, listening to my mother's throaty laugh. She knows these people. She asks a customer about his mother's recovery from hip surgery. She offers a few suggestions to a tourist looking for hiking trails with ocean views. I saw her beaming photo yesterday and got my proof of life through her vivid website, but seeing her here—smiling, happy, connected—is not a reality I could have prepared for. Because it proves the lie. It confirms she's alive and well, and fine without me.

I step forward and she looks at me expectantly. Her gray-blond hair is swept into a makeshift bun, her face tan and creased by laugh and worry lines in equal measure. Her right front tooth crowds the left, overlapping slightly. "Welcome. What can I get you?" she asks.

But I'm suddenly incapable of speaking, of acknowledging this moment. And if I'm honest, I'm waiting for her to know me. For her to recognize me through the molecular connection of motherhood that every piece of fiction fooled me into trusting.

I want her to remember me like I remember her—as an ache.

But nothing. A generic smile is offered in return. "I made a special batch of custard-filled croissants this morning. The bear claw is a local favorite. And there's always our specialty—the huckleberry scone."

I part my lips to speak but choke on every word that bubbles up.

Her worry lines etch deep, and I see my future. The way my forehead will wrinkle. The way my jawline will soften with age. The

The Truth Is in the Detours

way I might fail to figure my shit out, screw everything up, and hurt everyone who loved me.

"Yes," I hear myself say. She grins and tilts her head to study me. "Which one?"

"One of each, I guess," I say as her husband steps behind the counter to help the next customer.

"Are you here on vacation?" She turns to pull pastries out of the case with wax paper.

"My mother moved here." It tumbles out of my mouth—this truth that feels like a lie.

"Oh, how lovely," she says. "We've been here six years now. Never been happier."

The platitude, the meaningless expression, is a dull blade sawing at my breastbone. "Yeah, I can see that."

She freezes as she places a pink pastry box on the counter. She tilts her head, assessing me. My tone is strange enough that she looks unsettled. It's not like she recognizes me. Hell, maybe she's willed herself to forget I was ever hers.

I was wrong. The time is here, and I still don't know what I want to say to her. I haven't even had my coffee yet and I'm trying to find words to ask her why she abandoned me. Or command her to recognize me, fall at my feet, beg me for forgiveness.

I'm looking for closure. But there isn't any. There's no closed loop when the story is a sinkhole that's expanding faster than I can fill it.

"That'll be $19.43," she says.

There's only a ten-dollar bill in my wallet, so I hand her my credit card and she swipes it, still studying me as I grab my order.

"Have a great visit, Ms. . . ." Her eyes flash to my card and hang there for *one, two, three*. She drops it on the counter, swallows, and stills. And then she looks at me like she's calculating whether she can escape. Her breathing becomes uneven when her gaze snares on my pendant. I grab it, covering the face with my fingertips—as if I can guard the fairy tale of her from the terrible reality of her.

"Dad is dead," I say. And she chokes on a breath. "But I was surprised to learn you are not."

Her eyes widen before she begins blinking rapidly. One hand goes to her stomach and the other to her chest, and she steps back.

"I can't," she says. And it's a whisper, almost soundless. "I can't do this."

Jack Huckleberry steps beside her, an arm going to the small of her back. "Mare?" he asks—one syllable soaked with concern and comfort.

Mary stares at me behind her palm with something like fear or denial in her eyes.

"Yeah," I say, begging my voice not to betray my heartache, "I guess you never could." I slip outside as my breakdown stalks me like a predator.

I was stupid. I came all the way here, presenting myself to her like an opportunity for her absolution. But you can't make someone apologize or care about the hurt they've caused. You can't make someone love you who's made it clear they don't.

I lose my way as I race back to the cottage, overshooting the trailhead and backtracking a mile. By the time I return, Beau is pacing in the driveway in his running clothes.

He exhales and falls forward with his hands on his knees. "Jesus, Phe. You've been gone hours. You left your cell on the counter and didn't leave a note. Are you okay?" He strides over to meet me at the end of the drive, and I hand him the pink box, crushed under my arm. He reads the logo on the seal and moves to me, dropping the box and cupping my jaw in his palm. "What happened?"

I inhale, but the air is too thick for a full breath. "She wouldn't talk to me." And my knees buckle as I succumb to sobs. Beau catches me, holding me together with my nose against his chest and his chin tucked into my hair. His arms are wrapped, strong and sure, around my torso as my shoulders shake. Beau strokes my back with insistent palms, open and warm, buoying me through my sobs.

The Truth Is in the Detours

"I'm so sorry, Phe," he whispers, like a confession pressed into my hair, low and hushed, desperate to soothe me, but I am incapable of it. "So sorry."

My tears drench his shirt with salt, and I grip his waist with my fists and let him wring the grief out of me. Grief for a dad I thought I knew, for a mom I thought I'd already mourned, and for a history—bleak though it could be—that I thought I understood.

CHAPTER 35

Beau doesn't ask any more questions, and I don't offer any answers as we drive back to his house in Oakland. I sleep. I wake and stare out the window. He reaches out periodically to rub my shoulder, squeeze my thigh, hold my hand, until I recline the seat and fall into a deeper sleep, emerging into half consciousness as he exits the freeway. It reminds me of road trips with Dad, when I'd wake upon parking but fake sleep so he'd carry me inside.

I feel drugged—aware of the sun on my face, the steady strum of tires against city streets, but I'm in a partial dream state where I imagine we're pulling up to a new town filled with new truths where Mary's is the face of each confessor. I drift out again but am trying to claw my way back to consciousness when the car stops. I hear Beau say, "Phe," in a soft hush. A warm hand comes to my shoulder, jostling me. But my lids are so heavy.

There's shuffling beside me, the car door creaking open.

"Bianca, what are you doing here?" he asks, his voice muffled as the door closes behind him.

And I'm wide awake, going shock still on the reclined seat.

Bianca says something I don't hear. But then her voice is closer, clearer, and floats in through Beau's open window. "You said you'd be home days ago. You didn't answer your phone, and I was worried." She sounds like a concerned wife, like someone accustomed to his updates. For the second time today, I wish I could disappear into mist.

The Truth Is in the Detours

Why is she here? Has she been waiting on the porch for days? Popping in just in case he'd come home? Who would do that without reason to hope they'd be greeted with open arms?

"You can't keep coming over unannounced. That's not how this works."

I wish someone could tell me how it's supposed to work—how I'm supposed to handle myself. I can't *pretend* to be in love with Beau—now that I am. I can't be his wingman, because I have to be my own, and right now I feel like I'm flying solo without a parachute.

I take two deep breaths, smooth my hair away from my face, and open the door. Their voices silence as I step out.

"You're awake," Beau says. His eyes are wide behind his glasses. There's something in his expression I can't read—apology, sympathy, guilt? My meter is off. As I look from Beau to Bianca and back, I want to ask him again whether I'm getting in the way of their reconciliation. But my heart wants to ask a different question—whether she's getting in the way of ours.

Because whatever vows they made, she broke. And he feels like mine now.

I swallow and nod before turning to Bianca. "Hi," I say, unable to find other words. She's in periwinkle scrubs, as if she came straight from a long shift at the hospital. She has no makeup on but still looks pretty and composed as she inspects me. There's no malice in her expression—just hurt, confusion, panic, surprise. I know instantly that she didn't know I was still traveling with Beau. He must not have mentioned me when they last spoke—or maybe she assumed I was "out of his system by now."

"I didn't know you'd be here." Bianca tightens her arms across her chest, confirming my suspicion.

"Ophelia is my research assistant," Beau says, and there's an irrational part of me that hates him for explaining me away as anything other than, what—his girlfriend? We've made no promises to each other. But two weeks ago, he rushed to my side so Bianca would think

I was important to him. And now, just when I thought I was, he's made me feel insignificant.

But for some reason, I double down. "I transcribed the interviews."

For a few moments, the three of us say nothing, trapped in a stalemate. Bianca looks from me to Beau and back, and her eyes well up with tears. And despite how terribly she hurt him, despite how she may have the power to hurt me, too, I feel sorry for her. She wants him back. And if anyone knows how much it must hurt to lose him, it's me.

My phone rings, piercing the silence. I fish it out of my pocket and sigh when I see Ronald's name light up the screen. "I've got to get this."

Beau moves to me. I picture him wrapping me in his arms, giving me some assurance that we're okay, but instead, he hands me his keys, the house key clutched between his index finger and thumb.

"Thanks," I mumble, taking it without letting my hand brush his, without meeting his gaze. Bianca steps aside as I climb the steps.

The lock is merciful and allows me inside quickly. I close the door and pace across the polished wood floors as dust floats in panels of light, and Beau and Bianca pick up their conversation in the front yard.

"Ronald, hi," I say when I answer the call, my voice shaky and raw from my earlier sobs. I've said almost nothing since I admitted that my mother sent me away. It feels like a lifetime ago—as if it happened to some other broken version of myself.

~

A half hour later, Beau finds me on the back deck, sitting on the steps leading to the lawn.

When he closes the French doors behind him and turns to me, his expression is such a tableau of regret that I know something is off. I don't know what question to ask. But either way, I don't think I'll like the answer.

The Truth Is in the Detours

So I sidestep. "I agreed to the buyer's demands. I need to get back to sign the documents and grab the last of my dad's things I stored in the attic."

"How do you feel about it?" He sits next to me—but there's more space between us than there has been in days. It feels like a gulf.

"I bought my flight back to San Diego; I leave this evening."

He exhales, runs his hand through his hair. "Oh. Wow. I thought you said you'd stay?"

"Is Bianca gone?"

"I'm sorry, Phe." He slouches, leaning against the spindles of the railing like he can't keep himself upright. "She still has my phone hooked up to her tracking app. I didn't think to disable her access. So she rushed here when she saw I was on my way. She says she was worried because I stopped answering her calls, but I don't know."

"She still thinks there is hope for you two." It's obvious. And she's a smart woman—a doctor, for fuck's sake. She's not delusional or crazy. Something—someone—has given her hope.

Why didn't I ask him more questions?

Because I didn't expect to sleep with him. And I certainly didn't expect to fall in love with him. And what she did seemed unforgivable. She betrayed him, lied to him, made him believe her baby was his, and let him take the blame for her miscarriage. How could he possibly trust her again?

And the answer appears like a puzzle piece found on the floor, waiting to complete the picture.

A professor would seek to understand in order to forgive.

I've been so stupid.

"This trip wasn't about just understanding why she did what she did—it was about forgiving her. It was about reconciling." My voice is a rattle.

"No." He shakes his head and scoots closer.

"If you could understand her deception, then maybe you could forgive her and take her back."

"No," Beau says, but he stands and drums his fingers on his leg. I look at his hands, and he stills them, shoving them in his pockets as he paces in front of me. "Okay, maybe at first," he sighs, and then he unleashes like he's pleading a desperate case. "When Bianca finally spilled the truth, I asked for a divorce *that* day. I was done—unwilling to listen or forgive. And then after the miscarriage, I began to wonder whether I had given up too soon. Was I unforgiving? Too rigid? Too judgmental? Could I forgive her if I understood how people could lie and still love? And I made the mistake of mentioning it to Bianca in a moment of weakness—months ago. That's when she started all her games, her stalling tactics. She refused to sign the papers until I was back because—"

"Because you'd told her you might change your mind. That there was a chance you'd take her back." I don't recognize the thin sound of my own voice. This awareness, this recognition, has taken all the air from my lungs. Why the hell didn't I see it before?

He drops his head.

"Beau. How could you keep that from me? We promised each other the truth."

"You knew I wrote the book to understand," he tries.

"To understand—and maybe for closure. But not to take her back." I'm sick to my stomach, and my hands are shaking, but I don't want to show him how much his lie by omission has crushed me. Obviously, he was keeping his options open while pretending he was a real option for me.

"But it didn't matter, because I realized that maybe I could forgive her, but that didn't mean I should be with her again."

I stand, meeting him at eye level from where I'm perched on the second step. "But you wanted to?"

"No." His voice cracks on the syllable. "I didn't. Not since—"

"Since when? Since the last time we were here when you pretended we were together? You weren't trying to show her you'd moved on—you were trying to make her jealous."

The Truth Is in the Detours

"No, Phe. I knew before that."

I should have seen this coming. Beau married her. He vowed to love her forever in front of their families and friends. All he did was whisper confessions against my skin in private.

He's promised me nothing. But I've surrendered to him my whole heart.

He convinced me to drop my weapons and let down my guard and then took aim when I finally felt safe. What the hell was all this stupid growth for—the intimacy and honesty—other than to prime myself for the knife to slide in easier?

"You lied to me. I never would have . . ." I can't even say it. "If you told me there was a chance for your marriage."

"There isn't. Not now. Look . . ." He slides his hands through his hair. "You've never been married. It's complicated, and divorce is messy, and this year has been painful and confusing and—"

"So now it's complicated? You're confused?" Not only is he trying to justify his dishonesty, but he's using my sad relationship track record against me and implying it's my fault I don't understand. I want to find deflection or indifference—my trusty shields—but they're both failing me.

Beau stops in front of me, shakes his head, and tries to reach for my hand, but I yank it free. The hurt on his face makes me want to run away, to collapse, to rewind to the time when he was a sacred piece of my history and not the person breaking my heart.

"Beau, I just wanted the truth. The full truth. I didn't ask you for anything else." It's what we promised each other.

"I was embarrassed to admit that I considered taking her back after she got pregnant with another man's baby. That wasn't something I wanted to share with the woman I hoped would respect me."

"You lied to me to protect your pride?"

"Phe, please." His voice is desperate now. He steps closer, and the proximity makes my heart hurt from wounds so old that I can't distinguish between this moment and a million others. I've heard *Phe, please* too many times by the other man who broke my heart. Every time Matty dismissed me, belittled me, or cheated on me, it was *Phe, please. Overlook this, be cool, don't make it a big deal, feel less.*

I can't tolerate that from Beau of all people, who has been insisting that I stop ignoring my feelings and doubting my worth.

"You used me to even the score with your wife so you could take her back." My voice cracks on the words, and anger and mistrust are coursing through me, pouring from this gaping wound. This morning, I still had hope that the reason my mom left me—and my dad lied to me—was somehow forgivable. This morning, I had hope that the love Beau and I found could survive when we stopped running.

But there's nothing I can do to make the people I love choose me. I can chase them across state lines, forgive them for past transgressions, and open myself up to new hurt—but I can't make them love me back.

"Ophelia, it isn't like that. You *know* it isn't like that. I'm sorry I didn't tell you—but I didn't tell you because I knew it wasn't going to matter, not because I was hiding how I felt." He reaches for my hand, and I pull it back before his touch can burn me.

"Were you getting something out of your system? Was Bianca right?"

"No!" he yells, pacing again in front of me. "How could you ask me that?"

"I don't know, Beau. I don't have a stellar track record of knowing when someone is telling me the truth."

His chest rises and falls, his hands on his hips. "Well, here's the truth. When you came back into my life, I came alive again. And I want us to figure out how to be together. Finally."

"I don't believe you." I want to—I want his words to be the truth. But I'm the worst version of myself right now—scared, insecure, lost, and so fucking angry. And my memory reel is replaying all the worst versions of him, too. I see the Beau who avoided me after our first kiss. I see the Beau who begrudgingly rescued me from all my poor decisions but judged me for them. I see the Beau who tossed aside the last crumbs of our friendship when he moved away.

The Truth Is in the Detours

I see the Beau who asked another woman to marry him, and who considered forgiving the unforgivable to be with her forever.

I see the shiniest version of Beau, too—in soft-filtered shots beside his beautiful wife. What can I possibly offer Beau but nostalgia, but a broken girl trying—and failing—to figure out who she wants to be. I'm nothing more than a consolation prize.

"Phe—"

"But why?" I whisper. "Why would you want to be with me?" My only real relationship ended when he found someone better, smarter, more suitable.

And my own mother doesn't even want me.

"Why?" he sighs, exasperated. "Because I do . . . Because I have *always* wanted you," he stutters out, anger making his words hollow. "How has that not been embarrassingly clear?"

He is close enough to pull me into his arms but doesn't. His mouth is near enough that I could seek solace in his kiss. But I don't.

I love him. But not enough to trust him.

Or maybe not enough to trust myself.

"I don't know how to believe you."

He steps closer still, his toes touching the bottom step and leaning toward me like a trust fall. He finds my gaze and his well-deep eyes bore into me. "I don't know what more to say, Phe. If you don't believe you can be loved, I don't know how the hell to convince you I do."

CHAPTER 36

Beau's words play on a loop when I climb into my Uber a few moments later, leaving him in the backyard of his empty house. I didn't—couldn't—look at him as I left. Because I wanted to scream at him and comfort him and collapse into his chest. And I didn't trust any of my instincts. So I said I needed time—time to process everything that's happened since Dad died.

The dull ache in my heart becomes a sharp stab on each inhale when I arrive at the airport. So I keep my breathing shallow.

I wake to a replay of his words as the wheels touch down in San Diego. The words chant at me like an angry chorus as I pull up at my family home, which doesn't look like my home at all.

Dad painted the house dove gray when we moved in. But decades of salt air and sunlight transformed it to moss green, so it was the first upgrade that Ronald and his team completed before the house went on the market. Now, it stands proud—starched and pressed and dressed in stark white and black trim. The pathway is clean, revealing crimson brick, lined with a verdant row of infant hedges leading to the newly painted porch. I've been gone three weeks, and the home I knew for thirty years is gone. It is wiped of all memories and ready to contain someone else's joys, tears, deceptions, and confessions. I have two days to remove the boxes stashed in the attic, sign paperwork, and say goodbye forever.

The Truth Is in the Detours

But I can't obsess over that tonight. I have barely enough strength to fall into my old bed, which is staged with fresh bedding that no longer smells of home. Gone is the lingering scent of coffee and tea tree oil—the essence of Dad.

The next two days are a blur of signatures, walk-throughs, and a mad scramble to load the rest of Dad's stuff into my car. I don't have the fortitude to filter through the filth and feelings. I'll have to do that once I get it home.

I don't hear from Beau. Not the first day. Not the next. And I don't want to. Not really. Because I don't want to *feel*, well . . . anything.

I need time. I'm too raw to make a good decision right now. But somehow, I'm still heartbroken by every call that's not from him. I don't know whether I'm an idiot for walking away or an idiot for thinking he could love me in the first place. After all the lies and rejection that have marred my life, my trust meter is broken.

As I'm loading a box into my passenger seat, Lani appears on my right. She doesn't say anything before she pulls me into a hug, swaying on the concrete in the unrelenting glare of the sun. It's the first time I've let myself tear up since I walked away from Beau, since I caught him in my peripheral vision hunched over the railing of his deck with his head bowed.

"I can't believe you're leaving us," she says, and I wonder what she means—how much she knows—until she asks, "When does the house close?"

"Two days," I say, wiping my eyes with the back of my hand. "But I'm heading back to LA tomorrow."

She clutches my hands. "You always have a home here with us, you know. If you miss your hometown or Hawaiian food."

"Thanks," I whisper through the knot in my throat. But do I still have a home here? Did I cut this last tether, too?

"I'm so glad you and Beau have each other again, especially now." She wipes a strand of hair away from my face. "I always knew you'd find your way back to each other. Two peas, you two."

Beau is the first thought in the morning and the last image filtering through my haze as I fight for sleep. But still, the mention of him sends shivers along the surface of my skin and sinks a sour bomb in my gut.

"More like oil and water."

She laughs. "And sometimes bleach and ammonia. But always a pair."

"I don't know. I think we may have combusted for the last time."

She pats my arm. "Not possible." Her kind eyes crinkle at the corners, and she winks. It's as if she knows. Maybe not everything. But suspects—something? Because Lani always knows.

"I know that boy can be a bit hard to read. Sometimes too serious and guarded. But he has a soft spot a mile wide for you. You know why he was here so long after the funeral, don't you?"

I shake my head. I assumed it had to do with helping his parents, or hiding from Bianca, or working on his book. I remember how often I'd rush into the house those early weeks after Dad died, trying to avoid him.

She tilts her head, a sad smile tugging at her lips. "He postponed his interviews and stayed to make sure you were okay. Even after you ran from him at the hospital and the funeral. Even when you ignored every knock on your door. I told him you needed a bit of time. That you don't like to face your feelings head-on, but he kept going over. Every day until he finally had to storm in. He stayed in town because he couldn't leave without making sure you were taken care of."

When I stumble back inside, I have a hard time catching my breath. Beau made me think Lani was the instigator, that Beau came over on her orders—that our clumsy reconciliation was reluctant on his part.

I grab my phone and click over to messages, pressing play on the familiar recording: *"Ophelia, love, it's your dear old dad, checking in . . ."* I press my ear closer. *"Well, I love you. Call me. No matter how late."*

Then I replay the message that follows, one I haven't listened to since the day Dad died. *"Ophelia, this is Beau. Beau Augustin. I've called a few times. But it occurs to me you don't have this number and might not answer unknown numbers. I'm visiting my parents—your dad was here*

The Truth Is in the Detours

watching the Padres game with us. And . . . Phe." There's silence on the line for a moment. *"Your dad is being taken to UC San Diego Medical Center. I'm sorry to have to leave this message, but you need to come home. Now."*

I had run to my car before I'd listened to Beau's full message. The sky was cerulean and the clouds fluffy and cute—the kind of perfect weather no one had any right to enjoy on the day my dad left this earth.

But because Beau called, and kept calling, I made it in time to hold Dad's hand as he took his last breath. I made it in time to tell him I loved him back.

CHAPTER 37

Many of my worst decisions have been Cherry's idea, and this one is no exception. I'm too old for this. Too tired. Too weary. And I'm certainly too ancient for these shoes, which are a half size too small and digging into my heels. I feel like the oldest thirty-four-year-old alive. The depressing cocktail of grief and heartbreak will do that.

"You promised me," Cherry had wailed over the phone. "You have to spend your last night in San Diego with me."

I would have preferred to accept Lani's invitation for a family meal. I wanted to curl up on the couch in their family room and pretend my world hadn't tilted on its axis and tossed me on my ass. But I had promised Cherry, and I want to be a better friend. I've been angry with her about the stunt she pulled with Beau all those years ago—but I can't write her off for something she did at seventeen. We were all slightly crueler versions of ourselves then.

"Finally." She drops her purse on the stool next to mine. "I needed a night off. You have no idea how good you have it—only having to worry about yourself."

I slide her the Manhattan I ordered for her, and she moans. "How I've missed you," she says to the glass before taking a sip. "I'll have to pump and dump, but it's worth it. If I leave it to Austin, he'd never get my drink." She gestures to her husband, who is standing at the bar, riveted to a baseball game playing on the big screen.

The Truth Is in the Detours

"Cheers," I say, holding up my seltzer water. My stomach is in knots—food and alcohol aren't sitting well these days.

She clinks her glass to mine. "So tell me. Where did you go on your road trip? You left town without telling anyone."

"Up along the coast to Oregon. I had to get away." And leave a piece of my bruised heart on every interstate along the way.

She brushes her long brown hair over her shoulder. She's always had great hair, and tonight it looks like she's had a professional blowout. I couldn't produce those sexy waves with hair extensions and two stylists. "I wish. To be able to be so carefree."

I smile, but it's brittle, as if my lips might crack from the effort. I'd buried Dad only six weeks ago. Dad, who called her Cherry Blossom, who chauffeured us around town for years, who would make her aebleskivers when she'd spend the night. And it's like she's forgotten him.

Cherry waves to Simone and her wife, Alyanna, as they slip into the bar through the heavy wooden doors. Cherry didn't mention spouses were invited. I like Austin and Alyanna just fine, but I didn't know I'd be the fifth wheel.

Simone strides over in four graceful steps, balancing on red stilettos with a silver sequin clutch in one hand. She looks like she's dressed for the red carpet, not an evening out at Coach's Bar, the dive we frequented in our early twenties. She pulls me into a hug.

Alyanna is right behind her but is called over to the bar by Austin.

"Our nomad. We were worried you'd never come back." Simone hugs me.

"You know me. I can't commit to anything for too long—even aimlessness."

Simone laughs. "Too true. It's why we love you."

"Ophelia Dahl: saying fuck you to achievement culture long before it was cool." Cherry laughs.

I shouldn't be offended. I said it. They just agreed. I've always felt safer getting the barbs in before someone else launches them. But my friends have a knack for sinking them deeper. Maybe it's why I haven't told them about my mother or Beau. I risk multiplying my heartbreak by sharing it.

I wish I hadn't come. I yearn for the scratchy texture of motel sheets, a too-thin pillow, and a grumbling Beau complaining about the rom-com I've chosen on pay-per-view. I yearn for the person who knows me to the bone.

"You're so quiet, Phe. What's up?" Simone asks.

"Just tired."

"Tired?" Cherry says. "Childless people don't know tired. We haven't really hung out in eons. Austin's mom has the kids for an overnight." She drapes an arm over my shoulders and tilts her head against mine. "I need Fun Ophelia tonight."

Fun Ophelia. Who is that? She'd crack a self-deprecating joke. Maybe later, she'd sing bad karaoke. But that Ophelia hadn't lived through a personal apocalypse.

"I have to use the restroom," I mumble, and slink off the stool before either of them can follow.

The floor of the one-stall restroom is sticky. The walls are covered with sanctioned graffiti—elaborate sketches and statements that chronicle twenty years of cultural history. The lighting is dim, but I reapply lipstick—my favorite shade of blush pink that picks up the color still clinging to the ends of my hair. I brush on a bit more mascara. Perhaps if I play the part, I can get through the night. But the girl who looks back at me doesn't feel like me anymore—but like a wax figure.

I step into the hallway as a man enters the corridor. He's three paces away, and it takes me each stride to place him. The upturned blue eyes—although bordered by thin lines now. The wavy hair, still full despite Beau's sabotage.

"Dahl!" Matty envelops me in a hug, his hands curled against my spine and his forehead dropped to my neck. "Cherry said you'd be here." He pulls back, inspecting me. "Sorry about your dad."

"Thanks," I mumble on autopilot. Cherry invited him?

The Truth Is in the Detours

"How have you been?" He smiles at me—as if it's been a few months, not a decade since I changed my number and fled San Diego to commit to the fifth and final breakup.

"Fine." It's more truth than lie. Because until six weeks ago, I was fine. No highs. No lows. A job that paid the bills. Enough distractions to prevent me from yearning for more. Fine.

"You look good," he says.

"You too." But I don't mean it. He's still handsome enough. But his face has lost all its luster. Like a word you say so many times it becomes gibberish, a handsome face that spills toxicity too often becomes poisoned. He looks like my passivity, my poor boundaries, my regret.

He has a hand on my waist and drags his thumb over my bottom rib. The pit in my stomach expands, threatening to swallow me from inside.

I step back. "I'll see you, Matty." I slip to the side to return to the table, but he follows.

"Let me buy you a drink." He places his hand on my lower back, splayed across my spine like he owns me, leading me toward the bar.

I trip down the hall beside him but stop short as we enter the bar area. He turns toward me, ducking his head. "Baby Dahl." The old term of endearment curls off his tongue like a whip, as if he's been waiting to unleash it all this time.

There's no part of me that's been waiting to hear it.

"Don't," I say, and find space between us.

He chuckles and straightens to his full height, as if he didn't mean it anyway. "Still like mojitos?"

I shake my head. "I have a drink at the table." I almost escape, but Cherry appears at my side, sliding her arm around my waist and reaching for Matty's wrist.

"You found her," Cherry coos.

"He did," I bite.

"Do you need a drink, Cher?"

"Manhattan," she says.

Matty winks at me and heads to the bar.

"Cherry, what the fuck?"

"What?" she says, her doe eyes wide and innocent.

"You invited Matty?"

She waves a hand between us. "Oh, Phe. It's been so long. And he just broke up with Jace. And you're so lonely. I thought you might want to reconnect." Jace—the woman he cheated with last. I am somehow always the understudy for more deserving women.

"Matty is the last person I need to deal with today." How is this not a *given* to one of my oldest friends?

"Can't we all be friends again? It's a pain in the ass that we have to see you separately. Ten years. That's a long time to hang on to baggage better left in the past."

And in the dim light of Coach's Bar, it's clear to me. Some things *are* better left in the past.

Like this friendship.

Cherry hasn't grown up at all; she is just as cruel as she was when she drove a wedge between Beau and me in high school.

"You're right, Cherry," I say before I turn and walk out of the bar into the clear night.

∼

Dad's house is so unfamiliar. Glowing in the moonlight now, rather than sinking into the background like the wallflower it was. It strikes me anew when I pull into the driveway for the last time, anxious to crash after my shitty night. The car sputters and twitches in the quiet—a reminder I need a new car, in addition to new friends and a new life. I leave it gasping in the driveway as I trudge up the porch to wrangle with the lockbox the Realtor installed.

I startle at my name, turning abruptly and spotting a figure emerging from the car parked across the street.

"I'm sorry; I didn't mean to scare you."

The Truth Is in the Detours

I crane toward the woman's voice, my eyes adjusting to make her out, and my heart gallops, each beat coming faster than the last, until adrenaline surges.

"What are you doing here?"

Mary doesn't say anything for a moment, but hovers with a hand on the railing and one foot on the bottom step. She's backlit from the streetlamp, and her hair casts a halo around her silhouette. She's dressed in slacks and a cardigan, as if ready for a job interview.

"I looked for you," she says.

"What? When? Are you saying Dad kidnapped me or something?" I don't even try to iron out the skepticism. I saw the paperwork. Her rights were terminated. Whatever mistakes Dad may have made, he didn't commit a crime.

"No," she says, her voice shaking. "After you came to the café. I tried to find you on social media."

"My accounts are private," I say. I don't use my full name online.

She nods. "There's a private investigator who is a regular at the café. He found this address and one in Pasadena. I went there first."

She could have found me years ago had she wanted to.

"Why are you here?"

She takes another big breath and wipes a wispy strand of hair away from her face with the back of her hand. "To apologize."

I cross my arms over my chest, trying to hide that my hands are shaking. "I think it's a bit late for that."

But she is undeterred. "An explanation, then." Her voice is lower than I remember, but perhaps I've created the memory of her out of nothing. A fiction, like the rest of my life. "I didn't handle it well, last week. I was caught off guard and—"

"Should I have waited for an invitation?"

She holds up her hands in a gesture of ceasefire. "I should have handled it better."

"Okay."

"I'd like to explain, if that's something you're open to." She shifts her purse higher on her shoulder and pulls her cardigan taut as if bracing herself from the cold. But it's a warm night, almost too warm.

"Now?" I say with incredulity, because apparently, I think she deserves the worst version of me—petulant adolescent—as punishment for her absence.

Her words come out rapid-fire. "Or anytime. Whenever you're ready. I can come back. Here to San Diego. Or wherever you're going to be." She waves to the PENDING Realtor's sign perched like a countdown clock in front of the house.

I release an exhausted sigh and relent. Rock bottom is the best place to have this conversation. I finally feel like I'll know what to ask and how to respond, because I've lost all hope that the answers will address my pain. My anticipation has settled into resignation. She left me, and when I found her, she didn't weep in relief or beg my forgiveness. She sent me away. I'll let her talk because she owes me answers, even if it feels academic. "Now is fine."

She nods once, then again, and puts her weight on the step before drawing it back down, unsure where to go.

"I'd invite you in, but there's no furniture. Or lamps. Or anything, really."

"Here is good," she says quickly.

I sink onto the top step and wave her up. The porch creaks under her feet, and she crouches until she's seated on the other side. I have a pang—a flashbulb memory of Dad and me here in these same spots. Sometimes we'd start a conversation on a drive and pause here to finish, as if the house would swallow up the magic of the impromptu heart-to-heart.

"Okay." I swallow. "I'm listening."

"How much do you know?" she asks.

"Almost nothing," I say. "I found a portion of the parental termination document after Dad died."

The Truth Is in the Detours

She exhales. "Okay, I guess I'll start at the beginning." She dips her metaphorical toe in the truth, testing the waters.

I've seen this pattern. I think of our interview subjects: their fear, hesitation, expectation of condemnation. I channel my professional distance, but it's out of reach. I feel a momentary ache that Beau isn't here as a buffer, that I'll have to gather this most personal truth on my own. "It's usually the best place to start."

"I was a troubled kid—never got along well with my family. I was moody, impulsive, and often a bit erratic, I guess."

I blink, trying to focus. I anticipated "the beginning" might give me more immediate answers—and the spindles of the porch railing are jammed in my spine, the hard wooden steps uncomfortable on my tailbone. I shift, and Mary watches me before quickening the pace of her words.

"I left home when I was seventeen, and I met Henry, fell in love, and I was stable for a while. I was young and foolish and thought he was all I needed to be okay." She stops, looks across the lawn, toward the other side of the street, before stealing a glance my way. "Illness doesn't work like that, though. And when I had you—well, I got worse. I had postpartum psychosis, which no one understood all that well then. And I honestly don't remember much about that time. But I left you alone in the bath when you were a few months old." She drops her head in her hands, and her shoulders are hunched, her spine casting a thin shadow through her cardigan before she straightens to an unnatural posture—as if donning armor. "Henry came home, and . . . thank goodness. You were okay. But that's when I was hospitalized the first time.

"Henry did all the parenting from then on. When I got out, you two had this bond I couldn't penetrate. He tried to care for me, too. He did. But I was in and out of the hospital those first few years. That's when they said it wasn't just postpartum, it was triggered by undiagnosed bipolar disorder, and there was no cure."

She's silent for a few moments. But I don't have it in me to fill it. I search her mannerisms, voice, and face for evidence of me—like a scavenger hunt for belonging.

"I would come home with a plan. But I'd stop taking my meds and launch into another manic episode, followed by a depressive episode, and we'd be right back to where we started. In the end, your dad and I both chose to save you."

Emotions are pinballing in my chest faster than I can process them. Loss. Grief. Sorrow—that Dad spent a lifetime carrying the weight of our forged family lore on his shoulders. But mostly anger. At myself for being so gullible. At her for giving me up. At Dad for letting her.

"A mother doesn't leave because she's sick, because she refuses to take medication." My throat is constricted with an ache I can't clear, tight and scalding.

She looks away, folds her arms across her chest, and inhales, as if she's about to speak, but stalls out. On her third attempt, she speaks slowly. "I did a lot of dangerous things, Ophelia. During a manic episode, I pulled you out of preschool and drove all the way to Cannon Beach."

A memory appears—the sun on my face, the biting Pacific on my toes, my mom's laugh singing in the wind. "I remember that."

A smile passes across her face, but it's gone before she speaks again. "I didn't tell your dad we were going, or where we were. And before I could get back, the depression set in. We ended up in a dirty motel. Henry tracked the credit card and found us two days later."

I try to find that piece of the memory, but it's out of reach. Maybe it's for the best—that I only remember the high. I count my memories of her. I have a handful, but I always wondered how many were real and not conjured up by imagination and implanted by years of yearning.

"Henry gave me an ultimatum then. I'd get help, take my meds, or he'd leave and take you with him. But the illness—and mania especially—makes you think you're invincible, and the medicine is the enemy. So, eventually, I stopped the meds. And he left."

The Truth Is in the Detours

I've been listening, trying to collect her story like an impartial interviewer and pretend she's another Natalia, Jeremiah, or Alexander. But anger crashes over me like a tidal wave. How simple it would have been for her to take her meds and stay, swallow a pill and spare me a life without a mother.

Mary fidgets, picking at the cuticle on her thumb, and clears her throat before saying more. "It got ugly after he left. I'd show up at your apartment in the middle of the night. By that time, social services had been called in, and there was a case against me. It was clear I might even lose visitation." She falters. "When the courts threatened to come after my parental rights entirely, I showed up at your preschool, snuck onto the playground. By that time, Henry had told them I couldn't pick you up, couldn't see you. But you came to me, hugged me with your little chubby arms, and said 'Mama' in my ear. I took you and drove out of town. I kept driving for hours, through the night—until I lost control on black ice. I broke my leg in three places, had a collapsed lung, and a bad concussion. You got that scar. Ten stitches." She brings a fingertip to my forehead, and I jolt. She sighs and drops her hand.

"But telling me you were dead? Why? How could he?" Of all the choices he could make, he chose the nuclear option. Permanent. Agonizing. A hole he tried to fill with shifting sand. I reach for my necklace but flex my hand when I remember I'd taken it off two days ago. I drop my fist to my side.

"I was facing a lot of legal consequences and knew I was going to lose you. When Henry came to see me in the hospital, I wasn't in a good place. I told him that I was better off dead to both of you. I thought if there was a possibility that you were waiting for me, wondering about me, I'd keep coming back and eventually ruin you. I told Henry that I would rather you think I was dead than a deadbeat." She can barely get the last words out; her voice is frail and breathy. She takes in a gulp of air. "By the time I got out of the hospital, you and Henry were gone. Soon after, I found out I was legally dead to you. According to the law, I was no longer your mother."

I fight back the tears I'm not sure she deserves and let anger march out ahead. "That was such a permanent decision," I whisper. "And you're better now. You have a business. You're married. After you got well—"

"You were already grown by the time I got it under control with the right diet, meds, and therapy."

As if I ever stopped needing my mother. Missing her. Dreaming of her. My throat feels swollen—there is no way to get these next words out and still hold back the well of tears. "Did you ever think to come look for me?"

She shifts on the step, turning to face me fully, and takes a deep, steadying breath. "Those early years, I was in such a state that I was barely functioning. I tried to self-medicate. I was so ill." She pauses again. "I'm scared to tell you this, but I think you need to know. When I got into the treatment center, the one that finally worked—"

"In Redding?" I ask.

She looks startled, but then nods. "Yes. I was not . . ." She trails off. "Totally coherent when I arrived. And there was a mix-up with my medical records, and they couldn't find a next of kin. They found your dad somehow. It turns out billing departments are good detectives. A few days later, he showed up to visit me."

"What? He came to see you?" This betrayal feels like an even deeper cut. I figured—knowing Dad—he'd blocked it out, created a new reality and lived in it for the past thirty years. But this?

Her speech speeds up, and words come at me quickly. "He confessed he'd let you believe I was dead. That he'd lived in guilt over it, but when you were young, he was so scared that I'd reappear and take you, accidentally hurt you—or kill you—because I'd come close twice. He put distance between us to save you. But then he lived in fear that you'd find out the truth and hate him forever. You were his world, Ophelia." She takes a deep breath. "He was willing to risk telling you if I got better. But I was just starting my recovery and didn't fully believe that I *could* get better. And we made the decision not to blow up your world. To ensure you'd continue to have a solid, whole relationship with one parent rather than fractured ones with both."

Tears glisten at her lids, falling like raindrops she doesn't bother to wipe away.

"He gave me this, though." She draws out an envelope and pulls out a photo. It's of me and Dad on the beach at sunset, his arm draped over my shoulder. I'm thirteen, maybe fourteen. Beau is in the distance tossing a Frisbee with Arthur. The memory lands somewhere too raw to process. I hand it back. "And he paid for my treatment. I didn't know until I'd checked out. I didn't even know how he afforded it. And I never had the chance to thank him."

He didn't have money to shell out for in-patient mental-health treatment. But suddenly the second mortgage and debts make a lot of sense. But this is all too much right now. I don't have the vocabulary or the emotional range to absorb all that she's told me. I could have prepared for this conversation for years, but there's no way I could have anticipated how it would feel to have my history torn down and retrofitted with a new, disjointed foundation. The silence stretches out until she fills it.

"There isn't a day that went by that the decision hasn't haunted me. But I didn't doubt it was the right one, at least at the time. Maybe if I would have had you now, when there isn't such stigma, and the treatments are better. I could have been . . ." She trails off, swallows, and then takes a rattling inhale. ". . . a mother to you. I could have been better for you. But that was the only option I saw at the time—and the only one your father saw, too."

She swallows a cry and keeps going.

"I'm sorry. For lying. For abandoning you. I'm sorry that I couldn't get well for you. I'm sorry I asked your father to lie. I don't expect you to forgive me. I could never deserve that. But I hope you forgive your father. That you find a way to"—she sucks in a breath—"if not understand, perhaps accept his decisions, however flawed, because they were made out of love for you.

"We knew Henry would be a better parent. That he would give you a good life. And look at you. You're beautiful. You're not . . ." She hesitates. "You don't suffer from . . ." She can't say it. Even after she acknowledged the stigma was one of her biggest barriers.

I stare back at her. It's a little late for her to express concern for my mental health. She and Dad have given me a lifetime of trauma to unpack. "Why would you think that?"

"It runs in families, what I have. And we worried . . ."

She stops and looks away. Afraid of the unsaid.

But another puzzle piece clicks into place. "That's why Dad always had me in therapy. He thought I'd have it, too." This fact only occurs to me as I say it aloud.

"From the beginning, he promised me he'd watch you. Get you better care if, well . . ." She reaches for me but hesitates and pulls back, tears pouring down her splotchy cheeks. "I'm real glad. I'm so happy. He made sure you were fine."

Fine.

I wrap my arms around my shins and drop my forehead to my knees, rocking gently back and forth on the creaking step. The new coat of paint can't hide the familiar sounds—the memory of Dad bounding up these steps at the end of the day.

Neither of us says anything for several heavy minutes.

"I'm sorry about Henry, Ophelia. He was a good man. And a good father."

Can he be considered a good father? Loving, yes. Doting, of course. Devoted, definitely. But a good father? A good man? I'm not sure I know what that means.

"Well, it's late, and I've taken more of your time than I deserve." Mary leans forward, moving to stand, but hesitates. "I know it's too much to ask, but I'd really like to get to know you. When, or if, you're ever ready." She hands me a piece of notepaper, folded into a triangle, and our fingertips brush as I take it.

The Truth Is in the Detours

She hesitates a moment, and I think she wants to hug me, but I can't offer myself to her. I won't. I remember how much I'd longed for her hug as a girl—every time I saw a friend hug their mom after a fall on the playground, blowing out birthday candles, graduating from high school. I can't give away that hug I've been clutching like a long-held breath.

Her steps are silent as she walks down the stairs to her car. I notice there is someone in the driver's seat. He's in silhouette, but I assume it's her husband. She climbs into the car and collapses onto his shoulder before he wraps his arms around her shoulders. I'm simultaneously relieved and jealous that she has someone to process this with. She has someone to hold her. I retreat into the house to give them their privacy and absorb the information alone.

My parents made so many bad choices—leaving me without the power to make my own. I can't rewind or change them. All I can do is make my own choices from here on out. Right now, though, I'm not ready to make this one. I don't know if I will ever be ready to get to know my mother.

But at least the choice is now mine. I slide the notepaper into my pocket.

CHAPTER 38

There was a fire that ravaged San Diego when I was a teen. The Santa Ana winds propelled the flames from the inland mountains and threatened coastal towns, sending residents scurrying to evacuate. The hillside was left charred, seemingly dead.

But that spring, Dad and I stayed at a cabin in the eastern mountains, and I was transfixed by the emerald shoots and confetti of wildflowers already pushing through the seared earth. The original landscape was gone. But in its place was a new promise.

After kerosene burns down my life, I decide to be the shoots of grass, the lupines, and poppies too stubborn to die away. I will be my own promise. Because I've made a huge mess of my life so far, with a lot of help from the people closest to me. I figure I might have better luck cleaning it up on my own.

After I wake in Dad's house for the last time, I slip out and drive away without looking back. I go home to my apartment to find that my plant has died and the cobwebs have flourished. Over the next few weeks, I clean. I purge everything that does not spark joy. Marie Kondo has nothing on me.

I practice making decisions. Easy decisions. Tough decisions. Bad decisions. Good decisions.

Either way, I'm not going to let things happen to me anymore.

The Truth Is in the Detours

I go back to therapy. The first therapist I find intimidates me. She reminds me of my fourth-grade teacher, whose disapproving scowl was legendary. So I try another therapist. She has a full sleeve of inked wildflowers and an eyebrow ring. She reminds me of my hairdresser and makes me feel at ease.

And I start at the beginning.

I rescue the ugliest dog from the local shelter and name him Adonis. He is of indiscriminate breed with bald patches, one pointy and one floppy ear, and a snaggletooth protruding from the right side of his mouth. But he has kind eyes and was so grateful to be rescued that he's like Velcro against my heels. On the rare times I leave him, he celebrates my homecoming with a sneezing fit and cries of joy. He also dragged my new potted plant onto my bed and tore it to shreds, smearing mud all over my white bedding (one of the few possessions that did spark joy), and I worried he might wind up in the bad-decisions column. But then he bowed into a chastened posture as if he were my humble subject, and I, his queen. And I forgave him. He's the best decision, surely. He may never win a dog show or pass obedience school. But well-behaved dogs seldom make history.

I also try some fitness classes. First, I attempt goat yoga. I figured I like yoga. I like goats. It'll be perfect for me. But within the first five minutes, a goat pees on my mat. Two thumbs down. Do not recommend. Then I try pole dancing—inspired by the athleticism of the women at Pandora's Box. I'm even more impressed after trying to spin upside down on a chrome bar. The skin burn is real.

Within a month, I've signed five new clients and hired a part-time assistant to take on simple tasks so I can handle complex projects at a higher billable rate. Aiming to separate my work and home life, and force myself out of my PJs, I move into a coworking space. It comes with free coffee, snacks, and Wi-Fi and allows me to work beside other professionals. They consider me an entrepreneur rather than someone who couldn't figure out what the hell she was good at.

I cut my hair past my shoulders, and for the first time, I go natural. My hair is more honey than the platinum of my youth. My natural color deepened, darkened, while I was busy disguising it with every bold hue on the color wheel.

Six weeks after I return home, I receive a package from Jackson County, Oregon. It contains all ten pages of the legal document that changed my life twice. Once when it was filed. Once when I found it. It confirms the whole, harsh, ugly truth of my early years and the mother who didn't raise me. I read through it three times but toss it in the trash. Of all the mementos of my childhood, this is not one I wish to keep.

I make decisions. Brave. Minor. Definitive.

I practice not being fine. Some days, the grief creeps in like an arctic freeze, and my body aches, deep in my joints and muscles, and it's all I can do to get out of bed. On those days, I drive to the beach and toss sticks into the waves for Adonis to retrieve. I eat vegetables and drink water. I absorb sunlight and go for long walks. Or I curl up on my couch under an afghan and read the book Serena gave me. The collection of poems speaks to me on an elemental level—about grief, hope, joy, gratitude, and melancholy. The poems tackle every emotion but "fine." They sing about the extremes—agony and ecstasy coexisting in one embrace. And I listen.

And I let myself mourn Dad. He loved me and lied to me. He saved me and surrendered me to a lifetime of complex grief. I don't think I'll ever be "fine" again. But I hope someday I can think of his devotion without remembering his dishonesty, too.

I realize the search for answers was never about finding Mom. It was about finding Dad. It was about understanding his deceit so I could embrace or renounce my love for him. And I don't know whether I understand why he made the choice he did, but it has helped me understand how his choices shaped me. *Whatever makes you happy, Princess* was his mantra. He let me get away with everything. Chose my happiness—however transient and unearned—over everything else. He celebrated every milestone and modest achievement as if I'd climbed Everest. Whether he meant to or not, it made me feel like I wasn't capable of more. That I'd exceeded my modest capabilities.

But I know now that he was just relieved I wasn't sick.

He wanted me to be happy. Not in the happily-ever-after endgame that most parents wish for their kids. He wanted my happiness immediately and always. He wanted my happiness as a security against the looming threat that I would inherit Mom's illness.

But you can't will someone to happiness. You must let them find it, earn it. And whatever Dad's motivations—good, bad, or indifferent—he shielded me from the hard truths, wrapped me in rose-colored Bubble Wrap, and convinced me to settle for fine. Because if I reached for more, I might tumble over the cliff.

And I need to decide whether I'm willing to reach for more now that I understand why I never have.

In defiance of being "fine," I let myself think about Beau. I allow myself to miss him. To acknowledge that there is no such thing as the whole truth, only shards that catch the light at different angles and tell assorted stories.

Beau's first text comes when I've been home a week. It says simply: **Can we please talk?**

It tells me nothing about where his heart is, so I don't respond. He calls a few times, but I don't answer. I don't respond when he texts me a while later letting me know he sold his book and completed the first draft, that my notes were as hilarious as they were helpful. Actually, he says "our" book. But it feels like flattery.

Six weeks after I stormed out of his house, he sends me a text that says only: **I miss you. Please talk to me.** And it takes all my emotional strength not to respond. My phone feels like a grenade when I visit my therapist that afternoon. I toss it onto the ottoman in front of me and collapse on the couch.

"What scares you about replying?" Dahlia asks me once I've told her about the offending text.

"It doesn't scare me," I snap.

"Okay. Why do you think replying is a bad idea?"

"Because I miss him, too. Because I miss him so much, I may overlook why I left in the first place."

"Which was?" But she knows why. She knows the story—or my version of it anyway.

I sigh. "Because he didn't tell me the truth."

"Right," she says, nodding. It's a drawn-out "Right," but sounds like "and . . ."

"And I don't want to get in the way of him reconciling with Bianca, if that's what he wants."

"And you think that's what he wants." All her statements sound like questions.

"I'm afraid he never would have chosen me if he weren't beaten down by her. That I'm a consolation prize."

"Hmm," Dahlia says. And she is starting to remind me of my fourth-grade teacher, too.

"What's hmm?"

"Well, you seem to give a lot of credence to his choices. But what about yours?"

She's right. I'm doing all this work on myself—and yet, as I think about Beau, I'm still deferring to my stubborn insecurities, waiting to be chosen, waiting for proof of my value and his affection. Old habits with old friends die hard.

The next day, on our shared birthday, I wake thinking of him. Honestly, I'm never not thinking of him, but as the sun breaks through my curtains, his name is a drumbeat in my skull. I check the time. He'll be thirty-five in a few minutes, and I'll follow twelve hours later.

I don't want to celebrate without him. I don't want to spend another moment without him.

And that's when I make my choice. Whether or not he chooses me back.

CHAPTER 39

I hop in my car with a small overnight bag and Adonis as my copilot. It may be the last miles my poor car can carry me, but I'll deal with that later. I've already fought LA traffic and climbed and descended the Grapevine on my way to the Bay Area when Beau's first text comes in.

35 truths for your 35th birthday.

I'm ravished by curiosity but keep driving, even as my cell dings every twenty minutes or so, ratcheting up my heart rate each time. I pull over for gas at a rest stop and scramble to read as I take Adonis on a quick walk. He tugs on the leash to drag me to a trash can. I put my keys in my pocket to be safe.

1. The first time I fell in love with you, we were four years old.

2. The moving truck had just pulled up, and you had already spilled everything from the boxes all over your bedroom floor so you could make a fort out of the cardboard.

3. I thought you were the most beautiful and remarkable person I'd ever met.

And the next came in twenty minutes later.

The Truth Is in the Detours

4. The first time you broke my heart was when you chose Rupert as your second-grade reading buddy.

5. I think I've finally forgiven you.

I giggle, but it's muffled, because I'm also brushing away tears. My hands are shaking as I restart the car and get back on the road. The pattern continues. Every twenty minutes, Beau sends me another few truths.

I peek when I'm stuck in traffic on a bland stretch of the highway.

6. You really do have a nonsensical taste in music.

7. But a wonderful taste in pajamas.

8. And bathing suits.

A while later, traffic slows to a crawl, and I cheat.

9. I've traveled all over the world, but driving through the desert in the height of summer was the best trip of my life.

10. Even with the detours, dead ends, fires, and feuds.

11. Because you were with me.

I check when Adonis howls from the back seat and forces me to take another break.

12. I miss you.

13. It feels as though I've been missing you for years.

14. There's a piece of me that's been dormant while you've been absent from my life.

And when traffic slows to a crawl, I hazard a glance.

15. When you demanded I kiss you in the tree house, I was so overwhelmed that my heart stopped.

16. It didn't restart until you kissed me again all these years later.

I read more while I'm picking up coffee.

17. I outgrew my extreme ticklishness as a preteen.

18. But I kept pretending so you'd touch me.

19. I have no excuse for my hormonal former self.

I want to take them all in as he means to send them: a love letter, I think, or an apology at least.

20. I fell in love with you a little more as you nursed me back to health after my run-in with a mechanical bull.

21. And I was a goner the first time you cooked for me.

I release a soft laugh as tears collect at the corners of my eyes. I wait in the car before pulling out of the lot, addicted to his truths and waiting for a fix.

22. For our thirteenth birthday, I campaigned for a beach party.

23. Because I knew you'd wear a bikini.

The Truth Is in the Detours

I throw my phone in the back seat because I'm too tempted to check while driving, and getting into an accident would be just my road-trip luck. I make one last stop when I'm close. It is his birthday, after all, and I can't come empty-handed. I look at the next batch of truths as I wait at the bakery.

24. I never told you how I felt all those years ago because I couldn't imagine you'd love me back.

25. But I'm not stupid enough to make the same mistake now.

I pull onto his street as my phone dings again, several times in rapid succession.

26. I'm so sorry I didn't tell you the full truth about the original inspiration for the trip.

27. But there was never a risk I'd change my mind about the divorce.

28. There wasn't any chance I'd change my heart about you.

29. Especially not since the day you cried in your entryway and invited me back into your life.

30. Not since you slid into my car and took control of my radio and my goddamn heart.

31. Not since I saw you for the first time in years and realized there's never been anyone but you who I could forgive anything.

I park several houses down and wait. Maybe I should put him out of his misery, but I'm greedy now, rereading his confessions, brushing away my tears. I look like I've been traveling all day, but he's accustomed to me like this: a little messy—literally and emotionally. When the last texts come through, exactly as the clock turns to my birth moment of 7:57, I steel myself and inhale.

32. I love you.

33. I have always loved you.

34. And I will always love you.

35. If you give me a chance, I will finally love you right.

I collapse back on the seat and sob, and Adonis climbs in my lap, licking my face until I laugh out loud. "Okay," I say, "time for me to be brave."

CHAPTER 40

Beau could be out celebrating. He *should* be out celebrating. It's his birthday, after all.

We've surprised people on doorsteps all summer. It's only fitting that I have to wait on his porch, and I'm prepared for that. But as I approach, with the cake in one hand and Adonis's leash in the other, I see Beau's car in the driveway and am overcome with homesickness. Then I spot several others along the curb. A party. *Perfect.*

Adonis pulls me up the porch steps, and the door swings open before I can knock.

"Ophelia!" I'm wrapped in a hug so tight I almost drop the cake.

"Serena," I gasp.

She pulls back. "I hear it's your birthday, too. Did you two used to sing that Beatles song all the time?" She starts to sing in full rocker mode, banging on invisible drums. I wonder how many drinks she's polished off—she's a little loopy.

I shake my head and say, deadpan, "No."

"Oh," she says, straightening.

"I'm kidding. I sang it to Beau every year. It would irritate the shit out of him."

She bursts into laughter, leaning on my arm. "He's going to be so happy you're here." She squeals and then drops her voice. "We surprised him to try to cheer him up. But he's been a grump—messing with his phone most of the day."

I smile, but the small talk is making me more anxious, and Adonis is whining and wrapping himself around my legs with his leash. I stoop to untangle him when I hear, "Phe?"

Beau's voice sends goose bumps along my arms. I look up to find him in the doorway, his knuckles white against the doorknob. He steps through, and Serena squeezes my hand before disappearing into the house and closing the door behind her.

Beau hasn't shaved, and his hair is grown out and messy. He looks more like a mad professor than the uptight academic I teased mercilessly just weeks ago. He's disheveled—in a faded black T-shirt and Levi's that he's likely owned for a decade that are worn in all the right places. Thirty-five looks fucking good on him.

We stare at each other for a solid minute before Adonis growls and peeks between my shins. Beau startles.

"Who's this?"

"Adonis." I tug on the leash to force him out of hiding.

Beau does a double take, his eyes traveling over the snaggletooth, the patchy, wiry coat, and then he snorts, breaking the tension. "You have a sardonic sense of humor, Ophelia."

"Whatever do you mean? My baby is beautiful."

"On the inside, I'm sure."

Our gazes snag. "Happy birthday, Beau."

His smile drops to something more contemplative. "You didn't respond."

"It's not safe to text and drive," I say.

"You drove here?" His dimple appears. "You must have left hours ago."

"I owed you a carrot cake—and candles. I promise not to blow them out this year."

I hold the cake aloft, and he laughs, his eyes twinkling in the porch light. Relief is running through my veins with the strength of whiskey.

"Thank you," he says, and his eyes are warm and grateful.

The Truth Is in the Detours

I curtsy and slide the cake onto the porch swing. "It's not a list of profound and intimate confessions—but you've always been the overachiever between us."

He steps toward me, so close I feel the warmth of his skin, smell his familiar soap. "I'm sorry."

"I know," I whisper.

"No one teaches you how to handle betrayal—or how to start over with the person you've waited a lifetime for."

"Wait," I say, and step back. His face falls, but I add, "I came here to tell you something. To be brave and emotional and vulnerable. But you beat me to the grand gesture, so at least let me say it."

He takes a deep breath, bracing himself. "Of course."

"I came here to say that I've been working on me. I'm still a work in progress, but my goal is to not let life happen to me, and not doubt myself so much. I'm trying to figure out what I want and what I choose for myself. I've never really been sure of anything in my life. I'm not sure of my past or my future. I don't always know what will make me happy, or where to live, or what my calling is. But I'm sure about you."

The tension in Beau's face is replaced by a slight smile.

"I'm sure that you are the person I want by my side as I work my shit out. I'm sure that you have been my safe place for thirty years—and the person who brings me the most joy. And I know from the outside we don't fit. Because I didn't know the Oregon Trail was more than a low-fi video game, and I can't name more than like nine of the original colonies, and I really thought Samuel Adams was just a beer—and you're an actual history professor."

He winces but is still grinning at me. It gives me the courage to go on.

"So, I worried I didn't deserve you. That you couldn't possibly want me because of all the things I haven't figured out—and you've known who you are and what you want since we were four years old."

He reaches out and takes my hand, swiping his thumb across my wrist. I'm rambling and a little unhinged, but he's listening, even as the sounds of his birthday party filter out of the house. Someone cheers from inside, and then there's a chorus of laughter. But he never takes his eyes from me.

"Most of all, I worried that you hadn't chosen me. That maybe you were falling back on me by default. But I forgot to figure out what I wanted. To choose."

I stop for a moment and take a needed breath. My throat is dry from unleashing all my fears and inadequacies in a single rush. My skin is flushed, as if there are electrical currents fluttering across the surface. I swallow. "And I choose you, Beau. Whether or not you choose me back."

His face lights up, showing off my favorite smile—with his eyes crinkling at the corners and a deep dimple appearing right below his glasses. He steps closer, until our bodies are inches apart and I crane my neck to see him clearly.

"I've been broken for a long time, and you have a fresh, raw break. And I can't promise I'll do everything right, or that I won't have flashes of inadequacy that I'll project all over you. I can't promise that I won't irritate the crap out of you most of the time. But I'm working on not being fine. And I want to not be fine with you."

He quirks his head and chuckles. "I'm sorry?"

"I mean, I want to feel things with you. I want to let myself be euphoric, frustrated, joyful, and sad. I want to love you and make you laugh until you cry and fight with you over the music selection and make food that you sigh over. I want to dance with you at country-western bars and entice you to sleep through your workout. I want to complain about your history podcasts while I secretly crush on how adorable you are when you nerd out on some new fact. I want to meet your colleagues and pretend I know as much about the War of 1812 as I do about pop music."

Beau laughs and closes the remaining distance between us until our bodies are flush and our foreheads are kissing. He skates his hands along my hips, his fingertips pressed into the bare skin above my jeans, and I slide one hand to the nape of his neck. It's such a relief to touch

The Truth Is in the Detours

him, to be touched, and we release matched sighs. Adonis growls and scampers behind my legs.

"Are you done?" Beau asks in a whisper.

I think for a moment. "That last thing I said may not be the romantic finale I was going for, but I'll own it."

Beau chuckles before his expression straightens. "I choose you back, Ophelia. In fact, I chose you first."

My tears begin to fall when he ducks to kiss me. It starts as an exhale, his breath skating across my lips as my inhale draws him in. The kiss is fragile and careful, a nod to our first kiss all those years ago—and hopeful and grateful, a preview of the many that stretch out ahead.

EPILOGUE

Two Years Later

Beau hates to listen to himself in interviews—his aversion borders on phobic. So I download podcasts and cue up recordings to savor when he's gone. Two nights ago, Lani and Arthur forced him to watch the recorded episode of *The Daily Show*, and he cringed throughout, curled into the side of their couch with his hand on his forehead to cover his eyes. I kept his bourbon full, so he survived the experience. And nursed him back to health the next day.

The Truths We Tell Ourselves came out a month ago, and the marketing has kept him busy. Everyone wants the secrets behind the secrets—the salacious details Beau is reluctant to share. Instead, he launches into the implications of our misunderstanding of our own histories—how deception shifts the way we make choices, how lies change the chart of our futures. But the interviewers want to know whether any of the confessors are famous—politicians, Hollywood stars, CEOs. Beau is a bit stiff on camera, a tad serious, but he looks damn good. I suspect his bone structure hasn't hurt his bookings—that and the scandalous topic. But he really attracted attention when he admitted he fell in love during his research—that over the rubble of lies, he found the courage to share a long-held secret of his own.

I got roped into doing a few small podcasts with him after that. His publicist loved our chemistry and how I "humanized and humorized

The Truth Is in the Detours

the stories." But Beau worried it might ruin his academic credibility. He couldn't pretend to be stiff and clinical as I teased him about his mechanical bull injury. And frankly, I don't have time for it. I'm too busy with my own stuff to follow Beau around anymore—as much as I miss him when he's gone.

I turn up the volume on the podcast so I can hear it over the mixer. This one came out a week ago, but I've yet to finish it.

The interviewer segues from Beau's dry description of the psychology behind shame and asks, "You've said this book is uniquely personal, and I have to ask about the dedication and the woman behind it. 'For Ophelia, who holds my most cherished truth.' She was your research assistant?"

Beau credited me as a research assistant, and this interviewer sure makes it sound shocking, borderline unethical. Beau stammers before recovering. "Technically, she was a friend helping me out. My best friend from childhood, actually, and first crush."

The interviewer laughs, and Beau continues. "She'd just discovered a painful family secret. And I, well . . . I was going through a life change of my own. So she volunteered to help me with my research. It was part therapy, part archaeological dig, part self-discovery. We learned that people lie for all sorts of reasons—self-preservation, generosity, fear—and the reasons for telling the truth aren't always that different. And the research forced us to face the truth of *us*. So, yes. The dedication is hers. This book is fuller and more honest because of her shrewd insight. And, more importantly, my life is fuller and more honest now that she's back in it."

I'm startled from the podcast when warm arms slide around my waist. I flip off the mixer and pull out my headphones as Beau drops his face to my neck.

I lean back into his chest as he pulls me closer. "Where'd you disappear to?" I ask.

"Wouldn't you like to know," he teases, pressing a kiss below my ear.

"Taste this." I dip the spoon into the bowl for a dollop of frosting and spin to him.

When it touches his tongue, he closes his eyes and makes a sound typically reserved for our bedroom. "Mm," he says.

"It's your mom's guava cake recipe, with a little twist."

"If you repeat this, I will deny it, but this is better than hers." He leans down and kisses me, tasting sweet and tangy from the frosting. I expect it to be brief, chaste. But he presses me into the counter and cradles my face in his hands before a throat clears behind us.

"Ah, my keiki." Lani chuckles as she moves to the fridge, Adonis at her heels. My dog loves her; I suspect she's sneaking him snacks.

We freeze. Even now, I feel like a kid caught making out in the basement. I was prepared to stay in the guest room the first time we came home, but Lani laughed and dropped my bag at the foot of Beau's bed. "You live together, Ophelia," she'd said. "I'm not an idiot." When we curled up in his full bed later that night, surrounded by his Academic Decathlon medals and Spelling Bee ribbons, Beau pulled me over him and growled, "Make my adolescent fantasies come true, Ophelia." And I giggled, called him a pig, and complied.

When I moved to the Bay Area to be with Beau after we reconnected, I was careful not to get lost in his life. It helped that I didn't have to move into the home he shared with Bianca. In the end, they couldn't come to an agreement, so they sold the house and split the proceeds. Beau and I decided to find something together. The house we chose is perfect for us. It's small and cozy but has a gourmet kitchen and a wooded backyard strung with fairy lights, with a hot tub outside the primary bedroom.

The move was a fresh start—a gift, really. I had gotten unstuck in the months following our road trip, but the move increased my momentum. The proceeds from Dad's house gave me some wiggle room, and I used a portion to enroll in a culinary program. I didn't have an endgame, except to do something that brought me joy. And cooking—creating a sensory experience and sharing it—was the thing that always had.

And then I had an idea. I started small. When ordering groceries for clients, I'd share my recipes. For local clients, I began to book weekday meals, delivering a few custom recipes to be reheated. It was another convenience offered through my personal concierge service. Some hired me to cater dinner parties. A few told their friends. Now, 70 percent of my business is food—personal chef, weekly meal deliveries, curated recipes bundled with grocery delivery. I love to puzzle out how to feed a family with complex dietary needs—with vegetarian, eco-conscious, gluten-free, and paleo diets under one roof. One client hired me to give her weekly cooking lessons and equip her kitchen with knives, pots, pans, and gadgets. The business is a bit scattered, and a lot to manage—even with two associates to handle the simpler accounts. I'll need to specialize at some point, but right now, I'm loving the variety.

I've also visited Mary a few times. Beau and I stayed at the little cottage over the water and met Mary and Jack for dinner. It was awkward and loaded, with stilted conversation where the unsaid was so thick that understanding eluded us. On my second visit, I took a different approach. I showed up at Café Huckleberry and asked to be put to work. And as Mary taught me her famous huckleberry scone recipe, as we became flour coated and fatigued, we began to speak the same language. She and I are working on it and have the tentative start of a relationship. I'm hopeful that we'll have a future, even though she'll never hold my history—or be my home. But that's okay. That's here. With this family, who are the people who help me keep Dad's memory alive—and are the connective tissue stretched between my then and now.

Beau and I arrived in San Diego ten days ago, after he finished his spring semester and as the dreaded second anniversary of Dad's death approached. I was grateful to be here with the Augustins, next door to my family home, but not trapped within the mausoleum of memories. We visited the grave site on the anniversary, just as I did a year ago, and

I sat on the green lawn in front of his headstone for an hour while they waited patiently at the curb, and then they took me home, where I beat them all in a game of poker using Dad's heirloom chips.

Today is our last day of this nostalgic trip home, and Lani has planned a big Hawaiian dinner as a farewell. The kitchen smells of home cooking and Lani's love.

"Everything's ready," Lani says. "We'll eat in ten minutes." She looks meaningfully at Beau, but I can't read whatever passes between them.

"Just enough time," Beau whispers in my ear, and I smell the salt air and sunblock on his skin. He's always the most Beau when we come home to San Diego. "I have to show you something."

"But I need to frost the cake," I protest.

"It'll just take a minute." He tugs on my arm and drags me out through the patio doors and onto Lani's lanai. He covers my eyes with his palm.

"What are you—"

"Shh," he says. "Trust me, Phe."

He wraps another hand around my waist and leads me off the deck and onto the lawn. "Did you clean up after Adonis? Because Lord help me if I step in dog poop. I'm wearing flip-flops."

He grumbles, "Shh," but then laughs and stills, unwinding his hands.

I squint as the scene comes into focus. The tree house, faded and likely dry-rotted now, is lit up with fairy lights and draped in an arbor of wildflowers.

"What—" I start, but he leans forward and steals the words with a kiss, threading his fingers in mine.

He takes a huge breath and releases it in an uneven exhale, and then he sinks to one knee. My pulse incites a riot in my veins.

"The first time I knew I wanted to marry you was when I stood here beside you in a Spider-Man costume and said, 'I do.' But it took a lot of years, a lot of mistakes, and a lot of heartbreak to make our way

The Truth Is in the Detours

back to each other—back to where we belong. So I'm asking you, thirty years later, to marry me for real."

He releases my hand and reaches into his pocket. I think he's opened a ring box, but I can't be sure, because tears blur my vision. Adonis storms into the backyard and jumps on me, nearly knocking me over. From the distance, a camera flash fires, making stars swirl overhead at the same time they burst in my chest.

"Yes," I say, laughing, crying, and sinking into the grass to catch his face in my hands. He breaks into a grin even as he kisses me. "I choose you. I'll always choose you."

There are more clicks from the camera shutter, and I'm aware that Lani and Arthur have joined us to document the moment—a photo that will bookend that old, faded photo of us, which rests on our mantel at home. But I can't process anything but Beau and the way it feels to love him.

It feels like luck. Like hope. Like truth.

ACKNOWLEDGMENTS

As a reader, I devour the acknowledgments. I love learning about all the people who made the author's path to publication possible and a little less lonely. Thank you for being here to read mine and for taking a chance on a new author. I am eternally grateful that you have.

Writing can be a solitary endeavor, but I am blessed with friends and family who make it feel like a team sport. First, thank you to my parents, who encouraged me to follow my heart with reckless abandon, even when it meant quitting premed to major in literature three years into college (without any interest in teaching). Thank you to Dee Dee, whose weekly library hauls showcased how transformative reading could be. I hope you have unlimited books in the library of the afterlife, all marked with a big X to remind you which ones you've read.

Thank you to my sisters, Heather (my first reader) and Hilary (my most fanatical). It is not hyperbole to say I never would have completed a single book without you both. There are no words for how much I love you, sissies. To Kel, thank you for reading with such enthusiasm and joy—my books and all those I recommend. You are the best niece and book friend to boot. To my expanded sisters—Jenn, Becca, and Amanda—thank you for reading my work, encouraging me, and being loyal lifelong friends. Marina, you are a phenomenal beta reader and copyeditor. I'm so glad we can stay connected in this most unexpected way. And Rob, although our creative outlets are wildly different,

I've always been inspired by how committed you are to yours, and appreciative that you support mine.

I am eternally grateful to my agent, Melissa Edwards, who is steadfast, solid, and such a fierce advocate. Thank you for plucking my submission out of the slush pile and giving me a chance to do what I've always dreamed of doing. Thank you to my editors, Maria Gomez, Selena James, and Selina McLemore, for the thoughtful revisions, encouragement, and brainstorming. You've all made this book—and my future books—better. Thanks to my copyeditor, Jon Ford, and to my proofreader, Jill Kramer, for polishing this book until it shined. To Sarah Horgan, thank you for designing the cover of my dreams. A huge thank-you to Jen Bentham, Tree Abraham, Rachael Clark, and the entire Lake Union team for getting this book out into the world.

To Kevin Fisher-Paulson from the Outer, Outer, Outer, Outer Excelsior, your wit, empathy, and storytelling will live on in the writers and readers you've inspired. Thank you for the immense generosity and care with which you read my first words. You gave me the confidence to keep writing (and slay the adverbs). I promise to pay it forward in honor of your memory.

To my writing friends and loyal beta readers, what would I do without you all? A huge thank-you to Gina Banks, the A-plus student of publishing who sits in the front of every class and generously shares her notes, knowledge, and networks. I am so lucky to count you as a friend. To Jessica Banks and Isabelle Engel, I have loved going on this journey with both of you—thanks for the moral support, feedback, editing, and comic relief. Thank you to the Deep Dive Group: Lorene Straka for pulling us together, Amanda Hauck for your edits and encouragement, and the rest of the amazing crew for being cheerleaders and thought partners. To my critique partners, Aria Garnett, Megan Correll, and Jamie Factor, your monthly feedback and friendship were a lifeline. To Melissa Liebling-Goldberg, thank you for being such a phenomenal critique partner and helping me celebrate the small victories. To Heather Hecht, your phenomenal insights and encouragement over the years have been such a gift. To Becca Chapin and the other readers who have become friends, I appreciate the time you took to offer your bighearted feedback. Thank you to Holly James, Sierra Godfrey, Meredith Schorr, and Lindsay Hameroff for reading this book and answering all my industry questions—no matter how small. To all my Agent Siblings of the Slack, I'm so grateful you welcomed me and shared your wisdom with such generosity. I appreciate all the knowledge, humor, and support. I won the jackpot with all of you.

Finally, thank you to my amazing sons, Damien, Wyatt, and Levi, for sharing me with my daydreams and celebrating every milestone. To my dear daughter, Makenna, thank you for being my biggest fan and most candid critic. You make me brave, and you make me better. And to Kenny, thank you for the countless real-life rom-com moments of inspiration—mechanical bulls, mislaid keys, impossibly small motel rooms, and love letters written as lists. Most of all, thank you for letting me ride in the passenger seat on road trips to take in the view and draft from my mobile writing retreat.

ABOUT THE AUTHOR

Photo © 2024 Kevin Neilson

Mara Williams drafted her first novel in third grade on a spiral notebook—a story about a golden retriever and the stray dog who loved her. Now she writes novels about strong, messy women trying to find their way in the world. When not writing or reading, Mara can be found enjoying California's beaches, redwoods, and trails with her husband, kids, and disobedient dog. For more information, visit www.marawilliamsauthor.com.